# THE (IN)CONVENIENT TRUTH ABOUT THE WORLD YOU LIVE IN

NOLAN JAZIMREG

Paperback ISBN: 978-1-3999-4175-4

Cover design by: Nolan Jazimreg

PRISHTINA

A cultural grant from the Municipality of Prishtina has generously defrayed the editing costs.

www.nolanjazimreg.wordpress.com

This book is dedicated to you and no one else, all right?

"If you wish to become a philosopher, the first thing to realise is that most people go through life with a whole world of beliefs that have no sort of rational justification, and that one man's world of beliefs is apt to be incompatible with another man's, so that they cannot both be right. People's opinions are mainly designed to make them feel comfortable; truth, for most people is a secondary consideration."

Bertrand Russell, *The Art of Philosophizing and other Essays*

Truth is a dormant volcano, which never fails to erupt.

# ACKNOWLEDGMENTS

Warm greetings to the over 400,000 people who have read and complimented my Brexit insights as featured on my blog, nolanjazimreg.wordpress.com.

Writing a book is a solitary process that deprives an author of being there for their family. This book wouldn't have been possible without the support of my wife, Artushka, who understood my craving to write with its many ups or downs. From reading early drafts to providing suggestions for improvement to incessantly taking care of our children, whenever I was torturing my laptop's keyboard, she was as crucial in completing this book as I was.

When I stumbled from writer's block, and my confidence in completing this novel began to fade, the Municipality of Prishtina awarded me a vital grant to cover the expenses to get my manuscript edited and published, reinstating my belief that my novel is worth something. If it weren't for Linda, Yllka, Adrian, and other Prishtina municipal officials, this novel would have never been in the state it is, which is why I am eternally indebted to them for providing me with crucial financial assistance at a critical time.

Special thanks go to Klarita, Artushe, Bashkim, Dulani and Shaban for reading and rereading my manuscript throughout its various revision stages but also for continuously pointing out mistakes I've made in the writing process.

A big thank you goes to Sam, Yasmeen, Mira, David, Karmit, Florencous, Gerrit, Albin, Pierre, Fadil, Afro, Sead, Artan, Lekajlo, Lalito, Ardi, Krena, Dajkolino, Versho, Lili, including others who wouldn't fit on this page, for reading the early drafts and providing me ways to improve my writing.

Apologies to Doki, Pufki, Ibrau, Burim, Agonua, Mendi, Linke, my in-laws and other friends who had to endure my incessant talking about how this book will revolutionise our society.

And finally, I would like to thank Roxanne most cordially for the splendid job she has done editing my novel. I am truly grateful not only for her professionalism and insight, but also for the time she devoted to reading the book so attentively.

# Contents

# Meanwhile, in London – Part One

**W**ELL, BLOODY MARVELLOUS!
Turns out curiosity doesn't kill cats, but it just murders sleep in cold blood.

The sun is peeking over the horizon to announce the first day of spring 2070, and guess who's been awake all night? Yours truly, because apparently, according to the BBC, humankind is gearing up to do what it does best… fuck everything up.

But hey, let's not act surprised, because whatever comes out of a fuck will inevitably end up in something fucked.

# Chapter 1

In the aftermath of the allegedly "effective" negotiations between China, Russia, and the EU, discussions so "fruitful" that diplomats privately described them as a mixture of theatre, caffeine abuse, and barely concealed threats, Iran activated its nuclear enrichment program in 2029. The announcement hit global news cycles like a malfunctioning fire alarm, loud, repetitive, and mostly ignored by anyone who wasn't paid to care.

The following day, the US president, John Ryan, summoned twenty-seven journalists to a press conference in the White House's windy Rose Garden, where the weather seemed as irritated as Washington's political establishment. Camera flashes went berserk the moment President Ryan stepped outside, as though the journalists were trying to blind him before he could speak. He strolled toward them with the stiff gait of a man who hadn't slept for days, his shoes scraping against the stone path with an ominous finality.

Arriving behind the wooden lectern, President Ryan paused, tugged sharply at the hem of his grey suit, as if it were personally responsible for Iran's uranium levels, and straightened his white shirt. Then he lifted his head, revealing wide-open, bloodshot eyes that suggested he had spent the night negotiating with insomnia rather than world leaders. Speaking slowly, with exaggerated gravitas, Ryan thanked the journalists for attending this "urgent event," a phrase he delivered as though the fate of humanity hinged on their punctuality.

He launched into a 27-minute meandering monologue that ricocheted between historical grievances, selective outrage, and poetic reinterpretations of international law. As he spoke, he threw volleys of accusations at Iran with the gusto of a man throwing darts while blindfolded. Journalists exchanged glances, their pens pausing mid-note, silently debating whether he had rehearsed this speech or simply wandered off-script sometime between sentence two and three.

Then, smiling nervously, like a man who had just realised he left the oven on, he concluded, "I will not haggle over the serious threat to world peace from Iran's nuclear enrichment program. From the initially agreed 3.67 percent uranium enrichment level, Iran has now increased it to 18.75 percent and could soon produce its first nuclear warhead. The United States is committed to making the world safer, and if Iran doesn't stop its uranium enrichment program immediately, the US and our allies will."

President Ryan stretched out his hand, evidently to add something, perhaps a dramatic flourish or another completely unverified statistic, but then paused, dropped it to his side, and stared bleakly into the middle distance. The journalists erupted into a frenzy, shouting his name, demanding clarity, probing for meaning he clearly didn't have. Ryan ignored them entirely, turned around with the defeated posture of a man who had misplaced his own conviction, and walked back toward the West Wing with his head hanging low.

*** 

The US president's fiery statement triggered diplomatic shockwaves so intense that within hours Moscow resembled a disturbed beehive. guards rushing, aides whispering, doors slamming with the urgency only global crises can inspire. The Kremlin's marble corridors echoed with hurried footsteps as the Iranian, Russian, and Chinese leaders convened behind heavily guarded doors, their silhouettes flickering against antique walls lit by chandeliers that looked older than half the nations involved.

Four hours later, the suspense finally broke. The Russian president, Boris Chizov, lumbered out and positioned himself behind a white lectern adorned with a golden-plated two-headed eagle, a symbol so unsubtle it practically screamed, *"We're in charge here, whether you like it or not."*

President Chizov's appearance was a spectacle of deliberate contrast. He wore an immaculate white suit, blinding under the stage lights, paired with a crisp white shirt and black tie, making him look like a dictator attending a communion. Meanwhile, the Iranian president on his right and the Chinese president on his left stood draped in black, forming a colour-coordinated trio that unintentionally resembled a mafia council debating the ethics of extortion.

Chizov himself was a tall, obese figure with a large, clean-shaven face and a pronounced double chin that wobbled with every syllable. Coarse blonde hair clung awkwardly to the rims of his tiny ears, as if unsure where else to go. As he spoke about Iran's sovereign right to supply its people with electricity from a nuclear plant, a statement delivered with the passion of a man defending his right to a second dessert, his voice reverberated through the hall, thick with indignation.

Midway through his declaration, Chizov paused to wipe sweat from his neck with a white handkerchief. A futile gesture. The heat from the studio lights, combined with his rising anger, betrayed him; beads of new sweat surfaced almost immediately, glistening like misplaced pearls on his flushed skin. His pale green eyes were moist, not with emotion, but with simmering irritation, and his trembling hands gripped the lectern as he accused the US president of spreading "inflammatory fake news," each word sharpened and hurled like a diplomatic dagger.

Then, inhaling deeply, he pressed on, "To develop a nuclear warhead, Iran must have enriched uranium of at least 20 percent. Our agreed deal ensures Iran's uranium enrichment capacities remain below 20 percent. China and Russia won't allow another violation of international laws and shall hesitate in protecting Iran from any foreign military aggression."

The hall instantly erupted into chaos. Dozens of journalists sprang to life, their voices overlapping in a chaotic chorus of questions, theories, and thinly veiled accusations. Microphones lunged forward like hungry animals. But Chizov remained utterly silent. His laboured breath showed on his face under the bright lights as he pushed out his lower lip, exposing an unsettlingly large row of teeth. He stroked his shaking forehead with a sluggish, almost tender motion, as though trying to soothe a headache caused by the stupidity of the world itself, before turning away.

With a final dismissive glance, he vanished behind the tall wooden doors with his Chinese and Iranian counterparts, their retreating figures swallowed by the shadows of the hallway. The doors slammed shut with a dramatic boom, as if the building itself wanted no part in what was coming next.

Later that evening, the world received another unwanted update. Six Chinese and fourteen Russian warships began slicing methodically through open waters toward the Persian Gulf. Their decks bristled with missile systems, and four nuclear submarines glided beneath the water surface in eerie silence. Satellites captured their movements from above, the images going viral online under titles ranging from *"Apocalypse"* to *"World War Three is around the corner."*

This coordinated naval flex jolted the US president into action. He called an urgent United Nations Security Council meeting in a desperate bid to pass a resolution restraining Iran's enrichment activities. The proposal, however, died swiftly, smothered beneath the predictable vetoes of China and Russia, who rejected it with the casual confidence of people declining an invitation to a party they never intended to attend.

After this predictable diplomatic face-plant, the US president summoned NATO leaders to Brussels. They arrived at NATO headquarters tense, jet-lagged, and visibly irritated at being dragged into yet another crisis born from other people's initiatives. The ensuing discussions, held in a sterile conference hall humming with recycled air, lasted for hours.

Despite the intensity of the talks, raised voices, pointed fingers, and theatrical sighs, not all NATO leaders agreed to military action against Iran. Apart from the United States, the UK, and five new NATO states desperately eager to prove their worth, the rest flatly refused involvement. Their message was clear, *"Good luck with your war, but please leave us out of it."*

And with that, the alliance fractured into camps, enthusiastic, reluctant, and absolutely-not-under-any-circumstances, setting the stage for a geopolitical disaster only humans could manufacture with such consistency.

\*\*\*

Grey clouds sagged over Tehran like a damp wool blanket, promising torrents of rain that would soak anyone foolish enough to stand outdoors. But Iranians are a resilient bunch, or perhaps simply exhausted by being told to stay home, because over 200,000 of them packed into Azadi Square anyway. The square itself, surrounded by concrete buildings that looked embarrassed to still exist, pulsed with bodies, noise, and the smell of grilled corn from street vendors who had wisely decided not to let geopolitics interfere with business.

Tehran's Azadi Tower loomed dramatically above the crowd, its stark geometric frame slicing through the bruised sky. Normally a symbol of national pride, today it looked like an art installation titled "Impending Trouble." The flagpoles lining the plaza clattered loudly in the wind, as if joining in the national conversation whether they wanted to or not.

People waved Iranian flags with such enthusiasm it was a miracle no one lost an eye. Others hoisted portraits of Iranian President Ebrahim Jahromi, some of which were so heavily airbrushed they made him look like a saint or the winner of a very pious beauty pageant. Together they formed a heaving, chanting ocean of limbs and fabric.

The moment the president appeared on the elevated blue podium, paint already peeling at the corners, because obviously Tehran's maintenance budget had bigger concerns, the crowd detonated into hysterics. The fading light cast a golden halo over him, although that might also have been the reflection off a particularly shiny camera drone hovering nearby. Either way, the crowd bought it.

Jahromi waved with theatrical flourish, one hand raised, the other pressed dramatically over his heart, as though personally moved by the devotion of 200,000 people who conveniently forgot how much they complained about fuel prices last week. His smile widened, perfectly rehearsed and sturdy enough to withstand the coming rain.

President Jahromi bore a striking resemblance to Ayatollah Khomeini, right down to the intense gaze and the austere posture that suggested he had never once encountered a comfortable chair. Dressed in a flowing black cloak that caught the wind in suspiciously majestic fashion, he stepped toward the microphone, gripping it with the intensity of a man determined to bend world events through sheer vocal force.

He thanked his allies for safeguarding Iran's sovereign right to provide electricity to its citizens through nuclear fission, a phrase that had been repeated so often in state media it now triggered applause reflexively. And indeed, the crowd obeyed, wild roars erupted, tens of thousands shouting "Allahu Akbar" in a rhythm that rattled nearby windows and frightened a flock of pigeons into early retirement.

President Jahromi's face glowed with self-satisfaction, basking in the adoration as though he were personally responsible for inventing electricity. The chants of his name rolled through Azadi Square like waves, rising and crashing until finally, mercifully, the volume dipped enough for him to resume speaking.

His voice, hoarse but determined, blasted through the speakers, cheap but loud ones that crackled at every consonant. With the finesse of a seasoned orator and the subtlety of a hammer, he launched a blistering tirade against the US president. His words struck the air like darts, designed less for diplomatic communication and more for rousing an already overexcited crowd.

He jabbed his finger upward, slicing the air with all the restraint of an angry schoolteacher lecturing a room full of misbehaving students. Then he added, in tones rich with melodrama, "I implore the world to prevent the United States of America from attacking Iran. We don't want war, and I assume this is a stance most US citizens hold. Therefore,

I urge all US citizens to rise against their government's thirst for the energy resources of other nations and ..."

He paused, leaning closer to the microphone with an expression that suggested he was about to reveal the secrets of the universe, or at least deliver a sentence aimed to trend on every social media platform still functioning. The crowd leaned in with him, breaths held, flags frozen mid-wave, awaiting the next thunderous proclamation and the clouds rumbled ominously above as though Tehran's sky itself was bracing for whatever would come next.

*Marg bar Āmrikā, Marg bar Āmrikā ...*, the "Death to America" chant rolled through the courtyard like a violent tide. President Jahromi's supporters, men and women pressed shoulder-to-shoulder beneath the blazing Tehran sun, thrust their fists into the air, their faces twisted with the ferocity of battle-hardened zealots. The metallic crackle of the loudspeakers trembled under their voices as if the very equipment recoiled from the rage it was forced to amplify.

President Jahromi halted mid-sentence.

He lowered his chin and glared through his half-closed eyes at the mob before him. The deep lines of age etched across his face darkened as a scarlet flush crept from his neck to his temples. His jaw clenched; the sinews of his throat tightened. For a long moment, he stood motionless behind the wooden podium, gripping its edges until his knuckles blanched, as though wrestling his own fury into submission.

When he finally spoke, his voice was hoarse but cutting.

"My fellow Iranians," he began, struggling to rise above the relentless chant, "death isn't the objective here!"

The crowd's roar faltered, just enough for his words to snake through the tension.

"We must prevent the United States from inciting more Muslim bloodshed."

He looked down at his notes, the papers trembling slightly in his hands. He pressed his lips together, drew in a sharp breath, and raised his head with a renewed, almost explosive force.

"If the world fails," he said, now shouting over the restless sea of followers, "unless the United States is restrained from causing further loss of life among Muslim populations in our region, Iran may resort to closing the Strait of Hormuz, effectively severing the world from the region's oil lifeline!"

A gust of dry desert wind swept across the stage, scattering dust at his feet.

The crowd gasped, the chant dying instantly.

"The White House," he continued, voice booming with theatrical conviction, "is desperate to control Iran's oil and gas. Their economy, their currency itself, depends on forcing the world to trade with them. And they know it. Therefore, if the world must stop the US grabbing from the region's oil and gas, including Iran's, so that they could start trading it US dollars. If the world fails to prevent the US from attacking Iran will halt the trade of region's oil and gas traded in US dollars by closing the Strait of Hormuz and cause global economic mayhem."

A tense silence fell.

Only the faint rattle of a loose banner above the stage disturbed the air as President Jahromi stared out over his people, his chest heaving, awaiting their response.

***

Meanwhile, the US and the UK dispatched thirty-two battleships to the Persian Gulf, parking them neatly, like aggressive metallic ornaments, along its southern coastline to "safeguard the region's oil wells" from Iran's supposedly imminent attack. The admirals, undoubtedly pleased with their own grand choreography, stood ready for a war that even President Jahromi hadn't quite decided to start.

Though President Jahromi's infamous speech did *not* lead to the obliteration of a single oil well, tragically disappointing for those who thrive on chaos, the markets behaved as if he had already torched half the Middle East. Oil prices skyrocketed. Traders, those ever-reliable apostles of panic, stampeded to buy and hoard barrels as if they personally planned to bathe in crude oil. The US dollar, equally melodramatic, swelled by nineteen percent within days.

After several rounds of Vienna-style bickering, also known as "diplomatic debates", OPEC hiked oil production by fifteen percent. Oil prices sank, the dollar slowly deflated back to its pre-Jahromi size, and the verbal war drums in Washington and Tehran finally, and mercifully, got their well-earned coffee break. Unfortunately, recess never lasts long in global politics.

\*\*\*

The enormous, circular-shaped UN General Assembly Hall, an architectural triumph in resembling a high-budget lecture theatre, glowed under its dome of artificial lights. Golden panels arched overhead like the ribs of some celestial beast, while rows of desks formed neat concentric circles that forced world leaders to stare each other down whether they liked it or not. Delegates shuffled in their seats, adjusting earpieces, coughing into their microphones, and pretending to have read the briefing notes in front of them.

From time to time, a low murmur drifted across the hall like an indecisive wave, as ambassadors leaned toward one another to whisper the diplomatic equivalents of *"he's lying"* or *"this again?"*

The annual Session was already ablaze with tension. Some leaders defended Iran with polished righteousness; others accused it of undermining world peace with theatrical disgust. The hall smelled faintly of polished wood, stale coffee, and barely concealed hypocrisy, an authentic fragrance of international cooperation.

President Jahromi approached the rostrum with the solemnity of a man who believed the universe personally wronged him. His eyes shrivelled into narrow creases deep inside his dark, expressionless face. He carried his papers as though they offended him, gripping them tightly enough to wrinkle every page.

He raised one hand, his index finger extended like a tiny divine sword, and waved it about dramatically as he lamented the future apocalypse, he insisted Iran would heroically unleash "only if forced." His inarticulate words slithered out in a strained, weary voice, as though even he questioned whether they deserved to be spoken.

"We urge all the leaders of the UN member states," he began, pausing to glare meaningfully at absolutely no one, "to stand on the right side of history by opposing yet another US military aggression on a sovereign state, such as Iran."

A few delegates nodded gravely; others blinked at him, already mentally drafting their press releases.

"Your inability to avert this flagrant violation of international law will compel Iran to wreak worldwide environmental and economic havoc by obliterating the region's oil wells."

At the mention of "obliterating oil wells," three translators visibly stiffened in their glass booths. One pinched the bridge of his nose. Another scribbled something aggressively into his notebook.

"On behalf of the Iranian people," Jahromi continued, his voice quivering with what he presumably believed was righteous sorrow, "I implore you to prevent the US from mounting a military attack on our sovereign country."

He lifted his head, lowered his reading glasses, and surveyed the hall as if expecting the delegates to faint from the sheer profundity of his message. No one fainted. A few yawned discreetly.

After a long sigh, long enough to echo faintly around the dome he concluded, "Please don't force us to do something that will lead to a situation with grave consequences beyond repair, not just for Iran, but the entire world. Thanks for your attention and your support!"

He stepped back from the rostrum, placing his glasses back onto the bridge of his nose with a theatrical flick, as though he had personally saved the world.

After dozens of delegations addressed the UN General Assembly Session, came Russian President Chizov, waddling towards the rostrum with the solemnity of a man bracing for a dental appointment. He darted sharp green eyes across the audience, squinting like the lights were intentionally trying to assassinate him. His chubby fingers trembled as he brushed aside the stubborn blonde fringe from his broad forehead.

He exhaled heavily, Russians' traditional precursor to a lengthy monologue, and began reminding everyone about the Reykjavík

Summit of 1985. Several delegates stared at their translation headphones as if hoping they would misinterpret him on purpose.

Then Chizov launched into his attack on US foreign policy. His enormous stomach quivered with each impassioned burst, shaking like a loyal drum accompanying his rhetorical symphony.

"My honourable UN delegates," he boomed, "it was President Richard Nixon who instigated the current Iranian crisis!" A few diplomats exchanged glances, silently wagering how far back in history he planned to go, as the Russian President pressed on, "In the seventies, President Richard Nixon undertook the unilateral cancellation of backing the US dollar with gold reserves so that he could print additional money to finance the Vietnam war. This decision plunged the value of the US dollar by a third against other European currencies. To restore the global demand for the US dollar and prevent its further downfall, the White House persuaded the leaders of major oil-producing countries to trade their oil exclusively in the US currency. The late presidents of Iraq and Libya, Saddam Hussein and Muammar Gaddafi, terminated their oil trade in US dollars, and we are all aware of what happened to them afterwards. Therefore, oil trade in US dollars is vital to sustaining the value of the US currency. However, the US currency and economy will soon face a steady decline because unless the current global oil consumption of around 100 million barrels per day isn't substantially reduced, the world will run out of oil by the year 2080!"

When he paused to glance around, some delegates lowered their eyes solemnly; others turned to check whether their colleagues were still awake.

A pair of severe coughs, loud, and theatrical ones, pierced the hall, causing Chizov to tense. His pale face flushed crimson as he leaned heavily on the lectern, which groaned under his weight as if reconsidering its career choices.

President Chizov paused to glance at his audience. Some of them tilted down their grave faces, while others regularly turned their heads to look over their shoulders at their fellow delegates. A couple of severe coughs forced President Chizov's eyes to sink deep. He rested his elbows on the lectern to support his enormous weight before his pale face flushed red. President Chizov's eyes began shining with sudden anger when he added, "Considering that there will be no oil to trade in US dollars by 2080, the White House is now keen to snatch and trade Iran's natural gas, the largest world reserves in US dollars, too."

That did it. The US delegation stood up and marched out with synchronized indignation, followed by the British and Saudi delegations, all performing the diplomatic version of storming out of a family dinner.

Chizov watched them leave with visible irritation before delivering his grand finale, "Therefore, everyone here and across the world should be aware that Tehran's refusal to trade their natural gas in US dollars instigated the current Iranian crisis, not Iran's nuclear capacity. Two years ago, leaders of Armenia, Azerbaijan, Belarus, China, Cuba, India, Iran, Iraq, Kazakhstan, Kyrgyzstan, Northern Korea, Russia, Syria, Tajikistan, and Venezuela created a new intergovernmental military alliance, East Pacific Treaty Organization. Mirroring the NATO treaty, if one of the East Pacific Treaty Organization member states gets attacked by a foreign country, it constitutes an attack on all of its member states, whereby all member states are obliged to engage their military might to defend its fellow member state. If the United States of America attacks an East Pacific Treaty Organization member state, such as Iran, this will become an irreversible mistake with grave ramifications not only for the US but also for any other country participating in such an infringement of international laws. Thank you for your attention!"

He stepped down, breathing heavily.

Around twenty percent of the UN delegates clapped vigorously, eager to demonstrate their loyalty or at least to be seen doing so. Others booed with elegant indignation, loud enough to express disapproval but not loud enough to be quoted later.

The hall returned to its natural state, tense, divided, and ready for the next apocalyptic speech.

The US delegation returned with the dramatic timing of a theatre troupe re-entering the stage after an intermission, strolling back to their seats the moment their president appeared behind the lectern. President

Ryan walked with rigid determination toward the microphone, shoulders squared, jaw locked tight, as though preparing to physically wrestle Iran's nuclear program into submission. He cleared his throat, gripping the lectern with both hands, and launched into his address in a sorrowful, almost preacher-like lament about Iran's human rights violations.

At fifty-nine, President Ryan carried the weary look of a man who had battled several wars, most of them statistical. His face bore deep trenches of stress, and his sleepless red eyes shimmered under the glare of the General Assembly Hall's unforgiving spotlights. If exhaustion were an Olympic sport, he would have secured medals for three consecutive terms.

The attending UN delegates watched him with expressions blanched by apprehension, some leaning forward with rigid backs, others sitting frozen as though the air-conditioning had suddenly dropped to polar temperatures. Translators in their booths shifted restlessly, adjusting their headsets in preparation for yet another round of global melodrama.

President Ryan's face turned a fierce, blotchy red, as if someone rubbed it with sandpaper, when he pointed directly at the Iranian delegation with a trembling index finger. Gasps scattered like tiny firecrackers across the hall.

"Dear UN delegates," he thundered, "the United States and other nations have pursued patient efforts to enable Iran to develop its nuclear enrichment program for more than two decades without compromising world peace."

A few delegates blinked at him sceptically, but politely maintained their diplomatic poker faces.

"Unfortunately," he continued, tightening his grip on the lectern, "Iran's regime has a history of reckless and pertinacious aggression in the Middle East, as well as a deep hatred of the US and our allies. This was affirmed today when the Iranian president threatened to obliterate the region's oil reserves. Could you imagine if Iran could back these threats with nuclear weapons?"

He lifted his head, letting his gaze travel across the semicircle of delegates as if inviting them to share in the horror he imagined. Some nodded gravely; others glanced at their notes in the hope that they might find a hidden escape hatch in the text.

He inhaled sharply and resumed with renewed vigour, "Despite decades of our endeavours to find a mutually acceptable solution for Iran and the US, today Iran's leader issued a serious threat to the world."

The absence of cordiality in his tone could have sharpened knives. His voice boomed through the speakers with the authority of a man confident that microphones were invented solely for him.

"Therefore, I would like to clarify that unless Iran's regime doesn't abandon its nuclear enrichment program, it will result in military action to be initiated at a time of our choosing."

A couple of delegates gasped at the double negative; others flinched at the word *military*, anticipating headlines before dessert.

"I urge the world's nations to unite against Iran's current regime because free nations have a moral obligation to confront such existential threats."

The Iranian delegation exchanged stiff, venomous glances.

"I would like to remind all the Iranians that aren't part of Iran's current regime," he added with strained sincerity, "that if we must begin a military campaign, it will not be directed against you. On the contrary, we will tear down the dictatorship apparatus in your country and help you build a prosperous, democratic Iran."

A few eyebrows shot up at the word.

"Failure to act now," he warned, wagging a finger toward the ceiling as if lecturing a rebellious classroom, "will lead to an unstable world where the Kremlin and Tehran will control all the world's gas reserves and turn off its taps whenever a sovereign country doesn't comply with their demands."

At this, two European delegates exchanged knowing glances, the kind usually reserved for long-suffering neighbours discussing a noisy resident.

"We must stand united and act now," Ryan concluded grandly, raising his arms as if to bless the entire hemisphere, "so that whoever becomes the future Russian or Iranian president doesn't push his or her political agenda by cutting the gas supply to countries that will become reliant on this energy source over the next 300 years. I thank you for your attention, and may God continue to bless America and the entire world with long-standing peace."

Scattered cheers floated up from the delegates, more out of courtesy than conviction. The applause echoed awkwardly through the hall, punctuated by the faint hum of delegates whispering behind their hands.

Fifty minutes later, after many sighs and water top-ups, it was the president of the European Council, Ms Derikur Keshtu's turn. She ascended the rostrum with composed elegance, her light-blue suit shimmering beneath the dome's golden lighting and perfectly matching her striking deep-blue eyes. Compared to the preceding theatrics, she looked almost serene.

Ms Keshtu scanned the hall with cool confidence before adjusting the microphone. Her hands moved gracefully, slicing the air as she emphasised each point. A few delegates straightened in their chairs, sensing the shift from fire-and-brimstone to measured European scolding.

She began by underlining her grave apprehension about the never-ending refugee crisis, her voice steady yet firm. Hands interlocked, brows furrowed, she leaned slightly forward as if urging the world to finally pay attention.

"The European Union," she declared, "is at a critical point. We can no longer remain indifferent to the countries that refuse to provide a sanctuary for displaced immigrants upon entering their territories."

Several delegates stiffened, others rolled their eyes so subtly they deserved awards.

"Moreover," she pressed on, gesturing broadly with open palms, "given the real danger of a full-blown nuclear war, the UN organisation must urgently reform itself and provide a credible way that would prevent the Iran crisis from spiralling into a world-wide conflict."

Her tone sharpened ever so slightly at *reform itself*, evoking the collective guilt of an institution that had mastered the art of procrastination.

"While we request nations to refrain from war threats," she added, narrowing her eyes at no one and everyone simultaneously, "the EU member states won't take part in any military action that will please the imperial appetites of either the Kremlin or the White House!"

That line sent a visible ripple through the hall. Some delegates dared to smirk behind their papers.

"We want peace, not war," she insisted, "and to achieve this, we must establish an independent UN Reform Task Force to provide concrete recommendations for overcoming the concurrent Iranian and refugee crises!"

Her voice rang with defiant clarity, echoing softly around the curved walls.

"I want to appeal to world leaders to refrain from any military action until we obtain recommendations from the proposed UN Reform Task Force. Hereby, I urge the UN Secretary-General to process my request and seek from UN member states their vote as soon as possible."

She stepped back from the lectern, exhaling quietly, before descending the rostrum with dignified poise.

Her remarks were met with a strong roar of cheering and applause, though some UN delegates wore expressions somewhere between contempt and indigestion as they watched her walk away, evidently displeased with Europe's sudden backbone.

# Chapter 2

At the next UN General Assembly Session, mounting booing accompanied the UN Reform Task Force's Chairman, Professor Bashkim Bote, as he approached the rostrum platform. The UN Reform Task Force led by 24 experts from the non-governmental sector had worked arduously, concealed from the world leaders, over the last nine months. Instead of a report, the UN Reform Task Force prepared a Convention on the Secret of Divine Civilisation with its Script Protocol, which was issued to the UN delegates on the day its chairman was due to address them.

The Hall itself, circular, towering, and overwhelmed by gold leaf intended to inspire unity but usually provoking migraines, seemed to shrink around the unfortunate professor. He advanced stiffly, his gentle steps almost swallowed by the thick blue carpet. The UN emblem glared down from behind him like a disappointed parent.

The UN Reform Task Force had been extremely cautious in revealing *anything* concrete about the labour of its twenty-four non-governmental experts, who had spent the last nine months doing something no one quite understood and no one entirely trusted. Instead of a report, they handed the delegates a document titled Convention on the Secret of Divine Civilisation, accompanied by a Script Protocol so thick it could double as a blunt-force weapon. It had arrived that very morning, causing several ambassadors to mutter curses in different languages as they tried to flip through its pages without spraining their wrists.

Bemused and visibly trembling, Professor Bote positioned himself behind the marble-clad speaker's stand. He anxiously adjusted the microphones downward to accommodate his diminutive stature. His jacket, an unfortunate shade of brown that only deepened under the hall's merciless lights, rustled as he placed his notes on the lectern with careful precision.

Then, in a move that made several diplomats instinctively clutch their headsets in fear, he reached inside his jacket and pulled out a cell phone. He glided his thumb across its screen and held it close to the microphones. Instantly, John Lennon's *Imagine* began spilling into the enormous hall, its peaceful melody starkly at odds with the rising tensions and the delegates' general desire to escape to lunch.

A few diplomats blinked in disbelief. One Scandinavian representative whispered, "Is this performance art?"

But the song lasted only until the second verse, because the green lights on the microphones flicked off with a distinct and very intentional *click*.

Professor Bote tapped both microphones with his hairy fingers, baffled, then turned sharply toward the UN General Assembly President. They stared at each other with blank, frozen expressions, an awkward tableau of bureaucratic disappointment, until he made a small, desperate jerk of his head toward the silenced equipment.

"Honourable Professor Bote, the UN General Assembly rostrum isn't a DJ booth!" the President barked, provoking loud, rolling laughter across the hall. Even the translators snickered into their microphones.

Realising his error, the professor bowed stiffly and executed a formal apologetic gesture with both hands.

"The microphones aren't responding because I switched them off," the President clarified, eyebrows raised in exhausted authority. "I shall now switch them back on, but I implore you to adhere to the speech you submitted last week."

The professor nodded like a chastened schoolboy, adjusted his spectacles, and cleared his throat. The hall gradually settled into resentful silence.

In a serious tone, he began, "Monsieur President, Madame Secretary-General, distinguished delegates. Eighty years ago, your predecessors gathered in San Francisco to sign the United Nations Charter and gave birth to this organisation, but its pledges are visible only on its pages."

Several delegates shifted in their seats, some rubbing their temples, others already regretting their choice to attend in person.

"Instead of reflecting unity," he continued, "this hall endured division because of various renditions of truth. Therefore, today our Task Force has deposited a reliable blueprint for gaining a unifying truth through the *Convention on the Secret of Divine Civilisation*. It is named after Abdu'l Bahá's book addressed to the rulers and the people of Persia, which set the basis for establishing the United Nations."

His voice carried genuine devotion, but paired with an audience displaying the hollow-eyed despair of trapped elevator passengers.

Professor Bote paused, scanning the hall for traces of comprehension. He found mostly hopelessness, and mild hostility.

Sweat dripped visibly down the professor's flushed face. He dabbed at it with a white handkerchief, then bowed his head before continuing in a droning, almost priestly monotone.

"This Convention intends to be the basis for a new constitution that will transcend the United Nations into a united nation by globally broadcasting every second of the entire life of an adopted orphan."

Several delegates coughed, choked, or pretended to sneeze in disbelief.

"To secure long-lasting peace, economic prosperity, justice, and equality for his war-torn country, this orphan will draft a new global constitution after he turns 35."

A faint groan travelled around the hall.

"Then, his constitution will be subjected to national referendums in the UN member states," he continued, "by which time all its legal implications have been tried and tested in his fictitious state, under his supervision as its interim president."

This was followed by the longest, most excruciating minute of silence the UN had endured since the microphone failure during the 1989 budget session. The delegates sat frozen, their expressions drifting between horror and pity.

The professor, however, looked invigorated by his own words.

"The Srebrenica massacre commemoration reminded me of the importance of unity," he pressed on. "A local teacher asked me whether I knew the difference between the United Nations and the mafia. He asserted that, unlike the UN, the mafia is an organised establishment."

This produced scattered, uncomfortable tittering, half amusement, half diplomatic panic.

Then, to the horror of everyone, the professor once again pulled out his cell phone again.

"Professor Bote, please put your cell phone down!" the President snapped, her voice cracking through the speakers like a disciplinary thunderbolt. She switched Professor Bote's microphones off again.

Shaken, he nodded quickly. "Madame President, I assure you… I have no intention of playing music this time."

An audible sigh of collective relief passed through the hall.

"But," he added timidly, "I couldn't think of a better way to wrap up my little appearance here today than by borrowing a few minutes of genius from Charlie Chaplin's *The Great Dictator*."

A few diplomats perked up, as if at least this was a cultural reference they respected.

"I brought a printed copy with me, just in case my nerves outperformed my English… but I think you've suffered enough of my accent for one day. So instead of reading it, let's listen to Chaplin himself… the man who could say more in one minute of silence than most of us can in a lifetime of words."

The President sighed deeply but eventually gave a light nod, then switched the green lights back on.

With the solemnity of a man defusing a bomb, Professor Bote placed his thumb on the screen. Chaplin's impassioned call to unite echoed across the chamber, clear, powerful, and cinematic. The hall fell utterly silent, mesmerised.

When the playback ended, the chamber erupted into thunderous applause, far louder than anything the professor himself had achieved. Delegates rose to their feet, clapping in rapturous admiration, mostly for Chaplin, but the professor enjoyed the loud applause anyway.

\*\*\*

As if his humiliation in the General Assembly Hall had not been enough, an hour later Professor Bote found himself seated beside the UN Secretary-General, Ms Zyrtare E'Larte, in the UN's press conference room. The air vibrated with impatient chatter; camera shutters clicked like mechanical insects waiting to pounce.

The United Nations press conference room in New York looked exactly like the kind of place where global crises are announced with the emotional range of a malfunctioning toaster. A cavernous, over-air-conditioned chamber, kept at a temperature suitable for preserving either dignitaries or deli meat, bathed in a gentle, migraine-inducing wash of fluorescent light. The room tried very hard to look important, and instead succeeded only in looking expensive. Rows of pale blue seats stretched in perfectly aligned ranks, each one equipped with a tiny fold-up desk barely large enough for a notepad or a journalist's waning hope in international diplomacy.

At the front stood the iconic lectern, stamped with the unmistakable gold UN emblem, a sort of global participation trophy meant to remind everyone that although nothing gets solved, at least everyone *showed up*. Behind it hung a repeating backdrop of the UN logo on an ocean-blue fabric, designed not only to be visually recognizable but also to ensure that any photograph taken in the room resembles every other photograph ever taken there, thus guaranteeing maximum bureaucratic anonymity.

Cameras from every global news network perched like vultures along the back wall, their red lights blinking with predatory patience. Journalists sat poised with pens, laptops, and deeply suppressed exasperation. A few seasoned correspondents sported a glazed, existential expression unique to people who have spent decades years listening to diplomats answer questions without actually answering anything.

After Ms Zyrtare E'Larte's formal welcome, a skinny moderator surveyed the forest of raised hands and pointed towards a woman in the third row.

"Thank you," she said crisply. "Suzan Gerrard, BBC News. Madam Secretary-General, since the Task Force's proposal elicited no debate in the General Assembly, is there *any* support for this Convention?"

A faint sigh escaped Ms Zyrtare E'Larte as she lifted her comically thin eyebrows. "I cannot speculate on the future of this Convention. Next week, we will present it to UNESCO's Executive Board, who will determine whether it merits inclusion in their upcoming general conference."

Before the room could digest her evasive answer, another hand shot up, a tall journalist whose cranky voice carried an accusatory edge.

"Aziz Benzema, Al Jazeera. Professor Bote, are you proposing a global reality show modelled on *The Truman Show*? And wouldn't such a project require astronomical funding?"

Professor Bote leaned forward, elbows planted on the table, as if anchoring himself against the rising tide of scrutiny.

"Yes," he said with unnerving calm. "We are proposing a reality show akin to *The Truman Show*, where the orphan would be unaware, he is being broadcast to the entire world." He blinked, then added, "And regarding financing… yes, the Convention demands substantial resources, but only during its initial phase. The global fascination with reality television will quadruple the UN's existing budget once the project is underway, and…"

A thunderous outburst cut him off.

"This is *outrageous*!" roared the Al Jazeera journalist, his voice slicing through the hushed room. "You are violating human rights. What you're describing would rob an orphan of the one thing every human being is entitled to and that is free will!"

"You call the sacrifice of a single life 'outrageous,'" Bote replied, voice lower, colder, each word weighed and sharpened. "Yet you stand indifferent to the alternative, which is a potential nuclear holocaust that could extinguish millions, perhaps billions. Tell me... shall we let the world burn so that we can congratulate ourselves on moral purity? Or shall we accept that saving humanity may require a singular, tragic necessity?"

A shiver ran through the room.

The moderator's hand swept forward again and pointed toward a poised woman in the second row. She rose with a deliberate elegance that turned heads.

"Susan Robinson, CNN," she said. "Professor Bote, your orphan's constitution remains sealed until he turns thirty-five. Why? And what if he dies before then? Does the entire project collapse? Do you simply... start over?"

The silence that followed tightened like a noose.

Bote inhaled sharply, clasping his hands as though preparing for confession. "To draft a constitution that transcends bias," he began, "the orphan must first endure the full landscape of human existence... privilege and degradation, triumph and despair, hunger, loneliness, and the brutal clarity born of war... specifically, an ethnic war."

Gasps flickered across the room like sparks.

"He will receive the finest care and education," Bote continued, "but authenticity must be tested constantly. He must govern, struggle, fail, and ascend... all under the world's watchful eye. And if fate intervenes and he dies before fulfilling his purpose... then yes. We begin again. A new orphan. A new chance to get it right."

At this stage the professor's composure had begun to betray him. Sweat spilled down his temples; his fixed grin twitched at the edges, becoming something feral, unhinged, carrying the smile of a man who believed his nightmare blueprint was destiny.

A tall figure rose at the back.

"Alphonse Villeneuve, CBC News," he said. "How will this orphan interact with the world? You speak of transparency, but what does that mean?"

Bote dabbed his brow, his hand trembling. "For the constitution to be accepted," he explained, "the orphan must justify every decision, openly, before journalists, experts, and random voices from around the world." He leaned in, eyes glinting. "Actors will portray his friends, his colleagues… even his family. Every encounter a test. Every challenge a mirror. From that friction, we believe a unifying truth will emerge."

A wave of uneasy whispers rippled through the room.

The moderator pointed again, this time to a woman in the front row whose feline eyes gleamed with a predator's patience. She rose slowly, notebook poised.

"You keep calling him 'the orphan,'" she said, voice taut. "But who is he? And where does he come from?"

A small smile brightened Bote's sweating face, as though he'd been waiting desperately for this.

"Finally," he exhaled, "an easy question."

Anticipation rippled through the press room.

"The orphan," he declared solemnly, "comes from his mother's womb."

The room detonated with laughter, loud, and unrestrained, rolling across the walls like a crashing wave. Reporters bent double, cameras shook, a few journalists wiped tears from the corners of their eyes.

But Bote did not flinch. He adjusted his glasses with eerie serenity and scribbled something onto his notes, waiting patiently for the laughter to die.

When silence finally returned, he lifted his head with childlike poise.

"Unfortunately," he said, "I cannot reveal the orphan's identity, because he has not yet been born."

A stunned hush fell over the room.

Then, with the solemnity of a man delivering a verdict, Bote continued, "After an exhaustive genetic review of all ethnic groups, our board concluded that the orphan must be of Gypsy origin. This community, lacking a state of its own, is statistically less vulnerable to the inherited genetic afflictions of power and nationalism."

The laughter drained from the room instantly, before a tremor of disbelief.

A young journalist in a buoyant red tie rose next, the kind of tie that demanded attention even before its wearer spoke.

"Bob Simpson, CBS News," he announced briskly. "Professor, I'm referring to recent statements by world leaders who've already expressed doubts about an individual's capacity to bring forth genuine change or, as some put it, a better world. What's your response to them?"

Professor Bote blinked behind his thick lenses, the weight of the afternoon pressing visibly on his shoulders. His fingers began to drum against the table. Then, with a weary sigh, he leaned toward the microphone.

"One might expect such hypocrisy from ordinary citizens," he began, voice low and measured, "but not from politicians." He paused, letting the word hang in the air like an accusation. "Aren't heads of state themselves products of trust… the trust bestowed upon them by their voters?"

He removed his glasses, rubbing his eyes before continuing. "Imagine, if you will, what becomes of democracy when the world's electorate begins to doubt the very people they elect to improve their lives." His tone grew harder now, gathering conviction from exhaustion.

"I am confident," he went on, "that the world's leaders are aware this Convention merely mirrors the same democratic process they themselves once endured though scrutiny, selection, and legitimacy by consensus. The only difference," he said, slipping his glasses back on, "is that this time, democracy isn't just national. It's global."

He leaned back, the faintest trace of a brittle, unconvincing smile returning, "After all," he concluded, "this is democracy, but simply practiced on a larger scale."

The press conference moderator thanked the journalists and added, "I hope this press conference has adequately responded to your inquiries. I hope you will continue to show your interest in the United Nations' efforts to resolve global challenges. Until the next session, thank you and …"

"EXCUSE ME!" a shriek tore through the hall, shredding the

moderator's closing remarks in mid-sentence. Heads jerked up. Pens froze. Cameras stopped clicking.

"I've been raising my hand since the start of this conference," the voice quavered, rising to a fever pitch. "And I demand an answer from Professor Bote!"

A heavy, unnatural silence fell. Every journalist turned in unison toward the back of the room, where a dishevelled man stood trembling with anger, his press badge glinting under the fluorescent lights.

The moderator hesitated, as his eyes flicked towards the professor, who slumped in his chair, then gave the faintest nod. The moderator extended a single finger, a reluctant summons.

"Thank you," the man snapped, stepping forward. "Eduardo Neymar, Associated Press." His gaze locked onto the professor, not the moderator. "Professor Bote, you opened this conference with John Lennon's Imagine, a song that dreams of a world without wars, countries, or religions. Tell us, Professor… are you trying to create a world without God?"

Laughter burst from Professor Bote like a sudden, violent thunderclap, too loud and too sharp, the kind of laugh that made people shift uneasily in their seats. His thin shoulders shook as he bowed his head, his glasses slipping down the bridge of his nose.

"Most of my colleagues warned me not to play that song," he managed between strained chuckles. "They thought it would send the wrong message. So, thank you, Mr. Neymar, you've just lost me a bet and now I have to buy lunch for the entire board at Sushi Yasuda tomorrow."

A few awkward snickers scattered through the room. But the professor's smile was wrong, brittle, fixed, and desperate. It dissolved almost as soon as it appeared.

He leaned toward the microphone. His lips twitched. The humour drained from his face like blood retreating from a wound.

"Professor, are you alright?" the moderator asked quietly, his voice softer now, shorn of the earlier edge.

"Yes," Bote murmured. "Yes, I'm fine."

But he wasn't. Everyone could hear it, the tremor and the fragility threaded through each syllable. A flicker of guilt crossed his features. His eyes darted away, to the wall, to nothing, as if searching for an escape that wasn't there.

He cleared his throat. Slowly, almost painfully, he leaned back in his chair. His left fist rose to his chin, a thinker's gesture, but it looked more like a man shielding himself from his own thoughts.

"Your question," he said at last, "is fair."

The room stilled. Recorders angled forward in unison.

"But it isn't for me to decide whether the orphan's new constitution will yield a religious or a religiousness state." His voice grew steadier, anchored in conviction. "That choice belongs to the orphan... the child who will grow up in a town deliberately engineered from contradictions. A place where people will be initially banned and then allowed worship different gods beneath the same sky, where prayers rise together but never meet."

Bote lowered his eyes to his notes, then raised them again with something darker behind them.

"The Convention's Script Protocol specifies he will have a Muslim mother and a Christian Orthodox father."

A ripple of shifting bodies moved through the hall.

"They were meant to embody coexistence," Bote continued softly, "to prove that faiths once divided by centuries of bloodshed could live in one home. Under one roof. Bound not by dogma... but by love."

He paused. Something tightened in his jaw.

"But love," he said, his voice dropping into a funeral register, "will become the first casualty when the town descends into an ethnic religious war."

The lights overhead hummed faintly, as if the room itself were holding its breath.

"The promise of unity," he went on, "will drown in the cries of the faithful. Mosques and churches that once stood side by side will become fortresses. Neighbours will become enemies. And the couple who were once hailed as symbols of peace..." His breath hitched.

"…will be torn apart by the very doctrines they believed they could transcend."

Silence spread through the hall, thick as smoke. Even the cameras stopped clicking.

"The orphan," Bote whispered, "will be born from the ashes of their separation. He will inherit their faiths. Their wounds. Their silence."

He lifted his gaze, and for a brief moment, just a flicker, something like sorrow crossed his eyes.

"And when the time comes…" he said, voice barely audible, "it will be his decision whether religions will survive… or fade."

.

# Meanwhile, in London – Part Two

So, there you have it, the spurious *par excellence* of UN nonsense. Let's adopt a poor orphan, strip him of his humanity, and hand him over like state-issued property to whatever pair of psychopathic wannabe-celebrities are desperate enough to raise him under a global microscope. The United Nations, or the United Nutcases, as anyone sane might justifiably rename them, has once again proved incapable of grasping the human essence. It was written in neon during Professor Bote's obscene little performance; every word he uttered was a signature on a document that no rational species would ever draft.

In the face of such colossal imbecility, it's laughable to hope for any kind of immediate solution to the impending nuclear war. And into this carnival of idiocy marched Professor Bote himself, the self-proclaimed saviour, delusional visionary, occasional ornament on late-night talk shows, brandishing a proposal that sounded less like a peace plan and more like the transcript of a psychiatric episode dressed up in pseudo-scientific gibberish.

His grand "solution" to global annihilation?

Not diplomacy.

Not de-escalation.

Not even common sense.

No, Bote proposed that world leaders, instead of exchanging nuclear warheads, should participate in what he called "a mutually therapeutic act of physical surrender." According to him, if mankind could not rise above its destructive instincts, it might at least find salvation by collapsing beneath them. The idea was immediately hailed by the intellectually bankrupt as "provocative" and "refreshingly unorthodox," while the rest of the civilised world called it what it truly was: the deranged fantasy of a man confusing desperation with genius.

But undeterred, because delusion rarely knows when to stop, Bote insisted his proposal was not madness but "moral innovation." Proof, once again, that in an age of universal lunacy, insanity doesn't stand out, it gets tenure.

The world is what we make of it, and one thing is certain, there is absolutely no frigging way that another human, a member of the same species that screwed everything up, is going to fix it with a new constitution. Especially not one written under surveillance, parental trauma, and UN sponsorship.

And speaking of a new global constitution, let's talk about referendums, those glorious exercises in false equality where a wit and a halfwit are treated as political equals. Democracy is great, yes, but what good is it when the number of registered voters with the intellectual range of a coat hanger is steadily rising?

Take 2016.

The infamous Brexit referendum.

A national act of self-harm disguised as patriotism.

Quivering at the thought of the EU's new anti-tax-avoidance measures, the British establishment decided that Brexit was the perfect escape hatch. Britain, once a proud democracy, aimed to reinvent itself as the world's largest low-wage tax haven, a paradise for the super-wealthy and a purgatory for the rest. Of course, most of the EU Anti-Tax Avoidance Directive was already baked into British law. But three provisions threatened this fantasy.

First, the level-playing-field rule, which prevents countries from striking sweetheart tax deals that distort competition. Second, and far more terrifying to the British establishment, the jurisdiction of the European Court of Justice, the only entity with the teeth to actually enforce those rules. Third, the British Exit Tax was different to EU Exit Tax.

So, when Brexiteers like Boris Johnson, Jacob Rees-Mogg, and Nigel Farage wailed about the EU threatening British sovereignty, what they really meant was that the EU is threatening the sovereignty of the British tax-dodging practices by the wealthy elite. After all, the European Court of Justice forced Apple to repay €13 billion to Ireland and slapped Fiat Chrysler with a massive tax penalty.

Unable to maintain the good old British tax-dodging traditions under EU oversight, the establishment demanded a referendum. David Cameron initially said no, but then the next day, met the *real* powers of Britain, and suddenly "no" transformed into "let's ask 65 million people to burn down their own house." The Leave vote won. The country left the EU. And Cameron went down in history as the Right Honourable Twat, Dave Came'moron.

Came'moron's elected successor, Boris Johnson, arrived with "BJ" initials, which obviously was rather tempting to most of his male English voters. After all, what better metaphor for the national political mood than a man whose very monogram reads like the punchline of a pub joke? It was as if the universe decided that if the country was going to plunge headfirst into chaos, it might as well do so under a leader whose initials were very attractive indeed. It's almost poetic. Years of political decline culminating in a leader who resembled a malfunctioning scarecrow. By the time he entered Number 10, the whole spectacle resembled Britain auditioning for the role of "Most Chaotic Democracy" in a dark global sitcom. And it succeeded brilliantly. After all, any nation can elect a competent leader, but it takes a true pioneer of self-inflicted humiliation to elevate a man whose initials alone could fuel half the nation's late-night comedy shows.

And did we learn anything from that catastrophe?

Of course not.

By 2069, Britain staged yet another disastrous referendum, this time because the extreme tropical temperatures that turned the UK into a reluctant Mediterranean wasteland. At 45°C, London recorded its hottest May ever. Schools closed. Roads melted. Asphalt turned into treacle.

And in the midst of all this, the nation was asked whether to switch working hours from 9:00–17:00 to 20:00–04:00. Result? Sixty-three percent voted yes. Because, naturally, the country that once conquered half the planet is now perfectly content to live like vampires to escape the heat."

British children now attend school under moonlight, from 10 pm to 4 am. My sister Jane is inconsolable at the thought of raising her three children in nocturnal captivity. She wants to migrate to Siberia, one of the few remaining places on earth with tolerable summers, and Miny the new booming metropolis where my uncle Stephen already lives, But her husband, Paul, refuses to leave London. So now my sister is filing for divorce on Monday thanks to that referendum.

Unsurprisingly, we, the British government framed the nocturnal-work referendum as a "bold leap into climate-adaptive modernity," which is political code for, we've run out of ideas, please stop asking us for solutions. Instead of investing in infrastructure, cooling systems, or heaven forbid coherent policies, they simply pushed the entire population eight hours forward like a broken clock. The official slogan was "Beat the Heat: Work at Night!", which some enthusiastic MP assured the public was innovative, as if ancient desert-dwelling civilizations hadn't figured this out several thousand years ago without needing a referendum or a six-week BBC debate marathon. Britain, ever determined to remain the world champion of unnecessary plebiscites, marched proudly into its new nocturnal era. Instead of fixing anything, infrastructure, housing, climate policy, food supply, basic governance, the country chose once again to outsource all decision-making to an overheated public that can barely think straight when the temperature rises above 20°C.

So really, the UN should have seen the warning signs long ago, give humanity a referendum, and it will reliably choose the option that guarantees maximum inconvenience, psychological trauma, and irreversible chaos. In that sense, Britain has always been a trailblazer. It paved the way, or rather, melted it, ensuring that when the UN finally cooked up its global referendum fiasco, the rest of the world would be perfectly primed to follow Britain's shining example of climate-induced democratic self-harm.

Given this rich history of national self-sabotage, it's no surprise that the UN Reform Task Force, in all its brilliance, decided to top it with their "pièce de résistance", a referendum that gives nearly the entire planet a chance to screw everything up again.

# Chapter 3

Following massive opposition from human rights groups, significant changes to the original Script Protocol, and thirteen months since its ratification by 87 member states, the United Nations Secret of Divine Civilisation Broadcast Centres began their first uninterrupted broadcasts. Rather than one, the Convention began broadcasting 24 hours a day the lives of five orphans living in the brand-new town of Anitshirp, built on the Croatian island, Olib, which was inhabited by 65,000 actors and skilled individuals lured in by six-figure salaries. Every sane observer agreed that such an enterprise could not possibly endure. Yet, in a democracy, stupidity is a universal right, and millions exercised it every day by tuning in to this sanctimonious spectacle. What had been hailed as a humanitarian milestone quickly descended into the most elaborately funded moral disaster in broadcasting history. If the Convention achieved anything, it was the systematic destruction of five innocent lives for the sake of global entertainment and bureaucratic pride.

In fact, the UN insisted on calling the project "innovative social engineering," which in UN jargon simply means "we have no idea what we are doing but it's too late to cancel the budget." Diplomats beamed proudly as if they had personally solved world hunger rather than invented a dystopian talent show in which the only talent required was suffering. Committees held champagne receptions celebrating "historic transparency," blissfully unaware that the only thing transparent was the thin varnish of moral justification hiding humanity's insatiable appetite for voyeurism. If anything, the project served as an unexpected case study proving that when self-righteous idealism meets unlimited funding, the result is indistinguishable from a very expensive nervous breakdown.

The orphan appearing on UN-SDC-BC1 descended into alcoholism, his sole ambition reduced to securing two litres of vodka a day. By adulthood, his speech was a litany of profanity, and his marriage had become a theatre of violence. After breaking his wife's left arm in a particularly brutal domestic altercation, sixty-one UN member states held national referendums and promptly terminated his broadcast in their respective countries. Two years later, he died of cirrhosis, leaving behind a legacy of moral lessons ignored and headlines forgotten. In classic UN fashion, a special committee was formed to examine "the root causes of his behavioural decline," which concluded, after eighteen months of meetings at scenic resort locations, that he had been born with "insufficient resilience for global visibility", summing it up as his fault. This report, naturally, was praised for its "balanced analysis" and then quietly shelved, where it remains buried under decades of equally useless findings.

The orphan featured on UN-SDC-BC3 was a gifted driver, utterly obsessed with speed and danger. His youthful talent promised a glittering career in Formula One, only for it to end tragically in a fatal car accident before he even reached twenty-three. The world mourned briefly, then returned to its endless consumption of spectacle. The Convention responded with a solemn moment of silence that lasted exactly thirty seconds before announcing a new fundraising gala themed "Drive Toward a Brighter Future," complete with luxury cars displayed outside the venue. This profound tribute demonstrated that even in tragedy, humanity can still find a way to turn moral failure into an opportunity for corporate sponsorship.

The child on UN-SDC-BC4 evolved into a vicious Bresian nationalist. Rather than promoting unity, he incited ethnic hatred, undermining the very principles the Convention claimed to uphold.

Following a televised attempt to murder his Muslim neighbour during a staged civil war, fifty-four UN member states immediately pulled the plug on his broadcast. He was subsequently confined to a psychiatric ward, where he remains, a living monument to the perils of ideological engineering. Despite this, the UN held an emergency press conference insisting the programme had "largely succeeded," because, according to their spokesperson, "viewers were able to witness the dangers of extremism firsthand." The fact that the extremism had been manufactured for television was not mentioned. Nor was the awkward detail that ratings spiked during the attempted murder.

The UN-SDC-BC5 orphan became a global darling, a handsome, charismatic boy who captivated millions. But fame proved as toxic as any addiction. At his twenty-fifth birthday party, he snorted a dangerously excessive amount of cocaine, succumbing to the very indulgence that had fuelled his allure. Even in death, he retained a peculiar cultural immortality, people worldwide, including my mother, regularly held remembrance vigils, a tribute to the odd intersection of innocence, celebrity, and disaster.

There were even rumours that UNESCO considered designating his childhood bedroom a World Heritage Site "to commemorate the intersection of global media and emotional projection." Thankfully, the proposal was abandoned once someone realised that turning a memorial to an exploited orphan into a tourist attraction might appear "slightly insensitive," even by UN standards.

The only orphan to survive this global circus known as The Secret of Divine Civilisation was the one featured on UN-SDC-BC2. His name was Isa Iri, and, by any measure, he was the dullest of the lot. Though his every mundane activity was broadcast worldwide, his island home was arguably the most isolated place on Earth, completely cut off from the internet, cable television, and inbound or outbound flights. Moreover, the elderly living on this island constantly reminded Isa and every child living in Anitshirp Town of a big fat lie that their island was a small part of the vast Atheist Communist Federation of Vallsia, where 20 million people lived. Everyone who migrated to Anitshirp Town assumed new identities with awkward, unpronounceable names, a sort of administrative hazing ritual designed by people who believed that linguistic suffering-built character. They had signed lifelong contracts with UN-SDC-BC, agreeing to forfeit any semblance of dignity in exchange for residing on the island. Though they knew five orphans were being televised globally, they remained unaware of their identities. The only ones permitted to know Isa's true status were his adoptive parents, managers of public institutions, and law enforcement officers, the holy trinity of those who pretend to maintain order while ensuring chaos prevails.

This fictitious federation comprised the Republic of Ansobia, Bresia, Taorkia, and the Province of Ryllia.

It was a masterpiece of bureaucratic theatre, because an entire generation was raised inside a geopolitical hallucination invented by people who had never successfully organised even a lunch meeting. The Convention called it "identity immersion." Psychologists called it "collective gaslighting."

Isa resided in a modest two-storey brick house on the northern outskirts of Anitshirp Town. The building was barely visible from the street, hidden behind a riot of apricot, peach, plum, pear, apple, and cherry trees, which seemed determined to obscure both its architecture and its occupant from the world.

The neighbourhood was a curious patchwork of ethnic theatre, identical houses lined up perpendicular to a massive, ceremonial roundabout, each inhabited by families claiming Ansobian, Taorkian, Bresian, Ryllian, or Jewish heritage. Ansobians, Taorks, and Bresians spoke the same language, Vallsian, but distinguished themselves with accents so minor that they might have been invented purely for authenticity. Ryllians and Jews spoke another language entirely, though both had mastered Vallsian, which, in an ironic twist, was in fact just English with bureaucratic pretensions.

In this carefully orchestrated microcosm, diversity existed mainly on paper, as if the Convention had mandated it in a footnote. The town's architecture, language, and social arrangement resembled a badly designed board game, where every player was expected to perform their ethnicity correctly, lest the illusion of "multicultural harmony" crumble before the cameras.

\*\*\*

Ever since early childhood, Isa displayed an astonishing, almost performative stupidity. Most toddlers threw the occasional tantrum; Isa, however, was a bona fide drama queen, whose daily bouts of defiance would have earned him an Oscar if only someone had bothered to nominate him. His Ansobian mother, Nona, and Bresian father, Ati, struggled constantly with their resilient, theatrically obstinate child.

And of course, the UN's behavioural consultants insisted that Isa's theatrical idiocy was "developmentally enriching," as if throwing furniture, screaming at clouds, and bursting into spontaneous weeping fits constituted a meaningful contribution to human civilisation. In interviews, they praised his "emotional expressiveness," which is a polite way of admitting that even they could not explain why this particular child seemed committed to turning every minor inconvenience into a full-length opera.

During Isa's first month at the nursery, his eyes brimmed with tears every single morning as his mother handed him over. One particularly memorable day, Nona passed a tiny grey rucksack to Isa's teacher, who stood dutifully at the far edge of the entrance. Isa, displaying the obstinacy of a miniature monarch, plopped himself onto the hall floor and clutched his feet as if resisting gravity itself. The scene resembled a small-scale political uprising, one toddler seceding from all forms of authority.

Nona knelt beside him. "Every child hates their nursery at first," she explained patiently, "but you're in the excellent hands of Ms Mesuese. You two will get on just fine."

"We won't!" Isa shrieked. "She's constantly telling me what to do as if I'm one of her toys."

"That's a cruel observation!" Nona retorted, bending down to untie his stubborn little shoes. "You should apologise immediately!"

Ms Mesuese offered Isa a compassionate smile and extended a hand toward him. She maintained the serene expression of a woman who had long ago learned to outsource her sanity to meditation apps. Meanwhile, Nona, performing her own version of diplomacy, apologised on Isa's behalf before scooping him up into a hug. Isa resisted, pushing and squirming as though he were trying to repel the very laws of nature. Had Newton been present, he might have rewritten his laws of motion specifically to account for Isa's talent for generating chaos from a seated position.

The hallway buzzed with the typical morning symphony of half-awake parents and children, but Isa's operatic protests sliced through it like a foghorn. Other toddlers paused mid-cry to observe how true professionals conducted emotional meltdowns. Some admired him. Others, more strategic in temperament, took mental notes for future use against their own parents.

According to the Convention's Script Protocol, Isa was receiving exemplary care, with his adoptive parents dutifully following a rigid upbringing regime. Yet somehow, against all logic and human decency, Nona and Ati had succeeded in raising a child who redefined the term spoiled rotten, an extraordinary feat even for a global experiment designed to manufacture exemplary humans. Isa was not merely spoiled; he was a one-boy showcase of bureaucratic failure, a living monument to the absurdities of intention versus outcome!

And of course, the UN's psychological assessment team, those brave souls armed with clipboards, theories, and the kind of optimism that borders on self-delusion, insisted that Isa's daily theatrics were "healthy expressions of agency." They even drafted a 48-page report celebrating his "assertive emotional autonomy," which is precisely the academic phrase one uses when too embarrassed to write "this child behaves like a rabid goat."

Behind closed doors, even Ms Mesuese occasionally questioned her career choices. She would watch Isa wrap himself around door frames, radiators, and unsuspecting classmates like a crisis in human form, wondering how the world's most expensive social experiment had managed to produce a toddler who behaved like a mythological punishment sent by vengeful gods. Meanwhile, Nona and Ati clung stubbornly to the belief that strict adherence to the Script Protocol would eventually yield a well-adjusted adult, blissfully ignoring the mounting evidence that it was turning their child into an avant-garde performance piece titled *Anarchy in Preschool.*

\*\*\*

Isa's morning tantrums persisted for an entire month, until a Jewish girl named Eva enrolled at the nursery. From that day forward, his daily resistance to drop-offs vanished. Eva was a quiet, red-haired girl who spoke with a peculiar lisp. Isa, too, had a modest lisp, which had long discouraged him from conversing with his peers. Yet with Eva, he spoke freely, always in a shy, whispering tone, as if the lisp itself had been a secret handshake between them.

Beyond their shared lisp, both children had distinct ears, Eva's were small and subtle, rising only to her eyelids, while Isa's jutted proudly upward to his eyebrows, resembling external side-view mirrors mounted on buses, likely the reason his mother kept his hair long, hoping to obscure them from the world's judgmental gaze. His father, meanwhile, had suggested ear-friendly hats, ear-strengthening exercises, and even a visit to a cosmetic surgeon, before Nona reminded him, they were raising a child, not upgrading a second-hand vehicle.

Shortly after turning four, Isa discovered the joys of strawberries at the nursery, smearing juice across his face as though applying ceremonial war paint. Then, holding an empty plastic bowl aloft, he marched toward his teacher and, in a display of precocious mischief, tugged at her leather skirt.

The teacher turned calmly, suppressing a sigh. "What's the matter?" she asked.

"Could I have more strawberries?" Isa inquired, lifting the empty bowl with solemn expectation.

"And what's the magic word?"

"Abracadabra!" he answered promptly, eyes wide with sincerity.

The teacher laughed, pressing slim fingers against her mouth to stifle it. After a composed pause, she bowed theatrically toward him and swung her left index finger like a tiny metronome.

"Did I say something wrong?" Isa asked, glancing up with innocent bewilderment.

"Your reply is absurdly flawless," she said, "but that isn't the magic word I sought."

"Hocus Pocus?" Isa ventured, offering another wild guess, entirely untroubled by decorum or consequence.

The teacher laughed again before replying, "Wrong again! It's more like Hocus Pleasus."

Isa stared at her, lips parted, head slightly tilted, as if she had just delivered a cryptic prophecy meant only for the spiritually gifted. "Hocus... Pleasus?" he echoed, testing the phrase like a fragile artefact. It sounded to him less like a magic word and more like something one might whisper to summon a confused pigeon.

Eva, watching from her seat, clasped her little hands together and giggled into her collar. Isa's ears, his two proud satellite dishes, reddened instantly. To her, the scene was sweet. To Isa, it was a moment of destiny, the kind poets later describe as the beginning of everything and adults refer to as a harmless childhood crush that eventually ends in heartbreak and therapy.

Ms Mesuese knelt down, still smiling. "No, Isa. The real magic word is simply 'please.' You know that." Then Ms Mesuese looked back at Isa. "But next time, magic word first. Strawberries second."

Isa nodded solemnly, the weight of this cosmic order settling upon him.

But as he shuffled away, Eva smiled at him, the soft, conspiratorial smile only children can manage, the kind that promises lifelong friendship in three seconds.

Isa's chest puffed with pride. Finally, for the first time in his life, he had done something impressive enough to make a girl laugh.

Granted, it involved smearing fruit all over his face and misunderstanding a basic social cue, but for Isa Iri, this was monumental progress.

Behind them, Ms Mesuese muttered under her breath, "This is not what I signed up for," before refilling his bowl anyway, because even the Script Protocol could not withstand the combined power of Isa's earnest stupidity and Eva's approving giggle.!"

\*\*\*

As the days progressed, Isa's prodigious stupidity only intensified. Ten months after the infamous "magic word" fiasco, Ms Mesuese announced that each Monday would feature a different topic.

"This morning's topic is a calendar. Isa, could you please tell us what a calendar is?" she asked, leaning over with faint optimism.

Hesitant at first, Isa replied solemnly, "Calendar is this morning's topic."

Ironically, the nursery was called Bright Kids Academy.

The irony, in fact, had long overtaken irony itself. Parents of other children had begun complaining that the mere presence of Isa in the classroom risked lowering their own offspring's IQ by osmosis. Some even claimed their toddlers had begun speaking in broken, existential riddles after group activities with him. The administration, naturally, denied any such effect, but then again, this was the same nursery that awarded Isa a certificate of "Most Improved Thinker" simply because he finally learned not to eat crayons that weren't blue.

\*\*\*

Two weeks later, Isa wandered into the kitchen and opened the fridge door. He retrieved a carrot from the bottom drawer, closed it with solemn care, and marched into the front garden where his parents were seated. The sky had darkened, illuminated only by a full moon suspended in the cloudless expanse. Occasional car headlights briefly lit his face, but the grass beneath his feet remained shrouded in shadow. He clutched the carrot as if it were a precious dog leash.

Nona and Ati sat on elegantly sculpted bamboo chairs, sipping coffee. Ati's face was buried behind the morning newspaper, while

Nona observed her son with the focused intensity of a scientist monitoring a particularly perplexing experiment.

"Isa, why are you holding that carrot?" Nona asked, carefully setting her cup down on the glazed surface of the round outdoor table. "Are you looking for a rabbit?"

"No, Mum!" Isa shouted without glancing back. "I'm trying to find the red car you got me last month."

"But why the carrot?" Nona pressed, suspicion rising.

"Because it's dark out here," Isa replied, as if this explained everything.

Ati pushed aside his newspaper, narrowing his eyes. "I can see it's dark. But why are you holding a carrot?"

"Our teacher told us that carrots improve our vision, especially in the dark!" Isa explained, nodding with the absolute conviction of someone whose worldview had been shaped entirely by absurd authority.

The scene lingered in a kind of tragicomic tableau with a boy wandering in circles, armed with a vegetable, parents complicit in the theatre of absurdity, and the moon silently bearing witness to another day in the life of the Convention's only surviving, and spectacularly idiotic, experiment.

One could hardly blame the moon for keeping its distance. Even celestial bodies, one suspects, know better than to get involved with bureaucratic human stupidity. Somewhere, thousands of kilometres away, an astronomer might have pointed a telescope that night and noticed the faint shimmer of a lone carrot rotating in the darkness. Had he known the story behind it, he would likely have retired on the spot, despairing at humanity's intellectual trajectory.

Isa did an outstanding job in ravaging whatever expectations brainless people had from this convention. Either Isa's parents were exceptionally gifted in turning their adopted son into such an imbecile, or his stupidity was due to some genetic predetermination.

The Convention, of course, pretended to study such outcomes with scientific seriousness. Committees were formed. Graphs were drawn.

Experts, experts in absolutely nothing, were flown in to give PowerPoint presentations filled with arrows, flowcharts, and colour-coded stupidity projections. They spoke solemnly about "Outcome Maximisation Models" as if they were detailing a Mars landing, instead of chronicling the intellectual collapse of a child raised by paperwork.

\*\*\*

The Convention's Script Protocol meticulously outlined Isa's "critical development stages," one of which mandated that all orphans undertake a boat journey with their adoptive families, an excursion that was, by design, to end in a sinking vessel. When the event unfolded, Isa screamed his parents' names as tears carved clean paths down his face, flailing in the Adriatic Sea, battling for his very life.

The incident sparked immediate global outrage. Human rights groups denounced the Convention as barbaric, and protests erupted worldwide, demanding its immediate termination. Yet the UN-SDC-BC's Executive Producer, Ms. Drejtoresha, defended the atrocity with the clinical detachment of a bureaucrat who had mistaken sadism for protocol. In a now-infamous tweet, she wrote:

> *"To ensure that orphans would never leave the island, we had to abide by the Script Protocol's requirements and stage the drowning incident. With no flights into or off the island, sailing is the only ingress or egress. This horrendous act is intended to instil a permanent fear of the sea in the children, thereby deterring any attempt to leave."*

Her justification, couched in the sterile language of policy, only magnified the grotesque absurdity of the Convention: a meticulously organized tragedy presented as child development, a carefully choreographed horror packaged as pedagogy, and a drowning, orchestrated under the guise of "protocol compliance," celebrated on social media as a triumph of bureaucratic ingenuity.

In fact, Ms. Drejtoresha's tweet garnered over 200,000 likes from people who believed cruelty must surely be progressive if phrased in sufficiently technical jargon. Influencers made reaction videos praising the "boldness" of fear-based education. Some even suggested licensing the model to other institutions, because nothing says child welfare quite like intentionally traumatising minors under the warm glow of bureaucratic self-congratulation.

By the following week, the Convention had already begun planning the next stage of Isa's development, proving once more that in the world of international organisations, the capacity for embarrassment is not merely low, it is extinct.

***

Throughout his primary school years, Isa spent most of his afternoons playing football or cards with his neighbourhood friends Ryllian Shoki, Taork Ajtam, Ansobian Ojum, Jewish Joseph, Bresian Alexander, and Bresian Ocim. Their gatherings usually took place on the cracked concrete lot behind the row of red brick houses.

Shoki, Alexander, and Joseph were his closest companions, the ones with whom he spent most of his time outdoors, whether kicking a half-deflated football or trading insults over card games conducted at a wobbly picnic table. Unbeknownst to them, every joke, every argument, every triumphant shout of "goal!" and every muttered curse when Isa inevitably tripped over his own feet, was being broadcast to millions of invisible spectators. The children were blissfully unaware that their carefree afternoons doubled as international entertainment, a Truman-Show-meets-social-welfare fiasco approved by the world's most self-satisfied bureaucrats.

Isa ended up an entirely average pupil, harbouring a particular hatred for mathematics, a subject that never failed to provoke in him an operatic level of fury. His classmates often watched in awe as Isa threw tantrums with the dramatic bravado of a Shakespearean actor playing Hamlet in an underfunded school production. In response, his parents hired an "exceptional" private tutor to conduct additional one-on-one sessions, as if academic brilliance could be bought by the hour, like cheap therapy or premium cable subscriptions.

\*\*\*

Two months after Isa's eighth birthday, Nona, a tall woman now teetering on the brink of obesity, sat across from him at the dining table, methodically peeling potatoes. The dining room was bathed in the soft glow of late afternoon light filtering through the wide-glazed doors that opened onto a meticulously tended garden, complete with trimmed hedges, potted geraniums, and a stone path that led nowhere in particular, much like Isa's intellectual development.

Her long blond hair fell in careful waves over a pale face, showing only the faintest wrinkles around her unnervingly bright blue eyes. These eyes, depending on the moment, could either radiate maternal affection or beam a silent warning that mediocrity would not be tolerated under her roof, unless, of course, it came from Isa, for whom mediocrity was practically a lifestyle choice.

A large television screen presided over the room like an indifferent deity, reflecting distorted versions of their silhouettes on its glossy black surface. Opposite the garden doors, an antique mahogany cupboard dominated the wall, its narrow shelves crammed with souvenir plates emblazoned with European capitals. They were arranged with neurotic precision, as though compensating for the emotional disorderliness of the household. A bowl overflowing with summer fruits sat atop the cupboard beside a polished brass candlestick that gleamed pointedly, as if mocking the absurd seriousness with which this family performed their domestic rituals.

Nona returned to the dining room clutching a small brown bottle and a white plastic spoon. She poured the yellowish liquid into the spoon and extended it toward Isa with the solemnity of a scientist administering an experimental serum that might, if they were lucky, raise his IQ by half a point.

"Must I drink this horrible thingy?" Isa protested, pursing his lips and tilting backward like a man confronted with poison.

"You know what your doctor said. One spoon a day to keep your allergy away! Without this, you won't be able to attend your precious football training sessions," Nona reminded him, tone dripping with maternal martyrdom.

Isa grudgingly complied, swallowing the medicine with a grimace that suggested he had just bitten into a chunk of raw ginger dipped in regret. He then turned back to his homework, letting out a series of frustrated grunts before finally exploding, "Maths is driving me crazy!"

"I'll be right back," Nona said, disappearing into the kitchen with the sacred bottle.

When she returned, she circled to the other side of the table, crouched behind Isa, and threw her arms around his neck in a dramatic, overbearing hug that would have suffocated a weaker child.

"Maths drives you crazy, doesn't it?" she asked patiently.

"Yes! All it does, is tell you that two plus two is four," Isa replied with the solemnity of a philosopher confronting a cruel cosmic truth.

"And what's wrong with that?" Nona asked.

"Why must we learn to calculate when we could just use a calculator?" Isa demanded, as if presenting a groundbreaking solution to the world's intellectual burdens.

Nona laughed and ruffled his hair. "Mathematics is one of the few truthful subjects. If humans adopted the laws of mathematics and nature, our little planet might actually become a better place to live."

"But planet Earth is already a good place, isn't it?" Isa asked, his innocence hanging in the air like a timid balloon waiting to be popped.

"Oh, I'd love to be young like you again," Nona sighed, tickling him lightly. "When I was your age, I never thought about the world or what it could become. Enjoy your childhood and stop asking silly questions."

"Stop it, Mum!" Isa cried, flailing to escape her tickling hands.

"As you grow up, you'll spend much of your life trying to understand humans. Instead, I implore you to focus on the laws of mathematics, nature, and God."

"Mum! You just said the G-word!" Isa scolded, horrified. "Our teacher said people who say that end up in prison, like Lokin's father."

At that moment, Ati entered the dining room, his foul mood

practically dripping from his shoulders. His walk carried the defeated slump of a man who had battled both society and himself, and lost both fights. He planted a perfunctory kiss on Nona's cheek and another on Isa's forehead before announcing, "I'm off for my afternoon nap."

"Sweet dreams!" Nona called after him as he climbed the stairs.

"But Dad has diabetes, so he isn't allowed to have anything sweet!" Isa shouted after him, correcting the universe with the earnestness of a tiny, clueless bureaucrat.

His parents burst into laughter, but the sound rang hollow, echoing through the meticulously curated dining room like applause at a funeral. It wasn't funny. It was tragic. Isa, the Convention's sole surviving "exemplar," was meant to illuminate the world with brilliance and moral fortitude. Instead, he had achieved the impossible by becoming the crowning glory of the UN's long line of spectacular failures, a living monument to bureaucratic hubris, misplaced ambition, and the eternal absurdity of trying to manufacture perfection out of a child who could barely handle the concept of addition.

In that moment, the grandeur of the mahogany cupboards, the polished brass candlestick, and the souvenir plates of European capitals seemed almost sinister, standing as silent witnesses to the catastrophic mismanagement of human potential. The Convention had promised enlightenment, but it delivered mediocrity, neatly wrapped in protocol and broadcast worldwide for all to admire.

# Chapter 4

In strict accordance with the Convention's Script Protocol, Isa was required to watch the 19:00 news over dinner with his parents every single night, a ritual allegedly intended to cultivate worldly awareness, though in practice it merely fostered passive compliance. The Protocol insisted this routine would one day "mould future leaders." Instead, it moulded Isa, which should have been enough evidence to terminate the entire programme on humanitarian grounds.

Five weeks after his seventeenth birthday, Isa sat at the dining table with his parents, tucking into roast beef and potatoes under the unforgiving gleam of a sparkling glass chandelier. The chandelier, a monstrous arrangement of crystal teardrops and gold-plated branches, emitted a glare so bright it could have interrogated confessions out of war criminals. Its light bounced across their faces, illuminating every pore, wrinkle, and micro-expression of irritation, transforming an otherwise mundane dinner into a theatrical display of domestic pretence.

The dining room itself seemed complicit in the farce. The walls were covered in white wallpaper cluttered with small, repetitive flowers, thousands of them, creating the visual equivalent of being quietly smothered by lace doilies. The pattern felt almost predatory, leaning inward, as though to remind the family that the Script Protocol watched all, permitted nothing, and forgave even less. Even the air felt stiff with obedience.

Ati sat rigidly in his usual place, shoulders tight, posture erect, the embodiment of a man who had long ago surrendered emotional expression in exchange for the dubious honour of being "Protocol-compliant." His silence hovered over the table like smoke. Nona, as always, compensated for Ati's muteness by maintaining a relentless stream of chatter, verbal confetti that she sprinkled uninvited over every meal. Her energy was at once admirable and exhausting, a woman determined to narrate every fleeting thought as though the fate of the European continent depended on her commentary.

She wore a silky white top that softened the pallor of her skin, a skin that, under harsher lighting, often took on a ghostly hue, making her look like a well-dressed apparition on loan from a Victorian portrait. Her blond hair, which she insisted was naturally cooperative, bobbed and swayed with every sentence, forcing her to pat it down repeatedly in a battle she had not won once in seventeen years.

Ati's dark chestnut eyes bulged slightly, giving him a look of permanent astonishment, as though every moment of his life delivered yet another mild disappointment. The slight slant of his eyes was further emphasised by the constant strain of refusing to wear spectacles. He despised glasses with a fiery passion he reserved for nothing else, not even Isa's idiocy or the Script Protocol itself. His refusal was unwavering: better to misread the entire world than be caught looking scholarly.

Between the rigid décor, the choking floral wallpaper, and the chandelier that seemed capable of signalling ships at sea. Each family member performed their assigned roles with dutiful precision, Ati the stoic patriarch, Nona the sanitized chatterbox, Isa the reluctant heir to global disappointment. And all of them oblivious, or pretending to be, to the absurdity of the nightly performance.

"How is your Béarnaise sauce today?" Nona asked, as though the state of Isa's condiments contained some prophetic significance for his future.

Isa wiped the yellow flecks from the corners of his mouth, pressed the fingertips of his right hand together, then planted a dramatic kiss upon them before opening his hand wide toward the air, like a chef in a tacky cooking show concluding a recipe for mediocrity. He yawned expansively, stretching his jaw in a way that suggested he was preparing to swallow the chandelier. It was the universal sigh of a teenager trapped between parental scrutiny and global surveillance, boredom, despair, and existential fatigue all folded into one elegant, cavernous yawn.

Ati, in a gesture of ritualised resignation, lifted the remote and turned up the TV volume. The news presenter's hollow, overly enunciated female voice filled the dining room with the artificial urgency of a woman who had been trained to pronounce catastrophe as though reading poetry.

Her tone, sharp and sterile, sliced through the clinking of cutlery and the rustling of floral wallpaper. She announced the day's events with such breathless pomp that even mundane political scandals sounded like apocalyptic revelations. Each word infiltrated the chandelier-lit room with the cold precision of a bureaucratic sermon, reinforcing the absurd theatre of the Protocol-mandated ritual, a ritual designed not to enlighten Isa, but to remind him nightly of the world's dysfunction and of his accidental role in exacerbating it.

> *Good people of the Atheist Communist Federation of Vallsia, today, members of our Federal Parliament have enacted sweeping changes to our constitution. Henceforth, our nation shall be known as the Socialist Federation of Vallsia. These constitutional amendments will grant each republic the power to govern its own affairs, so long as they do not violate the overarching order of the Federation. Each republic will now maintain its own independent parliament, supreme court, and array of liberties carefully calibrated to inspire both pride and compliance. From tomorrow onward, Vallsian citizens will be able to claim rightful ownership of land and property, and ambitious entrepreneurs may register and operate private businesses under the vigilant eye of the state. Furthermore, citizens will no longer be prosecuted for invoking God's name; sacral buildings will reopen for regular prayers and other religious services, allowing faith to flourish under the watchful gaze of the Federations.*

Isa's eyes widened as he turned sharply to Nona, his pupils glowing with the kind of naïve excitement usually reserved for children discovering that Santa might actually exist after all. "Mum, does this mean we can finally use the G-word?"

"Yes!" Nona declared with theatrical grandeur, her voice lifting like a soprano hitting a triumphant note. "As of today, we no longer live in a communist Federation. From now on, you must stop using the G-word and say God instead!" She practically worshipped her own proclamation, as though announcing the Second Coming to an audience of two.

Isa's gaze swivelled to his father. Ati sat rigidly at the head of the table, framed by the halo of the ostentatious chandelier, a posture so solemn he could have been sculpted by a bored communist-era artist commissioned to create "The Ideal Judge."

"Dad, you're a district court judge," Isa pressed. "Does this mean the court will now release Lokin's father from prison?"

Ati's eyelids glided downward, slowly, like a theatre curtain closing over a performance he had not enjoyed. The question hovered in the dining room like a mosquito, irritating, insistent, and unwelcome. Rather than swat it, he took a long sip of wine. The dark-red liquid stained his lips momentarily.

He dipped another piece of the strikingly red meat into the glowing yellow Béarnaise sauce, chewing with painful deliberation. His face remained unreadable, an expression perfected over decades of state service and domestic survival.

Realising Ati planned to outlast the question through silence, Nona tapped her fork against her glass, producing a faint metallic ping that echoed through the chandelier-lit dining room. She peered at him through her thick lashes, lashes she fluttered with passive-aggressive precision, honed through seventeen years of marital diplomacy.

Finally, in order to escape Nona's gaze rather than answer Isa's, Ati turned toward his son. He set his slice of bread delicately on the rim of his plate, dusted crumbs from his fingers with the elegance of a man performing a royal tradition, then took yet another sip of wine, as if fortifying himself for philosophical combat.

"Dad, I've heard the state imprisoned Lokin's father only because he mentioned the G-word..." Isa ventured timidly.

"Isa, I told you not to use the G-word!" Nona snapped. "We're no longer an atheist communist country!"

"Sorry, Mum." Isa shrank back, clutching the correction as though it were a flotation device in turbulent waters. "I meant to say... God."

Ati wiped his lips with a napkin, his gesture firm, judicial, and exact. From the inner pocket of his corded jacket he retrieved a cigar, a thick, intimidating specimen he seemed to treat as a professional companion. He lit it with a wooden match, exhaling two dense clouds that drifted upward toward the chandelier like ghostly apparitions protesting the revival of religion.

His voice finally broke the silence.

"Yes, Lokin's father is in prison because he couldn't stop expressing his love for God," Ati said, his eyes fixed on the wine glass he spun clockwise with legalistic focus. Rising from his seat, he retrieved a ceramic ashtray from the cupboard, an oversized relic shaped like a seashell, and stepped toward the patio door. As he opened it, he added with rehearsed gravity, "Most likely, Lokin's father will be released soon. Lokin is a good kid and deserves to grow up with his father by his side."

The night beyond the patio was ink-black, illuminated by a dim porch light that cast Ati's silhouette across the tiles, making him look like a dictator delivering a midnight speech to the hydrangeas.

"But surely a declaration of love can't be a crime," Isa protested, his fork trembling slightly. "Lokin's father didn't offend anyone by declaring his affection for God."

"You're right," Ati admitted, returning to the table with the faintest sliver of pride, as though Isa's reasoning temporarily restored his academic faith in humanity. "But to uphold unity and brotherhood among all humans, communism scorned God's existence and prohibited divisive religious practices." His tone radiated the smugness of a man who believed he was explaining the meaning of life to people unworthy of the revelation.

Nona set down her fork with a click that resonated like a warning bell. "Your dad is a well-respected judge," she reminded Isa. "He earns a decent salary and enjoys many privileges. So, his affection for communism shouldn't surprise you."

"Isa, your Mum is right. Eat your food while it's warm," Ati added, re-entering the dining room with an air of self-importance. Then, slipping effortlessly into lecturing mode, he continued, "Nona, you seem to forget that communism liberated women from suppressive religious indoctrinations."

*"Communism liberated women from suppressive religious indoctrinations?"* Nona repeated, each syllable sharpened into a verbal dagger.

Ati burst into laughter, a loud, echoing laughter that ricocheted off the floral wallpaper. He threw his head back with such enthusiasm it looked as though he were auditioning for a revolutionary propaganda film.

"Why are you laughing?" Nona barked, her eyes narrowing into razor-edged slits.

After wiping imaginary tears, Ati declared, "You're lucky you didn't marry a Muslim who would have turned you into a ninja by placing a jihab over your head!"

Nona's expression hardened to basalt.

A chunk of potato disappeared into Isa's mouth as he cautiously ventured, "What's the harm in believing in God?"

Ati rested his cigar in the ceramic ashtray and resumed his seat. He dipped another piece of meat into the Béarnaise sauce and said with the smug smile of a man convinced the cosmos applauded him, "What matters to God is whether humankind obeys His commandments, something only communism ever managed to accomplish."

"Come on, Ati! That's not true and you know it," Nona countered.

"But it is true," he insisted, lifting his chin. "Communists enacted

God's laws without worshiping Him, whereas capitalists worshipped God without enacting His laws."

Nona leaned back, exasperated. "I think you've had too much wine."

"No, I didn't!" Ati snapped. "The God-forbidding communism is the only system coherent with Moses' commandments because it forbade perpetual land ownership."

"Yes, it did," Nona conceded reluctantly.

"Did God-worshipping countries forbid eternal land ownership?" Ati demanded triumphantly.

Nona stabbed a roasted potato, slicing it into four neat quarters like a surgeon preparing a demonstration.

"Did God-worshipping countries outlaw loans with interest? No! Communism did, through national banks that required no interest!" Ati's voice climbed dramatically. "Thus communism, not capitalism, is the political system in full harmony with God's laws."

"All right," Nona murmured, "perhaps a couple of God's instructions were followed, but…"

"Just a couple?" Ati interrupted, visibly offended. "Did you forget God's command not to appoint kings who have excessive amount of gold and silver? Communist leaders neither possessed nor hoarded extreme wealth."

"But they enjoyed plenty of privileges," Nona countered.

"Yes, but they didn't stash millions abroad! They left nothing but debt, broken furniture, and a medal of honour," Ati said, triumphant. "Therefore, my dear, Karl Marx is the promised Messiah because he enacted God's laws."

Nona burst into near-hysterical laughter, shaking her head. "How can you call Marx the Messiah when he denied God's existence?"

"The Scriptures foretold a Messiah who would unite humanity and bring new laws," Ati argued. "Marx did that. By uniting nations and races across borders."

"But he denied God!"

"The Messiah's mission is unity. Do you think he could achieve that while letting divisive religions persist?" Ati replied smugly.

"What's a Messiah?" Isa interjected innocently.

"The Messiah is God's anointed one who unites humankind and enforces Moses' laws, something the United States failed to do," Ati lectured, sounding like Moses' personal spokesperson.

"Ah, the United States!" Nona sighed. "It's rich, democratic, and the freest country in the world."

Ati burst into uncontrollable laughter again, nearly choking on his potato. He tugged at his tie as Nona thumped his back until the potato popped free like a rebellious cork.

"Are you alright?" Isa asked cautiously.

Ati nodded, pouring another glass of wine.

"You see what happens when someone utters falsehoods," Nona said, smirking.

Isa's gaze bounced between them as though watching a tennis match between ideological maniacs.

"But the United States is rich!" Nona insisted.

"The U.S. is among the poorest nations if you measure by national wealth, not billionaire wealth! And they top global national debt!" Ati retorted.

"Yes, but it's democratic!"

"And has the highest incarceration rate!"

"But they don't imprison people for beliefs!"

"Democracy allows both misleading and being misled. Communism enforces equality," Ati countered.

Nona exploded into laughter again.

"Mum, why are you laughing?" Isa asked, bewildered.

"Because despite your father's communist zeal, equality is a myth," she said, pointing at him. "Isa, how many students in your class?"

"Twenty-four."

"And your maths grade?"

"A five!"

"And your best friend?"

"A three."

"Exactly! Averaging marks doesn't produce equality, because if that's the case you'd all end up getting the same mark by adding and then dividing them with the number of pupils in your class to get same mark. Now, that's what I call equality." Nona exclaimed, as Isa nodded vigorously. "Therefore, Communist equality is a myth!"

Ati paled, rubbing his temples.

Nona pressed on. "This house belongs to the state. Isa goes to state schools. This isn't freedom... it's slavery!"

Ati opened his mouth, but his phone began vibrating violently.

He checked the screen and froze. "I need to answer this," he muttered, slipping outside.

Inside the garage's dim light, Ati answered stiffly.

"Hello, Ati. It's *Shefe* from production," a stern female voice barked.

Ati winced. "Yes, I recognised your number."

"Article 37 of the Script Protocol forbids criticizing specific nations," she scolded.

"I'm aware," he snapped. "But the script told me to praise communism and critique capitalism... what do you expect?"

"Systems, not nations! Am I clear?"

Ati muttered about memorising 56 pages of communist propaganda before finally yelling, "YES! CRYSTAL CLEAR!"

The call ended.

He re-entered the dining room with the defeated air of a man returning from a battlefield he didn't sign up for.

"Who was on the phone?" Nona asked.

Isa tilted his head. "Dad, are you saying the U.S. is a ghastly place?"

"I'm tired. Goodnight," Ati said abruptly, disappearing upstairs like a man fleeing prosecution.

Isa brushed crumbs from the tablecloth. "Mum, why is the U.S. God-worshipping but not God-abiding?"

"After reading the Holy Scriptures and studying law, you can decide for yourself," Nona replied.

"But where can I read them?"

"Once religious services resume, I'll take you to the mosque for a copy of the Holy Quran."

"What's a mosque?"

"It's where Muslims worship."

"So, you're Muslim?"

"Yes. Traditionally, Ansobians were Muslim before communism banned religion."

"And Dad and my friends?"

"Before communism, Taorks were Catholic, Bresians Orthodox, Jews Jewish, and Ryllians mixed. But communists shut every sacred building. That's why you've never seen a priest, imam, or rabbi."

"What's a priest, imam, or rabbi?" Isa asked, wide-eyed and hopeless.

And with that question, the chandelier seemed to flicker, either in sympathy or sheer exhaustion.

# Chapter 5

After receiving the news that he'd been accepted at the public university to study law, Isa invited Shoki, Joseph, and Alexander to meet at their local café at 6:00 pm, celebratory gathering that only Isa seemed committed to attending on time. He buttoned his linen shirt with the solemnity of someone preparing for a diplomatic summit, grabbed the thick book resting on his bedside cabinet, and headed out, half-floating on pride, half-dreading Shoki's inevitable nonsense.

Isa arrived first, naturally. The café's cosy interior attempted, with limited success, to mimic an old British pub, its walls coated in polished dark wood as if trying to obscure its chronic shortage of charm. A large TV screen hung opposite his table like a smug oracle of global mediocrity. The air smelled faintly of fried onions, cheap espresso, and the lingering despair of conversations repeated too many times by locals with nothing new to say.

He sipped his coffee, already his second, while flipping through the book with Arabic lettering embossed in gold on its dark green cover. He looked every bit the studious future lawyer, elbows tucked neatly, eyes half-narrowed, brow furrowed in concentration, radiating an aura that practically screamed I am mature, responsible, and above the idiocy of my peers.

Naturally, this illusion shattered the moment Shoki arrived.

A tall chap with a thick neck, a rugged jaw, and a face that appeared sculpted by a blacksmith rather than nature, plopped himself into the seat opposite Isa. Shoki's Scottish accent, an acoustical miracle that managed to sound like both a greeting and a threat, gravelled out, "Hello, amigo!"

Isa poked at his wristwatch with the offended dignity of a train inspector.

"Come on, Shoki! I've been sitting here since 6:00 pm It's almost 7:00 pm now, and I've finished my second coffee! I haven't seen you in weeks, and you're late!"

"Sorry, amigo! I was reading an intriguing book," Shoki replied with the remorse level of a cat knocking over a vase. "Where are the other two bastards?"

"Alexander and Joseph can't make it," Isa said, slapping his thick book onto the table like a righteous judge presenting Exhibit A.

Shoki leaned forward, stretching his neck to read the book's cover. His eyebrows practically leapt off his face.

"Aren't you too bloody old to read fairy tales?"

Isa's nostrils flared. "What book are you currently reading?"

"Unlike you," Shoki grunted, "I don't read lousy religious fiction."

"How dare you call the Holy Quran fiction?" Isa snapped, leaning forward so abruptly that nearby spoons vibrated. "Just because you don't believe in God doesn't mean millions worldwide don't know this book is real!"

"Apart from holding your spectacles, I don't see much point in you having those ears," Shoki shot back cheerfully. "They clearly aren't doing their job, listening. And since they make you look ugly, maybe consider plastic surgery and have them removed."

Before Isa could elevate the argument to homicide, a chubby waitress appeared. Her expression suggested she had been overworked since birth.

"What would you like to drink?" she asked Shoki, already half-regretting the question.

Shoki lifted a finger like a professor preparing to deliver a groundbreaking lecture.

"We were just…"

"I don't have time to listen to your conversation with all this noise!" she barked, gesturing to the café's lively hum, consisting of chattering couples, clinking glasses, and three teenagers at the next table laughing so violently that they seemed destined for respiratory therapy.

"I see you're busy," Shoki conceded in an accent wobbling between Glasgow and Aberdeen. "But please tell me whether you accept God or…"

"No, we don't accept God," the waitress interrupted with masterful sarcasm, "but we do accept cash, Visa, or MasterCard."

Isa and Shoki erupted into laughter so unrestrained that the three teenagers behind them momentarily halted their own hysteria to observe two teenage boys collapsing into it. Isa slapped his knee repeatedly like he was trying to exorcise a demon. Shoki nearly fell off his chair, arms flailing like a malfunctioning crane.

The waitress, producing the sourest smile in human history, scratched her head and huffed loudly.

"So," she barked, "what will it be?"

"My stomach is being held ransom by bacteria," Shoki gasped, pointing to his belly. "They demand an ice-cold draught lager and a juicy steak."

"How do you eat your steak?" she asked flatly while tapping her order pad.

"With my mouth," Shoki said triumphantly.

"I meant rare, medium…"

"Medium rare, please."

She typed rapidly and marched away, brushing past the three teenagers as they tumbled out the door in giggles.

Shoki jabbed a thumb in her direction.

"She's clever and knows that cash, Visa, or MasterCard determine our fate, not God. Yet here you are wasting your time on ancient nonsense. You're turning eighteen next month and can't stop talking about your imaginary friend no one has ever seen!"

"Half the world believes in God!" Isa protested, holding up his book like a sacred shield. "That's a hefty statistic!"

"That's a disgrace, not a statistic!" Shoki shot back. "Believing in invisible beings isn't my thing."

"Just because you can't see God doesn't mean He doesn't exist! If you came with me to the mosque…"

"Do me a favour," Shoki cut in, suddenly staring past Isa. "Get me the phone number of that blond girl under the old fig tree."

"Did you break up with Dashnorja?"

"I'm not into leaving girlfriends anymore," Shoki announced bravely. "I'm into adding girlfriends. And hopefully that stunning blond will improve my score."

"The one in the white shirt or the yellow dress?" Isa asked, scanning the area.

"No! The one with the precious assets sitting between her two friends," Shoki said, licking his lips like an idiot.

Isa twisted around twice, shielding his eyes from the sunset glare. "I see only two brunettes sitting there. Both drinking white wine."

Shoki pointed insistently. "Are you blind? She's right there. Lifting the cup now."

Isa squinted so hard he might have been trying to see the future.

"There are only two women there. No blond. No… assets."

Shoki leaned back smugly.

"As you said earlier, *just because you can't see* her doesn't mean she doesn't exist. So go get me her number."

"Fetch it yourself!" Isa snapped.

"But unlike you, I'm not skilled in communicating with invisible beings."

"You're going mental," Isa groaned. "I can't believe I'm still listening to your crap."

Shoki suddenly lifted his hand and waved at the bar like he was summoning a lost seagull.

"What now?" Isa asked warily.

A short chap in an ill-fitted suit barrelled toward them like a caffeinated garden gnome on a mission, scattering chairs, glaring at passers-by, and radiating urgent chaos.

"I'm trying to grab the waitress's attention because…"

"Blimey!" the chap chirped, voice too chipper for someone whose liver clearly hated him. "So, this is where you've been hiding all this time!"

The guy's face had been ravaged by excessive drinking, giving him a permanently confused expression as if he had just woken up in the wrong century. His solid black suit made him look either ready for a funeral or fresh from one he didn't want to attend. He had the goofy grin of a man who'd forgotten what teeth were for. Shoki stared up at him like a deer spotting a wolf.

"Cousin!" the man exclaimed, punching Shoki playfully in the right arm as if trying to infuse him with life energy. "I'm surprised you waved to me. Last time we spoke, you told me to fuck off forever!"

"Yes, Gin! I'm also surprised you've forgotten the meaning of the phrase *fuck off forever*! I wasn't waving at you. It's the waitress I'm after," Shoki explained in an uninviting tone.

"Which one?" Gin asked, scanning the café like a cat sizing up a buffet, then nodded toward the waitress. "The flabby one? She isn't your type, is she?"

Shoki ignored him with the determination of a monk meditating through a fire alarm.

"Why the long face?" Gin pressed, poking him with words. "Why're you still ignoring me?"

"I'm not ignoring you!" Shoki growled, his voice going up an octave as he waved his hand dismissively. "I'm just contemplating the timing of my food's arrival, as I would love to acquaint your ribs with an impeccably sharp steak knife!"

The waitress slid between Shoki and Gin to set the food platter on the wooden table and then exclaimed, "Here's your steak."

Upon reading the waitress's name badge, Gin addressed her amicably, "So, you're a Walker! Your cousin is a good friend of mine."

"Oh yeah? Which one?" she asked, sceptical eyebrow raised.

"Johnnie," Gin replied with a grin.

"Johnnie Walker, as in the Scotch whiskey?"

"No," he said, deadpan. "Johnnie Walker as the Scotch whiskey. I'm meeting him tonight at a wedding."

The waitress shook her head in disbelief before dashing off.

Isa looked at Gin and asked dryly, "Do you drink a lot?"

Gin grinned proudly. "There was this one period in my life when I didn't drink a drop for fourteen years."

Isa's eyebrows rose. "Really?"

"Yeah... then I started secondary school and haven't stopped since."

Isa sighed. "Maybe you should consider giving up drinking."

"But drinking is so much fun," Gin said, as if stating a scientific fact.

"You can have fun without alcohol, too," Isa insisted.

"I'm also confident you could walk barefoot," Gin replied, "but you still wear shoes, don't you?".

Shoki's steak and chips looked yummy, but he didn't appear impressed. He let out a sigh before beckoning the waitress again. After noticing him, the waitress rushed back to Shoki.

"What are you after *this* time?" the waitress asked.

Gin cut in behind the waitress with his arms folded, "Sweetheart, I've known this fella since his nappy years, and you're not his type!"

"Could you please taste this steak?" Shoki pointed at the muddy-looking meat.

The waitress craned her head down and asked, "Why?"

"Just a small bite. For science," Shoki pleaded.

"I'm not allowed to eat the customers' food!" she snapped, checking her watch as if hoping the shift would end out of pity.

Isa tried to mediate. "Why don't you just tell her what's wrong? Do you mind if I taste it and tell her?"

Shoki shoved the plate toward him.

Isa looked around. "Where's your knife and fork?"

Shoki exhaled dramatically. "Precisely, my dear Sherlock." He pointed at the waitress.

She slapped her forehead. "I forgot to bring them."

Isa chuckled. "That explains it." "Why didn't you just say so?" the waitress asked Shoki with a wide grin.

"Because," Gin interrupted, "he's a master at turning the simplest problem into a Shakespearean tragedy. Trust me, I've known him since nappies."

Shoki turned to Gin, glaring. "And Mr. Parrot here…" he jabbed a finger at him, "is a master at repeating himself!"

Gin smirked. "See? He's still doing it."

"What would you like to drink?" the waitress asked Gin.

"I'd love a drink with you, but I've got a wedding to crash. Give me your number, and we'll sort something next week," Gin said, brandishing his cell phone like a sword.

The waitress ignored Gin, turned and swiftly walked away.

Gin and Shoki looked at each other without saying a word. It was an unusual scene whereby the boys neither conversed nor moved, looking like statues amidst the buzzing café.

Then the waitress appeared next to Shoki with the controversial cutlery and a beer bottle. She placed them next to Shoki's plate and ran off.

"You don't have to be so rude to your cousin!" Isa scrutinised Shoki.

He's a scam, and his father's worst nightmare!" Shoki shot back, grabbing the cutlery with the intensity of a man defusing a bomb. He jabbed the first bite of steak like it owed him money. "Gin, did you ever make peace with your father?"

"Yes," Gin replied casually, "I've finally made peace with my motherfucker!"

Shoki stared, fork mid-air, piercing the steak as if performing a sacred ritual.

"Why are you looking at me like that?" Gin asked, mouth full. "Either he fucked my mother, or I'm someone else's bastard."

Isa, chewing a potato chip, burst into uncontrollable laughter. "I'm sorry… I know… I shouldn't laugh," he gasped between giggles.

"This is why he's no longer my cousin," Shoki muttered, swallowing his first bite.

"I'd love to chat more, but I've got a wedding to attend," Gin announced grandly.

"Who's getting married?" Shoki asked. "Anyone I know?"

"Stella and Jonathan," Gin replied.

"Who are they?" Shoki asked.

"I don't know them! All I know is that Stella is a nurse, and Jonathan is a doctor!"

"Well, if you don't know them, how come you're invited to their wedding?" Isa asked.

"They didn't invite me!" Gin said, shrugging like it was obvious.

"I know you're comfortable chatting shite, but why would you attend a wedding you haven't been invited to?" Shoki asked, bemused.

"To get drunk!" Gin replied, stretching out his hands as if the answer had been obvious.

"But … didn't you promise your parents that you'll stop drinking?" Shoki asked again, his mouth full of steak.

"If they didn't want me drinking, they shouldn't have named me after my Mum's favourite drink – Gin and Tonic!" Gin responded.

"So, your full name is Gin and Tonic?" Isa chuckled.

"No! His full name is Gin, Tonic, and Lime," Shoki exclaimed sarcastically. "They could have named you something that matches your character. Arse-ache would've been a perfect fit for you."

"Whatever," Gin said and resumed telling them how he'd crashed at least 30 wedding receptions, enjoying complimentary drinks and dinner. Next, he explained how he'd call venues, pretending to be interested in booking their restaurant for a wedding reception. Then, after identifying the restaurants reserved for forthcoming weddings, he'd call them back again and pretend to be the baker responsible for making their wedding cake. Finally, he explained that he would seek the bride and groom's names from the staff because he would have to write them on their wedding cake.

"After I've finished this complicated process, I slide into my Dad's suit and crash a wedding reception carrying an envelope like this one," Gin concluded, holding up a white envelope.

"What's the envelope for?" Isa asked suspiciously.

"It's for the bride and groom," Gin replied.

"Yes, but… what's inside it?" Isa pressed.

"Nothing!" Gin replied.

"Nothing?" Shoki asked.

"I'm broke!" Gin squalled. "So, until I get a job, I'll have to crash other people's celebrations and drink to their voluntary destruction of happiness."

"Surely, you must be joking!" Isa said.

"No, I'm not," Gin rambled.

"You're such an intelligent man," Isa said, pointing his index finger towards Gin.

"Please don't flatter me. I'm not that intelligent. I have a brilliant therapist who recommended this amazing biography of a former alcoholic, which reveals how he got drunk by attending wedding receptions of people he didn't know."

Isa laughed, shaking his head in disbelief.

Gin checked his watch, gave a dramatic salute, and sprinted off toward his next wedding-crashing adventure.

# Chapter 6

Isa had grown fond of Eva, his childhood sweetheart, whose lisp had miraculously vanished, along with her shy, wallflower tendencies. She'd transformed into a whirlwind of words, chattering nonstop like a radio host stuck on repeat. Eva was all bones and loose joints, but her warm, cozy face softened the bony frame, her tanned skin glowing like sun-kissed caramel. A curly red fringe flopped across her forehead, and her long, rabbit-like teeth flashed whenever she smiled. Her mocha eyes sparkled like coffee stirred with a hint of mischief.

Isa's own lisp had disappeared, too, leaving behind a reasonably handsome young man. He had slimmed down as he shot up taller, emphasizing his high cheekbones, square jaw, long black eyelashes, and thick black eyebrows framing piercing, pitch-black eyes.

The first time Isa and Eva got frisky under the orange tree, yes, that orange tree, they became inseparable. From then on, Isa's football academy days dwindled to nothing; his friends joked that he'd become Eva's permanent shadow, sticking to her like gum on a sneaker.

Nearly every night, after the 19:00 news, Isa would sneak off to meet Eva beneath the orange tree, chatting away between kisses. The rows of orange trees created a green-orange tunnel leading to breathtaking views of the blue sea, where even the sunsets seemed jealous of the couple's romantic shenanigans.

Weeks before graduation, Isa dropped the bombshell at dinner, when he informed them of intention to propose to Eva. His parents exchanged one of those parental glances that meant "Well, he's either in love or insane", then gave him their blessing. Overjoyed, Isa phoned Eva and asked her to meet him by the orange tree where their lips had first met, their sacred site now upgraded from "teenage make-out spot" to "potential engagement venue." She said yes, and he hung up grinning like a fool.

Then, like a general summoning his troops, Isa called Alexander, Joseph, and Shoki. "Tomorrow. Five o'clock. Café. Important mission," he told them, hanging up before they could ask questions.

The next morning, at exactly 09:35, Isa's radio alarm clock blasted Another One Bites the Dust. He slapped the green button, cranked the volume to "neighbour complaint" level, and moonwalked to the bathroom. Inside the shower, he unleashed his inner rock star. His deep, gruff voice mangled Freddie Mercury so brutally it could have been declared a war crime. Fortunately, he paused long enough to brush his teeth, a brief act of mercy for humankind.

After showering, Isa wrapped a towel around his waist and faced his reflection. For several seconds, he studied the battlefield of red spots on his face, picking at them with surgical precision. Then came the layering, deodorant underarms, cologne under the ears, and hair wax to sculpt the perfect "I woke up like this" look. When one rebellious lock drooped into a crescent on his forehead, he smirked approvingly, the hero's curl.

Satisfied, Isa strutted to his room, read from the Holy Quran for two hours, and then had lunch. Ever the gentleman, he placed his dirty dishes in the dishwasher. By 15:40, study time was over and it was now showtime.

He slipped into bright-blue stonewashed jeans, buttoned up a black shirt, and slid his feet into sparkling white All-Stars sneakers that practically glowed with optimism. Stopping by the hallway mirror, he straightened his hair, flashed himself a wink, and whispered, "Looking sharp, future fiancé."

As he stepped outside, the late-April sun greeted him like a spotlight.

Isa locked the door, took a deep breath, and smiled at the sky. It was a perfect day for love… or disaster.

Twenty minutes later, whistling to himself, he entered the mosque for his afternoon Friday prayers. Once the religious ritual ended, Isa rushed outside, placed his feet into his All-Stars again, and headed to meet his friends. Half an hour later, he arrived at the café. After Shoki shouted Isa's name, he turned and headed towards the outdoor table where his two friends sat. They happened to be physical opposites because Shoki was relatively tall and slightly overweight, whereas Alexander was short and slim, with a prominent forehead visible below his cropped brown hair.

Isa greeted them both, pinched some roasted peanuts from the tiny transparent bowl next to a green beer bottle, and sat down.

"How's it hanging?" Isa asked Alexander.

"Thanks to that stunning girl sitting there," Alexander replied, pushing his chin towards a blond woman sitting opposite him, and pointing down between his legs, "it is standing up and eager to get wet with her. She looks like she needs a bit of Alexing."

"Her *Alexing*?" Shoki asked. "Surely, there isn't enough wine in the world to make a stunning beauty like her sleep with a brute like you!"

Isa spotted Shoki hunched over his table, staring at his coffee like it had personally betrayed him.

"Why the gloomy look?" Isa asked, sliding into the chair opposite him. "I'm not late, am I?"

"Yes, Mr Rolex!" Shoki fired back, squinting at his watch. "You're thirty-seven seconds late. I should send you back to Switzerland for a full service, new gears, polish, maybe an ego adjustment."

Isa chuckled. "Sorry, the Friday prayer took longer than usual."

"Of course it did," Shoki said, lighting a Marlboro like he was auditioning for a noir film. The wind immediately stole the smoke, leaving him muttering curses about meteorology. "You know, every time you call us together with that stupid grin, something catastrophic follows. So, what's your latest disaster, Amigo? Did you accidentally marry someone again?"

Before Isa could respond, a tall waitress appeared, wielding a menu in one hand and a pen topped with a fluffy pink pom-pom that looked like it belonged in a teenage diary.

"Would you gentlemen like something from the bar?" she asked sweetly. "It's Happy Hour, so Margaritas, Piña Coladas…"

"Don't waste your breath," Shoki interrupted. "This one still talks to his imaginary friend named God. Pretty sure serving him alcohol counts as blasphemy. Bring the child a warm glass of milk. And a Margarita for me."

"I don't want milk!" Isa objected. "Just a bottle of still water, please."

"Water?" Shoki groaned. "Water is drink for plants, amigo, not people."

"Muslims live by a moral code that forbids drinking alcohol," Isa explained calmly. "Besides, there'll be plenty of wine waiting for us in the afterlife."

Shoki leaned back, smirking. "Perfect. So, you don't drink real wine now, hoping to drink imaginary wine later with your imaginary mouth. Brilliant business plan."

The waitress bit her lip, clearly fighting laughter, before escaping toward the bar.

Just then, Joseph strolled in, tossing his jacket onto a chair.

"Speak of the devil, and by devil, I mean the only sane one here," Shoki said. "We were just discussing how life is for living, not waiting for some celestial after-party."

Isa glanced at his watch. "I didn't ask you here to debate theology, Socrates. I've got to meet Eva in half an hour, so let's focus on my big announcement." "Of course, if you don't meet your *General Eva* exactly at 6 pm, it will lead to the pointless loss of Vallsian life," Joseph teased Isa.

"What are you on about?" Isa asked.

"Ever since you started dating Eva, you're no longer meeting us," Joseph replied.

"I met you last week," Isa said.

"Yes, you met me because you needed help moving your wardrobe,"

Joseph said, scratching his back.

"What can I say? You're an angel," Isa said to Joseph, placing his hand on his friend's shoulder.

"What can I say, Isa? You're also an angel whenever you need something from me," Joseph said with a frown.

"Joseph, I'm glad you said that because I thought Isa was hitting on you," Shoki added with a huge grin.

The waitress returned with a Margarita and a water bottle on her black tray. After placing them on the oak table, she reminded them that Happy Hour would end in eighteen minutes. Joseph ordered an Irish coffee.

"So, why did you invite us here?" Shoki asked.

After the waitress migrated towards the table near the café's entrance, Isa answered, "Shoki, I want to get married."

"Amigo, I'm flattered, but I'm not into gay marriages," Shoki replied with a cocky smile.

"Are you out of your mind?" Isa asked crossly. "I meant getting married to Eva. I will ask for her hand in less than 25 minutes."

"Why?" Alexander asked. "Has your right hand grown tired from wanking?"

"I'm not allowed to wank," Isa replied.

"Who told you that? Your imaginary friend?" Shoki asked, pointing towards the sky.

"Of course not! The imam told me," Isa replied firmly.

"Yeah, right! Imams get married and laid, so they don't have to masturbate. Have you ever tried asking a priest?" Shoki asked, and then lit up another cigarette.

"Could you please stop making fun of priests?" Alexander pleaded.

"You shouldn't defend priests!" Shoki exclaimed. "After all, a priest married you to Ajam and bound you to your misery."

Joseph waved away Shoki's smoke. "You ever thought about quitting cigarettes?"

Shoki rolled his eyes and took a slow drag. "I stub out thirty a day. Technically, I quit thirty times daily. That's world-class performance."

"Can we talk about my marriage?" Isa asked before gulping down his water.

"Bloody hell!" Alexander exclaimed. "You reminded me of what my uncle used to say whenever someone mentioned the word *marriage*."

"So, what he used to say?" Joseph asked Alexander.

"Bloody hell!" Alexander replied. "That's exactly what he used to say every time someone mentioned the word *marriage*."

Shoki snorted. "Alex, brains are awesome, shame you never got issued one."

"For a long time, I refused to believe that angels of death existed," Alexander confessed. "But then I got married and ended up living with one."

"It can't be that bad," Isa hinted.

"But it is!" Alexander exclaimed. "Tomorrow is her birthday, and she warned me that if I bought her a crappy birthday present again, she'll burn it!"

"So, what did you get her?" Shoki asked, lifting his hand.

"I got her a candle," Alexander replied.

"A candle?" Shoki asked with a light laughter.

"Surely, you and your wife must have something in common," Isa suggested.

"Now that you mentioned it, my wife and I have something in common," Alexander nodded. "We hate each other's guts."

Joseph burst out laughing. "Isa, don't let Alex scare you away from marriage. There's nothing wrong with it. I'm sure you'll do great with Eva, especially since when you marry a Jewish girl, you're basically marrying her whole family... plus their family friends, accountants, and real estate agents."

Shoki chuckled. "That's not a wedding... that's a merger."

"Having failed in marriage, could we continue talking about something I'm very good at," Alexander pleaded.

"Well since you're such an overachiever on this matter, you probably want us to talk about wanking, don't you?" Shoki asked.

"Can we please change the discussion into something more

nutritious for our brains," Joseph exclaimed.

Alexander sighed, and then added, "All right, I've got this idea about ..."

"Alex, you can't generate ideas. You need a brain for that!" Shoki interrupted Alexander.

Isa and Joseph suddenly broke into laughter just as the waitress returned, placing Joseph's Irish coffee beside him.

Once Isa calmed down, he spoke at length about his intention to marry Eva, his voice softening as he described her. When he finished, he paid the bill, glanced at his watch, and rose from his seat. After quick goodbyes, he hurried off.

He stopped at the supermarket, where he fetched a baguette, a wedge of blue cheese, red apples, white grapes, strawberries, green olives, a small chilled bottle of champagne, water, and disposable cups, cutlery, and plates. At the till, he tapped his foot impatiently, then stuffed the items into a bag, paid, and dashed out into the afternoon light.

Fifteen minutes later, Isa reached the orange tree, their orange tree, and sat beneath its shade. The sea below shimmered in the fading gold of the sun.

Soon, Eva appeared, climbing the hill toward him. A thin brown leather belt hugged her short floral dress, and a knotted red scarf fell loosely over her long neck. Her curls danced in the wind, scattering around her bronze, square face. When she drew near, she gave Isa an odd look.

"What's wrong?" she asked, her mocha eyes narrowing with a glimmer of doubtful concern.

"Nothing," Isa said, shaking his head as he reached for her. He pulled her close, but when she tried to speak, he pressed his finger gently to her lips. Eva frowned, puzzled.

"Close your eyes," he whispered.

She obeyed, her pink tongue brushing lightly against her white teeth. Isa knelt, plucked a single blade of grass, and took her right hand. Turning it palm up, he tied the grass around her engagement finger in a small knot.

"Open your eyes," he said softly.

When she did, Isa smiled nervously and dropped to one knee.

"Eva," he began, "we've been together almost eight years. If this grass ring could speak, it would ask if you'd marry Isa."

Eva's cheeks flushed red as her shoulders lifted in shy delight. She looked down at him through her lashes, her expression flickering between disbelief and joy.

"Are you proposing to me?" she breathed, her mocha eyes trembling.

"Yes, my darling," Isa replied, brushing her fringe from her eye. "Do you think you could put up with this annoying guy as your husband?"

"YES!" she cried, throwing her arms around his neck. Their lips met in a long, trembling kiss. Isa's hand moved gently over her back as he tugged at the zipper of her dress… and then the screen blurred.

The moment their nakedness began, their bodies dissolved into tiny coloured squares. Their voices turned into muffled static. The Script Protocol required that all erotic scenes on the UN–SDC–BC broadcast be obscured to preserve "the dignity and privacy of individuals involved."

An hour later, the picture cleared. Isa and Eva sat clothed again, faces glowing in the firelight opposite them. They stayed there for two more hours, whispering and laughing softly beneath the rustling orange leaves, until they parted at midnight.

***

The following morning broke with a rare brilliance, sunlight flooding the breakfast table where Isa spoke with unrestrained joy. His words tumbled over one another as he described his wedding plans, the music, the vows, the life he and Eva would soon begin together. His parents smiled, quietly warmed by his excitement.

Then Isa's phone rang.

He glanced at the screen, and his expression softened instantly. Eva.

"I must answer this," he said, rising from his chair with a boyish grin.

76

"Hello, future Mrs Iri!" he greeted, stepping into the garden, the air still scented with dew.

But the voice that answered was nothing like he expected. It trembled, fragile, almost breaking.

"I'm so… sorry," Eva whispered.

Isa froze. "Are you alright?"

"Last night," she began, her voice faltering, "was the happiest night of my life. On my way home, I stopped by the corner shop and bought a bottle of champagne. My parents and brother were still awake, so I poured four glasses and told them the news. Isa… are you still there?"

"Yes," he said quickly, heart beginning to pound.

"As soon as I told them about our marriage," she continued, her words dissolving into panic, "my brother began shouting… 'I told you she'd destroy everything I've worked for!', and he stormed out, slamming the door so hard I thought the house would collapse."

Her voice cracked. The sound of muffled sobs filled the line. She tried to steady herself, but her next words came broken, jagged.

"I'm… so… so sorry. I'm not… feeling well right now."

The raw sound of Eva's crying tore through Isa's chest.

"Eva, listen to me… we've got to meet. Now."

"Please, Isa," she murmured weakly. "Don't make this harder for me. I haven't slept. I can't think straight."

"Eva, I beg you," Isa pleaded, his tone desperate. "We need to talk… face to face."

"I can't." Her voice sank to a whisper. "I've already left the island."

Isa felt the blood drain from his face. "When will you be coming back?"

"I can't come back," she said and then came the sound of her breaking. Deep, wrenching sobs.

"What does that mean?" Isa's tone sharpened; his voice trembled with restrained fury.

"I'M NOT ALLOWED TO COME BACK!" Eva suddenly cried, the words echoing with unbearable pain.

Isa's pulse throbbed in his temples. "Why the sudden change of heart? We've been together for nearly a decade. Your parents never once opposed us."

"You're right," she said between ragged breaths. "But that was under the communist regime, which banned religious practices. There were no synagogues, no mosques, no churches…. we were free in our own way. But now… now that I practise my faith, I'm bound by it. I'm only allowed to marry a Jew."

Isa clenched his jaw. "So, all I'm hearing are your family's wishes. What about yours?"

Eva's reply came as a sob that barely formed words. "Please, Isa…" she gasped. "I love you. But I love my parents too. I can't hurt them."

A long silence followed. Isa could hear his own breathing, the faint rustle of wind through the garden leaves.

"Isa," she whispered after a pause, "please say something."

His voice was low, but heavy. "Then give me one chance… one chance to see you. To talk in person."

"I told you. I can't return!" she cried.

"Have you ever thought about what happens after your parents are gone?" Isa demanded, his tone darkening. "What happens to Eva then? To the woman who wakes every morning beside a man she doesn't love?"

"Please, stop," she begged, her voice shattering. "My brother's training to be a rabbi. If I marry a gentile, it'll destroy his reputation… destroy everything."

Isa's voice rose, edged with anguish. "And if he were in your place, would he give up the woman he loved to preserve someone else's pride?"

Eva struggled to suppress her mounting sobs. Isa pulled his cell phone away from his ear, shaking his head in frustration. Seconds later, Isa again positioned his phone to his ear and called her name, but Eva didn't reply. After looking at his cell phone's screen, Isa realised Eva had hung up. He redialled her number, but she didn't answer his call. Isa called her five more times but failed to get through to her. Eventually, Isa gave up and slumped his head against the garage door. His frowning face reflected nothing but repulsion and agony. He left his house, headed towards the orange tree, where he'd proposed to Eva, and remained there until the moon began climbing.

\*\*\*

In sharp contrast to typically vibrant debates during their evening meals. Isa entered the dining room, his steps heavy, his gaze low. His parents were already seated at the table, their faces lit by the amber glow of the chandelier. Silence reigned when Isa joined his parents seated at the dining table. Isa kept his head down while Nona stared at him intently. Then, finally, Ati forked up another piece of the pie and reminded Isa that he missed the 19:00 news. Isa drew his lips wide and sat down. Ten minutes had passed since Isa had sat down in his chair without taking a single bite of his spinach pie.

"Isa, you must eat! It's your favourite pie," Nona insisted.

Isa forced a faint stretch of his lips that vanished before it became a smile. He took his seat, his movements mechanical, and stared blankly at his untouched plate. Ten minutes passed, not a single bite.

"Isa, what's bothering you?" Ati asked.

Isa pulled his arms across his chest and replied in a stagnant voice, words sounding like a thunderclap, "Our … marriage ... is off."

"What?" Nona asked, raising her plucked eyebrows as she looked at her shattered son.

Isa flung his arms in the air and replied, "Her parents … disapprove ... of our ... marriage."

Isa dropped his eyelids, tapping the tablecloth with his index finger. He then picked up his glass of water and drew it closer to his lips. After moistening them, he placed the empty glass back on the table and prolonged his unsettling silence.

Ati wagged his hand to grab Nona's attention as she straightened her napkin, her shiny red nail polish glinting under the chandelier's light. She pretended not to have seen her husband and started dabbing her mouth smoothly with the napkin. Ati glanced at Isa to ensure he wasn't looking and quickly placed his index finger over his lips, pleading with Nona to let Isa be. She didn't abide and leaned toward her son to fill his glass with water.

"Besides Eva, did her parents take away your voice too?" Nona teased her son with the apparent intention of making him talk.

Isa's knees began to quiver.

"Isa, please start eating," Ati said.

"Oh, for God's sake, stop patronising me!" Isa burst out, his voice cracking with pent-up anguish. He still couldn't meet his father's eyes.

"It helps if you get it off your chest," Nona said gently.

Eventually, Isa began speaking, filling his lungs with long sighs between sentences. He was unable to talk cohesively about his last conversation with Eva.

"I'm sorry, Isa," Nona interrupted gently, "but I can't hear you. Could you please turn up the volume?

Isa shrugged clumsily, lifting his eyes and looking at Nona's red cheeks. He scratched his head and amplified his voice. He sounded like a prime suspect being interrogated by a public prosecutor, "I was hoping to discuss something else today... but I don't even know what to say anymore."

Ati sat motionless, back straight, lips pressed together, listening like a man witnessing a storm approach.

Isa spoke for another five minutes, fragmented and broken, before concluding with a single sentence that seemed to extinguish the air in the room, "That's why our marriage is off.

"Unfortunately, millions of heartbroken Romeos and Juliets across the work have parted ways because of their religious differences," Ati reasoned as Isa sipped his water.

Isa reached for the wine bottle with a shaking hand, poured hastily, and the crimson liquid spilled, bleeding across the white tablecloth.

"Oh, dear!" Nona gasped, rushing to smother the spreading stain with salt and napkins. "Muslims aren't allowed to drink wine."

"I'm fed up with religion's capacity to hurt people," Isa's tone rose.

"Isa, I sympathise with your situation, but you shouldn't talk like that," Nona pleaded.

He rose abruptly, his chair screeching against the tiles. "What's the bloody point of religion," he thundered, "when it preaches love but then destroys it?" He raised his glass and drank deeply. "As of tonight, I'm no longer a Muslim. I refuse to worship anything that forbids love."

"Isa, you shouldn't be drinking when you're angry," Ati interjected. "Or when you're hungry."

Isa gulped down more wine and lifted his index finger before replying, "I won't pretend to be enjoying myself drinking wine, but I'm an adult now, entitled to do whatever I please!"

Nona's voice trembled now, her earlier composure faltering. "I know you're hurting, my son, but anger and wine won't heal you. Becoming an atheist won't heal you either. You need rest. Next week, you'll come with me to Friday prayers… we'll talk to the imam, you'll…"

Isa laughed bitterly, cutting her off. "Prayers won't bring her back, Mother."

Nona pressed on, "But, Isa…"

"Argh! Give the kid a break!" Ati shouted. "Isa is an adult now and can do as he pleases."

Isa lowered himself back into his chair, his shoulders slumped as if carrying an invisible weight, as Nona reacted instantly, unable to contain herself, "We belong to different religions, yet, this didn't prevent us from being together and in love. Right, Ati?"

Ati nodded and reached across the table to rest his hand gently on hers, a gesture that felt both tender and weary. Then he turned his solemn gaze toward Isa.

"Your mother's right, son. Our parents came from different faiths too, but communism made it possible for us to marry. If the constitution had remained communist, you and Eva would…"

"You and your bloody communism again!" Nona erupted, her voice cutting through the room like a whip. "That godforsaken ideology trampled on human rights and bred monstrous dictatorships! Don't pretend it was a paradise!"

Ati's composure cracked. He leaned forward, his tone sharp, his eyes aflame. "You talk of civil liberties, but let me ask you something. Is Eva free to marry our son?"

"Yes, she is free to do that, and no law can prevent her from marrying anyone she wants. It's another matter that she decided not to marry Isa," Nona replied.

"Because religious confinements didn't exist under the communist regime, you could tie the knot with whomever you wished," Ati sighed, shaking his head.

"You're hilarious. You know full well what happened to the wives of the contra-revolutionary husbands who opposed the regime. Most of those men ended up in prison because they spoke with their hearts. While in prison, the regime forcefully divorced them from their wives. Under the new constitution, the state can no longer interfere with its citizens' marital status," Nona objected with unassailable contempt. "Perhaps you need some reminding of what happened to your nephew, Shivalls, after he publicly opposed the regime?"

Ati bowed his head submissively and leant back.

"Dad, what happened to Shivalls?" Isa asked curiously.

Ati opened his mouth to speak at one point but then shook his head silently, drawing deep sighs. He finished his third glass of wine and topped it up again.

Nona slammed her knife against her white plate and then pressed on, "Why don't you explain to Isa how your charismatic communist regime forcibly divorced your nephew from his wife, separating him from his two children, whom he never saw again?"

Ati reached for the cigar box with trembling hands, drew one out, and struck a match. The faint crack of the flame filled the silence that had swallowed the table.

He leaned back, exhaling a long ribbon of smoke that curled toward the chandelier. For a moment, he looked like a man preparing to exhume ghosts he'd long buried.

After several long drags, his resolve broke. "What can I say?" he murmured at last, his voice gravelly, tired. "Shivalls was... careless. Too honest for his own good. He spoke against the regime... loudly, publicly. I warned him, again and again, to be cautious, to hold his tongue. But he never listened."

He paused, staring into the smoke that hung above the table like a fog of memory. "His father was an Orthodox priest," Ati continued quietly, "a good man... too gentle for the world that replaced God with the Party. When communism banned all religious practice, he couldn't bear it. He... took his own life."

Nona's knife stilled mid-motion. Isa froze, eyes wide.

"Shivalls was sixteen," Ati went on, his tone flattening under the weight of the memory. "He found his father hanging in an abandoned church. That image burned itself into him. After that day, he could never forgive the world. He became... loud. Angry. A man constantly wrestling with ghosts."

He took another sip of wine, then another, as though trying to wash the taste of the story from his mouth. "Still," he said, "he built a life. Worked at the municipal urban department. He was good at his job, precise, and meticulous. But every now and then, the old rage would come flooding back."

Ati's eyes drifted somewhere far beyond the room. "I remember one rainy afternoon in Imreg Park," he said softly. "He and I walked under the bare chestnut trees. I told him, 'Shivalls, stop it. Stop attacking the communist order, or you'll end up in prison. Your children will grow up without a father... just like you did.'"

He drew a long breath, his gaze dimming. "I begged him to be careful. To keep his faith quiet. But he laughed in my face."

Ati took another drag, the ember flaring red. Then he let out a sigh that trembled between sorrow and guilt. "He had a wicked sense of humour," he said, a wistful smile flickering briefly. "I loved him dearly. But he drank too much. And when the bottle was empty, the anger came out... raw and merciless. He'd curse the regime, curse the leader, curse the silence we were all confined to."

Then, without warning, Ati burst into laughter of a man both haunted and incredulous at his own memories. It rang too loudly, too long, until he caught himself and waved a hand apologetically. "Forgive me," he muttered, his smile collapsing into a grimace. "Sometimes, the absurdity of it all just... catches up with you."

He turned to Isa then, eyes glistening faintly in the light. "Do you know," he asked in a voice almost gentle, "how he justified it all? His defiance, his recklessness, his endless need to provoke?"

Ati leaned forward, the tip of his cigar glowing like a tiny, defiant sun.

"He said," Ati whispered, "that silence kills the soul faster than prison ever could and then claimed that his vodka said those words and not him. Yet, he advised me to force defendants to answer the prosecutor's questions when drunk, too, because alcohol reveals their true colours. Shivalls believed Muslims were better liars because they didn't drink, so they never got to ..."

At that very instant, Ati's phone vibrated sharply on the table. A Yellow Code warning from the UN-SDC-BC Producers flashed across the screen. But before he could react, Nona's voice sliced through the thickening air.

"Ati!" she snapped, eyes flashing like blades. "I can't believe you're sitting here poisoning Isa with Shivalls' hatred against other faiths. How dare you laugh at such vile remarks about the Muslim population? Shivalls got what he deserved!"

Ati threw his head back and erupted into uncontrollable laughter. His eyes glistened under the dim chandelier, his movements clumsy and disjointed. He had clearly crossed the border into drunken madness.

"What's so damn funny, Ati?" Nona demanded, her voice trembling with rage as she twisted her engagement ring, not out of affection, but restraint.

Ati straightened his narrow shoulders, forcing his posture upright like a soldier trying to remember his rank. "You see, Isa," he slurred, his smile curdling, "deep down, your mother's no different from the communists she condemns. She preaches democracy, free will, tolerance, and yet she thinks my nephew deserved prison for speaking his mind."

"Ati, stop!" Nona snapped, but her voice faltered when she noticed Isa's hand scratching at his chest, just beneath his blue T-shirt. He looked distant, his face pale, eyes unfocused.

"Isa?" she asked, softening suddenly. "Are you alright?"

Isa didn't respond. His brimming glass of wine trembled in his grip, red liquid spilling across his hand like blood. A deep grunt escaped him as he tried to lift the glass to his lips.

"What's the matter, Isa?" Ati's laughter died in his throat. His voice shook, no longer defiant but afraid.

Isa drained the remaining wine in a single swallow. Then, with a violent motion, he threw the napkin from his lap onto the table. "I'm not feeling well," he said, voice hoarse. "I need to lie down."

He didn't wait for their reaction. He rose abruptly, chair scraping across the wooden floor, and strode toward the staircase.

Behind him, Nona and Ati's quarrel blurred into a muffled storm of voices. The stairs creaked under his weight until a loud thud broke through their argument.

"Isa?" Nona called out, alarmed. "Are you alright?"

No answer. Only the slow groan of the wooden steps as Isa dragged himself upward.

Moments later, he reached his room and collapsed onto the bed. Pulling out his phone, he stared at pictures of Eva, her smile frozen, unreachable, as his expression emptied into lifeless stillness.

# Chapter 7

Eva's departure struck Isa like a blunt silent weapon with the slow suffocation of meaning itself. His world stalled. The pulse of his life flattened to a monotone hum, and he withdrew into the shadows of his bedroom, where he read the Jewish Holy Scriptures as though they contained a cure for heartbreak. Finding the proof that would disprove Eva's rejection became his new faith, a private religion of obsession.

Each evening at precisely nineteen hundred hours, Isa would drag himself to the dining table, sit across from his parents, and eat a fraction of what was served, without appetite. The rest of his hours were surrendered to solitude. The university no longer saw him. The mosque no longer heard him. His friends, Joseph and Shoki, called again and again, their voices trapped in voicemail purgatory. Beyond reading, Isa's existence shrank to the barest mechanics of being, which consisted only breathing, eating, pissing, and shitting with an occasional weekly showering. He smoked two packs a day and drank eight beers to numb the edges of thought, supplies reluctantly procured by his mother, who watched her son's slow disintegration with helpless dread.

His heart sank into a lonesome, derided abyss, gnawed by the suspicion that he had nothing left to offer to anyone. Isa became a sinking vessel, rusted and forgotten, tethered to his room, as he drowned silently in the rising tide of wordless despair.

He wanted nothing but to be left alone. But solitude, like fate, is rarely absolute. His mother would still intrude, knocking timidly, her voice trembling through the door, "Isa? Are you alright, darling?" He would answer only with a silent nod. Whenever Nona turned up and instigated a conversation with him, Isa reduced his vocabulary to *No, Yes, Leave it here, I'm fine,* or *Could you please leave me alone?*

Eventually, even that fragile intrusion became unbearable for Isa. To avoid his mother, he began locking himself in the bathroom, his last sanctuary, a self-imposed prison cell where she could no longer reach him. There, amid the echo of dripping taps and the stale fog of cigarette smoke, he read the remaining chapters of the Jewish Holy Scriptures, searching for meaning among the ashes of his own faith.

The UN initiative, which was supposed to enlighten the world, instantly downgraded into the dullest televised show ever. People began using the term *Isaistic* to express depression. After having read the Jewish Holy Scriptures, Isa spent most of his time lying on his bed, lacking the impulse to get off it. His flat tummy turned curvy because of excessive beer drinking in his bedroom. Once a bright, spotless bedroom, now became a pigsty stuffed with dirty clothes over the carpet.

Then, one evening, Nona entered Isa's dimly lit room carrying a small tray of fruit, an act more of maternal desperation than nourishment. The air was thick with the stale scent of cigarettes and unspoken words. As she set the tray down, her eyes caught the empty space on Isa's bedside cabinet. The Jewish Holy Scriptures, once ever-present, were gone.

Her voice trembled with a mix of concern and curiosity. "Isa, where are the Scriptures?"

Isa leaned back against the wall, his face half-sunk in shadow. His answer came flat, hollow like the sound of something breaking quietly inside him. "I've finished reading them," he said. "And then I binned them."

Nona froze, staring at her son as though she hadn't heard him correctly.

Isa went on, his tone sharpening with bitterness, "Eva's parents were right. She can't marry someone who isn't a Jew. I finally understand.

Religion is made for people with an enormous ego, people who think they're too good for the rest of us."

Nona drew in a slow, weary breath, her eyes softening but her voice edged with quiet resolve. "You should never judge faiths by the failings of a few," she said. "No more than you would condemn all humanity for one broken heart."

She turned without waiting for his reply, leaving the room in heavy silence, the tray of untouched fruit gleaming faintly under the dying light, a silent testament to everything that had withered between them.

*** 

The following morning, Shoki arrived unannounced at Isa's house. The moment he stepped into Isa's bedroom, the state of ruin struck him like a sour stench of defeat. The blue suede curtains were drawn tight, choking out the morning light and trapping the air in a grey, suffocating haze. His eyes wandered slowly through the wreckage, piles of crumpled clothes scattered like forgotten lives, an ashtray overflowing with cigarette butts, a plate of rotting chicken wings, spinach, and roasted potatoes, and a small army of empty beer bottles standing guard across the patterned carpet. The air smelled of stale smoke, sweat, and massive neglect.

"Hey," Shoki greeted softly, his voice uncertain, breaking the heavy silence.

Isa raised his hand weakly from the bed in a gesture that could barely pass for acknowledgment. He didn't bother to get up. His body was there, but the man inside seemed absent.

Shoki stood still for a moment, his eyes narrowing as he digested Isa's state. His right index finger tapped rhythmically against his lips, a habit from the old days, when he'd think before saying something that might hurt. Finally, with a frustrated sigh, he strode to the window and yanked the curtains open. The sunlight burst in like an intruder, flooding the room with a brilliance so sharp it seemed to wound the air itself. Outside, the sea glittered in infinite shades of blue, crowned by a massive white mushroom-shaped cloud sailing lazily across the sky.

Inside, however, the light only made the squalor more obscene. It revealed the yellow haze of smoke suspended in the room and the red, vein-webbed eyes of Isa, who squinted at the sudden brightness.

Shoki coughed, fanned the air, and threw the window open. The soft sound of chirping birds filled the stale silence, an almost cruel reminder that life still went on somewhere beyond those walls.

Turning back to Isa, Shoki began pacing around the bed, his hands folded neatly behind his back like an anxious schoolmaster. Isa, still slouched, stared down at his twitching foot, the tapping sound echoing through the tense air. His nails, browned from nicotine, met his teeth between drags of his cigarette, the ember glowing like a dying heartbeat. Sweat stains bloomed darkly under his armpits, and his hair, wild, frizzy, and unwashed, clung to his temples like a crown of abandonment.

Even Shoki's own reflection had changed. The hairline that once framed his youthful face had retreated far beyond his forehead, giving him the weary appearance of a man twice his age. The remnants of his red hair were pulled into a tight ponytail, as if to mock the years he hadn't yet lived. His round belly pushed impatiently against his garish red Hawaiian shirt with a pattern of white palm trees an almost laughable contrast to the gloom around him.

At last, Shoki made a sarcastic remark about the splendid weather, a desperate attempt to puncture the silence. Isa didn't answer. He only lifted his head slightly, his face framed by a dense, black beard that swallowed his expression. His mouth hung open, lips dry and cracked, revealing teeth stained to the colour of old parchment.

With a resigned sigh, Shoki pulled a pack of cigarettes from his pocket. He lit one for himself and tossed the pack across the bed. Isa caught it, fumbled for a cigarette, and lit it with trembling fingers. He took a long, painful drag, eyes fixed on the smoke curling upward, as if they were thin ghosts rising toward the ceiling.

Shoki watched him, a mix of pity and frustration tightening his features. He shifted his weight, his shoulders tense, and in an abrupt, inexplicable gesture of rage or helplessness, he flung his head back and slammed it against the wooden cupboard. The bang echoed sharply through the room, a violent punctuation mark in their wordless despair.

Isa pinched one of Shoki's cigarettes, lit it up, and dragged it profoundly into his lungs. Isa's head sank again, focusing on the smoke wafting from his cigarette that circled above his head. Shoki looked down at Isa, swaying his shoulder forward. At one point, he pulled his head back and smashed it against the wooden cupboard behind him, producing a loud bang.

"Why are you here?" Isa asked in a deep gravelly voice.

"Because I love drama," Shoki replied with a cheeky smile. "I met your Mum yesterday. She told me you're feeling down, so I couldn't help but come here to see it live."

"Don't worry, man!" Isa said. "I am not feeling *down*. On the contrary, I'm feeling rather up."

"Well, the only *up* I can see on you is the one that comes after the word fucked!"

Isa glimpsed at his friend with a cold unimpressed gaze before adding, "You have always been slightly fucked-up too!"

"True!" Shoki replied and smiled again. "But I've never been so finely fucked-up … sorry, I meant to say … so fucked-down."

"Don't worry about me! It's all good," Isa said, crushing the beer can on the floor with his left foot.

"The fuck, it's all good!" Shoki blasted, unleashing his full voice. "If you're into fucking-up yourself, could you at least be happy that your effort isn't wasted?"

"I wish to be left alone and not be bothered by others," Isa muttered, closing his eyes and leaning his head against his left hand.

"No one wishes to get *bothered by others*."

Isa fidgeted on his bed with his cigarette clamped between his teeth and squinted at Shoki through the white smoke.

"Listen up, amigo! You're acting as if you're the epicentre of the world. Well, that's just fine and dandy, but at this stage, you should ask yourself which Isa you prefer, the one before or the one after Eva left you?"

A long, sagging cigarette ash fell into Isa's lap.

"I know, but I can't help it!" Isa brushed the ash off his shorts. "Eva and I could have had such a happy marriage."

"This is awesome. Alex is constantly complaining about his marriage, and now you can't stop moaning about not getting married," Shoki said with a generous grin, but when Isa didn't react, he added. "You speak about Eva as if she was a physical necessity, something you were entitled to like she was your indisputable possession."

A series of dry coughs seized Isa, but he finally managed to say, "Eva enjoyed being with me as much as I enjoyed being with her. But God took Eva away from me."

"You know what your problem is?" Shoki stepped towards Isa. "You worry too much about non-existent things, such as God, and ..."

"No, man ... I am done with God!" Isa interrupted Shoki, his tone implying admission of guilt and despair.

"Glad to see you've made some progress! It took you a long time, but you got there. You should divert your thoughts from Eva and focus on something else, so how about a punch in the nose?"

"What?" Isa growled.

"Yes, a good punch in the nose would remind you that physical pain is much stronger than emotional pain, and I'm willing to sacrifice my fist!" Shoki replied. "It's quite possible that something isn't quite right in your brain, and a hefty punch might shake it back to working properly!"

Isa smiled briefly, gazing over Shoki, whose eyes bulged.

"Listen up, amigo! You need to stop behaving like other people don't matter."

"YES, I KNOW!" Isa snarled. "I've seen the look on my mother's face, and ... it's unbearable."

"I got a perfect place for you, and it isn't far from here."

"The Psychiatric Ward?"

"No. It's a secluded ledge that's an ideal jumping place for you to end your misery," Shoki grinned half-heartedly, raising his eyebrows, looking like he expected a smile from Isa.

"Yes, I know," Isa paused, "it isn't like it never crossed my mind."

After noticing Isa's failure to smile, Shoki sat beside him and continued slowly, "Listen up, amigo. I don't see much point in thinking about killing yourself when you're going to die anyway!"

"Three weeks ago, I concluded that killing myself is the best way out of this misery. I'm struggling to understand myself, so I can't expect you to."

"Amigo, troubles are free of charge. You're entitled to take on as many worries as possible without having to pay for them. They never go away, and the only change you'll notice is that your worries get better at messing you up as time goes by!" Shoki explained and added, pointing at the empty green beer can next to Isa's left barefoot. "However, I'm happy to see that you've finally reached adulthood by giving up on your imaginary friend."

"After reading the Jewish Holy Scriptures, I realised that my imaginary friend is a fraud who enjoys messing up people. For example, God says that we must love each other and then forbids us from doing so. How fucked-up is that?" Isa sighed. "Most probably, we are here to entertain God, who is bored to death, so why not throw in some religions to mess up people and enjoy the drama!"

"I couldn't agree more!" Shoki paused to pull another cigarette from his pack with his teeth and lit it up. "Soon, you'll discover another Eva out there who's just as worthy of your love."

"I'm not sure if I want to fall in love again!" Isa objected, blowing smoke from his mouth.

"Alexander and Joseph want to see you too," Shoki said.

"Alexander can come over, but not Joseph."

"Why not Joseph?"

"It's clear that Jews think they are too special for my kind," Isa replied. "They treat other people like they're second-class citizens because they believe that they are way too superior compared to others, including me, which is why from this point on, they can fuck off into their superior world without me."

"Meaning what?"

"Meaning that from now on, Jewish people don't exist for me, and

I couldn't care less for them!"

# Meanwhile, in London – Part Three

As a Jew, Isa's offensive remarks about Jewish people were a turning point for me. I've always disliked Isa, but from this point on, I hated his guts. Jewish people are superior because we managed to brainwash others by inventing a contaminating fairy tale about a guy called Jesus Christ who walked on water. When the world grew tired of being brainwashed by the Christ story, we upgraded our ailing indoctrinating tradition by using the mainstream media, which perceives itself as the shepherd dog and its consumers as sheep, which need safeguarding from inconvenient truths. If people buy into a bullshit story about a guy walking on water, they will believe anything mainstream media tells them. Immediately after Isa suggested that Jewish people should fuck off into their superior world, Jewish people did precisely that. Thanks to mainstream media and social networks, Isa instantly became an anti-Semitic bastard. In a democracy, offending God is a profanity that might go unpunished, but speaking out against Jews, the chosen people, constitutes a profanity that shall not escape severe retribution. After all, Jews are the chosen people, not some fucking Gypsy cunt from Albania whom even his parents didn't want.

Human rights groups worldwide built an alliance to collect over ten million signatures calling for the termination of all UN-SDC-BC broadcasts. They submitted the petition to the UN and staged widespread protests across the world's capitals. Over one million people attended a large demonstration on Manhattan Island. Israel and the

United States demanded that the UN terminate Isa's global broadcast under the pretext that it was promoting antisemitism. However, the UN didn't comply because neither Israel nor the United States had ratified the Convention. Subsequently, Israel and the United States blocked all TV channels and online sites from broadcasting Isa's life within their territories. As a result, millions could no longer see it live on the internet unless they used foreign IP addresses, and the Convention became a pointless waste of time.

However, that wasn't the case with my family living in London. I can still vividly recall my parents' massive row over Isa. Although my parents were Jews, my mother was an adopted orphan with a weak spot for all fellow orphans. She became so addicted to UN-SDC-BC orphans' plight that we had a giant TV screen in the living room, dining room, a smaller one in the kitchen, and another in my parent's bedroom. Only my parents' walk-in wardrobe, the tiny toilet on the ground floor, and my bedroom didn't contain a TV.

Besides going to work, my mother rarely left our home, spending most of her time glued either to UN-SDC-BC live broadcasts or selected daily highlights after midnight. Before the UN-SDC-BC broadcast, my mother used to be a lively, talkative, and affectionate person. However, as months passed by, she became cranky and secluded. Not only did she rarely verbally engage with us, but most of my questions echoed in the air, unnoticed by my mother, as though she ended up living with us due to some accidental circumstances and that Isa was her biological son.

Things got worse as Isa's depression prolonged. During this period, my mother rarely left the leather sofa opposite the curved 55-inch TV mounted on the white wall in the living room. Gradually, she developed a robotic habit of tiptoeing around the house to avoid our attention. Every time I greeted her, she responded by waving and acknowledging me with a cold, forced smile without saying a word. Then, two months later, her solitary strolls were accompanied by almost inaudible sounds. I could never determine whether she was talking or humming to herself. Sometimes, she would sob with voiceless grief, trying to conceal it from

Dad and me. She constantly avoided contact with my father by retreating to their bedroom whenever my father was on the ground floor and descending into the living room whenever my father was in their bedroom.

My father was a pragmatic man. Something was either black or white to him, and grey didn't exist. So, although Dad despised the idea of a nuclear war, he'd always regarded the UN's antidote with suspicion.

Then, one July weekend evening, brightened by the full moon, while Mum was eating dinner on her own in the living room watching Isa on TV, Jane, Dad, and I were out on the garden timber decking, enjoying our dinner laid out over the chipped wooden table. Dad had been in a good mood, but it instantly vanished when my sister asked him if Mum was talking to herself. Dad settled back in his chair and remained silent, shaking his head. He then grabbed his beer and gulped it down. Dad's moist and lifeless eyes stared at Jane in disbelief. I'd never seen him in this state, exhibiting insecurity, bitterness, and anger. He looked obstinate as he tremulously pulled a packet of cigarettes from the outer pocket of his pink shirt, which Jane bought for him. He pulled out a cancer stick and lit it up, blowing out the thick, white smoke that filled his mouth.

When I asked him if Mum's mumbling was normal, he untied his blue tie with his hands and rolled up his shirt's sleeves. He put his cigarette in the glass ashtray, and it took him at least 20 seconds to let it go. Finally, he gulped down his beer, leaned forward, dropped his elbows to his knees and clutched his hair with both hands. Dad, Jane, and I remained silent, avoiding eye contact by looking down at the table as if we were watching a chess game. Dad lit another cigarette, took a deep drag, and began coughing as his cheeks turned pink. When his grey eyes began to water, Jane stood, approached him, and removed the cigarette from his hand. She ground out his cigarette in the ashtray.

Once Dad recovered from his rattling cough and wiped his eyes with his sleeve, Jane asked him, "Dad, are you alright?"

In an instant, Dad leapt to his feet and dashed toward the living room, loudly stomping his shoes on the garden's timber decking and then on the kitchen's ceramic tiles, shouting hysterically as he headed towards the living room, "ESTHER! ESTHER! ESTHER ..."

My sister and I followed him, and then all hell broke loose. Things became heated very quickly, and within a minute, I witnessed the bursting horror of a couple fighting before their marriage was about to collapse. Dad grabbed the TV remote control from Mum's hand, turned the volume off, and then threw it down on the brown cherry flooring, producing a loud bang. As plastic bits scattered across the floor, an unbearable fusion of fear and tension shivered through my spine.

"Why did you do that?" Mum asked, gazing over Isa's face on the TV screen.

"BECAUSE YOU ARE DESTROYING THIS FAMILY!" Dad yelled ferociously.

"We shouldn't have this conversation before them," Mum whispered, nodding towards Jane and me.

"SO, WHEN AND WHERE SHOULD WE HAVE THIS ARGUMENT? IN YOUR OFFICE?" Dad shouted. "In case you've forgotten, over the past four months, you have spent your entire spare time watching the damn TV!"

Dad was beside himself. He shook Mum by her wrists before pushing her violently onto the sofa. Her spectacles fell off her red face, her eyes blinking tears. She discharged a low-pitched moan as if it came from the pit of her stomach.

"You're ignoring your children to spend time with that nutcase who's living thousands of miles away from here!" Dad shouted at Mum, pointing at the TV screen.

There was a pause, during which Mum looked like she'd reached her boiling point and was about to snap at my father. She stood with her legs apart, keeping her arms crossed firmly over her breasts. The left tip of Mum's lips wiggled vaguely as she intensely stared into Dad's eyes. I ran over and hugged her. Her entire body was trembling. She glanced at me briefly before sinking back onto the sofa, began crying loudly, and then exclaimed with her face covered by both hands, "I don't expect you to understand what being an orphan felt like! You didn't end up spending the best years of your life in an orphanage waiting for someone to provide you with a normal childhood."

"You're bloody right! I don't understand, but I know someone who can," Dad pulled out his cell phone and called the emergency services.

Once he got through to an operator, Dad explained the current situation to the person on the other end of the line and requested an ambulance to sanction Mum at the psychiatric ward. Upon hearing this, Mum produced high-pitched screams, alternating with deep moans, much louder than before.

"Please, don't do this to me," Mum pleaded, her voice dropping as she stood.

She tried to persuade him to end this unpleasant conversation. Still, Dad's voice torrented out of his wide mouth, higher than before, "I've tolerated your behaviour for far too long, hoping that you'll realise the damage you're causing to our family, but we have now reached that point when ENOUGH IS ENOUGH."

Mum's startled glance radiated graveness before she shook her head and lowered her eyes, almost closing them. She released a loud grunt as she sat on the sofa and drew her knees up to her chest, embracing them with both hands. Her watery eyes glared down on the timber flooring, bowing her head back and forth, as Jewish people do when praying. Jane sat down next to Mum and patted her pale knee.

When the paramedics arrived, Mum and Dad had run out of mutual accusations, and both calmed down. The male paramedic asked Dad to leave the living room while his female colleague knelt opposite Mum and spoke to her in a calm, low voice. Mum sniffed ostentatiously and wiped her nose with her sleeve as she stared back at the paramedic with a grimace of pain. Then, after fifteen minutes of negotiations with Mum, the female paramedic injected Mum's left arm with a transparent liquid inside the plastic syringe.

Ten minutes later, Dad entered the room with the male paramedic, and both grabbed Mum by her shoulders to lift her off the sofa. Mum's curly white hair covered her eyes. The female paramedic pushed back Mum's hair, exposing her face moist with saliva and tears. As they carried her up the stairs toward the bedroom, Mum lifted her drowsy eyes from beneath, shrugged her eyebrows and whispered to me, "I'm so … so sorry."

After laying Mum in the bedroom upstairs and closing the door on their way out, the paramedics gave my Dad concise instructions on how to section my Mum to the psychiatric ward tomorrow morning. As they descended the stairs, the female paramedic urged my father to take my Mum to see her GP tomorrow morning, who would be able to refer her to the Royal Free Hospital's psychiatric ward. My Dad nodded, and the paramedics left our house. After waving farewell, Dad shut the door, and the three of us headed towards the garden. He stopped by the fridge to grab another beer and joined us in the garden.

"I apologise for what just happened, but Mum needs professional help," Dad whispered, barely moving his lips. "Tomorrow morning, I'll take her to the GP, and she probably won't be back for an extended period."

And that's precisely what happened. Mum's tranquilisers and sleep wore off when my Dad was in the kitchen downstairs preparing breakfast. After waking up, Mum locked herself in the bathroom and gulped down all the bleach she could fetch from the laundry room. When Dad finally tore down the bathroom door, Mum was unconscious but still alive. He drove her to the hospital, and six hours later, Dad returned to inform us that Mum hadn't made it and that they'd found a piece of toilet paper containing a note tucked inside one of her pockets.

Dad held it up and began reading it:

*I'm sorry, but I can no longer belong to a world indifferent to Isa's suffering. As a baby, Isa was deprived of his parent's love, and now again, he is being deprived of Eva's love because cruel people at the UN think Isa ought to have additional grieving. Isa already went through hell in the orphanage, and I can take it no more. Please forgive me!*

After my Mum's burial, I spent most of my weekends watching the weekly UN-SDC-BC2 highlights of the main developments in Isa's life, who flounced off into selfish depression, hoping that something horrible would happen to him. An echoing wail inside my mind was eager to see this egotistical elusive bastard exhale his last breath. Deep inside, I sensed that he was responsible for my mother's death, which had caused my family so much grief.

# Chapter 8

Since all their attempts to soften Isa's depression through medication failed, the UN-SDC-BC producers instructed his parents to get him a puppy, a suggestion not taken lightly by Nona. Besides being a clean freak, Nona also greatly feared dogs. After six intensive weeks of negotiations and counselling, Nona finally succumbed to the idea of a puppy living with them.

Twenty days later, it was Isa's 24th birthday. Shortly after it passed 10:00 am, Ati knocked on his son's bedroom door and opened it.

"Happy birthday, son!" Ati called but didn't step in.

Isa seemed shaken, disorientated, and unsteady as his Dad ushered in a golden retriever. Barking loudly, the puppy scampered into the room, stepping hastily over the dirty carpet stretched out on the floor.

"I didn't ask for a puppy," Isa said, looking at his father.

"I know you didn't, but since you can't stand humans, I supposed you wouldn't mind the company of a puppy."

Isa rolled his eyes and sighed, "But ..."

"Just make sure you take him out at 08:00 am and 08:00 pm!" Ati snapped and disappeared behind the door after closing it.

The cute puppy began sniffing the lowest wall and furniture edges before drifting towards Isa, wagging her tail. Within seconds, the puppy appeared in front of Isa, looking up at him with irresistible brown eyes and a pink tongue sticking out of her mouth. Isa stretched his hand towards the puppy's mouth. The puppy approached and began licking

Isa's long-nailed fingers. Isa lifted her, drew her against his chest, and placed his arm around the puppy's neck. They remained that way until Isa checked the time on the digital clock. Then, he stood up, dressed in greasy clothes, held his new friend on his shoulder, and rushed downstairs.

Once he stepped out into the front garden, Isa placed his puppy on the grass. He observed her running loose with his tiny ears flapping up and down.

Nona joined him outside and said, "Look at her! She's so excited. Watch out so she doesn't reach the road and get run over by a passing car."

In an instant, Isa ran over and stationed himself by the entrance gate. The puppy rushed to him, barking at him. She stopped a pace away from Isa and stared straight at him, stomping her feet on the grass. Isa lifted her, went to the garage and returned with an orange frisbee. He then kneeled, released the puppy and before sending the frisbee flying, Isa shouted, "Fetch it, Qeni! Fetch it!"

Their frisbee throw-and-fetch game lasted almost an hour until Nona informed Isa that breakfast was ready. Isa then picked up his puppy and stepped inside his house. He sat in the dining room, ate his dinner, and told his parents he had decided to call his puppy Qeni.

After receiving his tiny, hairy roommate, Isa loosened a bit. Initially, he began taking his Prozac regularly, something he hesitated to do in the past. In contrast to nine months ago, he started eating properly with his parents in the dining room and frequently communicated by phone with Shoki. Over the next five weeks, Isa dedicated most of his time to Qeni, either playing in the garden or strolling around the neighbourhood with her on the leash. At night, Qeni became Isa's bedmate, sleeping every night next to him with her head resting on his chest.

\*\*\*

Five weeks later, on Saturday evening, Isa left his house to meet Shoki for drinks at the local café. He placed the leash on Qeni and strolled through his quiet neighbourhood. His Bresian friend, Alexander, drove by and stopped his car to speak to Isa. They exchanged friendly words for about ten minutes. Before parting, Isa promised Alexander they'd meet up the following week.

When Isa arrived at the café, Shoki greeted him with an overly enthusiastic hug. Qeni approached Shoki and sniffed his leg. Shoki knelt and began rubbing Qeni's neck with both hands. After Shoki stood up and sat, Isa tied the puppy's leash to the gold-plated fence adjacent to their table.

"So, this is the little girl that took you away from me?" Shoki asked, looking at Qeni with her stomach resting flat against the concrete pavement of the café patio, seemingly without a care in the world.

Isa smiled and sat down, "Yes, she is. You've put on a bit of weight, haven't you?"

"I'm an energetic person, but unfortunately, trapped in a lazy body," Shoki replied.

"Don't you exercise at all?"

"Yes, I do! Every morning, I get off my bed," Shoki said sarcastically.

They were in a good mood and having a good time until a short fellow wearing yellow khaki shorts came over and addressed Shoki, "Hello!"

"Hi, Joseph," Shoki greeted him back.

Then Joseph turned towards Isa and held out a hand to shake his, but Isa declined. Joseph kneeled and stretched his hand toward the puppy. "I tried to call you at least a hundred times, but you neither answered my calls nor called me back," Joseph addressed Isa, looking up at him while patting the puppy's soft white head.

Isa didn't lift his head and kept his eyes fixed on Shoki without replying to Joseph. Isa's puppy sniffed gently at the hem of Joseph's trousers. Shoki looked at Isa with a worrying gaze when Qeni began barking and growling at Joseph. Isa unhooked the leash, lifted his puppy, and placed him on his lap.

"What's going on, Isa? Why have you been avoiding me all this time?" Joseph pressed on, thumping his chest over his heart.

Isa ignored him again. Shoki stood up and pulled Joseph aside. Squinting through Shoki and Joseph's faces, Isa noticed they were arguing but couldn't hear a word.

When Shoki raised his voice, he could make out a little of what they were saying to each other, "... and after spending almost a year in depression, this is the first time he's left his house. So now is not a good time to judge his behaviour or speak to him about ..."

"As far as he's concerned, there will never be a good time for Joseph to speak to me, so he's free to leave now," Isa stated with a sudden wave of fury, talking over Shoki.

Shoki's jaw dropped, astounded by Isa's belligerent tone. It was something he had never seen him do before.

"Come on, man," Joseph pleaded, raising his tone and tapping Isa's shoulder. "It's me, Joseph. Your childhood friend."

"LEAVE ME ALONE!" Isa shouted at Joseph, pushing his hand from his shoulder.

Joseph stretched out a hand to touch Qeni's neck, but the puppy pushed toward Joseph, barking at a high pitch.

Joseph looked like he might turn and run as he took several steps backwards. His body began to tremble when he exclaimed to Shoki, "Bloody hell, Shoki! What the hell is wrong with him?"

"GET OUT OF MY SIGHT!" Isa shouted. "JEWS ARE NO LONGER MY FRIENDS. NOW, GET THE FUCK OUT OF MY SIGHT AND LEAVE ME ALONE."

Joseph raised his voice, "Could you please, at least, tell me how I've wronged you to deserve this kind of behaviour?"

Isa stood and stomped towards Joseph, sounding exasperated, "You're a Jew, and since I'm not a Jew, I'm not worthy of your kind."

"FOR FUCK'S SAKE!" Joseph shouted back. "THAT'S UTTER NONSENSE, AND ..."

"KEEP YOUR FUCKING VOICE DOWN AND LEAVE US ALONE!" Isa lost his temper, pointing towards the door.

Joseph tried to reply but couldn't. Isa's angry stare deterred him from doing so. Joseph opened his mouth again to say something, but after noticing that onlookers seated in the café were staring at him and Isa, he refrained and left.

# Chapter 9

Six years had passed since Qeni entered Isa's life and soothed his depression. Meanwhile, Isa completed his bachelor's and master's law studies. Then, following a three-month internship, Isa became a public prosecutor and executed his cases promptly and meticulously, securing maximum jail sentences for the alleged offenders.

It was an unusually wet Thursday in Anitshrip Town as rain fell almost ceaselessly. Isa's assistant, Ndihmese, barged into his office and placed a small takeaway cup and a brown bag on Isa's desk. She was a short woman with a brownish scalp visible through the sparse blond-dyed hair slicked back off her face. Her plucked, thin-arched eyebrows gave her a constant confused look. She wore extraordinarily high heels and a dark red dress with tiny stains above her chest. Ndihmese's hips were broad, her bare legs were immensely swollen with thick lines of varicose veins.

Isa greeted her, and instead of greeting him back, Ndihmese sniffed the air and asked, "What's that nasty smell?"

"It's silicone!" Isa replied, looking down at the double-sided A4 printed papers in his hand.

"So, who had her boobs done... Jenny or Liz?" Ndihmese whispered as she closed the office door, and then sat opposite Isa.

"Over the weekend, some workers applied new silicone sealant to our windows. Besides, I don't think Liz or Jenny is dumb enough to do that."

"Are you sure about that?" Ndihmese asked in an overly confident tone. "Last week, I walked in on Jenny and Liz having their usual meaningless conversation. Jenny was ranting about her diet and asked Liz if she could see that she'd lost almost a couple of stones. Guess what was Liz's reply?" After receiving a silent shrug from Isa, Ndihmese mimicked Liz, "*How am I supposed to see something if it's no longer there?*"

Isa laughed hysterically before Ndihmese added, "Every time I bump into them and listen to their stupid remarks, I wonder how much fun it would be to live with them."

"Going back to the plastic surgery issue, I think it's a waste of time for insecure people who thrive on spending their money to please the eyesight of others instead of their own," Isa suggested. "They should spend their money pleasing their own eyes by sightseeing the natural marvels of planet earth."

"Aha! But you keep forgetting something," Ndihmese replied enthusiastically. "Plastic surgery is the only investment that no one can steal from you, something that remains with you even after you've died."

Isa shook his head anxiously.

"You disagree, don't you?" Ndihmese asked. "Suppose you buy your dream car and enjoy it for several months but then die from a heart attack. You can't take your dream car to the grave, can you?"

"No, I can't."

"But if you have your nose, boobs, or bum done, you can take them with you to your grave, which is why plastic surgery is the best investment!" Ndihmese concluded before walking out and returning to her desk.

Once Ndihmese left, Isa shook his head and turned his attention to the printed copies on his desk. Then, half an hour later, he dashed off to the court.

Isa didn't go back to his office until one o'clock. He held a white polystyrene tray and his briefcase. Isa dropped the tray on his desk, stripped off his jacket, hung it on a peg, and invited Ndihmese into his office.

She walked over, sat with her notebook, and placed her cell phone on Isa's desk. They discussed Isa's schedule for next week, and fifteen minutes later, Ndihmese left.

Isa pulled a newspaper from his briefcase and began reading as he ate his late lunch. He was on his eighth bite when Isa's boss, the Chief Public Prosecutor, Bythlepiresi Kryeprokuror, stepped into Isa's office with a yellow file case tucked under his arm. His head displayed large ears, an extended tip of a flat nose, and deep-set copper eyes. A tailored striped navy suit enveloped Bythlepiresi's body. He greeted Isa with a frown, swinging his right hand in front of his nose as if warding off a fly. "Would you mind if I open it?" Bythlepiresi asked, pointing at the window. He then pointed at the lunch tray on Isa's desk, "I'm off to an important meeting and don't want my clothes smelling of whatever that is!"

"It's chicken curry," Isa replied, "would you like some?"

"Thanks, Isa! I'm good," Bythlepiresi shook his glistening bald head and walked over to the exterior glazed wall to open the window. "You go ahead. I'm sorry, I didn't realise it was lunchtime."

"It's fifteen minutes past lunch, but I got stuck at today's court proceeding, which ..."

"Yes, I know! Your assistant told me that you were running late. It's the beach knife attack case, isn't it?"

"Yes, it is!" Isa replied.

"How is it coming along?" Bythlepiresi asked.

"It looks like the defendant will accept the deal for a three-year imprisonment with a possibility of parole after two years!"

"Very good!" Bythlepiresi sighed as he scratched his face, revealing a gold ring featuring a large red stone in the middle.

Isa's office seemed smaller due to a tidy row of files stacked beneath the windowsills. A large computer screen and a momentous pile of yellow files occupied most of the surface of his desk.

"Finished eating your curry?" Bythlepiresi asked.

Isa nodded, still chewing on his last bite as he placed the tray inside the bin.

Bythlepiresi walked away from the exterior glass wall, which revealed a stretch of rotating rusted cranes visible outside. As he approached Isa's desk, Bythlepiresi noticed a cell phone with a velvet cover on Isa's desk and added with a smirk, pointing at it, "That's an interesting choice of colour."

"It's Ndihmese's phone, not mine! She was in here earlier, and it looks like she forgot to pick it up," Isa blushed slightly, forcing a grin.

Bythlepiresi smiled, stepped closer to Isa and slammed the yellow folder on Isa's desk.

"They've assigned you to the drunk driver killing a nurse case. Are you familiar with it?"

Isa tweaked the flimsy photocopied sheets inside the yellow folder.

"Never mind! Read it and prepare a brief report on it by Friday," Bythlepiresi added, scratching his grey goatee beard. "Could you do this for me?"

Isa confirmed with thumbs-up.

"That's wonderful!" Bythlepiresi said and left.

Isa pulled a blue file from the wooden shelf and opened it. As Isa immersed himself in reading them, the papers began trembling in his hand. He worked until 11 pm when he printed five pages, slipped them into a white envelope and scribbled over it. Isa rubbed his eyes and limped out of his office. Before leaving the building, he dropped the envelope on the desk of Bythlepiresi's assistant.

\*\*\*

Isa left his flat at a quarter to nine the next morning. He navigated through buzzing streets to his office. Holding a folded newspaper under his right arm, he stopped to grab a cup of coffee, queuing behind two men in hard hats, fluorescent yellow jackets, and boots clogged with mud. It took Isa less than a minute to order an espresso and pay for it before fetching it to sit outside. Isa lit another cigarette and sipped his espresso, reading the newspaper. Fifteen minutes later, he stood and headed toward his office.

Upon entering his office, he opened the window but then closed it to prevent the unbearable noise of the cistern pouring cement into the adjacent building. Then, he sat down and browsed a pile of papers beside the computer keyboard.

After three-quarters of an hour, Bythlepiresi barged into Isa's office, looking down at him with menacing eyes, "How long were you doing this?"

"Doing what, sir?"

"Working on this case, we discussed yesterday?"

"Around fourteen hours."

"I asked you to prepare a brief report on this case, not a court proceeding!" Bythlepiresi said with a distinctive authoritarian edge.

"I was just doing my job, sir," Isa replied, glowing with pride.

Bythlepiresi moved around Isa's desk, and once he reached Isa's right shoulder, he snarled at Isa, "You are my employee, and I'm the one who tells you what your job is. This case must not reach the courts, so forget it ever existed and focus on other cases you're working on!"

"But this is a straightforward open-and-shut case ..."

"STOP THERE!" Bythlepiresi cut in with an overtone of determination. "This case isn't as straightforward as you think, and this is an off-the-record chat."

"But sir, we have four unacquainted witnesses, the police report, and most importantly, the camera recordings of the accident. This case could be closed within three months!"

"IS THERE SOMETHING WRONG WITH YOUR EARS, OR DO YOU NO LONGER UNDERSTAND THE VALLSIAN LANGUAGE?" Bythlepiresi growled.

Bythlepiresi's shouting penetrated the flimsy dividing wall, reaching Isa's assistant, who left her desk and walked toward Isa's office. She knocked and craned her neck to look inside Isa's office.

"Is everything all right?" Ndihmese asked, clutching the edge of the door.

"Everything is fine," Bythlepiresi replied through his teeth, dragging out the vowels.

"We're all right, thanks for asking," Isa added, looking embarrassed.

As soon as Ndihmese left and her footsteps were no longer audible, Bythlepiresi unbuttoned his white collar and tugged his tie away from his neck before approaching Isa. "Listen up! This is a sensitive case. We can't discuss it here. We'll continue this discussion at my house tomorrow from 01:00 pm. Can you make it?"

Isa shrugged, then nodded.

"Goooood!" Bythlepiresi sighed, and after looking at his watch, he rushed out.

\*\*\*

It was a cold Saturday afternoon with grey clouds sailing slowly towards Anitshirp Town, but that didn't deter Isa from cycling through the sounds of occasional shouting and the growling horns of queuing cars. Finally, Isa arrived at Bythlepiresi's house on the posh, sloping hill overlooking the Adriatic Sea. He locked his bicycle against a pine tree on the pedestrian path, grabbed the bottle of Shiraz from the front basket, and stepped into a gravelled forecourt. He stopped by a large wooden front door with a bronze sculpture next to it and pressed the doorbell, which produced a loud ring. Bythlepiresi appeared within a few seconds, opening the large door, almost twice his height.

Isa handed the bottle of red wine to his superior and stepped inside. Bythlepiresi closed the door and led Isa toward the living room. After crossing the living room, Isa sat down at the large wooden table for twelve. The host headed for the open-plan kitchen, grabbed a corkscrew from a white drawer and joined Isa. He uncorked Isa's wine, poured it into two glasses next to two rounded plates with spaghetti Bolognese, and sat opposite Isa.

"It's not wise to pursue with our yesterday's conversation on an empty stomach," Bythlepiresi suggested.

They remained silent, and then, five minutes later, they began discussing their favourite cooking recipes. It wasn't long before they finished their lunch when Bythlepiresi got back to the subject at hand.

"Yesterday, we got on the wrong foot. Please don't take it personally, but you must stall this case!" Bythlepiresi said in a manner so exaggerated and perverse, plausible enough to fill anyone with alarmed guilt. "There's no other way around it."

"Why?" Isa asked, blinking rapidly.

"Because that's what needs to be done!" Bythlepiresi responded, red colour rising on his face.

"But ..."

"I DON'T GIVE A FUCK WHAT YOU THINK! IF YOU DON'T DO AS YOU'RE TOLD, I'M PULLING THE FUCKING PLUG ON YOU! DO YOU UNDERSTAND? IT'S MY WAY OR THE FUCK-OFF WAY!"

No font type or size, upper case or bold, could capture Bythlepiresi's outburst as his breathing accelerated.

"But ..." Isa tried to reassure him, smoothing sweaty hair strands off his forehead.

"DID YOU FUCKING UNDERSTAND WHAT I JUST SAID, OR DO YOU NEED IT WRITTEN DOWN?"

Bythlepiresi blasted again, sounding much harsher as spit flew out his mouth onto Isa's jacket.

Isa nodded submissively, his knees bouncing up and down. From that point on, Isa remained silent, blending seamlessly into the dim monologue of his superior.

With furtive eagerness, Bythlepiresi drew his cell phone from an inside pocket of his trousers and showed Isa a photograph of a man in a suit, "Do you know who this is?"

Isa nodded and then replied, "Yes, I know. It's the Minister of Justice!"

Bythlepiresi paused for a split second to regain his composure and added, "He also happens to be the uncle of the drunk driver who committed this offence and the one who made me a Chief Public Prosecutor, and now I must return his favour by averting his nephew's prosecution."

Isa's right eyelid flickered as he replied, "But you're asking me to obstruct the law."

"No, I'm not! I'm merely asking you to postpone advancing this case to the court."

"You can call it whatever you want, but what you're asking me to do, is to break the law," Isa pressed on.

Bythlepiresi rose from his chair, walked around the table towards Isa, and exclaimed, poking his employee with his index finger, "God damn, man! It isn't my fault that voters are asked to determine whose lies they like more and vote for them every four years, including our Minister of Justice. If he were a decent man, he would have done a better job teaching his nephew not to drive his car at 60 miles an hour in the town centre when drunk. I don't like him, but he's my superior and tells me what needs to be done."

"This is a personal and complicated case for me," Isa exclaimed, keeping a curb on his temper while his hands began to tremble. "I don't want to be a part of something which isn't right."

"Next week, my family and I will be on holiday with the Minister of Justice's family. So here's the first thing you'll do on Monday morning. You'll either do as you're told or resign!" Bythlepiresi threatened Isa, then grabbed his cell phone from the table as he walked away. He rubbed his thumb against the cell phone's screen and held it against his ear. Within seconds he changed his tone and spoke in a courteous voice, "Hi, honey! I've just finished the meeting. Are you done with your shopping? Where do you want me to pick you up? See you soon!"

After sliding his cell phone back into his pocket, Bythlepiresi walked toward Isa with his palms up. "I must pick up my wife and then head over to the mayor's house. Do you need a lift?"

"No, thanks! I'll cycle back."

"Isa, please understand! I'm in a difficult position" Bythlepiresi pleaded, pulling up his protruding stomach to adjust his belt. "My term will end in six months, and if you don't do as you're told, the Minister will replace me with someone who'll comply with his wishes."

"So, instead, you would rather replace me!"

"I don't want ..."

"Me too!" Isa interjected and walked away. "I don't want to impede your precious arse-kissing career, so you'll have my resignation on Monday."

As soon as he was outside and hit clean air, Isa pulled his Camel cigarettes out of his pocket and lit one. He took a couple of drags and then called Alexander. After receiving Alexander's confirmation that they would meet in half an hour, Isa hung up and called Shoki.

"Hello, amigo," Shoki said, picking up after a single ring.

"Shoki, I need to see you," Isa said, his cigarette jammed between his teeth.

"Why don't you skip the small talk and get straight into the bit that explains how bad you fucked up this time," Shoki replied.

"Pretty bad."

"All right then, where and when do you want to meet?"

"At the café in half an hour." "All right, I'll see you in forty minutes," Shoki confirmed and hung up.

Isa unchained his bicycle and pedalled down the hill upon finishing his conversation.

Fifteen minutes later, Isa pushed open the door of the café, which was almost full, echoing with overlapping chatter and classical music playing in the background. The interior had changed and was sleekly modern, with a curved steel counter, red-dyed resin flooring, and bare white walls. After realising his friends hadn't arrived yet, Isa stepped back outside and strolled towards the only empty table, being wiped down by a discontented-looking young man in glasses with tattooed forearms. Isa sat down, facing a table occupied by three young girls. They giggled at something one had shown the other two on her phone. Isa ordered an espresso and asked the waiter to turn on the patio gas heater. The waiter did what Isa asked him to do and then left. Ten minutes later, when the waiter returned with Isa's coffee, Shoki had arrived, too, wearing casual clothes and a puffy jacket.

Shoki patted his friend's shoulder and then turned to the waiter, who set down Isa's espresso on the table, "Could you please fetch me a glass of chilled Pinot Grigio?"

"It's freezing out here, and you're drinking chilled white wine!" Isa exclaimed as Shoki sat down opposite him.

"What else am I supposed to do with chilled white wine but drink it?" Shoki asked with a trace of smugness.

The waiter nodded with a grumpy expression and withdrew towards the bar.

"Where did they find that guy?" Shoki asked Isa, observing the departing waiter with a malicious smile. "Judging from his Frankenstein-like face, he is better suited to work in a cemetery, digging graves."

Isa shrugged as he dipped the spoon into his coffee cup.

"You don't look much better yourself," Shoki said as he glanced suspiciously at Isa.

"I had a rough night and had trouble sleeping."

Shoki lifted his left eyebrow.

"Surely, sometimes you have trouble sleeping, too," Isa added.

"No, I don't." Shoki said and grinned, "Sleeping is an easy task. I can do it with my eyes closed."

Shoki and Isa briefly discussed Qeni before Alexander arrived, holding his phone. His eyes moved rapidly from left to right, searching for Isa and Shoki. After spotting them, he joined them at their table.

"Make it quick because I've got to meet my in-laws at three," Alexander said as he sat next to Shoki. After noticing Isa's miserable facial expression, Alexander asked him, "Why the long face? Don't tell me you've found the perfect girl again, but, fortunately, she won't marry you."

Isa unleashed a smiling sigh and lit another cigarette on top of the fourteen he'd already had that day. The waiter popped by again to place Shoki's Pinot Grigio and a small bowl of roasted peanuts on the table.

The cranky waiter asked Alexander, "What would you like to ..."

"I would like to be single again," Alexander bumped in.

"Come on, Alex! Perhaps you two should get away for a nice vacation," Shoki added.

"But, we're already away, having a long vacation at the fiery pits of inferno!" Alexander responded and then ordered a cappuccino.

After the waiter retreated, Shoki asked Isa, "So, why did you invite us over?"

"Sorry, but I'm not in a good mood!" Isa replied.

"Wait until you get married, and then you'll discover what a bad mood is!" Alexander added.

"Is it still that bad?" Shoki asked, looking at Alexander.

"Last week, she stopped talking to me, so there's been a slight improvement," Alexander replied, pinching roast peanuts from the glass bowl in the centre of the table.

"What did you do this time?" Shoki asked.

"She insisted I should start seeing someone," Alexander replied. "But when I asked her if she was fine with me seeing my ex, she went nuts!"

"She probably meant a marriage therapist," Isa hinted.

"Yes, that's what she shouted afterwards," Alexander said. "A bit too late if you ask me."

"Every marriage has its ups and downs," Isa said. "Have you ever considered taking a break from each other?"

"Yes, we did that once, but then my wife realised she didn't torture me enough, so she came back," Alexander replied. "If marriage is a good thing, surely God could have created a wife for himself and married her."

"Don't pay much attention to him," Shoki pointed at Alexander as laughter subdued and then lit the cigarette between his teeth, "he's a human version of diarrhoea who can't stop shitting out stuff about his marriage."

"You know what, Shoki," Alexander growled, "you're a heartless son of a bitch."

"I'm not a son of a bitch, but when it comes to you, I've decided to use my heart less than I tend to for others," Shoki concluded, leaning backwards and clasping his hands behind his head.

"But Ajam is a wonderful woman," Isa added. "What does she do that makes you so miserable?"

"She exists, and that's what makes me so miserable!" Alexander exclaimed. "For starters, she's a cleaning freak with capital letters!"

"It's such a shame your parents didn't name you Domestos or Ajax because if they did so, I'm confident that your wife would have loved you more," Shoki said, "Didn't you know that the word husband derives from the word *hushband* that refers to someone who's always on the hush frequency band."

"I've got just the right book for you," Isa changed the subject. "It is called How To Change Your Life In 15 Days."

"Excuse me, did you say how to change *your life* or *your wife*?" Alexander asked.

"I said *life*, not *wife*," Isa replied.

"My life is fine. It's my wife that I've got a problem with!" Alexander retorted.

"We're just not going to get a break from your marriage today, are we?" Shoki asked Alexander.

"I would love to get a break from my married life, too," Alexander exclaimed.

"I don't know how to put this to you delicately," Shoki exclaimed, facing Alexander. "But the best I could come up with is - you're an imbecile!"

"Before you end up saying something that might offend me," Alexander said. "You ought to wait until you get to your eight-marriage anniversary."

"Dear God, please make Alex stop talking about his wife?" Shoki asked, holding his hands together and looking up into the sky.

"Come on, Shoki!" Alexander shouted. "My wife's body contains so much poison that if she ever gets bitten by a snake, it will be the snake that'll end up dead."

"There goes your proof that God doesn't exist!" Shoki exclaimed.

"Marrying her was my biggest mistake ever," Alexander said.

"Perhaps, you should embrace your mistake and move on!" Isa suggested.

"I've tried, but she won't let me hug her," Alexander concluded.

"You could shape up your life a bit. Have you ever considered running?" Isa asked Alex.

"How is that supposed to help my disastrous marriage?" Alexander objected. "By the way, neither of you does any running."

"If you continue bragging about your marriage, you'll see me running away real soon," Shoki said, raising his voice.

"Why do you have to be so negative about your marriage all the bloody time?" Shoki asked Alexander.

"I'm not negative about my marriage all the time. For example, I'm positive that my marriage will end soon."

"I've had enough of listening to your incessant moaning about your marriage, so Isa, what's up with your I want to look older facial hair?"

"I'm growing a beard," Isa said, "does it make me look ugly?"

"Nope! It makes you look super ugly!" Alexander winked. "How is your dog?"

"Qeni is fine," Isa replied. "Dogs are the most intelligent creatures on earth."

"That's not true! Wives are the most intelligent creatures on earth!" Alexander pursued his ranting. "Did you know that if wives were to be paid for moaning, my wife would have been a millionaire by now?"

"Isa, please ignore him and tell us why we're here. What's the big announcement?" Shoki asked.

Isa sighed again before flatly announcing, "I'm resigning on Monday."

"Resigning from being a prick or ...?" Shoki asked, squashing his cigarette pack after realising it was empty.

"Resigning from my job as a Public Prosecutor," Isa responded in a slightly elevated tone.

"That is great news!" Shoki erupted with joy as he pulled a Marlboro pack from his trousers. "This is a double resignation, resigning from your job and being a prick too! So, you have finally decided to follow my advice to make more money by moving into the private sector."

"I promised my Dad I'd never leave the public sector, and I intend to keep my word!"

"As my grandfather used to say ..." Alexander interjected.

"Here he goes again!" Shoki bellowed, ripping the cellophane off the Marlboro pack.

"No, that's what my grandmother used to say every time my grandfather was about to say something," Alexander reacted promptly. "My grandfather used to say that lawyers are prostitutes who did whatever their clients asked of them."

Shoki shook his head and asked Isa, "So why are you resigning?"

"Do you remember Fqinja from primary school?" Isa asked.

Shoki gulped down his white wine and replied, "You mean the one that had a crush on you?"

Isa nodded and continued, "Last month, Fqinja was hit and killed by a drunk driver who happens to be the nephew of our current Minister of Justice."

"That's horrible!" Alexander said.

"So, my boss doesn't want me to proceed with this case to the courts because he wants to secure another term as Chief Public Prosecutor while the offender's uncle is still the Minister of Justice," Isa paused to finish his espresso. "I can't do this to Fqinja, hence my resignation."

Isa patted his pockets and pulled out his Camel pack but found it empty. Shoki grabbed his Marlboro pack and tossed it to Isa.

"That's a tough call, but if you resign, that won't bring Fqinja back, and you'll end up disappointing your father!" Alexander added, taking a sip of his cappuccino, his eyes on the large breasts of a woman seated on her own behind Isa.

"But Dad has always insisted that if I retain my decency in everything I do, everything will be fine, and that's exactly what I intend to do," Isa reached for Shoki's cigarettes.

"I hate to admit it, but your Dad is right," Shoki added, "by retaining your decency and resigning, it will eventually turn out fine for the murderer, but not for you. You'll be replaced with someone who'll do whatever they're told to do, so your decency will set the murderer free, and you'll end up unemployed. Nowadays, public servants are there to serve politicians instead of the public and ..."

"Don't worry about it, Isa," Alexander joined the conversation. "As my grandmother always used to say, *as one door closes, another one opens.*"

"So, your grandmother was a carpenter, too?" Shoki asked Alexander as his cell phone rang.

Alexander answered the call in an instant, "Hi, Ajam. I'm having a drink with Isa and Shoki. What? At two?" Alexander asked and paused briefly, looking at his wristwatch before venting his frustration. "But I thought you said they're expecting us at three o'clock? Now, hold on a minute! I've told you I suffer from vitamin S deficiency, but you don't give a damn about it, yet now you're complaining that I'm not paying any attention to what you say. I've already explained how a lack of vitamin S impedes men's hearing abilities. ALL RIGHT! ALL RIGHT! ALL RIGHT! Get ready to torture me because I'm on my way to you now."

"Is that love or what?" Shoki asked with a condescending snort of laughter after Alexander hung up.

"Judging from her yelling, she seems very upset with you," Isa hinted.

"Unfortunately, nobody invented the machine that converts human yelling into energy because if they did, my wife would have become a millionaire by now," Alexander sighed, sliding his phone back into his pocket.

Isa lit a cigarette and then waved to grab the waiter's attention.

When the waiter appeared, Isa pulled a tenner from his pocket and said to Alexander, "I'll get this! You can tip the waiter."

"Here's a generous tip for you," Alexander addressed the waiter, pointing at his wedding ring, "DON'T GET MARRIED!"

The waiter didn't look impressed as he placed a fiver on Isa's hand.

"Come on, Alex!" Isa admonished, "surely, you must have 50

cents on you."

"I used to, but then I got married. I've got to go now." Alexander replied as he rummaged through his jean's front pockets and then walked away.

"Could I have some change, please?" Isa asked, passing the fiver back to the waiter.

"I'm glad you finally decided to change," Shoki added sarcastically, pointing his index finger at Isa.

"What's vitamin S?" Isa asked Alexander.

"Vitamin S stands for Vitamin Sex," Alexander replied, without looking back. "Ever since my wife became pregnant, I haven't had any vitamin S."

"So how come lack of sex affects your hearing?" Isa asked as their friend continued to walk away.

Alexander stopped, turned, and answered in a loud, curt voice, "Old people also suffer from sex deprivation! Coincidentally, they can't hear much."

Most people drinking and chatting in the café casted sceptical looks at Alexander as he stepped out of the café's fenced outdoor area.

"Could you please say it louder?" Shoki yelled at Alexander. "I'm not sure if the entire café heard you."

\*\*\*

Had his evening gone as usual, Isa would have been at his parents for dinner, watching the 19:00 news. Instead, the evening found Isa excessively drinking red wine on the balcony of his flat, looking at the stars struggling to twinkle behind the patch of remaining clouds. He was in a limbo state, drinking initially from the glass and then taking swigs directly from the bottle. He lit up another cigarette, probably the thirtieth that day. Halfway into his second bottle of wine, Isa's eyelids drooped. Within seconds, his head sank sideways, and the wine bottle slipped out of his slack grasp onto the floor, producing a loud bang, which woke him up.

Isa grabbed the wine bottle from the floor and his cell phone from the table as he begrudgingly stood up, but his knees betrayed him, and fell, hitting the edge of his chair with his left eye. Isa produced a series of grunts as he got up slowly and headed toward his bedroom. He swayed like a palm tree in the wind, his pace slow and unbalanced. He dropped his cell phone. "Fuck!" he shouted to himself, struggling to pick it up. Upon reaching the bedroom, his right hand clutched the door frame just in time to prevent another potential fall. After composing himself, he swerved and dashed straight to his bed. Shortly afterwards, he slept still fully dressed.

\*\*\*

It was a chilly and wet Monday morning. The rain hammered violently against the window, disturbing Isa's sleep. As indicated by a series of grunts, getting out of bed proved difficult for him. He headed into the kitchen, drank two cups of coffee, and chain-smoked five cigarettes to sober up. He skipped his usual morning routine, showering and brushing his teeth. Instead, Isa took off his clothes, sprayed deodorant under his armpits, and dressed up in fresh clothes. He picked up folded cardboard boxes wrapped in plastic foil and left the flat.

Isa had spent 20 anxious minutes on his way to work, moving slowly under a black umbrella and looking down at the damp, slippery concrete pavement. His shoulder bag hung limply by his side while traffic rumbled to his right. Gloomy sky pledged an extended downpour and matched Isa's unshaven expressionless rough looking face.

He entered the building without customary friendly greetings to the cleaner and receptionist. Once inside his office, Isa closed the door and stood next to the exterior glass wall, looking out at wobbling umbrellas below. He placed his suit jacket over his chair and sat in front of his computer monitor, silently gazing at it. Isa sighed and then straightened his short hair looking at his reflection on the dark computer screen. Eventually, he turned on his computer, and soon after the monitor brightened, he began typing on his keyboard. After numerous sighs, he stood and murmured, pacing every office corner. Ultimately, Isa left his office and walked out of the building.

He stopped at the café, and since no one was queuing, Isa immediately ordered a takeaway espresso and paid for it. After being served, he poured a sugar spoon into his coffee, grabbed it, and instead of heading back to his office, Isa crossed the tiled ground floor and stopped on the other side of the building, a grim outdoor area used by the smokers working there. He fiddled inside his pocket for a cigarette, and after pinching one, he lit up. Isa then pulled out his phone and looked at the image of his father displayed on the screen. After finishing his coffee, Isa dropped his cigarette into the paper coffee cup, generating a brief hiss.

He returned to the entrance hall, queuing up behind several other people who waited for the lift to arrive. Two of them were discussing how they'd spent their weekend. Once the bell dinged and the lift doors opened, Isa was the last to enter. Isa got out of the elevator once it reached the fourth floor. The open-plan area was occupied by people sparsely spread in front of their computers. Isa walked past them towards his assistant, sitting at her desk reading a thick book.

"Is it any good?" Isa asked Ndihmese, pointing at her book.

"I've read better," Ndihmese replied before looking up at Isa. "You look terrible. Looking like that, you could probably bag yourself a part in a zombie blockbuster."

"I've got a black eye from hitting the edge of the chair last night."

"Actually, you've got two black eyes," Ndihmese said with a slight grin.

"I spent all night weaselling through the details of what to do next," Isa replied between two massive yawns. "Which book transformed your life?"

"The Wedding Registry Book." Ndihmese sighed. "That one completely changed my life!"

"Is this a bad time to ask you for a favour?"

"No, but I've got this painful hunch you are about to turn it into one."

"I would appreciate it if you could help me type my resignation letter," Isa responded.

"I assume you will pack this job for a better one?"

"No, I haven't got a new job, but I've had enough of this one," Isa turned and strolled towards his office. "I'm here to do my job, yet my superior tells me not to!"

Ndihmese and Isa entered his office. Then, after placing the folded cardboard boxes on the floor and removing the clatter on his desk, Isa gave way to his assistant so she could sit at his chair.

Ndihmese turned on the computer before asking Isa, "You sure you want to proceed with this? It isn't down to some bloody bump on your head, right?" Then, after noticing the strained look on Isa's face, she added, "You probably think it isn't my business, but it is! You're the best boss I've ever had. If you leave, the arsehole will hire someone with the brain capacity of an ant but with expansive political connections."

Isa laughed.

"It isn't funny! Ever since that arsehole arrived, he has filled our payroll with imbeciles who can't even properly write Vallsian but have an outstanding mastery in kissing the stinking arses of our politicians," Ndihmese whispered. "Do you know how Bythlepiresi got his flat nose?"

Isa shrugged.

"It isn't from boxing, is it?" Ndihmese asked, lifting her ultra-thin eyebrows. "No, of course not! He got his flat nose from pushing it against politicians' bums so that his lips could reach deep inside their arses!"

Isa burst into uncontrolled laughter. Once he composed himself, he said to his assistant, "I'll miss your sense of humour!"

Ndihmese paused when her cell phone screen lit up, indicating the arrival of a new message. "Excuse me! I must reply to this message," Ndihmese said without leaving the chair.

Isa nodded as his eyes looked over Ndihmese's shoulder on her phone screen as she tapped her reply. Just before finishing her reply, Ndihmese lifted her head to tell Isa she was ready to type, but after noticing Isa's eyes fixed on her cell phone screen, she asked sarcastically, pointing at her cell phone, "Would you like to add something to my reply, or should I just send it as it is?"

Isa apologised as Ndihmese pressed reply and turned to face the computer screen.

"Please press cancel on that popup window," Isa exclaimed as Ndihmese moved the cursor over a red icon.

"Why? Is it one of those applications that will set off a ballistic missile to the Bresian Republic?"

"Could we start typing my resignation letter?" Isa asked.

Ndihmese nodded before starting to pound letters on the keyboard. Once she finished typing the letter, she pressed the print button. Isa fetched the printed letter and signed it before slipping it into a white A4 envelope. Isa then added three condoms to the envelope and sealed it.

"What are the condoms for?" Ndihmese asked.

"To prevent him from reproducing arse-kissers like him," Isa replied, walking towards the Chief Prosecutor's office to hand in his resignation letter.

# Chapter 10

After the humiliation of losing his first job, Isa retreated back to his parents' home. He buried his disappointment beneath academic ambition, chasing a PhD that was supposed to mean something. His mentor praised his thesis on constitutional law, lavished him with compliments, then quietly tethered Isa to his side as an assistant. A reward disguised as servitude.

Isa's office was a cramped little box, more prison than workspace, with floor-to-ceiling windows behind his desk that only gave him a view of the world he wasn't part of. The walls groaned under shelves stuffed with books in every shade, stacked sideways, collapsing in on themselves, like everything else in his life. Papers smothered his desk, piled high enough to swallow his monitor whole, the chaos echoing the disorder in his head.

Yet when Isa lectured, he transformed. Gone was the quiet, apologetic voice that barely crossed a room. In its place, a booming performance, harsh, sharp, and demanding. He interrogated students every ten minutes, refusing to let them drift, forcing them awake, forcing them to see him. Every lecture began with a joke, a strained attempt at levity. If the students didn't laugh, he made them contribute their own, turning their silence into another reminder that the room belonged to him, not them.

He forged bonds with many of his students, warm, helpful, and almost friendly. But not with the Jewish ones. With them, the warmth froze. Their questions were deflected. Their excellence dismissed. Their grades suppressed. And Isa justified it all, silently convincing himself that it wasn't personal. But it was. Everything was.

Whereas most of his peers expanded their families, wives, children, stability, Isa remained single. A brilliant mind stuck in place. A man left behind.

One evening, the 19:00 news blared through the dining room, announcing that the Taork Republic had declared independence from the Vallsian Federation. Bergaz was burning. Taork police clashing with Vallsian soldiers. Thirty-three dead. On screen, history bled in colour.

The announcement cracked the brittle peace at the dinner table.

The Bresian Ati wore his age like defeat. Once handsome, now hollow-cheeked, veins tracing the ruins of his face. His hair, once proud, now greased back in a sad imitation of youth.

"These Taork idiots think they'll be better off alone," he spat.

Nona's eyes flared. "They want control of their own fate. People say the Ansobians will be next!"

"Smaller nations don't control anything," Ati growled. "They're puppets. The smaller they are, the easier to pull their strings."

"People want freedom!" The Asnobian Nona snapped. "They're sick of being ruled by Bresians."

Ati exploded from his chair. "Freedom? Thirty-three young men died tonight for that word you love so much! They'll never live to enjoy it. And this is only the beginning. Ethnic killing spreads like rot. More will die. I've lost my appetite."

Isa slammed his hand on the table. "Can you both stop?!"

But Nona wasn't done. She turned her fury back on Ati. "Why do you argue with every word I say? I didn't cause this war!"

Ati's voice dropped, sharp as broken glass. "And I refuse to believe you don't understand that as a Bresian, I won't be safe if Ansobia breaks away."

He left, choosing fresh air and silence over another listening to another word.

Isa sat trapped between them, between worlds, between futures.

Rooted in a life that moved on without him, powerless to stop any of it.

\*\*\*

Over the next three weeks, fast-changing political events proved them both correct because of an upsurge of nationalism in Vallsia. The news confirmed that the Ansobian Republic declared their independence too, and the Vallsian death toll almost quadrupled to 181. At that point, the news presenter said that the war between local police and armed forces had extended into the Republic of Ansobia. Thereafter, the silent conflict between Nona and Ati grew stronger. They ceased talking to each other. Ati had slept in the living room every night, leaving early each morning to avoid seeing Nona and returning after midnight when she was asleep. He didn't join Nona or Isa at dinner and disappeared from their sight during weekends.

On the first Saturday of October, the Anitshirp's Ansobian community staged a protest against the Federation's decision not to respect their republic's constitutional right to become an independent state. Isa and his mother entered the public square, observing a large crowd holding placards or banners with different colours and wording. After they passed the uniformed police monitoring the perimeter fencing, they joined the back of the crowd as Nona tiptoed and looked for somebody. Nona and Isa headed toward a woman with a large straw hat, after noticing her waving her hand at them. Ranks of photographers and camera operators stood between the stage and the crowd, which began singing the Ansobian national anthem. Nona and Isa greeted the straw-hatted woman when a young woman appeared on stage, clad in a navy skirt, red leggings, and a white T-shirt on which Free Ansobia was inscribed in curly black lettering. Panting audibly, she began reading her speech, both hands clutching sheets of paper. Enthusiastic applause followed as the leader of the Ansobian Democratic Party appeared on stage to greet the gathered crowd, "Hello, everyone, and thanks for coming today. For almost a century, Bresians have encroached and eroded Ansobians' freedoms. Now, the Bresians want to prevent us from becoming an independent state. Bresians speak of defending the

Federation, brotherhood, and unity among Vallsians, but, in fact, they are defending their supremacy over other nations. Bresians are deploying paramilitary forces to suppress our constitutional rights, so everyone capable of fighting must join the Ansobian Liberation Army. All Ansobians must rise for our freedom!"

Nearly everyone applauded, including Nona but not Isa. Most police officers encircling the protesters joined the crowd, shouting WHAT DO WE WANT? WE WANT INDEPENDENCE... WHAT DO WE WANT? WE WANT INDEPENDENCE...

Twenty minutes later, the police officers left after the crowd began to disperse quietly. As Isa, Nona, and her friend slowly strode away from the public square onto the road by the sea, 11 masked men in military outfits closed in on the remaining protesters surrounding the Ansobian leader and began attacking them. Shrieks of indignation were heard as the masked men punched and kicked the protesters who didn't manage to run away. The Ansobian leader's bodyguards encircled him, quickly moving him off the stage and into his waiting car. The screams became louder when the masked mob grounded four more protesters, kicking their bodies with their feet.

Isa, Nona, and her friend were well away when they heard the screaming and shouting coming from the public square. Over 30 protesters were on the ground, most of them bleeding, when 20 police officers rushed back toward the masked man and chased them away.

Isa and Nona bode farewell to her friend. On their way home, Isa stopped at the café after spotting Shoki sitting there alone. As soon as he sat down, they began a heated debate about the ongoing conflict.

An hour later, Isa returned home, headphones still humming with noise he didn't realize he needed to survive. He took them off. That's when he heard it, voices shouting. Rage slicing through walls that once held laughter.

He stepped inside, closed the door slowly, silently, like a man walking into a funeral, and listened. His parents were at it again.

"... What's that supposed to mean?" Nona roared. "That Ansobians aren't worth your time now?!"

Isa moved closer, just in time to see Ati's eyes sunken, skin blotched with stress, grey hair clinging to his skull, looking less like a father and more like a man ready to kill, or be killed.

Isa entered, and Ati didn't so much as blink. His fury was too far gone.

"How explicit do you want me to be?" Ati shouted. "It's your kind that's tearing the Federation apart. The Bresians are the ONLY ones fighting to keep these nations together!"

He scratched his scalp, flakes of dandruff falling onto his brown shirt like snow on rotten earth, then poured himself a whiskey. Drained it in one breath, as though it were water.

Nona fired back instantly. "Of course, you don't mind unity, as long as every general, every minister, every judge is a Bresian! You call that a Federation?! It's a cage!"

"Yes! And why not?" Ati countered, voice cracking under the weight of shouted history. "Bresians are 33 percent of the population, we're the LARGEST group, so the decisions are OURS to make!"

"Not in Ansobia!" Nona screamed. "In Ansobia, Bresians are barely 11 percent! Your kind rules a country your ethnic group barely lives in!"

The house shook with their hatred, twenty straight minutes of venom, spittle, and the kind of accusations that don't heal. They weren't arguing political theory, they were tearing each other apart, piece by piece, identity by identity.

Finally, Isa snapped. He stepped between them, eyes wild, voice raw, "What happened to you both?! Are you even LISTENING to yourselves? Does it ever occur to either of you that before being Ansobian or Bresian, you are HUMAN BEINGS? Because right now, you sound like the war you're pretending to hate!"

Isa's parents ignored him and carried on shouting at each other.

Isa raised his voice, louder and desperate, "Do you know what this is doing to me?! People out there choose a side based on their parents. But I have BOTH. So, tell me, who am I supposed to be?! Mum's Ansobian son, or Dad's Bresian one?!"

That's when Ati's limited restraint finally shattered.

"I've had ENOUGH of this marriage!" he shouted, and stormed out, without hesitation, no turning back.

"Dad… please!" Isa called after him.

Too late. The door slammed, a gunshot sound, and Nona flinched.

Isa rushed to the doorway, only to see the car skid into the street, tires screaming, smoke rising, as if even the asphalt rejected this family.

He came back inside, broken, shaking, burning, and something in him finally cracked open.

"FUCK GOD! FUCK RELIGION! AND FUCK THE ENTIRE VALLSIA!" he screamed.

"Mind your tongue, Isa!" Nona snapped, voice trembling.

"I've had enough of this fucking world!"

"What's wrong with you?" she demanded, but her voice was small now.

Isa pulled out a pack of cigarettes, retrieved a ciggie, and lit it up. He placed the cigarette box on the table and turned it nervously around with his index finger.

Isa crushed the cigarette into the glass ashtray with a harsh grinding twist, watching the ember die like the last thread of his patience. Without a word, he rose, shoved the door open, and slipped out into the evening heat.

The street was still, too still, lined with neat hedges and identical houses pretending the world wasn't falling apart. The air was thick with dust and the faint stench of something burning in the distance. He walked, jaw clenched, fists tight, each step a release of poisonous rage as he headed toward the main road.

When the mosque came into view, it felt like an accusation carved from stone. He paused before it, the same mosque where he had once prayed every Friday, before Eva left and God became just another lie. The green-painted wooden doors loomed over him, polished by devotion he no longer felt.

He didn't bow. He didn't enter. He spat. The spit splattered against the sacred wood, dripping downward like desecration in slow motion.

"Fuck this," he hissed and then louder, for the benefit of God and anyone else listening who happened to pass by, he shouted, "FUCK THIS PLACE."

He walked away, cursing it, cursing everything.

Twenty minutes later, the public square greeted him like a cruel joke. No protesters. No slogans, just its random setting with people quietly getting on with their daily routines.

It was infused with laughter, clinking glasses, shaded cafés filled with people sipping iced drinks under cheerful umbrellas. The smell of grilled food hung in the air. Families strolled by with bags of fruit and bread while children licked melting ice cream, unconcerned, untouched, unbothered.

"What the fuck are you all looking at?!" Isa roared at a passing family of five.

They flinched, sped up, dragging their children along as he stalked them with his eyes.

"Doesn't anyone care that our beloved country is AT WAR?" he shouted after them, voice echoing off stone walls.

An older man eyed him, warily, clutching the hand of a pale blond child.

Isa turned on him.

"No compassion? No sanity? You're SHOPPING while people DIE!"

The man hurried away. Isa's rage didn't. It swelled. It searched for new targets.

He spun in place, arms raised, veins bulging like cables under his skin, and screamed, "WHAT?! WHAT?! WHAT THE FUCK ARE YOU STARING AT? GO TO HELL... ALL OF YOU... WITH YOUR FAKE GODS, FAKE FLAGS, AND FAKE IDENTITIES! You're killing REAL people to protect IMAGINARY lines and INVISIBLE gods!"

The sun was blistering and turning his sweat to salt, burning his eyes into something feral. Shadows cut across his face like war paint.

A waiter with his thin apron flapping in the wind, stepped forward and said, timidly, "Sir, please... children are present."

"FUCK OFF!" Isa roared back, spit flying.

The waiter recoiled, horrified, and vanished.

Isa's eyes, once bright, now glowed with something wild, cracked, and broken. Then he spotted a Catholic priest crossing the square, robes flowing, face pale with concern.

Isa lunged forward.

"STOP RUNNING!" he shouted. "A hundred people are DEAD because of lies like yours! If it weren't for religion, this island would have PEOPLE and not ANSOBIANS, TAORKS, BRESIANS OR JEWS. Thanks to people like you, we have become labels, instead of humans!"

People froze. Forks paused mid-air. A waiter stood motionless with an ice cream half-raised toward a child's waiting hand.

Then a man approached. Broad shoulders. Black shirt. A thick gold cross hanging down his chest like a warning.

"What's your problem, mate?" he asked.

Isa didn't hesitate. "My problem is we're killing EACH OTHER instead of the liars like him who CAUSED THIS!" Isa added pointing towards the Catholic priest. "Got a cigarette? I left mine at home."

The man smiled, but it wasn't kindness.

"No, I don't have a cigarette, but I've got something else you crave," the young man replied, and within a split second, he punched Isa in the nose. Isa released an immediate shriek of pain as his body fell to the ground. As Isa's blood dripped from his nostrils onto the stone pavement, laughter could be heard in the background. He folded his shaking body and clamped his hands over his nose. He looked at his white shirt, where a dozen drops of blood glistened under the sun.

The violent young man bowed down towards Isa and then yelled at him, "I'M A PROUD TAORK, YOU FUCKING DICKHEAD, AND IF I SEE YOU INSULTING MY CATHOLIC PRIEST, RELIGION, OR NATIONALITY AGAIN, YOU'RE A DEAD MAN! DO YOU HEAR ME? I'LL FUCKING KILL YOU!" His shadow over Isa's shaken and bloodstained body retreated as he sprinted from the public square. After his attacker dodged out of sight, Isa got up and began shouting at onlookers.

Isa staggered to his feet, dizzy, blood running down into his mouth. He screamed not words, just sound. A wounded animal rejecting the world.

Two policemen rushed over, uniforms creased but not exactly urgent.

They asked for his name and address.

He answered with curses, a flood of them. At them. At Vallsia. At the crowd now pretending not to stare.

Someone yelled from afar, "TAKE HIM AWAY!"

The fat cop sighed, reached for the cuffs.

Isa panicked. Fought. Screamed. He was no longer a man, just raw nerves and rage.

The tall cop grabbed his wrists while the other wrapped an elbow around Isa's neck, dragging him down. His feet scraped across stone, his shirt ripping, his dignity torn apart.

"KEEP STILL!" the fat cop yelled, knee jammed into Isa's spine.

Isa's watch fell off, clattering onto the pavement. The second cop picked it up while they hauled Isa up like garbage.

"LET ME GO, YOU MORONS!" Isa shrieked. "LEAVE ME ALONE!"

They shoved him into the back of the patrol car, behind a metal fence meant for criminals.

The door slammed. Engine growled. The square returned to normal, just as quickly as it had erupted.

Isa was driven away, bleeding, furious, and utterly alone. Once they reached the police station, the tall one emptied Isa's pockets and rang the number displayed on his detainee's Recent Calls window of his cell phone.

Once Nona answered his call, the tall policeman briefed her on what had happened earlier at the public square.

Within twenty minutes, Nona arrived at the station and sat beside her handcuffed son in the corridor, watching him with heavy, mournful eyes. As she opened her mouth to say something to Isa, the tall policeman stepped out of an office and invited Nona and Isa over.

Nona stood, pulling her long skirt clear of her flat shoes.

Isa grinned at Nona, but only briefly before he grunted, possibly from the pain around his nose, although he exercised considerable self-restraint.

"Are you alright?" Nona asked.

After a long sigh, Isa nodded, a blue bruise visible across his nose.

"What happened to your face?" Nona asked.

Isa shook his head in silence.

He followed Nona as she stepped inside the small office, where the chubby police officer sat, and the tall one stood behind him.

She sat on a wooden chair opposite him and answered questions regarding her son. Nona explained to the chubby police officer sitting next to a rugged desk that her son was extremely upset about the ongoing war, including the marital crisis at home between her husband and her, "This is turning into a nightmare. I can't believe this is happening," Nona whispered. "My son has always been kind and wouldn't hurt a fly, but he's been through a lot lately. Isa is devastated by my incessant quarrels with my husband."

Nona's lips and eyes sagged. Her face appeared pale as if the flesh had been sucked down out of its blood. Her eyes turned red as her tears washed her mascara away when she pleaded with the police officers to section her son to a Psychiatric Ward instead of a prison.

"But he resisted arrest!" the chubby policeman reminded her.

"Yes, I know!" Nona replied with a nervous wave of her hands. "But, before his arrest, he didn't break the law."

The tall policeman, who had handcuffed Isa, nodded in agreement.

"My son wouldn't hurt a fly," Nona paused briefly to wipe her nose with a napkin she picked from the police officer's desk.

"All right!" the chubby policeman said, raising his palms. "We'll call the Psychiatric Ward of the Shendeti Hospital and have Isa transferred there. You're most welcome to join us on our journey there, Ms Iri."

Nona thanked them with an enthusiastic smile, which didn't last long.

On their way to the hospital, Nona tried to reason with Isa, whose body shook on the rear seat of the police car, "I know that you're having a tough time, and you have every right to be upset with what's going on at the moment, but as long as you have faith in God, everything will turn out fine in the end."

"GOD?" Isa shouted back at her. "GOD IS HUMAN FICTION AT ITS WORST! THEY SAY GOD CREATED EVERYTHING, BUT, IN FACT, HUMANS CREATED THE BLOODY GOD."

"You know that's not true. If ..." Nona objected in a soft tone.

"Come on, Mum," Isa snapped, but after noticing her terrified gaze, his face crumpled in the effort to hold himself together and speak normally. "If God exists and is almighty, as they say, why would God have to send down prophets to tell us what to do when He could make us do whatever He wants us to? They say God doesn't want humans killing other humans because it constitutes killing all humankind. Yet, God doesn't seem interested in imposing His will and finishing this bloody war."

Isa's naked hostility and resentment towards Vallsians, religion, and God were impossible to ignore or avoid. It disturbed many people in various parts of the world. Following protests in the predominantly Muslim-populated countries, Isa's recent disparaging misconduct killed UN-SDC-BC Board limited enthusiasm that their project will produce something meaningful. Isa became their intolerable burden of dread and suspense. The following day, the leaders of Iran, Iraq, Turkey, Pakistan, Indonesia, and Saudi Arabia appeared on the national news to announce that they would hold national referendums to terminate Isa's broadcast in their respective countries as well as future funding of the Secret of Divine Civilisation Convention.

# Chapter 11

The following day, Isa's face was a ruin, far worse than when he'd first been dragged into the Psychiatric Ward like a broken thing no one knew what to do with. The swelling in his nose had finally begun to retreat, but it left behind a violent halo of dark bruising, coloured in sickening shades of oil-slick blue and raw, mottled red. His skin looked thinner now, almost translucent, stretched over the bones of his face like parchment.

The ward itself was a prison disguised in white, too bright, too clean, and too quiet. A suffocating sterility hung in the air, mixed with the faint chemical tang of disinfectant and the lingering undertone of stale, recycled breath. Isa moved slowly along the corridors, driftwood in a current he didn't choose. The walls were painted a too-cheerful yellow that only made the despair more noticeable, as if someone had tried to paint over misery with a children's crayon.

Patients shuffled past him, looking like sedated ghosts in slippers. Their eyes were vacant, hollow, glassy and staring at things only they could see, or at nothing at all. Three of them muttered to themselves in unbroken streams of private confession or accusation, their cracked lips moving ceaselessly. The rest wandered like sleepwalkers, aimless, mechanical, and stripped of purpose.

Isa's face, gaunt, sharp, and skeletal was becoming terrifying to behold. In barely a week he had wasted into something that no longer seemed entirely alive. His cheeks were hollow, his skin waxy, and his eyes, huge, bulging, and fever-bright, looked ready to burst from their sockets, giving him the haunted appearance of a starving prophet or a resurrected corpse.

His clothes were stained, wrinkled, smeared, humiliation woven into fabric.

That was the state he was in when Dr Judith Mjekowitz approached him for the first time.

She emerged like someone stepping out of a different world. A white coat hung from her slim frame, half concealing elegant clothing that felt almost obscene in this place of unravelled minds. Her curly, wild red hair radiated in all directions, disobedient and untamed, and her fringe fell across most of her forehead, nearly obscuring thoughts that were too tired to hide. Her face, pale, touched by early wrinkles, held a beauty that was collapsing, slowly, with dignity. A dark beauty spot beneath her lip only sharpened the contrast between the weary and the once-youthful.

She approached with weary determination, voice even, manner calm, but eyes betraying fatigue. "Isa," she said gently. "Come with me."

He followed without a word, his shuffling steps slow and heavy, his body bent, always five paces behind her. A defeated animal learning the angles of captivity.

They stopped at a door with cold engraved letters:

## CONSULTANCY ROOM 8

Dr Judith retrieved a keycard from her coat pocket, an efficient motion, practiced, mechanical motion to unlock the door.

It was narrow, rectangular, and oppressively tidy. Five tall, thin windows were set vertically along the eastern wall, funnelling in morning light that was too sharp, too pitiless. When Isa looked out, he did not see freedom, but the skeletal metal scaffolding wrapped around a neighbouring building like a brace holding a broken limb.

The wind slashed through the slightly open window, slapping the blinds against the pane with a harsh metallic rattle, like someone knocking impatiently, demanding to be let in.

Judith crossed the room in determined strides and shut the window.

She tugged the blinds up with a controlled motion, and the bright sun rays spilled in, lighting the room in an unforgiving glare.

"Mr. Iri, you may lie down over there," she said, gesturing to a brown leather lounge chair.

Isa lowered himself into it slowly with hesitation, and without confidence. His eyes were empty, faraway, dulled by chemicals he never asked for. The sunlight stabbed him in the face. He raised one trembling hand to shield his eyes.

"Shall I lower the blinds?" Judith asked.

Isa nodded, barely.

The blinds fell with a hard clatter. The room dimmed. A shade of mercy, artificial, but still a mercy.

Judith pulled a cheap plastic chair close and sat facing him. Clipboard in hand, pen ready, voice trained into something reassuring.

"Right," she began. "Over the next few weeks... or months... I'll do my best to help you with the obstacle that brought you here. So..."

"My obstacle," Isa said, cutting her off with a voice made gravelly and strange by sedation, "is the cruel and... insensitive world. Can you fix this crazy world of ours?"

Judith wrote something down, clinical and detached.

"No," she said finally. "I can't fix that. But I can help rebuild your emotional strength to cope with it."

Isa gave a weary, bitter smile.

"Is this how you rebuild strength? By sedating me until I can barely speak?"

"You need rest, Isa. Rest from the world outside these walls."

She glanced at her notes and then added, "You're being given four milligrams of risperidone a day. We'll reduce the dose in time, don't worry. Your thoughts... and voice... will return to normal."

Isa's lips twitched with irony.

"And when they do... will the world be a better place?"

She paused. Not because she didn't know the answer, but because she did.

"No. I didn't say that. We're here to talk about you... not the world."

"So, you agree," Isa murmured, "that the world is cruel."

"Yes," Judith said. "It is. But we have to live in it anyway."

He studied her, as he narrowed his eyes.

"Your accent... Are you a Ryllian?"

"No," she replied quickly, almost proudly. "I'm Jewish."

The word cracked the air like a whip.

Isa stiffened. His expression curdled. Something dark flickered through his gaze, hurt, anger, betrayal, history.

"A Jew?" he said at last, quiet, hollow.

A beat passed. Then another.

He sat up. Slowly. Unsteadily. Every bone resisting the movement.

"I'm too tired," he said, voice thick with drugged exhaustion and disgust, "to speak to you."

Judith rose quickly, alarmed. "Isa... wait. The sedative makes you tired. That's normal. You don't need to feel ashamed..."

He cut her off with a raised hand.

"I'm tired because I am being sedated. And because," he added with a chilling calmness, "you are a Jew."

Colour flooded her face. Anger rose, but she held herself together. Barely.

"What," she demanded, "is wrong with being a Jew?"

Isa didn't turn. He stared at the door, one hand already on it.

"What's wrong," he said, voice almost gentle now, "with being... a human instead? Why can't people be humans again... before the war made everything a label?"

His breath quickened, but his tone remained eerily calm, broken into strange pauses.

"I will not speak to an Ansobian. A Bresian. A Taork. And definitely not you... a Jew."

Judith straightened, tightening her grip on the clipboard, face flushed and rigid.

"Fine," she said sharply. "I'll speak to my superior and assign you another therapist who isn't a Jew."

Isa gave no reply.

He stepped out of the room, leaving the door wide open behind him, a patient too wounded to belong anywhere anymore.

\*\*\*

The next day, Isa's father arrived at the ward, a man already worn by guilt and sleepless nights, but Isa refused to see him. He sat behind his locked door, staring at the blank wall, jaw clenched, breath hollow. When his mother came later, carrying a steaming container of penne arrabbiata that she had cooked with hands still trembling, he rejected her too. The food was left at the nurse's station, growing cold beneath the humming fluorescent lights, its smell eventually swallowed by disinfectant and institutional air. Isa refused to see her, eat food, or speak to clinical staff.

By Monday morning, the atmosphere in the staff meeting room was heavy, the stench of burnt coffee, sweat trapped beneath coats, rustling papers, and the undertone of exhausted resignation that filled every weekly briefing. One by one, clinicians reported on patients, the silent ones, the violent ones, the broken ones who wept into their pillows at night.

Near the end, Dr Judith cleared her throat, her notes stiff in her hands, her composure visibly fragile.

She described Isa not just as an unstable Neo-Nazi, but as someone who despised her existence, rejecting her not as a doctor, but as a Jew. Her tone trembled near the edges, though she tried to sound clinical, detached, and professional, but she failed.

Dr Sheruese, head of the Psychiatric Ward, wrote something briskly into her notebook, face expressionless.

"I'll see what I can do," she said.

But Judith knew from her tone, this was not a promise, only a postponement.

And it wasn't up to the hospital anyway.

The one with real power was who gets to decide over Dr Judith's request was not a doctor at all, but the Executive Producer of the UN-SDC-BC. The Script Protocol governed Isa's treatment more than medical ethics ever could. Article 96 had chained them all, regardless of Isa's medical assessment.

Just after lunch, the head of the Psychiatric Ward called the UN-SDC-BC Executive Producer, Ms Drejtoresha, to discuss the swap sought by Dr Judith. Ms Drejtoresha insisted that Dr Judith must carry on consulting Isa because Article 96 of the Script Protocol mandates it.

That afternoon, forty-five minutes before the end of her shift, Dr Judith was summoned.

She entered her superior's office in good spirits, still clinging to the hope she would be reassigned. The office smelled of stale paper, lavender disinfectant, and old air that had never tasted wind.

"Please sit," Dr Sheruese said, pointing to a chair covered in tired black fabric, threadbare along the arms.

Judith sat. Legs crossed. Shoulders tight.

"I've spoken to my superior," Dr Sheruese began, voice steady, distant, administrative, "and she rejected your request…"

"What?"

Judith shot up, her chair scraping violently against the floor.

"You can't expect me to continue consulting someone who despises me for being a Jew."

"Doctor Judith… sit down."

The words were clipped like scissors cutting thread.

She obeyed, barely, arms and legs crossing into a self-barrier.

"You shouldn't take a patient's hostility personally," Dr Sheruese said. "No matter how vile it is."

"Yes, but he is the one requesting another therapist… not me."

"You've worked here two years. You're respected. Admired. Competent."

A pause.

"It would be a shame to let a troublesome patient compromise that."

Judith swallowed her anger.

"And it is not," Dr Sheruese continued, "up to patients to choose their therapists. It's up to me. And I expect you not to disappoint me."

Judith blinked. Swallowed. Nodded.

"…I won't let you down."

"Good," Dr Sheruese said with a final nod. "That will be all."

Judith stood, forced a polite smile, shook her superior's hand, and headed to the door.

Her hand was on the knob when Dr Sheruese's voice rose again, "If he makes you feel unsafe, I can join your next session with Isa."

Judith didn't turn around. "No. I'm not afraid of him. He's a teddy bear… with the poisonous mouth of a snake."

The door closed behind her. And then came the corridor.

Long. Pale. Over-lit. Reeking of bleach and despair.

Patients shuffled aimlessly, some drooling, some mumbling, all stripped of a world that once made sense. Their slippers dragged against the linoleum floors in slow, mindless rhythm.

They were moving, but not alive. A parade of broken minds and hearts.

Judith walked through them, red hair catching the harsh light, eyes straight ahead.

\*\*\*

On Friday morning, Isa was escorted down the endless psychiatric hallway by a skinny nurse in a pale blue uniform. She walked without looking at him, her thumb scrolling across the cracked screen of her phone. The corridor smelled faintly of bleach and boiled vegetables; the walls hummed with fluorescent lights that never slept.

They stopped before Consultancy Room 8.

Without lifting her eyes, the nurse knocked twice, then opened the door just enough to speak inside. "Doctor, your patient is here. Should I let him in?"

A silent nod answered.

The nurse flicked her tattooed fingers toward Isa, a half-gesture, half-dismissal, then drifted away.

Isa stepped across the threshold, but the sight of Dr Judith, made him recoil. A tremor ran through him, almost invisible, but she caught it. He turned sharply and called after the nurse, now disappearing down the hallway.

"Are you sure this is the right room?" he demanded. "I'm supposed to see someone else. Hello? You've brought me to the wrong place."

The nurse threw a lazy thumbs-up over her shoulder without slowing, already swallowed by the corridor's white glow.

"You're standing exactly where you need to be," Dr Judith said, her voice silky but distant. "It's your *heart* that's in the wrong place."

Isa exhaled sharply, defeat in the motion. "Planet Earth is the wrong place for me, and I'm sick of it," he muttered, raising his hands and letting them fall, hollow. He tightened his grip on the doorknob. "I told you I don't want to speak to anyone Jewish. You don't seem to understand Vallsian."

He turned to leave.

But Dr Judith was already in motion, cutting the distance between them. "Obviously you're here because of your erratic behaviour," she said, breath slightly quickened. "And I'm here to help you…"

"Help me gather scraps of strength until world's religions tear it apart again?" Isa snapped, his voice quick and sharp, like a match striking. "I keep reminding everyone of the basic truth that we're humans. Not Ansobians, Taorks, Bresians… yet somehow, *I'm* the one labelled abnormal."

"People take pride in their nationality," Dr Judith replied, voice steady but tiring. "That's not unusual. You need to…"

"Our mother's *vagina* determines our nationality!" Isa was rolling now, unstoppable. "But you never hear those Bresian flag-waving lunatics say *'I'm proud of my mother's superior Bresian vagina,'* do you?"

Dr Judith pressed her pen against her lips, fighting a laugh that threatened to escape at the worst moment.

"You're not wrong," she admitted carefully. "But it doesn't mean much when our country is at war. Families are tearing themselves apart. My sister and her husband no longer speak to each other."

Isa's rant stopped mid-air.

He lifted his head slowly, searching her eyes with unexpected stillness.

"Why?"

"He's a Taork. She's Jewish," she answered. "Two daughters. And they might lose both parents to this madness."

Silence. A rare one.

Isa closed the door behind him.

"Aren't Jews are supposed to marry their own," he said, almost gently.

"That was before," she replied. "During the communist era, when religion was banned. They married, because the religion didn't exist back then."

Isa moved toward the lounge chair, then paused. "Sounds familiar, doesn't it?"

She blinked, twice. "Your mother said your parents' divorce is what pushed you here."

"No," Isa said, voice tightening. "It's the war. The stupidity. Everyone blaming everyone else instead of themselves."

"So, you're saying…"

"They've forgotten they're *human*," Isa cut in. "They're Ansobian or Bresian first. Being human is secondary to them."

He gestured to the chair.

"May I?"

"Of course."

He sat, barely occupying only the edge, fingers restless, knee shaking with residual fury.

"But humans *can* be both," she said. "Human and Taork or Jew, or…"

He sliced the air with a finger. "No. That's exactly how we create these war-craving and hateful nationalistic monsters."

Dr Judith didn't argue. Not this time.

"When dogs bark," Isa continued, "they don't say 'Hello Jew' or 'Hello Ansobian.' They just *live*."

"Hm," she replied with over-bright enthusiasm. "But humans aren't animals…"

"That's the attitude that got us into this mess!" Isa exploded. Then, breathing hard, he softened. "We could learn from animals. They don't need or crave for flags. The world is in such a mess simply because humans created these unnatural identities, which are unimportant to animals."

For several minutes, Isa spoke in what the staff would later describe as philosophical delirium, railing brilliantly, tragically, against national identity itself. Dr Judith wrote it all down, page after page. A transcription of chaos.

When she finally checked her watch, his voice was hoarse.

"We'll stop here," she said. "Next Thursday. Same time."

She walked him to the door. Didn't touch him. Didn't smile.

Days passed.

She avoided him in the hallways, her eyes gazing on the floor or on distant nurses. But after their talk, after the revelation about her sister, something shifted.

The next session, he showed up early.

The one after that, he smiled when she entered.

His hostility dissolved, replaced by something unexpected. Trust. Maybe even affection, the fragile, reluctant kind that forms only in rooms where pain is spoken aloud.

*** 

By their fifth session, the formal ritual of Doctor Judith and Mr. Iri had dissolved into Judith and Isa, spoken more like reluctant allies than patient and consultant. The air in Consultancy Room 8 always smelled faintly of disinfectant and dust, a room where hope came to die or resurrect itself depending on the hour.

They spoke of Shoki and Alexander, the only two friends Isa still dared to speak of, because talking about anyone else felt like poking a bruise that hadn't healed. His voice carried a bitterness that wasn't loud, yet it echoed.

Judith sat across from him, legs crossed, a green rubber band holding her red hair back just barely, as if she might snap at any moment. Her pink-and-white complexion stood in stark, almost mocking contrast to

Isa's brownish skin, two different climates forced to share a room. Her pale blue eyes blinked slowly, steadily, like someone trying to remain calm in the middle of a battlefield.

She squinted at her cramped handwriting and finally looked up. "Surely, you must have other friends besides Shoki and Alexander," she commented, raising her eyebrows.

"I used to have many friends, but after I started dating Eva, I didn't spend much time with them, which has continued to this day. I guess it's my fault! Friends are plants that look after you if you look after them!"

"Who's Eva?" Dr Judith asked tentatively, as though she was unsure whether she had the right to ask. "According to your mother, she had an enormous impact on your life."

"She was my first love!"

"And your second love ..." Dr Judith asked with a cheeky smile, pausing her scribbling.

"I don't have a second love. After Eva left me, I was no longer interested in getting hurt again."

"Are you sure that you don't have any other friends?"

"I guess I'm not wealthy enough or married to a stunning wife to have more than three close friends."

Dr Judith chuckled at Isa's last remark and pulled her chair forward to lay a light hand on his sleeve. Her gentle touch was a rather peculiar and unconventional form of therapy. This was the first time both of them had laughed delightedly. She looked at her watch and wrapped up the session.

***

Their subsequent consultation found Isa lying flat on his back, speaking about Eva again.

"So, Isa, why don't we begin with Eva?" Dr Judith asked, peering at him through her fringe. "How did she make you feel?"

"Love can't be dissected by words. It's one of those things that's felt and can't be explained."

"Why don't you explain how Eva made you feel?"

Reluctant at first, Isa began telling her how Eva had made him feel. She listened curiously to his torrent of thoughts about Eva, stumbling here and there. From the day he first saw Eva at the nursery, he described every detail, the first kiss under the orange tree, funny situations that had made them laugh, including how his skin felt when rubbing against hers. Dr Judith blushed slightly. As Isa progressed explaining how he'd felt after Eva left him, Dr Judith's eyes remained fixed on Isa's lips, glancing at them with a concealed sympathy.

Isa enjoyed her undivided attention for another half an hour before disentangling from her warm and compassionate gaze. She appeared struck in amazement listening to his love story. Occasionally, she would interrupt him with specific questions, but most of the time, she remained silent, listening to Isa's confession about his first and only love.

Isa's voice became more slurred, and then he stopped talking. His hands trembled slightly. "Although she wasn't the most attractive human creature I had ever seen, she gave me everything I needed."

"In what way did she provide you with everything you needed?" Dr Judith asked, tossing back her head to remove the uneven fringe from her blue eyes.

"Up to the moment I met Eva, I had been preoccupied with being the ideal son to my parents, trying to please them so they would be proud of me. Eva made me feel like I was the ideal person and accepted me for whom I was instead. We all crave acceptance by others throughout our existence, and this tormenting longing ceases only after we fall in love."

After a moment, Dr Judith turned vehemently to Isa and said in a slow and shy voice, "You should consider yourself lucky to have experienced love. A lot of people live and die without falling in love, so you ought to feel privileged rather than depressed."

"Love is rain to a thirsty soul, but when that feeling comes to an end, it becomes a storm that leaves a wreckage behind," Isa responded and then asked. "Have you ever been in love?"

Dr Judith's eyes flickered, as though Isa's question had pulled her back into a memory, she had long buried. She hesitated, her lips parting but no words escaping at first. Finally, she whispered, "Yes... once. It was the kind of love that makes you believe the world was created just for the two of you. But it ended, and with it, a part of me seemed to vanish."

Isa leaned forward, intrigued. "And did you regret it?"

Judith shook her head slowly, her voice trembling yet resolute. "No. Even in its ending, love taught me more than any book or lecture ever could. It showed me the fragility of happiness, the courage it takes to trust, and the inevitability of loss. Love is not meant to be owned, it is meant to be lived, even if only for a fleeting moment."

Isa sighed, his gaze drifting toward the window where the rain tapped gently against the glass. "Then perhaps the wreckage is not the end, but the beginning of something else. Maybe storms clear the ground for new seeds to grow."

Judith smiled faintly, her sternness softening. "Exactly. Love is both the rain and the storm. It nourishes, it destroys, and yet it always leaves behind the possibility of renewal. The question is not whether we survive love, Isa, but whether we allow ourselves to grow from it."

For a long while, silence filled the room, heavy yet comforting. Isa finally murmured, "Maybe I am lucky after all. Lucky to have felt the rain, even if the storm followed."

Judith reached out, placing her hand gently over his. "And lucky still, because you are here, alive, with the chance to love again."

Isa shrugged, while Dr Judith restlessly lifted herself off the chair, placed one leg above the other, and sat back down. Then, she replied defensively, "We are here to discuss your life, not mine."

"But, for you to be able to help me, you ought to have experienced the agony that people experience after love reaches the end of the road."

"Oops! It's already four," Dr Judith said, looking at the clock above the door. "We'll have to leave it there and continue next week."

\*\*\*

As Isa's hospitalisation progressed into almost a month, Dr Judith's affection for Isa grew. Dr Judith's susceptibility to Isa developed every passing day after his confession about how he'd felt about Eva. Although medications wiped out whatever handsomeness Isa had, his therapist appeared impressed by him. From here on, she intensified her sessions and began consulting him three times a week.

Dr Judith's high-heeled footsteps echoed loudly down the hall as she approached Isa, who was waiting outside Consultancy Room 8 for their next session. She greeted him with an enthusiastic wave as she got closer to him. He waved back with an amiable smile as their eyes met. Isa appeared different, in a good mood, as if he'd just finished the finest marijuana joint. Perhaps it had to do with how she'd helped him soothe his anger and utter disappointment with people, including his parents. Or it could have been because he couldn't avoid her vastly improved stunning appearance, provided his spectacles still did what they were meant to do. She looked different that time. She appeared slightly taller with her shiny high-heeled red shoes, unlike the same low heels she'd worn at their previous sessions. Her waxed legs stretched from under her leather mini-skirt, her nails manicured and polished in red. The improvement in her appearance was startling, especially with the addition of mascara on her long eyelashes. With a few adjustments, she had become much prettier, far more feminine, and far younger-looking. After entering Consulting Room 8, Dr Judith sat in her plastic chair with her legs slightly overexposed.

"Isa, I'd like to talk about the outburst that got you here," Dr Judith said, placing her notebook on her lap. "Is that all right with you?"

Dr Judith listened to Isa attentively as he moaned and lamented the world for at least half an hour.

"Judith, why is the world so messed up?" Isa asked. "How can we be so cruel to one another? Why do people fail to understand that, above everything else, we're humans?"

Dr Judith got to her feet, walked towards the window, and gazed outside.

"Judith?" Isa tried to grab her attention but failed. Isa called her name repeatedly, more loudly, but she ignored him. As he approached Dr Judith from behind, Isa noticed her trembling shoulders. He stopped two paces away and looked at her handsome profile, silhouetted against the incoming light from the windows. "Judith?" Isa said in a voice barely louder than a whisper.

Dr Judith pretended not to have heard Isa. He paced himself and stood opposite her. "Judith, are you alright?" he asked, rubbing her right shoulder.

Dr Judith was suddenly crying, with her head bowed, covering her eyes with her fingers.

Isa lifted her chin with his index finger, his clear sparkling gaze on Dr Judith's face. She rubbed her tightly closed eyes, and an expression of the most intense pain pervaded her long face as tears sparkled down her red cheeks.

"I'm so sorry! This is awful … I'm sorry …" Dr Judith sobbed, trying to conceal it beneath her shaking hands. Then, finally, she turned around, disclosing her pinkish eyes full of tears, her mascara sliding down her smooth pale cheeks and onto her white coat, before gasping on a strangled note. "This isn't… I shouldn't… I'm not supposed to …".

Isa slid his arm around her shaking shoulders and drew her closer. She cried inconsolably as he squeezed her body tightly. "Don't worry, Judith. Just let yourself be."

She searched her pocket, pulled out a handkerchief, mopped her eyes, and then blew her nose.

"It's all my fault," Dr Judith added in a thin, cracked voice, indicating embarrassment or discomfort. "I know this is … all my … fault."

Isa's arms clasped his hands tightly around her shoulders, but Dr Judith resisted. She placed her arms against his chest, pushing him away with all her strength.

Isa held her tightly, placing his right cheek on top of her right cheek, his eyes moist with compassion. "It's alright … it's alright," he whispered, his lips barely moving. His eyes moved down Dr Judith's neck, onto her breasts, and then to her mouth and eyes again. Isa slid his hand around Dr Judith's waist. He moved his upper leg between her legs and pressed his body against hers with his eyes shut. Her breathing pattern paced up as Isa stroked her hair gently. He kissed her on the left cheek several times before pulling his head backwards to observe her face turning red again. Then, before she could stop him, Isa kissed her mouth.

"Hold on a second!" Dr Judith whispered as she shrank away, shuddering with involuntary posture and moving her hands nervously. "What are we doing?"

"Nothing! We're just sharing our grief," Isa responded with a generous wide smile that had been conspicuously absent since Eva had left him. She hastily wiped her face with her handkerchief and shivered. He winked at her as she examined his face in an unusually warm, friendly silent gaze for several seconds before a brief giggle escaped from her lips. Dr Judith slouched sideways into his chest and remained silent for a few minutes. Isa placed his finger on her chin again to lift it. She didn't hesitate and went along, meekly pulling her head forward. His lips moved slowly towards hers, leaning into a kiss. She lifted her mouth and opened it against his. Isa slipped his tongue inside her mouth. Both were breathing fast as their heads pivoted around their joined lips. Isa placed his hand beneath her red shirt and rubbed her back.

"Please, stop it!" she bellowed, pushing his chest away. She looked at him with an expression between amusement and disapproval, then stepped back, but Isa reached out and seized her arm. He moved closer to her and tightened his hand on her slim waist as he bent his smiling face to whisper something in her ear. Dr Judith smiled, colour rising on her face. Isa stared at her with drowsy eyes as if he had just woken up. She walked towards the other side of the mahogany desk with her hands crossed over her chest. "We must end these sessions!" she finished breathlessly.

"Here we go again! So, you don't want to see me anymore because I'm not Jewish enough for you?"

Dr Judith laughed, her body shivering as Isa looked at her with widened eyes.

"I had a long, turbulent relationship with a possessive Jewish businessman. He was interested in material things, while I was interested in spiritual things, which is why I became a psychiatrist," she explained. "Since then, my sister has tried to fix me up with almost every desperate bachelor or widowed Jewish man she knows. I decided to meet them to please her, but eventually, I grew tired of it. I've met at least eight Jewish men who have wanted to hook up with me, but none of them made my heart beat this fast."

Isa loosened his shoulders, unleashed a smile, and asked Dr Judith, "But why do you want to stop seeing me?"

"I want to see more of you and to accomplish that, I must discharge you from the hospital. I've studied hard to get to this place and earn this white coat," Dr Judith said, tapping her finger on the external pocket above her heart.

"So, we'll continue seeing each other then?"

"Yes, but under one condition!" Dr Judith said. "The moment you walk out of that door, you must convince others that you are ready to face the grim world again."

Isa tried to talk, but Dr Judith covered his lips with her palm and pressed on, "Therefore, next time you see your mother, you should ask her to bring some fresh clothes and a shaving machine. You should also reassure her that everything is all right with you."

Isa nodded and hugged her again, his eyes sparkling between winks.

\*\*\*

Over the next six days, Isa followed Dr Judith's instructions with great submission and commitment. He greeted every passer-by in the long inpatient corridor with a generous smile that extended to his glistening eyes.

When their last session reached its end, Dr Judith told him that for the first three months, they'd meet up two times a week and that no one must know about their relationship during that time. Then, after noticing Isa's excited grin fade out, Dr Judith reassured him that everything would turn out fine if he followed her instructions.

"All right," she said, smiling softly, leaning her head towards his. "Kiss me."

Isa pressed his full lips against hers for at least four minutes. Considering that she might lose her job and profession, it seemed a reasonable request to any considerate person, but not Isa. Instead, he insisted on seeing her more often. Ultimately, she agreed to meet him secretly at her place three times a week. Dr Judith kissed him passionately after writing down her phone number and address before Isa disappeared behind the closed door.

\*\*\*

The following morning, the wind whistled through Isa's hair as he stepped out of the hospital with Nona. His mother pointed at her car, and they slowly walked toward it. A slender young woman with a barking poodle walked in their direction. She was a tall girl whose dominant features were an anorexic body and a pair of large oceanic blue eyes. As she approached, the barking got louder, the dog pulling its owner towards Isa. He knelt and stretched out his hand. After climbing onto Isa's lap, the dog went manic, initially licking his hand and then his face.

Isa laughed softly, his voice carrying a warmth that contrasted with the sharp wind. The poodle's frantic affection seemed to dissolve the heaviness that had lingered in his chest over the past six weeks. Nona watched with a faint smile, though her eyes betrayed a quiet unease. She had always worried about Isa's tendency to attach himself too deeply, too quickly.

The young woman tugged at the leash, embarrassed by her dog's enthusiasm. "I'm sorry," she said, her voice delicate yet firm, as though she had rehearsed politeness to mask fragility. Isa looked up, meeting her gaze. For a moment, her oceanic eyes seemed to pull him into a depth he hadn't expected.

"No need to apologize," Isa replied, stroking the dog's silky fur. "He's just... honest. Animals don't hide their feelings the way people do."

The girl tilted her head, intrigued by his words. "That's true. They love without fear." She paused, then added almost shyly, "I'm Elira."

Nona cleared her throat, reminding Isa of her presence. "We should get going," she said, her tone protective. Isa rose reluctantly, brushing off his coat. Elira gave a faint smile, pulling her dog back to her side.

As they walked toward the car, Isa glanced over his shoulder. Elira was still watching him, her figure fragile against the wind, her dog tugging impatiently at the leash. An unspoken story etched into her thin frame and those vast, piercing eyes.

Inside the car, Nona started the engine. "You attract trouble, Isa," she muttered, half-joking, half-serious. Isa leaned back, closing his eyes as the poodle's playful energy replayed in his memory. The threads of his life were weaving into a tapestry of secrets, desires, and unexpected encounters.

The wind outside howled like a restless spirit, and Isa wondered if love was destined to follow him everywhere, sometimes as rain, sometimes as storm, and sometimes as a sudden, barking interruption in the middle of an ordinary morning.

# Chapter 12

Isa walked down Rruga Street through the quiet residential neighbourhood with his head down. He passed seven brick-clad four-storey apartment blocks listening to the chirping birds and the throttle of car engines passing by. Before reaching a section of terraced houses, Isa lit a cigarette and took three drags. Then he turned right, walked over the concrete path, and stopped by the entrance to the apartment block. After reading the names next to the numbers on the interphone, Isa pressed the number 16. The door unlocked after a loud beep, and Isa pulled it open. After stubbing out his cigarette on the ground, Isa stepped inside the building and climbed the stairs. Once he reached the second floor, Isa turned left after spotting Judith standing by the door to her flat.

Isa slid an arm around her, drew her close, and kissed her. Judith's breathing accelerated as she pulled him over to the doorstep, her lips still against his. Their lips parted when Isa coughed. He lifted his head, staring around the large, minimalist-furnished living room. "Nice place," he commented brightly, his arm still around her.

"Thanks," Judith said and disappeared into her bathroom while Isa stood in the middle of the room, his eyes travelled slowly across the limited objects around him. A sizeable seaside painting with an old couple lying under a red umbrella rested high above a sizeable black sofa, which could accommodate four people comfortably. High above it, a wooden shelf hung from the dark navy wall with Herman Hesse's books neatly arranged over it.

Isa heard running water and walked hastily toward its source. He walked down a carpeted hallway lined with six oil paintings of women from different races. Isa stopped by the bathroom door, watching silently as Judith washed her hands. She wasn't aware of his presence until he moved behind her, and their eyes met in the mirror. Isa pushed her red hair away from her neck before smelling and kissing it gently. Judith grabbed Isa's hand and led him to her bedroom. She stretched her body over the bed, looking stunning and inviting, her long hair spread over the pillow. Isa climbed over Judith.

As soon as Isa tried to take her top off, Judith pushed him off her, "I've got this rule about not having sex on the first night."

"I thought you were a psychiatrist, not a nun," Isa grinned.

"Next time, we'll do it. But not tonight."

Isa kissed her cheek and glanced at Judith. Her face looked slightly pink with faint circles under her blue eyes. After several pleasant sighs, Judith checked her watch, turned over, and slid out of bed.

She hummed her way into the kitchen to put the kettle on.

"Tea or coffee?" she called from the kitchen.

"Coffee, please! Black, no sugar!" Isa answered, his dark eyes fixed on a happy family picture on the bedside cabinet.

Isa fumbled to grab the photo. Judith's happy face was recognisable, standing between a thin older woman in a long dress and a round man with a kippah pinned to the remnants of his grey hair.

Judith returned to her bedroom carrying two cups of coffee and a bowl with chocolates on a plastic tray.

"Is this your family?" Isa asked, showing her the photo in his hand.

She nodded with a courteous grin as she placed the tray on the bedside cabinet on Isa's side and sat down next to him.

"Are you sure your father will be all right with me not being a Jew?" he asked after downing his Risperidone with water.

"Steady now!" Judith reacted, her mouth full of chocolate. "Nobody must know about us. I don't know how things will pan out for the two of us, but we must keep our relationship a secret from everyone, including our families, at least for the first three months."

"You ought to be true to yourself and stop caring about what others make of us."

"So, we have switched positions now by you becoming my psychotherapist?" Judith asked.

"You're wonderful as you are, but considering my experience with Eva's parents, I'm desperate to know what will happen when your parents find out you're dating an atheist!" Isa's voice cracked, his dark brows furrowing as he leaned forward. His tall frame seemed restless, shoulders tense beneath the worn leather jacket he had thrown on without care. His eyes searched Judith's face for reassurance, but found only a blank expression.

Judith sat across from him, her posture rigid yet fragile, like porcelain on the verge of breaking. Her pale hands trembled slightly as she looked at her family photo. The dim lamplight flickered against her red hair, catching strands that framed her delicate face. She grabbed the photo and rubbed a finger over it, tracing the edges as though it were a talisman.

"Don't worry," she whispered, her voice soft but carrying a strange conviction. "They wouldn't mind us being together!"

Isa's chest tightened. He leaned closer, the faint scent of rain clinging to his clothes from the storm outside. "What makes you so sure?" His tone was sharp, almost pleading, as though he needed her words to anchor him against the uncertainty gnawing at his heart.

Judith's lips parted, but her voice faltered. She lowered her gaze, her long lashes casting shadows over her cheeks. "He passed away fourteen months ago," she replied in a dithering voice, each syllable heavy with grief.

The room seemed to shrink around them. Outside, the wind rattled the windowpanes, carrying with it the distant hum of the town centre. Isa's breath caught in his throat, his anger dissolving into quiet shock. He reached out, his hand hovering above hers, hesitant to touch.

"I didn't know…" he murmured, his voice softer now, almost breaking. "Judith, I…"

She shook her head gently, forcing a faint smile that never reached her eyes. "It's all right. You couldn't have known. He was… everything to me. And losing him felt like losing the ground beneath my feet." Her fingers tightened around the photo, knuckles whitening.

Isa finally placed his hand over hers, his warmth steady against her trembling skin. "And yet you're here," he said, his voice low but resolute. "You're still standing. That means something."

Judith looked up, her ocean-green eyes glistening with unshed tears. "It means I've learned to carry ghosts with me," she whispered. "And maybe… maybe you're the reason I can bear it."

The silence that followed was not empty, but thick with unspoken promises, grief, and the fragile hope that love might heal what loss had shattered. The dim light from the bedside lamp painted the room in amber hues, shadows stretching across the walls like silent witnesses to their confessions.

"What about your Mum?" Isa asked softly, his voice carrying both hesitation and tenderness. His tall frame leaned forward, his broad shoulders tense beneath the thin cotton shirt he wore. His dark hair fell slightly over his forehead, and his eyes, deep, restless brown, searched Judith's face with an intensity that betrayed his fear of the answer.

Judith's lips trembled before she spoke. "She passed away three years ago," she whispered, her voice breaking like fragile glass. Her eyes shimmered with tears, the kind that seemed to hold entire oceans of sorrow.

Isa opened his mouth to say something, but the words dissolved on his tongue. He froze, watching as Judith's tears spilled silently down her cheeks. Her slender shoulders shook, her hands clutching the photo she had been holding earlier as though it were the last anchor to her past.

Unable to bear the sight of her pain, Isa lifted his shoulders and embraced her body. His arms wrapped around her with a firmness that contrasted her fragility, pulling her close against his chest. She buried her face into him, her sobs muffled by the warmth of his embrace.

"Judith…" he murmured, his voice low and trembling. "I'm so sorry. I didn't mean to reopen wounds." His hand gently stroked her hair, the strands soft against his fingers, as though he were trying to soothe not just her grief but the years of loneliness that had carved themselves into her soul.

She clung to him, her fingers gripping the fabric of his shirt. "It's not your fault," she whispered between sobs. "It's just… sometimes the silence reminds me of them. And then I realize they're gone, and I'm left here, trying to make sense of everything."

Isa tightened his embrace, his heartbeat steady against her ear. "You're not alone anymore," he said firmly, his voice carrying a quiet strength. "I'm here. And I'll stay, no matter how heavy the silence becomes."

Judith lifted her tear-streaked face, her eyes meeting his. For a moment, the grief softened, replaced by a fragile spark of hope. "Promise me you won't leave," she whispered, her voice trembling but resolute.

Isa cupped her face gently, his thumb brushing away the tears. "I promise," he said, his words carrying the weight of both love and determination.

Judith sobbed silently with her lips pressed inwards for a couple of minutes before she cleared her throat and then apologised to Isa, "Now, where were we?"

"In your bedroom, I suppose," Isa responded, trying to sound funny but failing to make Judith laugh.

"I'm not blind," Judith added, slapping Isa's chest, "I can see we're in my bedroom."

"At which point in life did you have the surgery to remove your sense of humour?"

Just as Judith's face blushed and smiled, Isa's cell phone rang. He stretched his hand towards his jeans, lying on the floor. She grabbed Isa's hand, asked him not to pick it up, and emphasised the importance of keeping their relationship secret. After she finished her justification, Isa searched the jeans for his phone, and after locating it, he exclaimed, "It's Mum!"

"Please don't pick it up!"

"But she is going through a rough time with my Dad, and the last thing she needs is to worry about me, too," Isa replied, still holding his phone.

"Please don't mention our relationship to anyone, including your mother, all right?" Judith responded immediately. "Head over to the beach and once you get there, call her back and tell her you've spent the entire afternoon there, clearing your thoughts."

"You're the one who kept telling me not to worry, and now you're the one worrying," Isa replied. "Give it a break! Being in love isn't a criminal offence." Isa pushed his mobile back into his pocket and glided his lips onto Judith's neck. After finishing his coffee, Isa got up, and as he was about to place his feet inside his jeans, Judith insisted that he shower before he left.

"We don't want your Mum getting suspicious after smelling female perfume on you," she added.

Isa stripped off his T-shirt and hurried away to take a shower. Ten minutes later, he joined Judith in the kitchen with a black towel wrapped around his waist. He took hold of her belly with both hands, terrifying Judith, who yelped. She was breathing fast as Isa apologised and embraced her. They kissed for a couple of minutes before returning to the bedroom to get dressed. Before leaving her apartment, Isa kissed Judith's lips and descended into a parking space where children shrieked as they chased a ball.

It was barely four o'clock when he reached the beach and called his mother to inquire if she needed something from the pharmacy. Then he strode off, looking up at the setting sun with a permanent grin. On his way home, Isa stepped inside a jewellery shop. After discussing various jewellery pieces with the sales assistant, Isa chose a pair of round silver filigree earrings and a matching bracelet. He asked the sales assistant to wrap them separately in different colours, paid for them, grabbed the presents, placed them inside two bags, and headed home to find his mother finishing her dinner.

"You're late!" Nona said as soon as Isa stepped inside the house.

"Yes, I know. Give me a minute," Isa replied and climbed the stairs.

He entered his bedroom, placed the small pink jewellery bag inside his wardrobe, and returned to the dining room, holding the other bag, as Nona was halfway toward the kitchen. He listened to her muffled footsteps receding into the kitchen, the sound of the running water, the bubbling of boiling water against a kettle lid, and then the tinkling of a teaspoon against a mug. Once Nona returned to the dining room, holding a steaming mug with both hands and settled on her chair, Isa placed the gift in front of her.

"This is for you!" Isa exclaimed, sounding uncharacteristically cheerful as he placed a tiny green bag on the table next to Nona's mug. His voice carried a brightness that seemed almost foreign, his smile stretching wide across his face, his dark eyes glistening with an unusual spark.

Nona's eyes spun with curiosity as she pulled out a small-wrapped box. The kitchen light reflected off her silver hair, neatly tied back, and the faint steam rising from her mug curled into the air between them. She sighed after opening her present, her fingers brushing over the delicate filigree bracelet.

"What's going on with you?" she asked, her tone caught between suspicion and concern.

"Meaning what?" Isa leaned back in his chair, his tall frame restless, tapping his fingers against the wooden table.

"You've changed," she said, pausing to clasp the bracelet around her wrist. Her expression softened, but her brows furrowed with worry. "Are you taking drugs?" she asked, her voice low, almost pleading.

Isa snapped, rolling his eyes dramatically. "What makes you say that?" His shoulders stiffened, his lips tightening into a defensive line.

"You seem much happier. There has to be a reason," Nona replied, her gaze steady, the kind of maternal stare that could pierce through any façade.

Isa laughed suddenly, waving his hands in exaggerated gestures, his energy filling the small kitchen. "No, Mum! I'm not taking drugs, just the medication the doctor prescribed." His voice was loud, almost too loud, as though he wanted to drown out her doubts with sheer enthusiasm.

He leaned forward, his eyes wide, his grin unshakable. "I've been diagnosed as bipolar, and according to my psychiatrist, I'm currently undergoing a manic episode associated with feeling absolute happiness."

Nona's lips parted, but no words came. She studied him, the way his cheeks flushed with excitement, the restless rhythm of his tapping fingers, the way his laughter seemed to echo longer than it should. Her heart tightened. The bracelet on her wrist suddenly felt heavier, as though it carried not just Isa's gift but the weight of his confession.

"Isa…" she whispered, her voice trembling. "Absolute happiness isn't always safe."

Isa's grin faltered for a moment, but then he leaned back, folding his arms across his chest. "Maybe not safe," he said, his tone softening, "but it feels real. And for once, Mum, I don't want to question it."

The kitchen fell silent, save for the faint hum of the refrigerator and the ticking of the clock on the wall. Nona reached across the table, her hand resting gently on his. "Then promise me you'll let me walk through this with you," she said, her eyes shimmering with both fear and love.

Isa nodded as he retained an inexplicable animosity about his secret relationship with Judith, even though Nona's tone had made it clear that she had been concerned about Isa's unusual jolly state.

"So, do you like your present?" Isa asked in an effort to change the subject.

"Yes, I do! Thanks!"

"It looks nice on you," Isa said, pointing at the bracelet with a broad smile.

"Something is wrong with you," Nona said, gazing at Isa with scrutinising eyes. "Your smile reminds me of the Isa before Eva left you, and I need to know what has led to this transformation."

"I don't understand you! Whenever I'm down, you ask me what's wrong with me, and now that I'm feeling happy, you're still asking me the same question," Isa replied, and after a tiny pause, he added. "Aren't you at least happy that I'm happy again?"

Nona nodded, rolling her weary eyes.

"It must be the medication, so there's nothing to worry about!" Isa concluded.

Once Isa finished his meal, he revealed his plan for his thirty-fifth birthday.

"What? With the ongoing conflict and hatred, I don't think it's a good idea to invite any of your non-Ansobian friends over."

Isa tried to persuade her to change her mind. After failing to do so, he finished his late dinner and disappeared upstairs to his bedroom. The room was dim, lit only by the soft glow of the bedside lamp. He lay back on the bed, staring at the ceiling, his mind restless. The silence pressed against him until his phone buzzed on the nightstand.

Judith's name appeared on the screen. His heart skipped. He answered quickly, his voice hushed but eager.

"Judith..."

Her voice came through, low and tender, carrying a warmth that immediately softened his frustration. "I couldn't sleep, Isa. I kept thinking about you."

Isa smiled faintly, running a hand through his dark hair. "I thought you were certain about your decision of me not sleeping over tonight. Why call me now?"

"I was certain," she admitted, her tone wavering. "But certainty doesn't silence the heart. I keep hearing your voice in my head, and it makes me wonder if I'm being too harsh."

Isa shifted on the bed, his tall frame curling into the pillow as though it could hold her presence. "You're not harsh. You're cautious. But I wish you could see how much I need you. Every time you pull away, it feels like the ground beneath me disappears."

Judith sighed softly, the sound brushing against his ear like a caress. "Isa, you don't realize how dangerous this is for me. My career, my reputation... everything could collapse if anyone finds out."

"Then let it collapse," Isa whispered fiercely, his eyes glistening in the dim light. "What's a career compared to love? You're all I want, Judith. Nothing else matters."

There was silence on the line, broken only by the faint hum of her breathing. Isa imagined her auburn hair falling over her shoulders, her green eyes shimmering with the same conflict he heard in her voice.

Finally, she spoke, her words trembling. "You make it sound so simple. And maybe it is. Because when I hear you, Isa, I feel alive again. I feel like the grief I've carried for years is finally loosening its grip."

Isa closed his eyes, clutching the phone tighter. "Then let me be the one to carry it with you. You don't have to face it alone anymore."

Judith's voice softened into a whisper. "Promise me you won't let go, no matter how complicated this gets."

"I promise," Isa said, his voice steady, his chest rising with conviction. "I'll hold on to you, Judith, even if the whole world tries to tear us apart."

She laughed faintly, a fragile sound that carried both relief and longing. "You're impossible, Isa. And yet… I think I love that about you."

Isa's lips curved into a smile, his heart pounding. "Say it again."

"I think I love you," she whispered, her voice breaking into a sigh.

Isa lay back against the pillow, the weight of the day dissolving into a quiet joy. "No, you love yourself, because of me."

***

As soon as he woke up the following day, Isa had a shower. The hot water cascaded over his shoulders, washing away the heaviness of the night before. He lingered longer than usual, letting the steam fog the mirror and loosen the tension in his muscles.

Once outside the bathroom, Isa padded barefoot across the wooden floor of his bedroom. The morning light filtered through the half-drawn curtains, painting stripes across the unmade bed. He tossed his damp towel onto the chair in the corner, then sat at the edge of the mattress, running his fingers through his still-wet hair.

His room smelled faintly of soap and the lingering musk of last night's dinner. Books lay scattered across the desk, a notebook open with half-finished thoughts scribbled in uneven handwriting. Isa picked up the notebook, glanced at the words, and sighed before closing it again. He reached for his phone, hesitated for a moment, then dialled.

Shoki answered almost at once, his voice brisk and alert. Isa leaned back against the headboard, stretching his legs out across the bed.

"Hello, amigo!" Isa greeted his friend in high spirits, lying down fully now, the phone pressed against his ear.

"Who's this?" Shoki asked.

"It's Isa, amigo! Didn't my name appear on your screen?"

"Yes, it did, but you sound different!"

"How different?"

"You sound … alarmingly happy?"

"Funny you should say that. Something is on the horizon, but that's all I can say for now." Isa replied, absentmindedly tracing invisible patterns across the blanket, his mind already racing ahead to what Shoki might say next.

"Besides, this is the first time you ever called me *amigo*."

"Guilty as charged. Lately, your amigo has been feeling *alarmingly happy*. Nona has noticed it too."

"I could do with some of your medication. What is it?" Shoki asked.

"Four milligrams of risperidone a day."

"Could you save some for me?"

"All right, I can give you some this Saturday at my birthday gathering."

"What? The last one I got invited to was when you turned 21 or 22."

"For a long time, I wished birthdays had never been invented," Isa replied and then added as if he was rapping. "Nothing keeps old age away like skipping your own birthday parties. Considering that I haven't celebrated my previous birthdays, technically, I'll be 23 on Saturday!"

"Hey, make sure you bring two boxes of your medication. This is the first time you've made me laugh in a long time!"

"I can't wait to see you guys again this Saturday at the café!"

"Who else is coming?"

"It depends on who you are still in contact with!" Isa replied, his voice steady but his mind swirling with unease. "Considering I haven't been in touch with any of them for a long time, could you please invite

Ajtam, Ocim, Ojum, and Joseph."

"What?" Shoki asked, sounding apprehensive as he raised his voice. "You want me to invite Joseph too. Are you having a stroke or something?"

"No, I'm not having a stroke, and yes, I want to invite Joseph too!" Isa said, forcing calm into his tone, though his chest tightened with guilt.

"Joseph, our Jewish classmate, the one you stopped speaking to after Eva left you?"

"Yes, that's the one!" Isa admitted, his throat dry. Memories of cold silences and bitter words flashed before him, moments he wished he could erase.

"Did Joseph change his religion or something?"

"No, he didn't," Isa said, his voice cracking slightly. "I changed my Jew-hating religion, which made me miserable for a long time." He paused, feeling the weight of his own confession. "For years, I had carried that anger like a shield, convincing myself it was righteous. But now, all I can see the wreckage, the hatred and the despair it left behind".

"All right, amigo! I doubt he'll come, but I'll try."

"Thank you!" Isa whispered, almost too softly. He appeared as if wanted to say more, how sorry he was, how much he regretted letting prejudice dictate his choices, but the words stayed trapped inside.

"Your Highness, is there anything else you want me to do?" Shoki asked.

"No, thanks, amigo! That's all for now," Isa replied before hanging up. He stared at the phone for a long moment, his reflection in the black screen accusing him silently. Joseph had been nothing but kind, and Isa had repaid that kindness with cruelty. All because of his own pain, his own weakness.

Isa then called Alexander to invite him for his birthday drinks, trying to shake off the heaviness in his chest.

"Where are you?" Isa asked after Alexander answered.

"At the men's cemetery," Alexander replied promptly.

"Men's cemetery?"

"Yes, the municipal building, where men get married and voluntarily bury their happiness."

Isa laughed wholeheartedly. "Oh, come on, it can't be that bad. I'm sure that many couples are happy together."

"You're probably thinking of Adam and Eve. But they didn't get married, did they?"

Isa grinned. "True. No paperwork, no lawyers, no alimony. Just a garden and an apple."

Alexander snorted. "Exactly! The moment you sign that paper, you're basically signing up for a lifetime subscription to arguments about curtains."

Isa laughed louder. "Curtains? That's the hill you're dying on?"

"No, amigo, curtains are just the appetizer. The main course is the eternal debate about the air-conditioner's settings. I swear, I live in a climate war zone."

Isa shook his head, amused. "Sounds like you need a UN peacekeeping force in your living room."

"Forget peacekeepers. I need a divorce lawyer on speed dial and a therapist who works weekends."

Isa teased, "Come on, you're exaggerating."

Alexander sighed dramatically. "Exaggerating? Yesterday, I asked if we could order pizza. She gave me a TED Talk on healthy eating. I just wanted pepperoni pizza, not a PowerPoint presentation."

Isa burst out laughing. "Man, you make marriage sound like a corporate job."

"It is! There are performance reviews, budget meetings, and if you're lucky, a Christmas bonus in the form of silent treatment."

Isa wiped tears of laughter from his eyes. "You're killing me."

Alexander groaned. "Marriage doesn't kill you, Isa. It just makes you wish you were dead… quietly, in a corner, with your dignity intact."

# Chapter 13

**D**ue to the ongoing mainland war, ethnic hatred, and simmering insecurity, the café patio wasn't as crowded as previous years for a warm June evening. The square beyond the patio stretched wide and quiet, its cobblestones glowing faintly under the amber streetlights. A few pigeons strutted lazily near the fountain, pecking at crumbs left behind by hurried passersby. The air was mixed with cigarette smoke drifting from a corner table.

Isa navigated through the mismatched wooden chairs, their legs scraping unevenly against the stone floor, and sidestepped a wobbly table where two old men hunched over a chessboard. He ordered a beer from a waiter passing by, a thin man in a wrinkled white shirt balancing a tray of half-empty glasses, and then settled outdoors at a large table near the railing. The chair creaked under his light weight as he sat, stretching his legs and drumming his fingers against the weathered tabletop. His eyes wandered aimlessly across the square, tracing the silhouettes of shuttered shops and the faint glow of neon signs flickering in the distance.

An ongoing conversation at the adjacent table soon absorbed Isa's attention. A large man with a vast black cross tattooed on his sizable forearm leaned forward, his elbows planted firmly on the table as he spoke with fervour. His voice carried easily across the patio, rough and sharp like gravel. He looked like a boxer, due to his slightly crooked nose with his dense, dark curly hair adding to the impression. The other two men were younger, their posture stiff, their hands wrapped around sweating beer bottles. They remained silent, nodding occasionally as they listened to his rising tone, which grew more aggressive with every sentence. The boxer's chair screeched as he shifted closer to them, pounding his fist lightly on the table for emphasis. Finally, when he began spitting out words like "fucking Bresians" and "fucking Ansobians," Isa felt a knot tighten in his stomach. He grabbed his pint, the glass, cool and damp against his palm, stood up abruptly, and moved to the farthest table from them, his footsteps echoing faintly on the stone floor.

When Alexander turned up, carrying a bag slung carelessly over his shoulder, Isa waved at him. Alexander's pink V-neck top, stretched tightly over his chest, looked almost comical against his pale complexion. His forehead glistened with sweat, and he wiped it with the back of his hand as he approached, weaving between chairs with the grace of someone too tired to care. He waved back to Isa before collapsing into the chair opposite him, producing a long sigh that seemed to drain the last ounce of energy from his body. The bag slid off his shoulder and thudded softly against the floor. The waiter popped up again, his tray now empty, and retreated after Alexander ordered a Margarita cocktail in a voice that sounded more like a plea than a request.

As their conversation about Alexander's miserable married life progressed, the patio lights flickered briefly, casting long shadows across the uneven floor. A tall man with a protruding belly and a dense beard approached Isa, his heavy boots thudding against the stone as he closed the distance, his eyes scanning the table with an expression Isa couldn't quite read.

"Salam Alaykum, brother," the tall man said in a flat tone, his voice cutting through the hum of distant traffic and the faint clinking of glasses from the café patio.

Isa stood, and hugged the tall man tightly. The man's coarse beard brushed Isa's cheek, "Hi, Ahmed! What a pleasant surprise. Long time no see!"

"Yes, brother. It's been what... six... seven years since the last time I saw you at the mosque?" Ahmed asked, his broad smile revealing teeth slightly stained from years of strong coffee and cigarettes.

"Yes, I know," Isa sighed, his shoulders slumping as he glanced briefly toward the glowing streetlights that framed the square.

"Are you attending a different mosque nowadays?" Ahmed asked, tilting his head slightly, his eyes narrowing with curiosity.

"No, he isn't!" Alexander joined the conversation, leaning back in his chair with a smirk. "He's an adult now."

Unamused, Ahmed turned slowly to Alexander, his thick eyebrows knitting together. "And who might you be?"

Alexander straightened his posture, resting his elbows on the table and clasping his hands dramatically. "I might have been a happy man, but instead, I'm just a married man," he replied, his voice dripping with sarcasm.

"Are you a Muslim brother?" Ahmed asked, his tone flat but his gaze sharp.

"No, I'm just a Christian husband of a soul-sucking Christian wife," Alexander replied, throwing his hands up as if surrendering to fate.

Ahmed lowered his eyebrows, looking unimpressed, his lips pressing into a thin line. He shifted his weight from one leg to the other, the leather of his boots creaking faintly.

"Could I have a brief chat with you in private?" Ahmed asked Isa, his voice dropping slightly.

Isa nodded, pushing his chair back and following Ahmed as he walked away. The two men weaved through the scattered tables, their footsteps echoing softly against the cobblestones. The night air was warm but carried a faint metallic tang from the nearby tram tracks. They stopped by the traffic lights at the nearby crossroad, where the red glow reflected off the polished hoods of parked cars.

"Listen up, brother, and listen carefully!" Ahmed said in a low voice, stepping closer until Isa could feel the heat radiating from his body. His shadow stretched long across the pavement under the flickering streetlamp. "What I'm about to say is strictly confidential, so please don't mention it to anyone. As you know, the Vallsian civilian conflict is spreading fast and could soon spill onto our island. We must protect our Ansobian Muslim brothers and sisters from potential attacks by Catholic Taorks or Orthodox Bresians. Therefore, we're contacting our Muslim brothers to recruit them into our Ansobian Liberation Army. Would you be interested in joining?"

Isa sighed deeply, his breath fogging faintly in the humid night air. He looked past Ahmed toward the square, where a stray dog sniffed at an overturned trash bin. "When will we ever learn?"

Ahmed drew his eyebrows closer, his jaw tightening, but didn't respond. His fingers tapped impatiently against his thigh.

"Nationalism is a cover-up for our leaders who cling to power by blaming other nations for their failures," Isa added, his voice calm but firm.

"You could be right," Ahmed said, his tone sharpening, "but when this ethnic conflict hits our town, who will defend you from the Catholic Taorks or Orthodox Bresians?"

Isa turned his gaze back to Ahmed, his eyes steady. "Others can do as they please, but I came to this world as a human without a specific religion or language," he replied. "I intend to live the rest of my life as a human, not a Muslim."

"So, you're no longer a Muslim?" Ahmed asked, his voice rising slightly, his hands balling into fists at his sides.

"No, Ahmed! I'm a human," Isa replied swiftly, his tone cutting through the night like a blade. "Now, if you'll excuse me."

"But everyone in town knows you're Muslim, and you could be killed because of this!" Ahmed insisted, his voice now elevated, drawing a few curious glances from pedestrians waiting at the crosswalk. "You don't want to mess around with this ethnic war and let events develop on their own. Bresian paramilitary troops don't bloody care if you consider yourself human. There's a reason why they're called the Zombie Squad."

"Listen up," Isa said, pointing the finger at Ahmed, "I'd rather die as a human than kill somebody else as a Muslim or any other brainwashed religious product. Bye now!"

Isa walked away, ignoring Ahmed, and joined Alexander, who sipped his Margarita.

"Boy, oh boy!" Alexander waved his hand around his nose, "Did you bathe in that perfume?"

Isa shrugged.

"Why the long face?" Alexander asked.

"Nothing. People have lost their minds in this town. Everyone is talking about the war all the time."

"Things aren't looking good. Yesterday, 20 people died in mainland Ansobia, 11 Ansobian police officers, and 9 Bresian paramilitary troops," Alexander said with a concerned look.

At that point, Isa noticed Shoki ushering Ojum toward him through the soft hum of conversation. Shoki moved with a calm confidence, one hand lightly resting on Ojum's shoulder as they approached Isa.

Once they reached him, Isa pushed back his chair with a slow scrape against the floor and rose to his feet. His smile broadened as he stepped forward, arms opening in welcome. He embraced Ojum first, pulling the shorter man into a firm hug that spoke of long friendship, then turned to Shoki with equal warmth, their shoulders briefly pressing together before Isa let go.

Isa shifted aside, his movements deliberate, and extended a hand toward his table. Shoki placed Isa's present, a box wrapped in shimmering silver paper, on an empty chair with a soft thud, then pulled out another chair opposite Isa and settled into it, his posture relaxed yet attentive. Ojum slid into the seat beside the birthday boy, the legs of his chair scraping lightly as he adjusted it closer.

Ojum was the shortest and hairiest of the lot, his presence marked by a quiet energy. His large brown eyes darted curiously around the room, catching the flicker of candlelight from a nearby table. His slightly yellowish teeth flashed as he grinned, and his short, curly brown hair framed his face in unruly waves that matched the chest hair peeking through the open collar of his purple shirt. The fabric shimmered faintly under the lights, its top buttons undone to reveal a casual confidence that contrasted with the festive neatness of the setting.

"Wow, Alex," Ojum exclaimed, leaning back slightly as if to take in the full view, "you look great!"

Alexander puffed out his chest like a proud rooster, his greyish goatee twitching with smugness. "Thanks! Finally, I got some weightlifting machines to impress single women with my biceps."

Shoki, who had been swirling his glass of water like it was fine wine, burst out laughing. "What a waste of money!"

Alexander's eyebrows shot up. "A waste of money?"

"Yes!" Shoki leaned forward, tapping the table for emphasis. "Frequent use of weightlifting machines to impress girls worked in the communist era. In capitalism, frequent use of ATMs is what impresses women, not weightlifting machines!"

Isa chuckled softly, while Ojum shook his head, his thick curls bouncing. He turned to Isa, his voice warm. "You don't look bad either. It's been eight years since I last saw you, and you haven't changed much. So, what's your secret recipe?"

"There's no secret recipe," Isa replied, adjusting his chair slightly, the legs scraping against the floor.

"His secret recipe is called avoid marriage at any cost!" Alexander interrupted, wagging a finger at Ojum like a schoolteacher delivering a hard truth.

Ojum's rugged face softened as he smiled, his rough skin contrasting with the crisp, finely ironed purple shirt that shimmered faintly under the lights. He raised an eyebrow. "I take it your married life isn't going well?"

Alexander groaned theatrically, running a hand over his goatee as if polishing his misery. "If I ever find the guy that invented marriage, he'll end up dead. Marriage is the longest surviving scam."

"I guess you were too young when you got married," Ojum teased, leaning back and folding his arms.

"I'm not so sure about being too young," Alexander said, his voice dripping with sarcasm. "But I must have been way too drunk."

The group erupted in laughter, their voices bouncing like playful echoes. Even the waiter, hovering nearby with a notepad, cracked a smile before stepping forward to take their orders and retreating like a silent ninja.

Isa leaned in, his elbows resting on the table. "Come on! Your marriage can't be that bad, can it?"

Alexander sighed dramatically, shaking his head so hard his goatee wobbled like a pendulum. "Honestly, I don't know why they call it marriage. We ought to call it what it is... *torturriage!*"

"Alex, could you please stop nagging about your marriage?" Shoki asked, rolling his eyes so far back Isa thought they might get stuck.

"So, I'm just a boring nag now," Alexander muttered, his lips curling downward.

"Obviously, I've underestimated you. You're a boring nag too!" Shoki shot back, glancing at Alexander out of the corner of his eye with a sly grin.

"Thanks, Shoki! As if I'm not already depressed enough," Alexander grumbled, stroking his goatee like it held the answers to life's problems.

"Who isn't nowadays?" Shoki replied, forcing a loud yawn so exaggerated it could have won an Oscar. He faced Alexander, who began shaking his head in disbelief. "All right, Mr Sourman! Please don't be greedy and enlighten us with your matrimonial misery."

Isa sighed, his fingers drumming lightly on the table. "Come on, Shoki, give the guy a break!"

"There was a time when people could moan about their marriage," Shoki continued, his face turning red with mock passion. "Nowadays, people are entitled to a divorce."

"I can't abandon my son," Alexander said, his voice suddenly serious, a trace of defensiveness creeping in. "I would rather kill myself!"

"Now that's a dazzling option you should consider," Shoki exclaimed, spinning his glass dramatically. "But, I guess, I'm not that lucky."

Isa coughed loudly to redirect the conversation. "Ojum, how has life been treating you lately?"

"I've been all right," Ojum replied, scratching his chin thoughtfully.

"I've been having trouble with my old car, so I bought Alexander's last week."

"Did Alex's car come with a Stanley Knife?" Shoki asked, his lips curling into a mischievous grin.

"Why a Stanley Knife?" Ojum asked, his face lighting up with curiosity.

"So that you could slit your wrists after finding out what a crap car you bought," Shoki replied, smirking like a cat that just stole the cream.

Isa and Ojum burst into laughter, while Alexander shot Shoki a look so sharp it could slice bread. His crossed arms and clenched jaw made it clear he didn't find the joke amusing.

Ojum scratched his chin again and turned to Isa. "I heard you haven't been feeling good lately."

"Lately?" Shoki snorted. "I don't remember Isa ever feeling good!"

"On my way here, Shoki told me you ended up in the hospital. Is that correct?" Ojum asked.

"How is Isa supposed to know what Shoki told you when he wasn't present when you two had this conversation?" Alexander deadpanned, his voice dripping with sarcasm.

Ojum ignored Alexander, and lifting his eyebrows, he asked Isa, "So?"

Isa pulled a cigarette from his pack, but it slipped through his fingers and tumbled to the floor, spinning like a tiny white baton before landing near the leg of the table. He muttered something under his breath and bent down, his chair creaking as he pushed it back. A waiter passed by balancing a tray of steaming plates, giving Isa a quick glance as if wondering whether to offer him a broom.

"Yes, I was in the Psychiatric Ward of Sherimi Hospital," Isa replied, straightening up and brushing imaginary dust from his trousers, cigarette now safely in hand.

"How long did you stay there?" Ojum asked, leaning forward slightly, his elbows resting on the edge of the table. His long hair slid over his shoulders like a curtain, and he tucked it back with a flick of his fingers, looking like a rock star interrogating a fan.

"His doctor examined his brain for four weeks, and after realising Isa lacked one, she decided to let him go," Shoki intruded, grinning wickedly. He raised his glass in mock salute, nearly knocking over the salt shaker. "Cheers to medical miracles!"

Isa laughed, shaking his head, before replying to Ojum, "I was in the hospital for a couple of months."

"Why did you end up there?" Ojum asked, his voice tinged with curiosity.

"He realised that Isa wasn't Isa's type after all," Shoki cut in again, pointing dramatically at Isa like a prosecutor delivering the final blow. His finger hovered in the air for a moment, then he used it to scratch his chin, pretending to ponder Isa's romantic preferences.

"So, how are you feeling now?" Ojum asked Isa again, ignoring Shoki's theatrics.

"Much better!" Isa replied, snatching a few crisps from a transparent bowl in the centre of the table. The bowl wobbled dangerously as his fingers dug in. "Besides, I've met someone special."

"That's great news!" Ojum exclaimed, his eyebrows shooting up as he tidied his hair again, this time with both hands like he was preparing for a photo shoot.

"Hold on a minute. Is this someone special a *she* or a *he*?" Shoki asked, leaning back in his chair with a sly grin. He tapped the table rhythmically with his fingertips, as if drumming up suspense.

"What do you mean by a *she* or a *he*?" Isa asked, cheeks puffed slightly as he chewed his crisps.

"For some time now, I've suspected you were gay," Shoki replied, maintaining a cheeky smile. "As far as I know, Eva was your only girlfriend, and when was that... nine years ago? Back when dinosaurs roamed the earth?"

"He can't be gay!" Alexander snapped, pointing at Isa with a fork like a knight wielding a sword. "He isn't that good-looking."

"Where did you meet her? At *Lunaticus Anonymous*?" Shoki asked, his grin widening. "Or perhaps she responded to your newspaper advert, impressed by your extremely low sex mileage?"

"No, I didn't place an ad," Isa responded, tilting his finger like a professor correcting a student.

"So, who's this unfortunate creature?" Shoki asked again, leaning forward now, his elbows planted firmly on the table.

"She's brilliant, charming, and loving!" Isa replied, puffing his chest slightly as if reciting poetry.

"Are you sure this creature is a woman?" Alexander asked, squinting suspiciously.

"Yes, she is!" Isa replied.

"Could I have her phone number?" Alexander asked, deadpan, making Ojum choke on his drink.

Isa laughed and added, "I'm in love with her."

"And I think you've forgotten to take your reality pills," Shoki replied, waving his hand in the air like he was hailing a taxi, trying to catch the waiter's eye.

"Come on, amigo," Isa said, spreading his arms wide as if embracing the entire café. "I'm in love, eternal love."

Shoki laughed loudly, his voice booming across the room and attracting sceptical looks from Alexander and Ojum. A couple at the next table turned their heads, clearly entertained by the drama unfolding.

"Money is the only thing that attracts eternal love," Shoki said, wagging his finger like a wise old sage.

Isa sipped his beer slowly, letting the foam linger on his lip before adding, "We are happy together and have many things in common, like ..."

"Let me guess!" Shoki intercepted, raising his hand again to summon the waiter. "You were both born in a hospital?"

"There are other things," Isa said, rolling his eyes.

"Please don't tell me she's as stupid as you are?" Shoki teased, grinning like a mischievous child, his hand still raised high as if he were in school asking for permission to speak

"I can't reveal much about her right now, but soon, you'll have a chance to meet her," Isa answered with a flat tone.

The waiter popped up again to ask Shoki and Ojum what they would like to drink. They both ordered beers, and as the waiter was about to leave, Shoki exclaimed, "Excuse me, but this table is too wobbly."

"I'll have it fixed straight away," the waiter said and then adjusted the table by rotating it slowly.

"Is there a chance you could fix my friend too?" Alexander asked. "He's about to turn 35 and still believes in love."

The waiter laughed as he finished adjusting the table. Then he grabbed Alexander's empty Margarita glass and, pointing at it, he asked Alexander, "Would you like another one of these?"

"Why would I want another empty glass?" Alexander asked, grinning at the waiter.

"I meant ..."

"Yes, I know what you meant to say." Alexander interrupted him. "I'll have another Margarita, please."

The waiter scribbled on his pad, lips pressed tight, and retreated like a soldier escaping a battlefield. The tension at the table was thick enough to choke on.

"Shoki, where's the rest of the gang?" Isa asked, voice sharp, eyes darting like blades.

Shoki leaned forward, his tone dripping venom. "You might not know this, but since the mainland conflict started, Ajtam's gone full nationalist. Won't answer my calls. Probably saluting flags somewhere."

Isa slammed his palm on the table. "But we aren't Ajtam's political opponents!"

Shoki barked a bitter laugh. "Tell that to Ajtam! He's chained to the Taork Party now. Won't even share a drink with me because I'm not Taork."

Ojum's voice cracked like a whip. "He's sold his soul to politics! He's not the same man."

Isa's fists clenched. "What about Joseph?"

Alexander snorted, kicking Isa's presents off the chair. "When life was calm, you hated Joseph's guts. Now the world's burning and suddenly you want him back? You're a bloody hypocrite!" He bent to grab the gifts, muttering curses.

Then Shoki froze, eyes narrowing. "Speak of the devil." He jabbed a finger toward the entrance. Joseph stood there, smug smile slicing through the smoke, scanning the room like a predator. When Shoki waved, Joseph's grin widened and began his slow march toward them, each step deliberate, like a man walking to an execution.

"Isn't that Joseph?" Isa asked, glaring at the short, round man in a white shirt stretched tight over his belly.

"Yes," Shoki said, rising so fast his chair screeched like a scream.

"How come you invited Joseph?" Ojum demanded, voice sharp as broken glass. "He told me you hated his Jewish guts."

"That was then," Isa shot back, his voice trembling with rage and desperation. "I've now buried that personality!"

Shoki sneered. "You never had a personality to bury."

Joseph's approach was slow, his eyes darting like knives. Isa rose, forcing a smile, stretching out his hand like a man offering peace before war.

"How are you, Joe?" Isa said, voice cracking. "Long time no see."

Joseph's eyes were ice. He nodded without interest, stepping back as if Isa's touch was fire. Isa opened his mouth, but Joseph's glare slammed it shut.

The waiter broke the moment, sliding drinks onto the table. Joseph ordered a double whiskey, his voice flat as a blade, then dropped into a chair beside a loud woman who shot him a look of disgust.

Ojum tried to lighten the mood. "Guys, remember when Onjarf fouled Ajtam and Joseph said, 'You didn't touch him, because you used a remote control snatch the ball away from him!'" He laughed, pounding the table.

Alexander roared. Isa chuckled nervously. Joseph? A thin smile, lips locked like a vault.

"Oh, come on, Joseph!" Shoki barked, gripping his arm hard. "It's Isa's birthday, not his bloody funeral!"

Joseph's fake smile shattered. His eyes burned with fury. "Sorry, I need to pee," Shoki muttered, grinding out his cigarette and sliding away.

Ojum leaned in, voice sharp. "Why can't you be happy about this reunion? Last time we all met was before graduation."

Joseph's sigh was venom. Then came the coughs, jagged, and angry. "You forget," he spat, eyes locked on Isa, "after Eva left him, this bastard refused to speak to me because I'm a Jew. I called him. Again, and again. Our Nazi friend ignored me!"

"Joseph, you're overreacting!" Ojum snapped.

"Yes, Joseph!" Alexander barked, slamming his fist on the table. "If you hate him so much, why the hell are you here?"

Joseph's voice dropped to a chilling calm. "Because Shoki promised good news. I hoped it was a terminal diagnosis."

The table froze. Isa laughed, wild, manic, like a man on the edge.

"You're joking, right?" Ojum whispered.

"No," Joseph hissed, shoving his chair back so hard it crashed into the woman behind him. She cursed. He didn't flinch. "We'd all be better off without this Hitler-loving fanatic!"

Voices erupted, overlapping like gunfire. Isa slammed his beer bottle with a lighter clang, , demanding silence. Smoke curled from his cigarette as he spoke, voice low, dangerous.

"I don't blame Joseph," Isa said, eyes glinting behind his glasses. "For eleven years, I've been an arsehole. Especially to him." He inhaled deeply, then exhaled like a man releasing demons. "The good news? Post-Eva Isa is dead. Along with my hatred. I invited you here to apologise."

Joseph sneered. "Clear your conscience, huh?"

Isa stretched out his hand, trembling but firm. "Unless you forgive me, I'll never make peace with myself."

Ojum and Alexander stared at Joseph, breathless. Joseph's eyes narrowed, suspicion dripping like poison.

"For Christ's sake," Joseph growled, "Isa lacks a conscience. He's sedated, grinning like a lunatic."

Isa's smile faltered. Shadows carved deep lines into his face.

"It's his birthday," Ojum tried weakly.

Isa cut him off, voice cracking with manic energy. "Something's changed. Maybe the meds. Maybe love. But I'm done hating. Done being that horrible and despairing man."

The waiter slid Joseph's whiskey onto the table. Glass clinked. Silence fell like a blade, as Shoki returned to their table.

Joseph swivelled his eyes, glancing at Ojum and then Isa before raising his voice, "Yes, but this arsehole didn't denigrate any of you by shouting at you," Joseph said before mimicking Isa's accent, "*... get out of my sight! An Ansobian-Bresian guy like myself isn't worthy of your Jewish superiority!*"

Three women seated at the table behind Joseph turned, throwing covert glances at him. The smile vanished from Isa's face as he bowed his head. Seconds passed in faintly unbearable silence.

"Come on, Joseph!" Shoki tried in a lofty tone.

Joseph ignored Shoki and looked at Isa vaguely, who chewed his nails vigorously.

After Joseph's outrage, nobody expected Isa to chase his forgiveness. "You shouldn't blame Joseph," Isa paused to light up another cigarette with trembling hands. "You've been a true friend to me, and you didn't deserve the things I said to you. Unfortunately, since Eva's departure, I managed to expand it further by hating you and other Jews rather than relieving myself of this pain. As a result, I've lived a miserable, lonely life. I am 35, unmarried, and still living with my parents, who are on the brink of a divorce. You're not the only one that I have hurt in the past. My parents have also suffered from the Isa you despise. I'm now aware of how much pain this hatred has caused me and others around me. I seek your forgiveness now because I miss my old self, the one that was worthy of your friendship."

Joseph remained speechless, staring at Isa with undisguised suspicion. "All right," Joseph drank his whiskey and got up. "I need some time to think it over."

"What's there to ..." Shoki tried to reason with Joseph.

"Goodbye, everyone," Joseph stood up and disappeared into the crowd.

# Chapter 14

Although the entire world saw them kissing and pleasing each other, Judith and Isa kept their relationship secret from their acquaintances. In a short while, Isa transformed from an angry stallion into a mellow pony, as if a twin brother had replaced him. His joy became endless, his goodwill limitless. At work, Isa radiated such warmth that even the most reserved colleagues found themselves drawn to him. His students, once intimidated by his sharp tone and rigid manner, now adored him. They lingered after lectures, eager to share ideas, basking in the glow of his newfound patience and humour. Isa listened to them with genuine interest, his laughter echoing through the corridors like music, and his compliments, once rare, flowed freely, leaving his students inspired and confident.

A generous smile reflected from his entire face, with love pouring out of his glistening eyes. He consumed Judith's love and generously gave it back to everyone he came across. His lectures became vibrant, sprinkled with anecdotes and gentle jokes that made even the driest topics sparkle. Students whispered among themselves that Isa had finally become "human", and some even speculated about the secret behind his transformation.

Outside the classroom, Isa's happiness spilled into his personal life. He began spending staggering sums of his savings on new clothes, gadgets, and presents for Judith, each gift carefully chosen, wrapped with a tenderness that mirrored his devotion. Occasionally, he would buy presents for his parents, although they no longer lived in the same house. He visited them more often now, arriving with flowers and laughter, filling their homes with the warmth they had long missed.

Isa also spent more time with his childhood friends, including Joseph, who ultimately forgave Isa after years of bitterness. Their reunions were lively, full of shared memories and laughter that Isa had once thought lost forever. Despite his brilliant job in offending billions worldwide and terminating this global spasm of madness, people began to change their minds about Isa, which was a pity. If it hadn't been for Judith, Isa would have vanished from our lives, and the Convention would have come to an end, saving us all a lot of trouble.

Judith remained the quiet centre of his universe. Every glance she gave him seemed to ignite a spark that kept his soul alight. Her presence softened his edges, and her laughter stitched together the torn fabric of his past. Isa often caught himself staring at her, overwhelmed by gratitude, silently promising never to let go of the miracle she had brought into his life.

Due to his transformation, the UN member states, which pledged to hold national referendums to terminate Isa's broadcast or their financing, held their nerve and declined to do so. Isa's happiness had become contagious, a force that rippled through his work, his family, and his friendships, leaving behind a trail of reconciliation and hope.

Judith's and Isa's three-month secrecy vow finally ended, and Isa spent his first night at her flat. The morning light streamed through sheer curtains, painting soft golden stripes across the room. The faint aroma of coffee drifted from the kitchen, mingling with the lingering scent of Judith's lavender perfume, a fragrance Isa now associated with comfort and desire.

Judith appeared at the doorway, her hair tousled like a halo of rebellion, her voice soft and intimate. "Coffee?" she murmured, her eyes glowing with the warmth of someone who had shared a secret night.

Isa blinked, his heart swelling as he took in the sight of her. For a moment, he wanted to freeze time. "I'd better make a move," he said, though his voice lacked conviction. He sat upright, the sheets sliding down his bare shoulders, and Judith's gaze followed him like a gentle caress.

"This is our first morning together," she whispered, stepping closer, "and you can't wait to leave?" Her tone carried a playful sting, but her eyes betrayed a flicker of vulnerability.

Isa smiled, reaching for her hand briefly before standing. "I told you, I've got to meet my mother and tell her about us." His words were bright, almost boyish, as if sharing a secret, he could no longer contain. Judith watched him move about the room, pulling on his shirt, his energy radiating like sunlight. He spoke animatedly about how he intended to tell his parents how much he loved her, his voice trembling with excitement.

Judith perched on the edge of the bed, her lips curving into a reluctant smile. She didn't like the idea, but Isa reminded her that their secrecy vow had ended, and he would no longer lie to his mother, who, according to Isa, was already "highly suspicious, like Sherlock Holmes with maternal instincts."

"My parents are getting a divorce," Isa said, his tone softening as he turned to her, eyes earnest. "And I must avert it by telling them everything I've learned from being with you." His words carried a weight that made Judith's heart flutter, because in that moment, she realised he saw her as more than a lover; he saw her as a reason for hope.

Judith sighed, her resistance melting under the sincerity in his voice. "All right," she whispered, "but please make sure they keep our relationship to themselves." Then, with a mischievous glint in her eye, "Kiss me."

Isa crossed the room in two strides, cupping her face with both hands before pressing his lips against hers. The kiss was slow, deliberate, a promise disguised as a touch. When he pulled back, he grinned, teasing, "Why do you look at me like I've stolen your credit card?" Judith laughed softly, her fingers tracing the line of his jaw as he grabbed his belt and headed for the bathroom.

When he returned, his hair damp and his face glowing, he kissed her again, this time with a passion that left her breathless, before tossing his phone charger and deodorant into his backpack like a man late for destiny. Isa then hurried to bid her a goodbye kiss, lingering at the door as if torn between leaving and staying forever.

"Could you at least refrain from telling your parents that I was your therapist at the hospital?" Judith asked, her voice tinged with worry.

"I can't carry on lying anymore!" Isa called out from the hallway, his voice echoing like a vow.

Judith's eyebrows knitted together. "But…"

"No buts!" Isa exclaimed, popping his head back in with a grin. "I must tell Mum and Dad the truth about us! I've seen her suffer far too long, and now I must help her."

Judith inhaled deeply, her chest rising and falling like waves before a storm. She held her tongue, watching Isa slip his feet into his shoes with the urgency of a man escaping a crime scene, but his eyes, when they met hers one last time, were soft, full of love. He blew her a final kiss, whispered something about eternal love, and set off, leaving Judith staring at the door, her heart pounding with equal parts fear and longing.

Twenty minutes later, Isa stepped inside his home. The heavy oak door creaked shut behind him. Sunlight streamed through the tall windows of the living room, illuminating the polished floor like shards of glass. The silence was thick, until it shattered.

"WHERE WERE YOU LAST NIGHT?" Nona's voice thundered from across the room, ricocheting off the walls like a gunshot. She stood rigid near the mantelpiece, her arms folded tightly, nails chipped against her otherwise immaculate appearance. Her mascara framed eyes glared at Isa with a mixture of fury and exhaustion.

Isa froze for a heartbeat, then forced a smile that barely masked the tension. "I've got some good news for you," he said, stepping forward slowly, his shoes tapping against the floor like hesitant drumbeats.

Nona tilted her head, one eyebrow arching high. Her chipped nail varnish betrayed the cracks in her polished façade. Isa could feel her eyes slicing through him as he loosened his scarf and tossed it onto the armchair.

"I've met someone special with whom I've spent the night," Isa added, his voice calm but carrying an undertone of defiance.

"Anyone I know?" Her words were sharp, each syllable like a blade.

"She's my therapist… Dr Judith Mjekowitz." Isa's confession hung in the air like smoke after an explosion.

The room seemed to shrink as Isa launched into a ten-minute explanation, pacing back and forth, his hands carving shapes in the air as he spoke. Nona remained still, her gaze fixed on the large bay windows overlooking the front garden, where the plum tree's twisting leaves danced in the wind like mocking whispers.

"I knew something was going on with you lately," Nona said finally, her voice brittle after Isa's long pause.

Isa dropped into the armchair, leaning forward, his elbows on his knees. "Could we please stop discussing me and start talking about you?" His tone sharpened. "Have you forgotten what hatred did to me? Do you want to live a miserable life like I did after Eva left?"

Nona's resentment deepened, her lips tightening as she turned her head away. She looked extremely tired, her shoulders sagging under invisible weight. "Of course not," she murmured, her eyes roaming the vast living room before settling on the garden beyond the glass, a world that seemed freer than the one inside.

Isa rose abruptly, his voice climbing. "If you pursue this breakup, you'll end up hating not only Dad and all the Bresians on the planet but yourself too… pretty much as I hated myself." He forced a smile, though his eyes burned with urgency. "Hatred is a contagious disease, Mum. It will strip you of happiness and lock you in a cage you can't escape."

"Why can't you just let me get on with living without your Dad?" Nona's voice cracked, seized by a desolate desire to end the conversation.

Isa shook his head helplessly, then slid off the armchair and walked to her on his knees. The carpet brushed against his trousers as he crawled closer, his hands trembling as they clasped her shaking shoulders. Her lips parted as if to speak, but instead, she pulled Isa into a sudden embrace. Her body quivered against his, and when tears prickled her eyes, she covered them with her hand, desperate to hide her vulnerability. But the sobs broke free, heaving gulps escaping as tears rolled down her pale cheeks.

"Mum?" Isa whispered, his voice softening.

"You act as though nothing has happened out there," Nona said, wiping her tears with jerky movements. "But there's an ongoing war whereby every ethnic group wants to wipe out the other."

Isa inhaled sharply, his chest rising like a storm tide. "I sympathise with your reasons for not wanting to be with Dad," he said, lifting a finger as if to punctuate the truth. "But I must remind you of my miserable journey when I hated Jewish people… not for who they were individually, but for what they were collectively. Hatred blinded me, Mum. It enslaved me."

Nona's voice trembled with anger. "But your father belongs to the bloodthirsty Bresian control freak ethnic group."

Isa's eyes flared. "Dad's a Bresian, but he isn't bloodthirsty!"

"Ati might not be bloodthirsty, but he's definitely a control freak!" Nona shot back, her voice slicing through the air.

Isa rose to his feet, his temper boiling. "Deep inside, I know that if you start to hate him and other Bresians, you'll end up miserable, just like I was after Eva left me." His voice cracked, raw with emotion. "Besides, Dad has always stood against this ethnic-hating madness!"

Nona descended into trembling breaths. Her hands slid down from her face, revealing eyes swollen and glistening like rain-soaked glass. She stared at Isa for a long moment, her lips parting as if the words were too heavy to lift.

"I'm scared, Isa," she whispered finally, her voice fragile, breaking like thin ice. "Not just of your father… but of everything." Her gaze drifted to the large bay window, where the plum tree swayed under a restless wind. "This war… this madness outside… it's poisoning everything. People I trusted now speak of blood and vengeance. I hear it in the streets, in the news. It's like the world is collapsing into hate."

Isa tightened his grip on her hands, his own pulse racing. "Mum, you don't have to carry this alone," he said softly, his voice steady but charged with emotion. "You're not powerless. You're not trapped."

Nona shook her head, tears spilling again. "You don't understand. If I stay with your father, people will brand me a traitor. They'll spit on me, Isa. They'll call me a Bresian sympathiser. I'll lose friends… family. I'll lose myself."

Isa leaned closer, his forehead almost touching hers. "You won't lose yourself," he said firmly. "You'll save yourself. You'll save us. Hatred wants you to believe that love is weakness, but it's the only strength we have left."

Her breath hitched, and for a moment, silence filled the room, broken only by the distant hum of traffic and the whisper of leaves outside. Isa brushed a tear from her cheek with the back of his hand, his touch gentle, almost reverent.

Isa's argument spiralled, colliding like clashing swords. Nona's downward gaze betrayed her breaking point as tears trickled again. Isa reached out, his arm wrapping around her shoulders, pulling her close as if to shield her from her own despair.

"I'm here for you," Isa whispered, his tone softening into a plea. "Life is about happiness, not misery. Identity means nothing if it shackles you to pain."

Nona muttered irritably, her mascara smudging into dark rivers. Isa's voice rose again, fierce and trembling. "No, I won't stop! I can't let you go down the same path of hatred I walked."

"This is different!" Nona snapped, her head twitching in defiance.

"No, it isn't!" Isa roared, his hands slicing the air. "By splitting up with Dad, you're splitting up with yourself!"

The room fell into a tense silence, broken only by the rustle of plum tree leaves outside. Isa's voice returned, low but sharp as a blade. "Are you even aware that you're becoming someone else, someone consumed by judgment?"

"Listen up, Isa!" Nona cut him off, her temper snapping like a whip. "There are things you'll never understand."

Isa's eyes blazed. "You're wrong! We think we're free, but we're enslaved by pain. Hatred reigns over our lives, obliterating happiness.

Don't you see? Every time I saw a Jewish person, my joy vanished instantly."

"Isa, you don't make sense!" Nona cried, her voice cracking.

Isa exhaled hard, his chest heaving. "Perhaps this will help you understand why I'm happy again, something you've been dying to know since I left the hospital." He strode to the kitchen, his footsteps pounding like war drums, then returned with a glass of water, sitting beside her.

"You've always defended democracy," Isa said, his voice calmer now, though his eyes still burned. "But hatred enslaves us. It kills joy."

"Please don't get into that now!" Nona pleaded, her voice trembling.

Isa leaned closer, his tone urgent. "If not now, then when? When it's too late?"

Her eyes searched his face, catching the strain etched into his mournful expression. "What's the matter, Isa?" she whispered.

Isa swallowed hard, his voice breaking as he confessed, "I loved Eva. When she left, I hated her, and every Jew. I let pain enslave me. I killed the jolly Isa. I became a monster. And every time I saw a Jewish person, my happiness died. You can't imagine the agony I inflicted upon myself."

An unsettling silence closed around them. Isa bowed his head, shaking it as he began sobbing. Nona appeared confused, preferring not to speak about her scripted divorce from Ati or listen to Isa dwell upon it. On numerous occasions, she'd opened her mouth, wishing to make some statement to ease Isa's worrying about her. Nona looked at him with a despairing gaze before tactfully grabbing her cell phone without Isa noticing. Unable or uncertain of how to proceed with this improvised conversation, based on anything else but honesty, Nona discreetly texted the UN-SDC-BC Producers, informing them she could no longer watch Isa suffer like this and asked them to relieve her from this unbearable scene. She knew that if Isa understood the bitter truth about himself, the magnitude of his role in shaping the future of the entire world, her son would most likely end up in the Psychiatric Ward again, and she would end up being blamed for terminating the UN-

SDC-BC broadcast before Isa had a chance draft his global constitution. To alleviate herself from this painstaking conversation, Nona felt she owed him the information about his true identity, but the Script Protocol forbade her from offering her son the simple truth that she was still very much in love with her husband but had to act as if she wasn't. Nona blamed herself for failing to tell Isa the truth. If she did so, she would receive a Red Code and end up being expelled from the island without the possibility of ever being part of Isa's life again. Her legs began to shake when she checked her cell phone to see the producer hadn't answered her text. Nona issued a second text seeking an end to this agonising conversation. She waited a few minutes for instructions from the UN-SDC-BC Producers before hugging Isa and rubbing his shoulders. Then, tears began to well-up again in her eyes. She wiped them away to prevent them from rolling down her cheeks so Isa wouldn't see them. Nona cleared her throat and finally dried her eyes with the back of her hand. "Oh, my lovely Isa … deep down ... I don't want to leave Ati," Nona whispered to him in anguish.

The living room was cloaked in a tense stillness, broken only by the faint hum of the refrigerator in the adjoining kitchen. Sunlight streamed through the tall windows, so Isa's shadow stretched long and uneasy across the polished floor. The plum tree outside swayed violently in the wind, its twisting branches scratching at the glass as if echoing the turmoil inside.

"Then why are you inflicting this pain on us all?" Isa asked, lifting his head from her trembling shoulder. His voice cracked like brittle glass, his eyes searching hers for an answer that wouldn't come.

Nona's lips quivered, her breath uneven as she dissolved into incoherence. "Because my relationship with Ati is extremely complex. External forces are driving our divorce, and we must accept this." Her voice faltered, breaking into sobs. "I don't deserve this… you don't deserve this… you don't know everything… you don't know…"

Isa's pulse throbbed in his temples. He gripped the armrest, leaning forward, his voice sharp and urgent. "What don't I know?"

Nona's mascara-streaked cheeks glistened under the harsh daylight.

Her words spilled out in jagged fragments. "I'm tired... I'm so bloody tired... tired of seeing you suffer again. It's as if you came to this life... to this miserable life... only to suffer for others."

Isa's chest tightened. He reached for her hands, his fingers trembling as they closed around hers. "Come on, Mum," he whispered, his voice softening, "it isn't that bad. I suffered a lot when Eva left me, but now I'm happy again, and the only thing that prevents my full happiness it is your decision to divorce Dad."

The silence that followed was heavy, punctuated by the distant rustle of leaves outside. When Nona's sobs subsided, she lifted her head, her voice pitched and brittle. "It's inhumane to press him into further distress when he has undergone so much misery already."

Isa blinked, confusion flickering across his face. "I agree! Dad has been stressed lately, and you need to calm down."

Nona shook her head slowly, her eyes darkening like storm clouds. "I wasn't referring to your father..." Her voice dropped to a chilling whisper. "...or speaking to you."

Isa stiffened, his breath catching. "Come again?" He turned his head sharply, scanning the room from one corner to the other, his gaze darting like a trapped animal. "Who were you speaking to?"

Before Nona could answer, her phone buzzed violently on the coffee table, its vibration rattling against the glass surface. She snatched it up, her fingers trembling, eyes narrowing as she read the screen. Expecting a producer's response, she instead saw the stark message from UN-SDC-BC Producers, a Yellow Code Warning. A surge of resentment flared inside her, burning through the fragile calm she had fought to maintain.

She shot to her feet, her chair, almost tipping over, as she added, "There comes the point when enough is..." Her voice cracked like a whip, but before she could finish, Isa's phone rang, slicing through the tension like a blade.

Isa answered, his tone brisk. "Hello?"

A calm, authoritative voice flowed through the receiver. "Am I speaking to Mr Isa Iri?"

Isa straightened, his grip tightening on the phone. "Yes, this is Isa speaking."

"This is the UN Secretary-General, Ms Erdhi Koha. I'm in Anitshirp Town, trying to secure a peace deal for the ongoing war in Vallsia. Your involvement is essential for this to happen, which is why we must meet tomorrow morning in the Anitshirp Municipal Building."

Isa froze, his breath catching in his throat. His eyes flicked to Nona, who stood rigid, her face pale and taut. "Yes… right!" Isa forced a smile, though his pulse hammered in his ears. He hung up, his hand trembling slightly.

"Who was that?" Nona demanded, her voice sharp with impatience.

Isa exhaled, feigning nonchalance. "It's one of those Alex pranks. He got a female friend to pretend she's the UN Secretary-General, as if she's in Anitshirp Town and wants to meet me."

Nona's eyes widened, her voice rising. "But she is in Anitshirp Town! Didn't you watch the news last night? The UN Secretary-General is here to end…"

Isa's phone rang again, cutting her off. He snatched it up instantly. "Hello."

"Mr Iri, it's me again… the UN Secretary-General, Ms Erdhi Koha. Unfortunately, I was cut off earlier."

Isa swallowed hard, his voice faltering. "Please accept my apologies. I thought your call was a prank. I've got a silly friend who pulls stunts like this incessantly."

Her tone remained calm, but firm. "Is there a chance for us to meet tomorrow?"

Isa hesitated, his mind spinning. "I guess so… but what's the purpose of this meeting?"

As their conversation unfolded, the gravity of her words sank in. The meeting wasn't a formality. It was pivotal to securing an UN-brokered peace deal for the Vallsian war. Isa's initial reluctance melted under the weight of responsibility pressing against his chest. Finally, with a deep breath, he agreed.

"Tomorrow, 10:00," he said, his voice steady now, though his heart thundered like distant artillery.

Isa stood frozen, the phone still warm in his hand, its screen gone dark like a sealed verdict. The silence in the room was suffocating, broken only by the howl of the wind. Outside, the plum tree bent violently, its branches thrashing like skeletal arms against the glass, a storm brewing both inside and out.

He turned slowly toward Nona. Her face was pale, her mascara smudged into dark rivers, her eyes hollow yet burning with something Isa couldn't name for fear, anger, despair, all tangled like barbed wire. She gripped the edge of the coffee table so tightly her knuckles whitened.

"Tomorrow morning," Isa said, his voice low, almost trembling. "They want me in Anitshirp. The UN Secretary-General herself. She says it's crucial for peace."

Nona's eyes flashed with anger.

Isa stepped forward, his pulse pounding like war drums. "Mum, listen to me. This isn't a prank. This is real. They need me."

Nona laughed bitterly.

Isa's jaw tightened, his hands curling into fists at his sides. "If I can stop this war, if I can save lives… how can I say no?"

"All you can do, is do your best!"

. He stared at her, the weight of her words pressing against his chest like a stone slab. For a moment, neither spoke. The air between them crackled with tension, thick and electric.

Isa stood rigid, his breath shallow, his mind spinning as the weight of her words sank in. The room felt smaller, darker, as if the walls were closing in.

# Chapter 15

If it wasn't for the clusters of brown leaves clinging stubbornly to the branches, the October morning could have passed for summer. The air was mild, and the sun played hide-and-seek behind puffy white clouds drifting lazily across a patchwork of brightening blue sky. Isa's legs burned slightly from the steady rhythm of pedalling, his breath misting faintly as he coasted to a stop after fourteen relentless minutes.

He rolled his bicycle onto the concrete pavement by the main entrance of the municipal building, its imposing façade gleaming like a modern fortress. Compared to the lined-up brick structures flanking the street, this building stood out with its floor-to-ceiling glazed panels catching the sunlight and throwing them back like polished steel. Isa chained his bicycle to a nearby lamppost, the metal clinking sharply in the stillness, then reached into his jacket pocket, pinching a cigarette between his fingers. The flick of his lighter sparked briefly, and soon thin curls of smoke spiralled upward as Isa drew in a long drag, his shoulders relaxing against the chill of the glass exterior.

For a moment, he stood motionless, watching the reflection of passing cars ripple across the building's mirrored surface. The faint hum of traffic and the distant chatter of pedestrians blended into a muted urban symphony. When the alarm on his phone shrilled, Isa flinched, silenced it with a swipe, and crushed the cigarette underfoot, grinding it into the pavement with deliberate force. Squaring his shoulders, he strode toward the entrance, his footsteps echoing faintly against the polished stone.

Inside, the municipal building exuded a sleek, almost futuristic vibe. The red resin flooring gleamed under the bright overhead lights, contrasting sharply with the pristine white walls. The reception area looked more like a tech start-up than a government office, glass-topped tables stood immaculate, free of clutter, their surfaces reflecting the sterile brilliance of the space. Isa's eyes swept across the room, catching the faint hum of printers and the rhythmic tapping of keyboards from beyond the open-plan workstations.

As he approached the reception desk, he noticed an obese elderly woman perched on a swivel chair, her voice animated as she spoke into the phone, her free hand gesturing wildly as if conducting an orchestra. Isa cleared his throat softly, then spoke with measured politeness.

"Excuse me!" His voice cut through her chatter like a blade. The woman jolted, her eyes widening as she turned toward him, startled by the interruption. Her lipstick was smudged slightly at the corner, and her chipped nail varnish glinted under the fluorescent lights.

"I've got an appointment with the UN Secretary-General at ten o'clock," Isa said, his tone calm but firm.

The receptionist blinked, then glanced at her wristwatch with exaggerated slowness before hanging up abruptly. "And you are?" she asked, her husky voice carrying a note of suspicion as she reached for the phone receiver again.

"Isa Iri," he replied, flashing a generous smile that softened the tension.

"What's the purpose of your visit?" she pressed, her tone gravelly, eyes narrowing.

Isa tilted his head, his smile sharpening into playful sarcasm. "Obviously, I'm not here for a haircut."

Her lips twitched, but she said nothing as she dialled four numbers with stubby fingers. After a brief exchange on the phone, she gestured toward a yellow sofa opposite the desk. "The UN Secretary-General will be with you in a moment."

Isa lowered himself onto the sofa, its cushions firm beneath him. He reached for a municipal brochure from the oval glass table, flipping through its glossy pages without really reading, his mind racing ahead to the meeting. The hum of conversation and the faint scent of disinfectant filled the air, mingling with the sterile chill of the space.

Minutes later, the receptionist heaved herself up with visible effort, her chair groaning in protest, as a short, grey-haired woman approached. She was dressed in an elegant white suit trimmed with black stripes, her posture radiating authority. Isa rose swiftly, smoothing his jacket as she extended a hand.

"Hello, Isa," she greeted warmly, her voice rich and confident. "I'm UN Secretary-General Erdhi Koha."

"Pleased to meet you, UN Secretary-General Erdhi Koha," Isa replied, his tone formal.

She laughed lightly, covering her mouth with manicured fingers. "If you keep addressing me like that, we'll miss lunch," she teased, her smile disarming. "Please, call me Erdhi."

Isa nodded, and she led him through a corridor lined with glass partitions, past rows of desks where officials hunched over glowing screens, their faces taut with concentration. The air buzzed with muted urgency, the click of keyboards punctuating the silence like distant gunfire.

When they entered her office, a spacious chamber bathed in natural light, Erdhi gestured toward a brown leather armchair beside a low wooden table. Isa sank into its supple embrace, the leather creaking softly under his weight. Erdhi settled opposite him, her movements precise, controlled, as she picked up her phone.

"What would you like to drink?" she asked, her thumb gliding across the screen.

"A short espresso, please," Isa replied, his voice steady though his pulse quickened.

She ordered an espresso, a cappuccino, and a bottle of still water with two glasses before setting the phone aside. Then, leaning forward slightly, she began outlining her career trajectory, her words flowing with quiet authority until a sharp knock on the door fractured the calm.

"Come in," the UN Secretary-General commanded, her voice sharp, eyes fixed on the heavy oak door as if expecting destiny to walk through.

The door creaked open, and a tall, slender woman entered, balancing a silver tray that glinted under the harsh fluorescent lights. The air smelled faintly of polished wood and strong coffee. She moved gracefully across the room, her heels clicking against the marble floor, and placed the drinks on the low glass table between two deep armchairs. Her smile flickered briefly at Isa before she vanished like a shadow, leaving behind the aroma of cappuccino and tension.

The Secretary-General leaned back in her chair, her posture regal yet taut, and stirred sugar into her cappuccino with slow, deliberate movements. "Tomorrow," she began, her voice calm but charged with authority, "I'll meet Ansobian, Taork, Ryllian, and Bresian representatives to present our overly ambitious peace deal." Her eyes glinted as she spoke, the teaspoon clinking softly against porcelain. "Our proposal consists of a new constitution drafted by a local legal expert endorsed by all conflicting sides. After the stakeholders rejected the four experts we proposed yesterday, someone suggested you would be the ideal candidate. Therefore, Isa, would you consider drafting a new constitution to end this dreadful war?"

Isa exhaled heavily, his shoulders sinking as if the weight of the world had just been dropped onto them. His gaze drifted to the vast map of Vallsia stretched across the opposite wall, its borders marked in crimson ink like open wounds.

"Dear Isa," she continued, leaning forward, her voice softening but her eyes unwavering, "everyone who knows you speaks highly of you. They call you a man who stood against the madness of war. This is your chance to end it." She stirred her cappuccino again, the rhythmic motion oddly soothing against the storm brewing in the room.

The silence that followed was thick, broken only by the faint hum of the air conditioner. Isa raised his espresso cup, his fingers trembling slightly, and took a slow sip. Then, a deafening bang erupted outside, rattling the windows like gunfire. Isa flinched, his body stiffening, the cup clinking against its saucer as he set it down. The Secretary-General shot to her feet, her heels hitting the floor like hammer blows, and strode to the window, pulling the blinds aside with a sharp snap. Her silhouette framed against the glass looked like a sentinel bracing for war.

Isa's voice cracked the silence, low and strained. "Did it ever occur to you that drafting this constitution would impose an enormous strain on me?" His eyes flicked from her tense figure to the blood-red borders on the map. "You do realise what you're asking will have unalterable consequences for millions. It isn't easy to decide how 22 million Vallsians will live in the future."

What Isa didn't know is what loomed like a shadow behind her words that his constitution could shape the fate of four billion people living in the UN member states tied to the Secret of Divine Civilisation Convention.

The Secretary-General turned slowly, her face pale but resolute. "Unless you agree, this war will never end. On the contrary, it will spread, infect this island, drown it in blood." She blew gently across the frothy surface of her cappuccino, as her eyes locked on Isa like a hawk. "After all, you want this war to end, don't you?"

Isa swallowed hard, finishing his espresso in one gulp. "Yes... but am I the ideal candidate?" His voice was brittle, almost mocking. "I was recently sanctioned to the Psychiatric Ward and diagnosed with bipolar disorder. Does that sound like the man you want to write your constitution?"

She lowered her cup slowly, her lips curling into a wry smile. "We're all lunatics, Isa... crazy enough to survive in this forsaken world. But that doesn't matter. What matters is that they trust you. Ansobian, Taork, Ryllian, Bresian... they all want you because you're impartial."

Isa leaned back, his fingers gripping the armrest like claws. "I'm honoured," he said, his voice taut, "but because of what I experienced during my bipolar setback, my vision of society is... different. Radically different. I doubt Vallsians will accept a constitution based on animal behaviour."

Her laugh was short, sharp, almost chilling. "It doesn't matter whether they accept it or not. What matters is that you produce a constitution that secures peace, equality, stability, prosperity." She set her cup down with a decisive clink and leaned forward, her eyes blazing. "That's precisely what Vallsia needs... a daring constitution."

Isa raised an eyebrow, and pressed on, his tone edged with defiance. "Are you after a constitution that won't be adopted because my peers can't grasp it?"

Her reply was swift, her voice slicing through the tension. "Once you submit your draft, we'll send it to appointed experts and UN reviewers. In four weeks, you'll argue your case publicly. This is your moment, Isa."

The air grew heavier as she pleaded with him, her words tumbling out like lifelines thrown into a storm. Isa sat rigid, his mind a battlefield of doubt and duty. Twenty minutes later, he rose slowly, his decision still shrouded in uncertainty. She stood too, her movements brisk but tinged with desperation, and stepped forward, wrapping him in a sudden embrace.

"You're an honest man," she whispered, her voice trembling with conviction. "Most would seize this to build their legacy. But not you."

Isa managed a faint smile, acknowledging the compliment without surrendering to it.

She walked to her desk, her heels echoing like distant gunfire, and retrieved a blue folder. "Here's what your assignment entails," she said, pressing it into his hands. "This might be our only chance to bring peace to Vallsia."

Isa nodded, the folder heavy in his grip like a verdict. She rummaged through her green leather handbag, pulling out a matching wallet and a crisp business card. "Here are my contact details," she said, her voice taut with urgency. "Call me before one o'clock."

Isa slipped the card into his wallet, his fingers cold. "I'll call you," he murmured.

Her eyes lingered on him, fierce and pleading. "If you take this on, you'll have the world's best minds behind you. But without you, Isa..." Her voice faltered, then hardened. "Without you, this war will devour us all."

She escorted him to the door, her steps quick, her breath uneven. Outside, the wind had picked up again like a warning with Isa stepping into the storm, blue folder in hand, the weight of nations pressing against his spine. After placing the blue brief inside the front basket of his bike, Isa paused for a moment, feeling the chill of the late morning against his cheeks. The street was alive with, cars honking impatiently in the distance, pedestrians weaving through the narrow pavements, and the faint aroma of roasted chestnuts drifting from a nearby vendor. He pulled his phone from the inner pocket of his navy corduroy jacket, its fabric warm against his fingertips, and dialled Judith's number, holding the phone between his ear and shoulder as he bent to unchain his bike. The metal links clinked sharply against the frame, echoing in the crisp air.

Judith didn't answer.

Isa exhaled slowly, his breath curling into the wind like smoke. He slid a cigarette from the pack, cupped the flame with his left hand to shield it from the gusting wind, and lit up. The first drag filled his lungs with a bitter calm as he leaned against the lamppost, watching the restless town pulse around him. By the time he finished his cigarette, Isa's phone vibrated in his palm. Judith's name glowed on the screen like a beacon. He answered instantly.

"Hello, darling," Judith's voice was warm, velvety, carrying a smile he could almost see.

"Hello, sweetie," Isa replied, his lips curling as he pulled out another cigarette, the match flaring briefly against the grey sky. "I've got something important to discuss with you."

"Something good or bad?" Her tone teased, but there was a thread of curiosity beneath it.

"Something good that could turn into something nasty," Isa murmured, blowing smoke into the wind.

"When do you want to meet?"

"We could meet for lunch."

"All right, how about noon at the Uria Restaurant off Qendra

Street?" Judith suggested.

"I can cycle over to a restaurant nearer to your work."

"No," Judith exclaimed quickly, her voice tightening. "I don't think it's a good idea for my colleagues to see me having lunch with my former patient."

Isa chuckled softly, flicking ash to the pavement. "That's fine with me. See you in twenty minutes."

"Bye now."

"Bye," Isa said, slipping the phone back into his pocket.

He locked his bike again, grabbed the brief, and tucked it under his arm like a secret he wasn't ready to share. He crossed the street, moving around others on the pedestrian crossing, then turned left, ambling beside the snarled traffic on Qendra Street. The air buzzed with horns and chatter, but Isa walked with a quiet pride, his chest swelling with something he hadn't felt in years. Five minutes later, he turned right and stepped into the back garden of the Uria Restaurant, where the scent of jasmine mingled with the aroma of grilled seafood. The waiter, dressed in crisp white, led him to a secluded table at the far end, shaded by a canopy of vines. Isa set his mobile and the brief on the table, shrugged off his jacket, and draped it over the chair before sinking into the soft cushion. When the waiter arrived, Isa ordered a glass of white wine, then opened the brief, its pages whispering promises of power and peril.

At ten past twelve, Judith appeared like a vision. Her tight red dress clung to her curves, shimmering under the dappled sunlight, and her matching high heels. Heads turned from half a dozen men in business suits paused mid-conversation, their eyes following her like moths to a flame. Isa's breath caught. He rose quickly, his knee catching the corner of the table, sending drops of white wine splashing onto the pristine cloth. He leaned forward, his hands trembling slightly, and kissed her cheek, inhaling the faint scent of her perfume.

Judith smiled, her lips curving like a secret, before sliding gracefully into her chair. They exchanged pleasantries about the weekend weather, their voices soft, intimate, as they browsed the menu. When the waiter returned, Isa ordered seafood spaghetti, while Judith chose sea bass and a glass of white wine. As the waiter retreated, Judith placed the napkin on her lap and leaned forward, her eyes glinting with curiosity.

Isa reached into his bag and placed a small wrapped box on the table. "What's this?" Judith asked, her brows arching.

"It's a thank-you present," Isa said, his voice low, almost tender.

"Thanks for what?" she teased, fingers brushing the glossy paper.

"For freeing me from my long Jew-hating misery," Isa replied, his words heavy with sincerity.

Judith unwrapped the box slowly, her nails grazing the ribbon, and when she lifted the lid, silver filigree earrings shimmered like captured moonlight. She sighed softly. "They're lovely." Rising from her chair, she crossed to Isa and bent close, her lips brushed his ear, warm and lingering. "Thank you," she whispered before kissing it gently.

Isa's pulse raced as she returned to her seat, her movements fluid, elegant. "So, how was your day at work?" he asked, his voice husky.

Judith sighed, her fingers smoothing the napkin. "I've told you... I can't discuss my work. Confidentiality clause." Her tone softened. "Let's not talk about work... yours or mine."

Isa nodded, though disappointment flickered in his eyes. "I understand. But... could I tell you what happened this morning?"

Judith hesitated, then smiled faintly. "All right. One last time."

Isa leaned forward, his voice dropping to a conspiratorial whisper. "Today, I met the UN Secretary-General. She asked me to draft a new constitution for our war-torn country."

Judith's eyes widened, her lips parting. "Wow. That's incredible!" She gestured eastward. "I heard she's here to broker peace."

"I haven't agreed yet," Isa murmured, sipping his wine.

"Why?"

"Because it could turn bad."

Judith tilted her head, her gaze locking on his. "What happened to the Isa who wanted to change the world?"

Isa smiled faintly, but his eyes were shadowed. "I'm not sure the world is ready for my vision."

The waiter arrived with Judith's wine and a basket of warm bread.

She lifted her glass, her fingers brushing Isa's as they toasted. "Unless you try," she said softly, her voice like velvet, "you'll never know."

Isa lit a cigarette, the flame flickering between them like a fragile promise. "Judith," he whispered, his eyes dark, "why are you with me?"

She slid her chair back slightly, her breath catching. "That's not the right question."

"Considering my bipolar disorder… what do you see in me?"

Judith's lips curved into a slow, enigmatic smile. "What do you see in me?"

Isa leaned back, his fingers raking through his hair. "Until I met you, I wanted peace from love's wreckage. I wanted solitude. But you… you changed that."

Judith's eyes softened, her hand reaching across the table to brush his. "Then don't waste this chance," she murmured. "Do it."

Isa stared at her, the cigarette trembling between his fingers, then crushed it into the ashtray. His voice was low, resolute. "All right," he said. "I'll do it."

Judith smiled, her eyes glowing like embers. Outside, the garden shimmered under the noon sun, and for a fleeting moment, the world felt still, balanced between chaos and hope, held together by the fragile thread of love.

It took him less than five seconds to reach for his phone, pull the UN Secretary-General's business card out of his valet, and press her telephone number.

"Hi, Erdhi, it's Isa," Isa announced once the UN Secretary-General answered.

Their conversation didn't last long and ended with the UN Secretary-General's request for him to return to the municipal building to sign his contract.

Half an hour later, Isa turned up at the same office he'd visited that morning and signed the agreement to prepare a new constitution for Vallsia.

# Chapter 16

After drafting his constitution, Isa was obliged to meet with international experts who specialised in governmental sectors, legal matters, human rights, and relevant stakeholders, which could be affected by it. Their role was to assist Isa in steering his constitution in the right direction. Over the next three weeks, Isa held 18 meetings on the top floor of the municipal building, where experts scrutinised his constitution and deemed it as something that was bound to fail.

When Professor Bote unveiled his utterly obscene idea at the UN headquarters in New York, I anticipated no one with an average IQ would give it any credence. However, his fallacy continued to thrive.

Believe it or not, as if human evolution bypassed him, Isa justified his outrageous constitution by claiming it was based on natural laws and, more specifically, animal behaviour. As a result, the UN Convention on the Secret of Divine Civilisation turned into an epic failure. Due to his insane ideas, Isa became something that went well beyond the classifications of insanity as defined in mental health dictionaries. Isa's constitution would create a society where people would live like animals, causing immense scepticism about his ability to grasp how a state actually functions. His vain attempts, journeying through different past constitutions, emphasising the advantages and disadvantages lurking within them, were not that impressive. Although he did genuinely try his best to justify his decisions, Isa's fucked-up vision for a new constitution backfired badly because his ideas were utter bullshit. Worldwide surveys showed that only 21.94 percent of the constituents of the UN member states that had ratified the Convention liked his constitution.

Owing to the brilliant spin by the British mainstream media, such as the BBC, only 17.63 percent of UK respondents supported Isa's constitution. Despite the UN's strong claims, the Convention would avert a nuclear war the negative press coverage meant it was doomed to fail

The last meeting on Isa's agenda was the most controversial, a tense encounter with the religious representatives. Considering Isa's outspoken anti-God sentiment displayed months earlier, the UN-SDC-BC Board dreaded the fallout. The stakes were monumental, and the air in the Executive Board's chamber felt heavy, as though the walls themselves were bracing for impact.

The Board convened in a sleek, glass-walled conference room overlooking the sprawling town. Outside, storm clouds gathered ominously, casting fractured shadows across the polished mahogany table. The members sat rigid in their high-backed chairs, their faces taut with worry. Fingers drummed nervously on tablet screens, papers rustled like whispers of dissent, and the hum of the air-conditioning seemed louder than usual, a mechanical heartbeat echoing their unease.

For an hour, voices clashed in subdued tones, punctuated by sharp gestures and furrowed brows. Some leaned forward, gripping the edge of the table as if to anchor themselves against the tide of uncertainty, while others reclined stiffly, arms folded, eyes darting toward the clock ticking mercilessly on the wall. The possibility of postponing Isa's meeting loomed like a forbidden fruit, tempting yet unattainable.

Finally, the heavy glass doors swung open, and Ms Drejtoresha, the Executive Producer, strode in with commanding presence. Her tailored navy suit gleamed under the recessed lights, and the click of her heels against the marble floor silenced the murmurs instantly. She approached the podium at the far end of the room, where a cluster of cameras and microphones waited like predators ready to pounce.

The press conference began. Flashbulbs erupted, bathing the room in staccato bursts of white light. Ms Drejtoresha gripped the podium with both hands, her knuckles pale against the polished wood. Her voice rang out, steady but edged with tension.

"Despite our wish to postpone Isa's meeting with religious leaders," she declared, her gaze sweeping across the sea of expectant faces, "Article 4, paragraph 4.3 of the Script Protocol forbids such measures. It explicitly states that during the preparation stages of the new constitution, neither the Executive Board nor the Executive Producers can censor, influence, change, postpone, or cancel any activities scheduled by the designated drafter."

She paused, inhaling deeply as the weight of her words settled over the room. Behind her, the UN emblem loomed like a silent judge, its golden wreath glinting under the lights.

"In the past," she continued, her voice tightening, "we faced public scrutiny for prolonging the Vallsian conflict, a decision that contributed to Isa's nervous breakdown. But the Script Protocol commands us to comply with its provisions. Today, we face a similar undesired situation. Regardless of its much-dreaded impact on our viewers, we must adhere to these rules."

Her hands shifted slightly, fingertips grazing the edge of the podium as if drawing strength from its solidity. "We will monitor the religious leaders' behaviour meticulously to uphold Isa's integrity and well-being. This encounter has been classified as a highly vulnerable event and therefore we will adopt zero tolerance of any infringements. If any representative violates the Script Protocol, we will issue a Red Code alert immediately and have them removed."

The room erupted in a flurry of camera clicks and hushed whispers. Ms Drejtoresha stepped back, her jaw set, her eyes hard as steel. Outside, thunder rumbled faintly, as if the heavens themselves were bracing for the storm to come.

As Ms Drejtoresha stepped back from the podium, the press conference erupted into chaos. Reporters surged forward, their voices colliding in a cacophony of urgent questions. Camera flashes lit the room like lightning, illuminating tense faces and the sheen of sweat on foreheads. The air was thick with the smell of coffee and adrenaline.

"Ms Drejtoresha, do you seriously believe Isa can handle this meeting given his past anti-religious statements?" shouted a correspondent from *The Times*, her microphone thrust forward like a weapon.

Another journalist from *Global Peace Network* barked over the din, "Isn't this a reckless gamble? What if Isa provokes the religious leaders instead of uniting them?"

The Executive Producer raised a hand, her diamond ring catching the light as she gestured for calm. "We are fully aware of the risks," she said, her voice slicing through the uproar. "That is why we have classified, as a highly vulnerable event. Every second will be monitored."

But the questions kept coming, relentless and sharp. The sound of shutters clicking was deafening, punctuated by the frantic tapping of keyboards as journalists live-blogged every word.

Ms Drejtoresha's jaw tightened as she leaned into the microphone, her voice calm and steely. "We are not here for spectacle. We are here for peace. Isa's integrity will be protected at all costs."

Her words hung in the air like a fragile shield against a storm of speculation, as she delivered her final statement, "This meeting will proceed as planned. And history will judge us not by our fears... but by our courage."

The room fell silent for a heartbeat before erupting again, a frenzy of flashing lights and shouted questions chasing her as she turned and strode out.

*** 

The next day, Isa stepped into the meeting room as the late afternoon sun slanted through the tall, dust-streaked windows, its golden rays crawling across the eastern wall and illuminating faint indentations and cracks like scars on a battlefield. The silence inside felt oppressive, as though the room itself was holding its breath.

Isa's polished shoes clicked against the worn parquet floor. He entered the room each step echoing faintly in the cavernous space. His movements were deliberate, smooth, and commanding, a stark contrast to the room's neglected state. The sizeable table at the centre bore the marks of time, its chipped edges and peeling varnish spoke of countless arguments and fragile truces. Along its western side sat the rabbi, imam, Catholic priest, and Orthodox priest, their chairs unevenly spread, their posture stiff, their eyes flickering with unease. Isa extended his hand to each of them in turn, his grip firm, his smile thin and unreadable, while their fingers hesitated before meeting his, as though reluctant to seal an unspoken pact.

As with all his meetings over the past three weeks, Isa looked immaculate; his shiny, combed-back hair gleamed under the muted sunlight, and his striped blue three-piece suit clung elegantly to his slim frame, exuding an aura of precision and control. Yet the room around him was a study in disarray, scattered pens and papers, and a radiator that hissed intermittently like a warning. Dust motes drifted lazily in the shafts of light, swirling above the table like silent witnesses to the tension brewing beneath.

A peculiar silence inhabited the room as Isa circled to the opposite side of the table, his footsteps measured, his presence magnetic. All eyes followed him as he lowered himself into the chair between two assistants, the leather groaning under his weight, and leaned back slightly, to face the religious representatives. They shifted nervously, their gazes darting across the cluttered space, as though searching for an escape route. Isa's face, however, remained a dispassionate mask, devoid of expression, his eyes cold and calculating.

"Thanks for being here today," Isa began, his voice calm yet carrying an undertone of steel that sliced through the stillness. "Our population is devastated by the recent bloodshed of Ansobsians, Bresians, Ryllians, and Taorks. So, I've invited you here today to seek your unreserved commitment to facilitating the vital stepping stone that will provide peace, unity, and concord among the Vallsians."

The rabbi's thick eyebrows arched sharply, his fingers tightening around the armrest of his chair. "What exactly do you wish us to do, Mr

Iri?" he asked, his voice low but edged with suspicion.

"What exactly do you wish us to do, Mr Iri?" the rabbi asked, raising his thick eyebrows.

"To safeguard the future harmony among Vallsians by setting up a brand-new Holy Scripture that will unify our nations," Isa replied. "Throughout the atheist communist reign, Ansobsians, Bresians, Ryllians, and Taorks enjoyed peace, accord, and harmony. But unfortunately, soon after the communist reign collapsed, religions resurfaced, and the bloody war erupted. According to the news, 150,000 Vallsians have died in the recent war, and an additional 4 million have fled the country."

The rabbi said nothing, but his brown eyes narrowed. "Surely you can't hold religion accountable for instigating the war," the Orthodox priest argued with a desperate tone.

"Perhaps religious beliefs did not spark the war, but they were the wind that spread its flame," Isa said softly.

"Armed Ansobsians, Bresians, Ryllians, and Taorks caused this war, not the religious clerics," the priest objected. "You claim that the Vallsian war isn't a religious conflict, but my dear priest, could you please confirm how many Orthodox churches and monasteries were ravaged during the war?"

"According to our records, 28 buildings belonging to the Orthodox Church have been destroyed since the war started," the Orthodox priest responded, his eyes shifting between Isa and his fellow religious representatives seated to his left.

"If it isn't a religious conflict, can you explain why spiritual buildings are being destroyed? The Vallsian War was not a war of conflicting ideologies. Since they share the same language, if it weren't for their different religions, Ansobsians, Bresians, and Taorks would all have belonged to a single Vallsian nation, wouldn't they?" Isa asked the priest, stretching out his palms towards him.

"I guess they would," the Orthodox priest succumbed, scratching his grey beard.

"Other than religion, are there other national distinctions between the Ansobsians, Bresians, and Taorks?" Isa inquired.

"Besides their dialects or alphabets, I can't think of any," the priest answered.

"If Vallsians had one religion, there would be no Ansobsians, Bresians, and Taorks, and this repulsive war could have been avoided. Could you please look beyond your religions and place yourselves in the graveyards of Vallsia? How do you comfort the grieving mothers who lost their sons in the war?" Isa paused briefly to take a sip of water from a plastic bottle in front of him. "Perhaps you deceive them by claiming it was God's will?"

Realising that his question would go unanswered, Isa continued with a scornful voice, "Or perhaps, you have the honesty to tell them the truth that their sons were killed solely because of religious differences and that if all Vallsians practised one single faith, they would still be alive today."

"I'm not sure I understand what you're implying, Mr Iri," the rabbi leaned towards Isa.

"Dear rabbi, are you actually saying that their deaths were worthless to us and that there is nothing we can do about it?" Isa asked.

"But Mr Iri, there's nothing else we can do," the rabbi answered, leaning forward. "If it were up to me, I would end this war today."

"You could ease the grieving families by telling them that their deaths meant something to you and that, in their remembrance, you're committed to wiping out all future religious persecutions by setting up a new Holy Scripture," Isa suggested.

"The Vatican will most definitely not approve the drafting of a new Holy Scripture," the Catholic priest objected.

"I'm asking you to stand up for the community you serve, not your establishment. We've gathered here to discuss Vallsia's future, not the Vatican's future," Isa responded swiftly.

"*Mon Dieu, il ne comprend pas rien,*" the Catholic priest muttered.

"Excuse me, Monseigneur, but I did not understand what you just said," Isa confessed, his voice calm but edged with curiosity. The words hung in the air only interrupted at that very moment, by the muted hum of mobile phones vibrating across the room. The UN-SDC-BC Producers had issued a Yellow Code warning, its sharp urgency flashing on every phone screen except Isa's. The Catholic priest's name glared back at him in stark letters, and as his eyes locked on it, a shadow of dread flickered across his face.

The priest's fingers tightened around the armrest of his chair, knuckles whitening as he hesitated. His lips parted, then closed again, as though the truth itself was a venom he dared not release. If he revealed that Isa's constitution could decide the Vatican's fate, the Red Code would follow, a summons that would see him escorted out by security guards. Beads of sweat glistened at his temple, catching the dim light.

"We're here as representatives of religious establishments," the Catholic priest finally replied, his voice thin, tentative, almost trembling. His eyes darted sideways to the rabbi and imam, seeking silent allies, but found only rigid faces carved in stone.

Isa leaned forward, his elbows resting lightly on the chipped table, his gaze piercing through the priest like a spear. "Your cause is to serve God and your community, is it not?" His tone was smooth, almost soothing, yet beneath it pulsed an unyielding force. After a brief pause, he added, his words deliberate and heavy, "Thus, as a God-serving man serving your community, I'm asking you to unite Vallsians by preparing a new Holy Scripture exclusively for the Vallsian nation."

The imam shifted in his seat, his robes whispering against the wooden chair as he leaned forward, his brows furrowed in disbelief. "But Mr Iri, why do we need another Holy Scripture when such sacred texts already exist?" His voice carried a tremor, betraying the storm brewing beneath his composed exterior.

Isa's reply came like a hammer striking iron. "I've been assigned the noble task of creating a constitution that will unify all Vallsians, and to achieve this, Vallsia requires a new Holy Scripture that will amalgamate all religions into one."

The Orthodox priest, who had been silent until now, suddenly stirred. His long fingers uncoiled slowly, like a serpent awakening, then curled tightly into fists as he leaned forward, his chair groaning under the strain. His eyes blazed with indignation. "This is outrageous! We aren't prophets!" His voice thundered across the room, rattling the fragile calm.

Isa's expression remained unflinching, his voice a blade of reason cutting through the priest's fury. "Excuse me, but our country is at war and on the brink of drawing unnatural borders. Besides, I'm not so sure that you have been serving them to the best of your collective capabilities because while you all claim that there is one God, each of you represents a different version of God." He paused, his gaze sweeping across the table like a predator surveying his prey. "I'm not suggesting you become prophets or invent a new Holy Scripture from scratch. Instead, I'm asking that you jointly review the existing Holy Scriptures and establish a new one that incorporates them all."

The rabbi, who had been silent, suddenly interjected, his heavy eyebrows knitting together as he leaned forward, his hands gripping the edge of the table. "Surely, there is nothing wrong with choosing a preferred religion," he said, his voice taut with restrained defiance.

Isa's triumphant smile flickered like a blade catching light. "According to your Holy Scriptures, God is one, and it isn't exactly a product you choose from a grocery store shelf, depending on which one suits you most."

The rabbi hesitated, his breath shallow, his gaze scrutinising Isa with a mixture of contempt and disbelief. After a long pause, he spoke, his voice low but firm, "People are blessed with different religions and Holy Scriptures. Therefore, it's wrong to force people into worshipping God in one specific way."

"I also agree with the rabbi that a brand-new Holy Scripture is completely unnecessary," the Catholic priest added, his chin lifting defiantly, though his fingers trembled against the table's scarred surface.

Isa's eyes narrowed. "Do we all agree that the existing Holy Scriptures provide sufficient information on God and that a new one is not required?" His emphasis on the last word was a challenge, a gauntlet thrown across the table.

The religious representatives exchanged uneasy glances before nodding in reluctant unison. The imam spoke for them all, his voice heavy with resignation, "I agree, and I believe everyone here feels the same."

"That's great!" Isa exhaled sharply, pushing his chair backwards with a screech that clawed at the silence. His next words detonated like a bomb. "Since you all agree that the current Holy Scriptures sufficiently explain the nature of God, then rabbis, priests, and imams are no longer needed to interpret them. Therefore, the new constitution of Vallsia will foresee the closure of all the synagogues, churches, and mosques. Thank you for attending this meeting."

The room froze. Their courteous smiles shattered like glass. Then, chaos erupted.

The Orthodox priest's fury ignited first, a volcanic eruption of rage. He slammed his Bible against the table with a deafening crack, sending loose splinters and dust into the air. His chair was pushed back violently as he surged to his feet, his cloak billowing like a storm cloud. His face turned crimson, veins bulging at his temples as he stormed toward Isa. His index finger jabbed the air like a dagger as he roared, "YOU... YOU... WHO THE HELL DO YOU THINK YOU ARE TO INVITE US HERE AND TELL US WHAT TO DO?"

Isa's breath quickened, his chest rising and falling as he stared at the priest's contorted face, saliva glistening at the corners of his mouth. The imam and rabbi joined the fray, their voices tumbling over one another in a torrent of condemnation, accusing Isa of being the Satan, Antichrist, Dajjal, echoed like curses in a haunted hall. Isa tried to speak, but his voice was drowned beneath the storm.

The Orthodox priest's chair crashed into the radiator with a metallic clang, reverberating through the room like a gunshot. Isa recoiled, bowing his head to avoid the priest's blazing eyes, which seemed ready to burst from their sockets. The priest lunged forward, fists clenched, his beard whipping against his chest as he bellowed, "YOU'RE NOT A PROPHET! YOU CAN'T TELL THE ENTIRE WORLD WHAT WE CAN AND CAN'T DO!"

Phones buzzed frantically, their shrill vibrations slicing through the chaos. Faces paled as screens lit up with the Yellow Code warning, Father Mosme Le Papune. The air crackled with dread. The other clerics rushed to restrain him, their hands clawing at his arms, their voices pleading, but Father Mosme roared back, his defiance shaking the room, "NO, I WILL NOT CALM DOWN!"

Isa's attempt to reason was swallowed by the tempest. The imam stepped between them, his hands raised in futile pacification, while the priest's body jerked like a marionette possessed, his rage spilling unchecked, his words pounding like war drums, "YOU THINK YOU CAN TERMINATE 2,000-YEAR-OLD CHRISTIANITY IN FIVE MINUTES, JUST LIKE THAT?"

The room had become a battlefield, using words as weapons, faith as fire, with Isa at its epicentre, silent now, his mind racing as the storm raged on.

He opened his mouth to respond, but a sudden, deafening bang shattered the ongoing turmoil. The sound ricocheted through the room, making Isa's body jolt so violently that he knocked his glass causing the water to slop over the rim, splattering across the table. His breath caught in his throat as he whipped his head towards the venetian blinds, the slats trembling faintly from the shockwave. Outside, the late afternoon light fractured into harsh stripes across the floor, casting shadows that seemed to crawl toward him.

In that split second, the room was pierced by the shrill buzz of mobile phones. The UN-SDC-BC Producers had issued a Red Code. The words glared on every screen like a death sentence, and beneath them, the name, Father Mosme Le Papune. The Orthodox priest's face drained of colour, then flushed crimson in a violent surge. His chest heaved, his nostrils flared, and his trembling hands clenched the edge of the table as though to anchor himself against the storm brewing inside.

The Catholic priest dragged his palms over his bald head, his fingers leaving streaks of sweat glistening under the dim light. He exhaled sharply, the sound almost a hiss, before glancing at his phone and shaking his head in despair. Leaning toward the imam, his voice dropped to a bitter whisper, "This is just great! Thanks to that lunatic priest, we'll no longer be able to have our say on Isa's constitution."

The door slammed open with a force that rattled the cracked plaster walls. Five figures stormed in, four young men and an older one, all clad in matching black uniforms, their boots pounding against the floor like war drums. Each carried a walkie-talkie clipped to their bulletproof vests, crackling with static. Two of the younger guards, faces taut with urgency, flanked Isa instantly, their eyes scanning the room like predators scenting danger.

The eldest guard stepped forward, his voice erupting in a thunderous command that swallowed the chaos, "We are under attack! Additional security forces are on their way to protect you. Meanwhile, we need to evacuate you to the bunker located in the basement. Leave everything behind and follow me… NOW!"

"Get your hands off me!" Father Mosme Le Papune roared, his voice raw with fury as the older guard seized his arm. The priest's cloak whipped around his legs as he twisted violently, his face contorted in rage.

"Your lives are under threat!" the guard barked back, his nose almost grazing the priest's forehead, his breath hot and acrid. "Failure to obey will result in you being forcibly removed!"

Across the table, Isa scrambled to gather his papers, his fingers trembling as sheets scattered like startled birds. He lunged to retrieve them, but a guard's iron grip clamped around his wrist. "Sir, we must leave right away," the guard growled, his voice low and urgent. "There's no point dying over a pile of paper."

Isa froze, his eyes locking with the guard's, a fleeting moment of silent defiance, before he spun toward the open door. Another guard seized his shoulder, steering him firmly into the corridor.

The group split into two columns, Isa and his assistants surged ahead, flanked by two guards whose boots thudded against the marble floor in a relentless rhythm. Behind them, the rabbi, imam, and Catholic priest followed under the watchful eyes of the remaining guards, whilst a security guard detained Father Mosme Le Papune in the meeting room. The corridor stretched long and dim, its flickering lights casting jittery shadows that danced like spectres along the peeling walls.

A tall, nervy guard with black tattoos snaking across his arms and neck slipped between the imam and the Catholic priest. His grip clamped onto the priest's arm as he leaned close, his voice a harsh whisper, "Excuse me, Father, do you mind telling me what the fuck just happened ..."

"Mind your language, young man!" the Catholic priest snapped.

"I'm sorry, Father!" the tattooed guard composed himself, and pointing at Isa, he asked. "What was that dickhead up to this time?"

"That lunatic is trying to turn us into messiahs!" the Catholic priest replied.

"What?" the tattooed guard asked. "The Producers are going manic today."

"He wants us to write a new Holy Scripture," the imam added.

"And if you don't comply?" the tall guard asked.

"That bloody infidel wants to end religious practices by shutting down all religious institutions and subjecting the entire world to atheist communism again," the imam replied.

"He's gone mad again! If Christianity is banned, what the fuck am I supposed to do with this?" the tall guard grunted, tapping his finger on the large cross tattoo on his arm.

"Just because religion impeded his desire to get laid with his childhood sweetheart, that lunatic has no right to deprive the entire world of religious services," the Catholic priest replied after Isa disappeared behind the closed laminated doors.

The shortest guard, walking discreetly behind them, burst out laughing. The Catholic priest, the imam, and the tattooed guard walking between them turned and looked at him as he apologetically extended his palm to them.

The Catholic priest walked towards the short guard, who couldn't suppress his laughter and asked him, poking his finger onto his protruding chest, "That lunatic wants to terminate religious practices, and you find this funny?"

"I'm so sorry ... Father ..., but it is funny!" the short guard apologised.

The tattooed guard approached his colleague, grabbed him by his shoulder and asked him, "Then why in the hell are you laughing?"

The short guard lifted his hands and pushed the man's hands off his shoulders and replied with a smirk, "I mean no disrespect, but having never made love to a woman, the priest isn't the most qualified person to judge another man's desire for a pussy!"

"Mind your language!" the priest objected, looking at him square in the eye.

"Yes, you damn motherfucker! Mind your language when you speak to a priest!" the tattooed guard stepped towards the short guard, pushing his chest against his colleague's flat nose.

The radio clipped to his bulletproof vest went ballistic, "Zulu, where the heck are you?"

"This is Zulu. We'll be down there in nine seconds!" the tall guard replied instantly. He turned to the Catholic priest, "We need to move now, but please, Father, be extra vigilant when speaking to Isa. The Producers are infuriated with the way the meeting has gone today."

Back in the meeting room, the atmosphere was suffocating, thick with the acrid scent of dust and old varnish, the air vibrating faintly from the distant echo of boots pounding in the corridor. The blinds rattled against the cracked windowpane as a gust of wind swept outside, Father Mosme Le Papune stood rigid, his chest heaving, his scraggly grey hair clinging to his damp temples like wild vines. His eyes blazed with defiance as the guard loomed over him, muscles taut beneath the black uniform.

"If you don't leave straight away, I'll have to force you out," the guard warned, his voice a low growl that reverberated through the tense silence.

"You can't force me out!" Father Mosme roared, his voice raw and harsh, echoing off the peeling walls. He jabbed a trembling finger toward the door, his nails yellowed and cracked. "I'm not finished with that Antichrist yet!"

"Oh yes, you are," the guard snapped, impatience flashing in his narrowed eyes as he stepped closer, the weight of authority radiating from his stance. "Now that you've received the Red Code, you won't be allowed to set foot near Isa again."

Father Mosme Le Papune's breath came in incoherent bursts, his words tumbling out in a torrent of fury as he tried to justify his refusal. But the guard's patience shattered. With a swift, brutal motion, he seized the priest by the shoulders, his fingers digging into the coarse fabric of Father Mosme Le Papune's cloak. The priest staggered, his sandals skidding across the polished floor, leaving faint streaks of grime. Papers fluttered from the table like startled birds as Father Mosme Le Papune flailed, his arms thrashing wildly.

Dragged toward the door, Father Mosme Le Papune lunged sideways, his fingers clawing for purchase. He clamped onto the doorknob with both hands, his knuckles whitening under the strain. His body arched like a bowstring, muscles trembling as he unleashed an animal-like howl that ripped through the corridor beyond. The sound was primal, a cry of rage and despair that made even the guards outside stiffen.

The guard gritted his teeth, his jaw clenched as he wrestled with the priest's iron grip. "Let go!" he barked, yanking hard, but Father Mosme Le Papune clung to the handle with a strength born of desperation. The metal groaned under the pressure, vibrating against the door as if protesting the struggle. Finally, with a savage wrench, the guard pried Father Mosme Le Papune's fingers loose one by one, the priest's nails scraping against the door's wood in a futile bid for resistance.

Father Mosme stumbled forward, his cloak wrapping around his legs as the guard dragged him into the hallway. Outside the main entrance, the chill wind swept through the open doorway, carrying with it the distant wail of sirens. Standing sentinel was a huge bald man, his presence dominating the threshold like a monolith. Six linear scars slashed across his face, pale against his weathered skin. A thick gold chain gleamed around his neck, catching the weak light, while four heavy rings glinted on his clenched fists. His arms were folded high across his chest, muscles bulging beneath the black fabric, and his expression was carved in stone, a silent warning.

Father Mosme's voice erupted again, raw and venomous, "HOW DARE YOU EVICT ME LIKE THIS? HE'S THE ONE YOU MUST EVICT, NOT ME!" His words tore through the air, his scraggly hair whipping against his stooped shoulders as he twisted violently in the guard's grip.

"You know the rules," the guard shot back, his tone clipped, his breath steaming in the cold draft. "Once a Red Code alert is issued, we are obliged to detain the person whose name appears in it." His eyes flicked briefly to the looming figure at the door before returning to Father Mosme's contorted face. "If you'd behaved earlier, the Producers wouldn't have triggered the Red Code, or staged that blast to make Isa believe the building was under attack."

Father Mosme spat his reply like venom, his voice cracking with rage, "You should detain Isa, not me! DON'T YOU REALISE HE IS THE ANTICHRIST?"

The guard opened his mouth, but Father Mosme surged on, his words tumbling like stones down a cliff, "The Holy Scriptures warned us of his coming! That Antichrist must be stopped by whatever means necessary! We must oppose the rules he wants to impose upon the world before it's too late!"

The guard's jaw tightened, his eyes hardening like flint. "Perhaps in two years, the world will vote against his constitution," he said coldly, stepping forward until his shadow swallowed Father Mosme's trembling form. "But right now, we obey the Script Protocol. And that means evicting you... by force if necessary."

He paused, his voice dropping to a deadly calm. "So, with all due respect, Father, you're leaving. NOW."

Meanwhile, inside the municipal building, the guards hustled Isa and his assistants down a narrow flight of concrete steps. The air grew colder and heavier as they descended, thick with the smell of damp stone and rust. The dim corridor stretched ahead like a tunnel into oblivion, its walls streaked with water stains that glistened under the flickering glow of the overhead bulbs. Shadows clung to the corners like lurking predators.

The group moved quickly, their footsteps echoing in the confined space. Isa's polished shoes slipped slightly on the slick floor, and one of the guards gripped his elbow firmly, steering him forward. Behind them, the rabbi, the imam, and the Catholic priest followed in tense silence. Their faces were masks of unease, eyes darting nervously as if expecting the concrete to crack open beneath their feet. Not a single word passed between them, only the sound of laboured breathing and the distant hum of security radios.

At last, they reached the underground chamber, a stark, oppressive room that reeked of neglect. Opposite the heavy steel door stood a rusted sink, its tap dripping steadily, each drop echoing like a ticking clock in the silence. Patches of peeling linoleum curled away from the floor, exposing the rough screed beneath. Eight harsh neon tubes buzzed overhead, their cold light casting shadows across the concrete ceiling. Against one wall, black polypropylene box files were stacked like tombstones, looming over four guards who stood rigid, their hands resting on the grips of their holstered weapons.

The imam tilted his head back, his eyes tracing the water stains that spidered across the ceiling like veins. The rabbi lowered himself onto a wooden chair with a grunt, his fingers brushing the ripped upholstery of the armrest, sending a puff of dust into the stale air. The Catholic priest, his lips pressed into a thin line, pulled a white handkerchief from his sleeve and wiped the rusted surface of the table, his movements slow and deliberate, as though cleansing something profane.

Isa cleared his throat, the sound sharp against the oppressive quiet. "Where is the Orthodox priest?" His voice carried a note of urgency that made the guards glance up.

"He had an urgent matter to attend to and had to leave immediately," Isa's female assistant replied, her tone clipped, her eyes avoiding his.

Isa's brows knitted, his voice tightening. "But he isn't safe out there. He shouldn't have left the building." He exhaled, his gaze sweeping the bleak chamber. "I apologise for keeping you inside this horrible room. I hope the attack will be averted, and you'll soon be able to leave safely."

"That's all right, Mr Iri," the rabbi said, his voice gravelly as he shifted on the hard chair. "But considering that I couldn't contribute much to our earlier discussion, would you mind if we continued talking about your constitution?" He grunted again, adjusting his weight, the chair creaking ominously beneath him.

Isa gestured toward the top shelf, where a dusty chessboard sat forgotten among the files. "Apart from using that to play a game," he said dryly, "I guess there isn't much else we can do right now."

"Thank you," the rabbi sighed, his shoulders sagging. "Vallsians will undergo a difficult process of bandaging their traumatised souls caused by this horrible war. If the new constitution prohibits religious activities, it might undermine their spiritual healing process facilitated by our services."

Isa leaned forward, his fingers tapping lightly on the rusted table, his voice calm but determined. "Rabbi Leibovitz, if your religions did not exist in the first place, we wouldn't have this bloody war going on, and consequently, we wouldn't end up with traumatised souls to heal." His eyes glinted under the harsh neon light. "Centuries ago, there were no doctors or medications. Then religious establishments and representatives facilitated the healing of traumatised souls. In contrast to past centuries these days, we have qualified psychiatrists and psychologists trained to deal with traumatised souls." He paused, his jaw tightening. "I was also deeply affected by the recent war, and a psychiatrist helped me overcome my nervous breakdown."

The imam shifted uneasily, "But many Vallsians will resist your plans to shut down religious institutions, especially Ansobians," he objected, his voice taut.

Isa's reply came slowly, reluctantly, as though each word was a weight he had to lift. "I don't intend to shut down religious institutions in an instant. You'll continue offering your services over the next twenty years." His gaze swept across their faces, cold and unwavering. "It would be unfair for current religious leaders to end their religious services abruptly. However, during those twenty years, you won't be allowed to offer your services to people aged twenty-five and younger."

The Catholic priest's back straightened, his fingers tightening around the edge of the table. "What do you intend to accomplish by shutting down religious institutions to people aged twenty-five and younger?"

Isa's lips curved into a faint, enigmatic smile. "The people of Vallsia need to self-reflect and return to their natural state."

"Meaning what?" the priest pressed, his voice sharp.

"Meaning…" Isa paused, his eyes narrowing as he leaned forward, his voice dropping to a near-whisper that nonetheless sliced through the silence. "You don't see any Muslim, Catholic, Orthodox, or Jewish dogs around, do you?"

The priest blinked, his mouth opening, but Isa cut him off, his tone rising. "Or Muslim, Catholic, Orthodox, or Jewish trees?"

The rabbi's heavy brows furrowed as he leaned in, his voice low and tense. "But we're humans, who happen to be very different from trees."

"Yes," Isa said, his voice smooth, almost chilling. "We're humans… creations of amazing Mother Nature, same as dogs and trees."

The rabbi's eyes narrowed further. "Excuse me, Mr Iri, but do you believe in the existence of God?"

Isa's answer came like a thunderclap, startling in its certainty. "Of course, I do!" His voice rang out, echoing against the concrete walls. "It's absurd to deny God's existence when there's overwhelming evidence of His existence."

The religious representatives exchanged startled glances in disbelief. For a moment, the imam seemed frozen, his lips parted but no words emerging.

"That's a relief," the priest murmured, his tone softening, almost cheerful. "So, you're not an atheist, after all."

The rabbi leaned forward, his eyes sharp as blades. "Which particular evidence are you referring to?"

Isa's gaze swept across them, his expression inscrutable. "Actually, there are two concrete and indisputable pieces of evidence that prove God's existence," he said, his voice calm, deliberate. "Both of them can be found in our sleep."

"Sleep?" the rabbi echoed, his voice tinged with suspicion.

"God's undeniable direct connection with people is depicted in the Holy Scriptures, but most are still unaware of this. Verse 42 from Chapter Ez-Zumer of the Holy Quran explicitly states that God does not take human souls only when we die, but also whenever we are asleep."

Isa inhaled deeply, the stale air of the underground chamber filling his lungs as he fixed his gaze on the elderly men seated opposite him. The harsh neon lights cast cold, angular shadows across their lined faces. The room felt claustrophobic, its concrete walls closing in like a silent jury. A faint drip from the rusted sink punctuated the silence, each drop echoing like a countdown.

The imam sat rigid, his shoulders hunched, his eyes lowered to his clasped hands as though seeking refuge in their stillness. His fingers twitched slightly, betraying the tension he tried to mask. The rabbi's brown eyes, framed by heavy brows, flicked from the imam to the priest and back again, searching for a spark of solidarity, his lips pressed into a thin, uncertain line. The Catholic priest shifted in his chair, the wood creaking under his weight, his damp forehead glistening under the unforgiving light.

When no one spoke, Isa leaned forward, his voice cutting through the oppressive quiet. "For a very long time, Vallsians thought that God takes one's soul only after death." His words hung in the air like smoke. "However, the Holy Quran explicitly states that God also takes our souls whenever we're asleep. Consequently, people experience heaven or hell whenever they are dreaming or experiencing nightmares." He paused deliberately, his tone sharpening as he emphasised the words *heaven* and *hell*, his eyes locking on each man in turn.

The imam's head jerked up, his eyes flashing with alarm. "But Mr Iri, Allah takes human souls only after their death," he objected, his voice taut with urgency. His hands lifted slightly, palms open as if to push Isa's words away. "This perception is upheld by many scholars who have devoted their lives to studying the Holy Quran. Their commentaries provide a detailed explanation and a genuine interpretation of that verse."

Isa's chair scraped against the floor as he leaned in. "Imam Abbas, what is there to comment about?" His voice cracked like a whip. "The Holy Quran is very explicit in its phraseology. It isn't some poetry produced during the communist regime, relying on metaphorical descriptions to convey its concealed true meaning."

The imam swallowed hard as he tried to steady his voice. "But, Mr Iri, heaven or hell are experienced only after we die," he insisted, desperation bleeding into his tone.

Isa's eyes narrowed, his jaw tightening. "I don't dare to claim that the Holy Quran has failed to convey the truth nor the arrogance to interpret its obvious verses." His hand slammed lightly against the table, sending a puff of dust into the air. "I just cited its verse, which clearly states that besides when dying, God also takes our souls when we sleep. What's there to add or comment on?"

The imam's shoulders sagged, his breath escaping in a defeated sigh. He shrugged silently, his mouth curving downward in a feeble gesture of discord.

Isa seized the moment, his voice rising with renewed force. "Verse 60 of Chapter Al-Anaam inside the Holy Quran also reiterates that God takes our souls whenever we are asleep and is well aware of what we have been up to during the day." He jabbed a finger against the table for emphasis, his eyes blazing. "Therefore, depending on our actions or projected thoughts, God takes our souls during sleep and subjects us to heaven or hell while we're asleep."

The priest lurched forward, his chair groaning under the sudden movement. His bloodshot eyes burned beneath his sweaty brow, his fists clenching atop the table. "This is outrageous!" he thundered, his voice reverberating off the concrete walls. "One experiences heaven or hell only after death and not before!"

The room crackled with tension, the neon lights buzzing louder as if amplifying the discord. The rabbi's fingers drummed nervously against the armrest, the imam's lips moved in silent prayer, and Isa sat motionless, his gaze cold and unyielding, a storm gathering behind his eyes

"But according to verse 12 of Chapter Âl' Imrân inside the Holy Quran, people who reject faith end up being vanquished and gathered together to Hell, which constitutes an evil bed to lie on!" Isa sighed, moving his stretched palms horizontally. "This verse clearly identifies the *bed* as a place where individuals experience *hell*. Besides that verse, there are other ones in the Holy Quran, which associate *hell* to something experienced in *bed*, when sleeping," Isa argued, again emphasising the word hell.

The chamber felt like a pressure cooker, the air thick with hostility. Isa inhaled deeply, his chest rising slowly as the neon lights buzzed like angry hornets. Every sound seemed amplified, the scrape of a chair, the rustle of a sleeve, each one a potential spark in the tinderbox of silence.

The priest sat rigid, his knuckles bone-white as he clenched a crumpled handkerchief, his jaw grinding like a millstone. His voice erupted, sharp and venomous, "Mr Iri, figuratively speaking, the bed refers to the final resting place... the grave!" His words cracked through the air, stirring the dust that floated lazily under the buzzing lights.

Isa leaned forward, his voice calm but laced with steel. "That particular verse relates to bed... as in furniture," he countered.

The priest's eyes flared, his lips curling in contempt. "That isn't true. Who do you think you are to tell us where one experiences hell?" His voice rose, trembling with fury as he slammed the handkerchief against the table. "You aren't a prophet!"

Isa didn't flinch. His posture remained composed, but his eyes burned with an unsettling certainty. "I recognise that you are reluctant to accept this revelation that God controls our pleasant dreams or heaven and nightmares or hell depending on what we did during the day." His words were deliberate, heavy, like stones dropped into a still pond. "But didn't God communicate to His prophets and messengers in their dreams?"

The silence that followed was suffocating. Isa's question hung in the air like smoke, curling into every corner of the room. When no one answered, he pressed on, his voice sharpening, "Or is it also outrageous to claim that God communicated with His prophets through dreams?"

The rabbi's restraint shattered. He surged forward, his palms slamming against the table with a force that rattled the rusted legs. "No, Mr Iri!" he thundered, his voice echoing like a gavel. "All religions uphold the fact that God communicated to His prophets and messengers through dreams or visions. For example, the Book of Genesis features Joseph's story, with whom God communicated through dreams."

Isa's lips curved into a faint smile, his eyes glinting like shards of glass. "Exactly, my dear rabbi."

"But Joseph was a prophet chosen by God," the rabbi shot back, tightening his fist. "It's blasphemy to compare ordinary people to God's prophets and messengers!"

Isa leaned in, his voice smooth, almost chilling, his shadow stretching across the table like a predator's silhouette. "However, you seem to forget that the Book of Joseph reveals that God also communicated through dreams to his two prison inmates and the Pharaoh, who weren't prophets." He exhaled slowly, his breath misting in the cold air. Then, with deliberate calm, he turned to the priest. "Don't you experience dreams?"

The priest shifted in his chair, the wood groaning under his weight. His eyes narrowed, his voice dripping with feigned annoyance. "Yes, I occasionally do."

Isa's next words struck like a hammer. "If dreams are created by God exclusively for prophets, then who generates your dreams?"

The Catholic priest lunged into the conversation, his voice taut with objection though lacking conviction. "But Mr Iri, scientists credit dreams and nightmares to the individual's subconscious mind."

Isa's gaze flicked to him, his tone sharpened. "I'm familiar with the scientific hypothesis of dreams being linked to real-life events." He pivoted back to the rabbi, their eyes locking his. "But, my dear rabbi, do you truly believe that the unconscious mind can project a dream that will eventually come true within a short period of time?"

The rabbi hesitated, his brows knitting together, his lips parting soundlessly. "Excuse me, Mr Iri, but I'm not sure I follow you."

At that point, Isa leaned back slowly, the chair creaking under his weight like a warning groan. His head dropped, his hand covering his mouth as silence swallowed the room. The neon lights buzzed louder, the drip from the sink echoing like a metronome counting down to something inevitable. His female assistant leaned forward, her voice tentative, slicing through the tension. "Are you alright?"

Isa raised his left palm without looking up, his breath coming in long, deliberate pulls. Then, after a pause that stretched like a taut wire ready to snap, he lifted his head, his eyes dark and resolute. "I invited them here today, hoping they would understand that over the centuries, they have failed to reveal God's nature to Vallsians." His voice deepened, resonating with controlled fury. "Now, more than ever, Vallsians need a new Holy Scripture to open their eyes and bring them closer to God, but they reject it under the pretext that it's sacrilege."

He rose slightly from his chair, his shadow looming across the table as he continued, his words pounding like war drums. "I've emphasised specific Holy Quran verses that reveal God's intimate and direct interaction with humans. Surely, if Vallsians knew that nightmares experienced during their sleep are manifestations of hell, a consistent reminder of what awaits them in their afterlife, they would refrain from causing harm to others. Because of your failure to explain how God interacts with us, many good-hearted individuals are lost, misled into sacrificing themselves erroneously for God."

The rabbi shot to his feet, his chair screeching across the floor like a wounded animal. His face blazed crimson, his voice erupting like a cannon. "This is outrageous! You feel sorry for those cold-blooded murdering terrorists of countless victims, who in God's name have brought destruction on earth, inciting fear, chaos, and division amongst the people!"

Isa's reply came like a stab, swift and merciless. "Dear rabbi, they're victims of human manipulation and a twisted interpretation of the Holy Scriptures, which all of you were supposed to prevent." His finger stabbed the air, his voice rising like a storm. "You should have told worshippers that as long as they experience nightmares, they aren't acting in God's way. Most of them have erroneously self-sacrificed themselves, motivated by idealism for a better life and a place in heaven, but for as long as they experience nightmares, they'll end up in hell instead."

"But Mr Iri, what makes you so confident that they experience nightmares?"

Isa's eyes blazed, his voice cutting through the charged. "Judging from their frantic public addresses with angry faces, it's apparent their souls are under immense torment and sleep deprivation associated with hell. A person truly in God's way is supposed to feel enlightenment, not anger."

"I'm not entirely convinced," the imam muttered, his voice full of resistance, his fingers drumming a frantic rhythm on the table.

Isa straightened, his tone cold and final, his words detonating like a bomb. "This is why in twenty-five years, my constitution foresees the closure of all religious institutions in Vallsia."

The words hung in the air like a gas ready to ignite the room. The religious representatives recoiled, their chairs scraping violently against the floor as they shook their heads in unison.

"Why would you do that?" the rabbi demanded, his voice cracking under the weight of fury.

Isa's reply came in a heartbeat, his brows arching like drawn blades. "Because you failed to provide ordinary Vallsians a single piece of evidence that proves God's existence."

The imam's fist slammed down on the table so hard that a box file toppled from the shelf, hitting the floor with a dull thud. "But we are continuously doing so!"

"No, you haven't!" Isa roared, his finger stabbing toward the imam like a spear. "Let's assume that I'm an agnostic who does not believe in God and finds it absurd that someone still believes that nothing in this world happens without God's knowledge. How can you prove that?"

The flow of talk suddenly dried up, leaving the chamber steeped in a suffocating silence. Isa's blank, dark eyes darted left and right between the three robed figures, their faces half-hidden by the harsh glare of the neon lights. The air was heavy with unspoken hostility. A single drip from the rusted sink punctuated the quiet like a ticking clock.

The religious representatives leaned toward one another, as they embarked on a hushed discussion. The rabbi's fingers tapped nervously on the armrest, his nails scraping the frayed upholstery. The imam rubbed his forehead with the heel of his palm, his lips moving in silent prayer. The priest clenched his handkerchief tightly like a safety blanket, his chest rising and falling in shallow bursts. Isa sat motionless, his fingers drumming a slow, deliberate rhythm on the scarred tabletop, his jaw tightening with every passing second. Three minutes crawled by like an eternity, the tension thick enough to choke on.

Finally, the priest straightened, his chair creaking under the strain, and delivered his verdict, "Therefore, something exists only because something else created it."

Isa's eyes narrowed. "Excuse me, my dear priest, but that does not constitute proof of God's existence." His tone was cold, clipped. "It's an interpretation of something that one cannot verify. I'm after verifiable evidence."

The rabbi shifted in his seat, his voice blunt and unyielding. "God works in mysterious ways. God's awareness about everything that happens on earth is apparent in the Holy Scriptures. Therefore, it's true."

"Based on what proof?" Isa's eyes glinted with a poignant mood, his words deliberate and heavy. "I have asked you specifically to point out the proof that God exists, a verifiable piece of evidence. But you can't, can you?"

The rabbi's shoulders sagged as he shrugged, his gaze sliding toward the imam like a silent plea.

The imam exhaled slowly, "It's impossible to do that," he admitted, his voice strained with resignation. "We aren't prophets to point out the evidence that proves Allah's existence. Only prophets can do that."

Isa's head dropped, his breath escaping in a long, weary sigh. He turned to his assistant seated to his left, her posture rigid, her eyes lowered to the floor, her hands clasped so tightly they trembled.

"You see?" Isa said, his voice rising, sharp. "When asked to point out the evidence that proves God's existence, they can't do it, and yet they want to pursue their preaching about Him."

His assistant swallowed hard, her gaze sinking deeper.

"As the imam explained," she murmured, "only prophets can point out the evidence that proves God's existence."

Isa's palm slammed against the table with a crack that reverberated through the chamber. As he shot to his feet, his voice erupted, harsh and commanding, like a drill sergeant bark, "I don't have to sit here and pursue this conversation with a bunch of incompetent people!"

The priest flinched, his hand tightening around the handkerchief as he rose halfway from his chair. "Mr Iri," he reasoned, his voice trembling with suppressed anger. "I believe we are more qualified than you to speak about God. We have studied hard to get…"

"Studied what? Mechanical engineering?" Isa's words cut like a whip, his tone dripping with scorn. He leaned forward, his shadow looming across the table. "Obviously, neither of you has studied your religions, because if you did, you would know that prophets already pointed out the evidence that proves God's existence."

The rabbi's eyes narrowed, his voice sharp as a blade. "What evidence are you referring to?"

Isa's lips curled into a grim smile, his voice steady, deliberate. "Holy Scriptures claim that no sparrow or a leaf fall without God's knowledge. This clue is the evidence that proves God's existence, and it is clearly depicted in the Book of Joseph." He paced slowly behind his chair, his footsteps, hovering menacingly as his footsteps fell on the concrete floor. "The Pharaoh and his two inmates experienced three different dreams that later on turned into reality. Therefore, God informs people through dreams about future events, and this is verifiable proof that God exists."

He stopped abruptly, his hands gripping the back of his chair. "God informs us about certain events that are bound to happen before they actually happen, as described in the Book of Joseph." Isa's voice softened, almost chilling in its calm. "I don't expect you to believe this, but days before I was asked to draft the new constitution for Vallsia, I had a dream, in which I was addressing thousands of people in a large square." His eyes locked on the rabbi, dark and unwavering. "Do you think my unconscious mind is powerful enough to project future events?"

The imam leaned forward, his voice betraying his suspicion, his fingers gripping the edge of the table hard.

The silence that followed was electric, crackling like a storm about to break. The neon lights seemed to buzz louder, the drip from the sink now pounding. The rabbi's fingers twitched against the armrest, the imam's lips moved in silent prayer, and the priest's chest heaved as he continued to grip the handkerchief like a lifeline.

# Meanwhile, in London – Part Four

That debate became permanently engraved in my memory. The living room was dimly lit, the pale afternoon light filtering through the half-drawn curtains and casting long shadows across the worn carpet. Shortly after Isa claimed that God informed people of future events through dreams, my father furiously flung his newspaper onto the coffee table, sending a porcelain coaster skittering to the floor. He shot up from his armchair, his face flushed crimson, and screamed at the TV, his voice cracking with rage, "You pathetic piece of shit! Why can't you just shut up, you fucking cunt? Why must you torment us like this?"

The television flickered silently in the background, its glow dancing across the framed family photos on the wall.

"Dad, can you please stop offending cunts? Cunts have depth, and that lunatic lacks it!" I quipped, forcing a grin on my Dad's face that felt brittle.

I thought my response would cheer him up, but my father ignored me completely. His jaw tightened, and without a word, he shoved the armchair back and strode out of the living room, his heavy footsteps echoing down the hallway.

I followed him quietly, my socks gliding across the cold tiles and stopped at the kitchen doorway. Through the open door leading to the garden, I saw him pacing like a caged animal. The November air was sharp, and the garden smelled faintly of damp earth and fallen leaves.

He walked frantically along the stone path, his slippers slapping against the slabs, whispering something to himself, his hands fluttering in the air like startled birds. Occasionally, he would stop abruptly, clench his fists, and yell at himself, his voice carrying through the stillness, "Damn you, John! Damn you, stupid fool!"

The wind rustled the bare branches, carrying away fragments of his anguish. Ten minutes later, his movements slowed. He wandered toward the timber deck, shoulders sagging, and sat down heavily, the boards creaking under his weight. Then he called my name, his voice hoarse.

"I'm coming," I replied, stepping into the garden. The grass was slick beneath my shoes, and the chill bit at my skin.

He pinched a cigarette from the pocket adjacent to his heart, his fingers trembling slightly. After several false starts, the gold-plated lighter finally sparked, and the flame danced briefly before kissing the tip of the cigarette. He inhaled deeply, the smoke curling upward like ghostly ribbons. After three long puffs, he said, his voice steadier now, "Son, could you please fetch me the bottle of scotch from the bottom shelf?"

After Mum's funeral, he would occasionally sip two scotches before dinner but never before lunch.

"Dad, isn't it too early for a scotch?" I commented as I approached him, my breath visible in the cold air.

"Please fetch another glass for yourself and sit next to me. I need to get something off my chest," he replied, the cigarette stuck in the corner of his mouth, its ash trembling precariously.

I stepped back into the kitchen, the warmth inside feeling almost alien now. I grabbed the scotch bottle, two glasses cool against my palm, and headed towards the garden. Then, I sat next to my father and poured the amber liquid into two tumbler glasses.

"Here you are," I said, handing him his whiskey. I sat beside him as he lit another cigarette, the lighter's metallic click punctuating the silence.

He lifted his head slowly and reached for the glass. Absolute silence ensued for a moment as he sipped his scotch, the liquid catching the pale sunlight like molten gold.

"Are you all right, Dad?" I asked softly.

He bowed his head, inhaling smoke from the cigarette between his fingers before grabbing the scotch bottle again. His hands shook slightly as he poured.

I tapped his shoulder gently. "You said you wanted to get something off your chest?"

"Just give me a minute," his voice trembled as he topped his glass with the light-brown liquid. He finally turned and gazed at me with watery grey eyes. Then, wiping tears from his cheeks with the back of his hand, he said, his voice breaking, "Ben, the night before your mother killed herself, she appeared in my dream dressed in white, standing between my deceased mother and father."

Dad placed his cigarette between his thin lips. After releasing three dense puffs of smoke above his head, he sighed deeply, the sound heavy with grief. He stretched out his hand and placed it on my shoulder, his grip weak but desperate. Then he started sobbing like a child, his body shaking.

"I guess ... God was... trying to tell me ... that she'd part from us and join our deceased ..." His words faltered, and suddenly he produced a loud grunt as he clutched his left shoulder with his right hand.

"Dad, are you alright?" Panic surged through me.

"I feel exhausted," he replied, his breathing accelerating, each word a struggle.

Despite the cold sweat beaded on his forehead, glistening in the pale light. He seemed to be having difficulty breathing.

"Dad!" I yelled, my voice cracking.

"Don't worry ... I'm all right," he gasped, his chest heaving. "There's a sharp pain ... in my left shoulder and ... pressure in my chest ... as if someone ... is standing on it." His words dissolved into a strangled groan as he collapsed onto the timber deck, his head striking the boards with a sickening thud.

I shouted his name several times, but he didn't respond. His eyes were wide open, glassy, and his mouth frozen, breathing erratically. I screamed his name again, my voice echoing through the empty garden. I pulled out my cell phone with trembling hands and dialled 999, clutching it between my ear and shoulder as I tried to revive him, pushing my palms against his chest in frantic rhythm.

The ambulance arrived some fifteen minutes later, its siren piercing through the quiet street. The paramedics spilled out, their boots crunching on the gravel, and asked me where the patient was. I pointed toward the garden, my voice barely coherent. They rushed past me, their equipment clattering. First, they wired Dad's chest to an electrocardiogram machine, its screen blinking with jagged lines. Next, they placed an oxygen mask over his face and poked a needle into his vein, pumping morphine to ease his pain. After checking his blood pressure and pulse, the young paramedic pulled a defibrillator out of his bag, its paddles gleaming, and applied around ten electrical shocks to my Dad's chest, his body jerking violently with each surge.

Then I helped them lift my Dad, his limbs limp, and rest him on a trolley. Together, we pushed the stretcher into the ambulance, its interior smelling of antiseptic and urgency. I sat next to my Dad's stretcher, fastening the seat belt with trembling fingers as the four of us embarked on the short, harrowing journey to the hospital.

He was placed in intensive care. I sat in the corridor and happened to see on the TV screen mounted in the waiting room hall Isa's delighted face smiling at Judith. As I watched the grinning face of the person responsible for my mother's death having breakfast with his girlfriend, a tall doctor approached to inform me that my father had passed away.

# Chapter 17

The morning sun streamed through the east-facing glazed balcony door, splashing golden light across the dining room and making the polished wooden floor gleam like it had been buttered. Judith and Isa sat at the glass dining table, eating breakfast in a silence so thick you could spread it on toast. The eyes of a lion painted on a large canvas hanging on the wall adjacent to the balcony door glared down at them with majestic disapproval, as if wondering why these two humans were so glum when there were grapes to eat and omelettes to devour.

On the table, a glass bowl brimmed with plump white grapes that looked like they'd been handpicked by angels. Two tall glasses of orange juice stood like obedient soldiers beside three types of cheeses lounging on a chopping board. Two large plates held omelettes accompanied by sliced baguettes arranged with the precision of a military parade. It was a breakfast fit for royalty, yet the atmosphere felt more like a funeral for joy. They both remained silent, as if they had argued earlier, or were telepathically arguing now.

Judith finished her omelette with the solemnity of someone signing a peace treaty, then rose and headed to the kitchen returning with two steaming black coffees, their aroma cutting through the tension like a diplomatic envoy. She placed them on the table and sat next to Isa, who was still glued to the Vallsian Daily on his tablet, his face illuminated by the screen like a monk meditating on holy scripture. Judith grabbed her own tablet and began reading the Psychiatric Science Quarterly, perhaps hoping to diagnose the silence.

The disconcerting hush that had lingered for over fifteen minutes ended abruptly when Isa tossed his tablet onto the glass table with a bang so loud the lion in the painting seemed to blink. Judith flinched, her coffee cup wobbling dangerously.

"What's wrong now?" she asked, her voice calm but her eyebrows performing a small interpretive dance. She looked up at Isa, whose face was now saturated with blood-red frustration.

Isa smiled to himself, covering his face with his hands like a magician about to reveal a trick. Unable to see his expression, Judith swung her chair toward him with the grace of a queen turning to address a court jester. Her stare was unmistakably charged, but her posture relaxed as she glanced at his crimsoned face, which looked like it was been marinated in confusion. Isa hastily lowered his eyes without replying, his knee jerking up and down beneath the table like a nervous drummer auditioning for a rock band. Judith opened her mouth to speak but hesitated, then placed her hand on Isa's shoulder and rubbed it gently before whispering, though they were alone, "What's the matter, Isa?"

Isa remained silent for several seconds, as if the article he had read earlier had clogged his mental plumbing. Finally, he yanked a cigarette and lighter from his shirt pocket and leapt out of his seat with the drama of a Shakespearean actor.

"I've already told you!" he whined in a pitched tone, stomping toward the balcony like a man marching to war. "Vallsia isn't ready for my constitution!"

Judith let her hands fall into her lap and asked in a soothing voice, "Says who?"

Isa jammed the cigarette between his lips, his other hand buried deep in his trouser pocket, and began pacing toward the balcony, his footsteps thudding on the wooden floor like angry punctuation marks.

Judith watched him with gracious calm, her eyes following his every move like a cat tracking a laser pointer. When he reached the balcony and lit his cigarette with his back turned, she shouted, "Isa!"

Isa spun around dramatically, planting his feet wide on the grey ceramic tiles like a gladiator preparing for battle. His voice trailed off as he declared, "Some local and international experts."

"What do they say?" Judith asked, rubbing her chin with the back of her palm like a detective about to crack a case.

"They say my constitution won't work," Isa replied without looking back, his cigarette clenched between his teeth like a pirate's dagger.

"Did they say why?" Judith pressed on, smiling affably as if humour might soften the blow.

Isa pivoted to face her and jabbed a finger toward his tablet. "It's all written down in that lengthy bloody article."

Judith smiled calmly, two faint lines running down from the corners of her mouth like parentheses enclosing her patience.

"Couldn't you give me a summary of why they oppose your constitution?" she pleaded.

Isa lifted a hand and waggled his index finger in the air like a conductor cueing an orchestra. A forced grin plastered on his face as he stood silent, shoulders hunched like a guilty schoolboy.

"I'm sorry, but after reading it, I'm not in much of a mood to talk about it," he muttered, shaking his head like a malfunctioning bobblehead.

Judith's mouth creased into a modest smile as she grabbed Isa's tablet and began reading.

"You may not want to read it," Isa warned, his cigarette hand flapping like a hummingbird's wings. "The last thing you want to do is find out how incompetent your boyfriend is!"

Judith ignored him and continued reading, her face a mask of concentration occasionally cracked by vague smiles. Meanwhile, Isa placed his cigarette on the ashtray, strutted back to the table for his coffee, and returned to the balcony like a man rehearsing for a tragic opera. Scratching his chest absentmindedly, he pinched his cigarette again and tilted his head skyward, observing the grey clouds sailing away like ships abandoning a sinking nation.

"Did you actually suggest that all the newly enrolled pupils must be taught exclusively in the Vallsian language at school?" Judith asked suddenly, her eyes widening like saucers.

Isa nodded, staring into his coffee cup as if it held the secrets of the universe.

"So, you want to force Ryllian and Jewish pupils to be taught in Vallsian instead of their mother tongue?"

"Yes," Isa affirmed, his eyes steady, his tone as firm as a judge delivering a verdict.

"But what will you accomplish by doing that?" Judith asked, crossing her arms over her chest like a sceptical statue.

Isa stubbed out his cigarette with exaggerated drama, then pressed his palms together and moved them up and down like a monk praying for linguistic harmony. Finally, leaning against the balcony door jamb, he replied with his eyes tightly shut, "Remove imposed differences between all Vallsians by establishing a unified language for future generations."

"Though I'm no expert, I think that's way too harsh," Judith countered. Then, scrolling through the tablet, she added, "It says here you're trying to assimilate other people's culture!"

"That's not true!" Isa barked, dragging the last puff of smoke before stabbing the cigarette into the ashtray. "A language is a communication tool... like a screwdriver! Instead of screws, it serves to place words into someone else's eyes or ears."

Judith laughed softly, shaking her head. "I disagree! Language is a pivotal component of culture passed from generation to generation."

Isa rolled his eyes so hard they nearly did a full orbit, shook his head wildly, and marched toward Judith with his coffee cup sloshing dangerously. "A language is only a tool to communicate thoughts and feelings, and that's what constitutes culture, not the language itself!"

Rubbing her hands together, Judith asked, "Meaning what?"

"Excuse me," Isa said and headed towards the kitchen. Once he reached the sink, he turned on the tap and splashed water over his red face. He then filled a glass of water and gulped it avidly. After returning to the dining table, Isa stood behind Judith, knotted his hands and said,

"Culture is an expression of certain behaviour, such as saying to others *I love you, je t'aime*, or *ani ohev otkha*, whereas the tool used to do it, is Vallsian, French or Jewish language. On the other hand, you have expressions that others use, such as *son of a bitch, fils de putain*, or *ben-zonna*, and although they are used in same languages as the other kind words, as I've mentioned earlier, they represent an entirely different culture of a particular human being. Therefore, what you say matters, not what language you use to say it."

"But I'm fond of my Jewish language. If we end up having children, I would like them to be taught in Hebrew, as most Jewish children currently are," Judith objected, sipping her coffee like it was liquid courage. "Why would you subject our future children to being taught exclusively in Vallsian and not Hebrew?"

"Well, isn't it obvious?" Isa smirked and planted a quick kiss on Judith's cheek, the kind that says *I'm about to annoy you further.* "So that our future children don't end up having such a needless unpleasant discussion when they reach our age. Besides, the best education is paramount to our future children, not the language they'll be taught."

Judith stared at him, absorbing what her ears had just endured, then resumed browsing Isa's tablet. Two minutes later, she giggled so suddenly that Isa nearly spilled his coffee.

"What?" Isa probed, narrowing his eyes like a detective interrogating a suspect.

"It says here you've claimed that your constitution aims to create a state compliant with laws of nature by reinstating Vallsians to their natural state," Judith replied, struggling to hold back laughter. "How does forcing Vallsian pupils who speak another language at home to get taught exclusively in Vallsian fit your vision of a natural state compliant with laws of nature?"

Isa sighed dramatically and cast his gaze at her, a smile creeping across his face as he began stroking Judith's hair like a philosopher petting his muse. She tilted her face up, and they kissed twice, because once wasn't enough for this level of absurdity.

"Darling, you need to go back to your natural state and self-reflect,"

Isa said, carrying a vague smile as he headed for his chair.

"What natural state are you referring to?" Judith asked, arching an eyebrow.

"The one you experienced soon after you were born."

"Meaning?"

"Meaning that as a baby, you communicated with your parents in the same language as that of a Chinese, Egyptian, Indian, English, or Vallsian baby, not Hebrew."

Judith shook her head, her lips drooping before springing into an instant smile. "You're not suggesting that future generations should communicate the way babies do, are you?"

Isa grinned like a man who thinks he's winning an argument. "We might not necessarily understand it, but that's a uniform natural form of human communication, whereby every baby that comes into this world speaks the same language, regardless of where they were born. And this is exactly what my constitution aims to accomplish. By establishing a single unifying language, future Vallsians will be reinstated to their natural state."

Judith burst out laughing. "So, your grand plan is to turn Vallsia into a nation of babbling toddlers? Brilliant. Shall we add mandatory nap times and pacifiers to your constitution?"

Isa waved his hand dismissively, as Judith pressed on, "No other country did it!"

"The US did it!" he declared with a broad smile lighting up his face as he sat down. "Various wars were fought throughout history, but although they led to pointless loss of human lives, we've never managed to obliterate their true cause… national and religious identities."

"Yes, but I doubt this generation of Vallsians will consent to giving up their national identities!" Judith exclaimed, her voice rising like steam from her coffee.

Isa lowered his head, puffing away like a frustrated dragon. "I've already told you that what determines our nationality is our mother's vagina. However, I've never come across any nationalist Ansobian, Bresian, Taork, Ryllian or Jew with a tattoo of their mother's vagina instead of their national flag."

Judith laughed so hard she nearly snorted. "Isa, that's the most disturbing... and oddly creative argument I've ever heard."

Isa shrugged. "Perhaps I wasn't clear enough. My proposal to teach Vallsian pupils exclusively in Vallsian only applies to those whose school enrolment commences from next year, not the existing ones. I'm not implying banning other languages or forcing our existing pupils to be taught exclusively in Vallsian. After all, my constitution isn't about us and our myopic desires. It's about the future Vallsian children who will build a unified Vallsia, insulated from mindless wars and human sufferings that will come and go for as long as national identities exist."

Judith sighed, standing up and grabbing her cup. "I need more caffeine to digest this insane idea of yours. Would you like another coffee?"

"Yes, please," Isa replied, lifting his cup. "Could you please fetch me a Grappa as well?"

"Isn't it a bit early for a shot of Grappa?" Judith asked, snatching Isa's cup from his hand.

Isa frowned, his lofty forehead creasing like a roadmap. He sighed, buried his face in his hands, and groaned. "What's wrong now?" Judith asked, heading for the kitchen.

"Considering the past stressful meetings and experts' inability to grasp what I'm trying to accomplish, I should be asking for bottles of Grappa, not a shot," Isa replied, stomping toward the balcony like a man preparing for exile.

Judith returned two minutes later, balancing a round plastic tray like a waitress in a sitcom. On it sat two steaming cups of coffee and a lonely shot of Grappa, glinting like liquid mischief. "Where do you want them, on the balcony or dining table?" Judith asked, lifting the tray with exaggerated grace.

"Over there, please," Isa replied, pointing at the dining table with the solemnity of a king demanding tribute.

Judith set the tray down, then raised an eyebrow. "One shot of Grappa? Isa, you look like you're about to start a Liquor Party instead of a political one."

Isa ignored the jab and reached for the Grappa like a man clutching salvation. He sniffed it dramatically, closing his eyes as if inhaling the essence of courage. "Ah... the aroma of victory," he declared, before tossing it back in one gulp and shuddering like he'd just swallowed molten lava.

Judith smirked. "Bravo. Shall I fetch you a medal or a mop for the tears in your eyes?"

Isa coughed, pounding his chest with the theatrics of a Shakespearean actor dying on stage. "This... this is what fuels revolutions!" he croaked, wiping his mouth with the back of his hand.

Judith rolled her eyes and slid his coffee toward him. "Here, revolutionary. Before you start drafting a manifesto on napkins."

Isa grabbed the cup, sloshing coffee dangerously close to the rim as he gestured wildly. "Judith, you don't understand! These experts... they're blind! Blind as bats in sunglasses!"

Judith leaned back, crossing her arms with a grin. "And you're sober as a judge... who just downed a shot of Grappa at nine in the morning."

Isa waved her off, pacing toward the balcony with his coffee in hand like a general inspecting his troops. "If they can't see the brilliance of my constitution, then maybe I should write it in smoke signals!" He puffed on his cigarette, sending a cloud skyward.

Judith chuckled, sipping her coffee. "Careful, Isa. At this rate, your smoke signals will say, *Help, I've lost my mind and my liver.*"

Isa turned dramatically, pointing his cigarette at her like a wand. "Mock me all you want, but history will remember me!"

Judith grinned. "Oh, it will. As the man who tried to unite a nation by turning everyone into babbling toddlers and then drowned his sorrows in Grappa."

Isa froze, then broke into a reluctant smile. "You're impossible."
Judith winked. "No, Isa. I'm bilingual. That's what makes me dangerous.

Judith tilted her head slightly, sniffing her coffee like a wine connoisseur evaluating a vintage, without even glancing at Isa. "It says here that you're proposing to ban the use of cash and switch to a digital currency with an expiry date. So how does this digital thing fit with your state compliant with laws of nature?"

Isa chuckled, leaning back in his chair with the smugness of a man about to deliver a utterly nonsense lecture nobody asked for. He dragged another smoke from his cigarette, exhaling a cloud so thick it could have its own postcode. "As we have evolved, we've drifted away from the laws of nature and, consequently, from our true natural being. Thus, we consistently seek solutions from human experts, whereas the best solutions are outside the human realm."

Judith raised an eyebrow, still swirling her coffee like it held the secrets of the universe. "Such as?"

"The animal realm and their behaviour, which remained faithful to their natural state without changing their living patterns," Isa declared, waving his cigarette like a professor wielding chalk.

Judith smirked, scrutinising his eyes. "As far as I'm aware, animals don't use digital or any other currency," she remarked light-heartedly. "Unless squirrels have started using contactless for acorns."

Isa grinned and wagged his index finger at her, releasing a puff of smoke so dramatic it could have been a scene from a noir film. Judith leaned back, arms crossed, her expression screaming, *Well? I'm still waiting for an answer.*

Isa opened his mouth to respond, but a loud ambulance siren wailed from the road below, drowning his words. He froze mid-gesture, cigarette poised like a conductor's baton, then sighed theatrically. The heated conversation fizzled into stony silence. Judith stared at him, half amused, half exasperated, while Isa stubbed out his cigarette with the solemnity of a man burying his dreams.

He returned to the dining table, kissed Judith's cheek like a peace offering, and plopped down beside her. "What an animal prey is to an animal, money is to a human," he began, gesturing grandly as if unveiling the theory of everything. "Animal preys go rotten if not used by a certain time, which is why money should also become unusable if not used by a specific date."

Judith blinked, her lips twitching. "So basically, you want money to expire like yoghurt?"

Isa ignored the jab and pressed on, his voice swelling with conviction. "In the wild, a pack of lions hunts a zebra, an animal good, and the entire pack eats it after they kill it. In our system, wealthy people hunt for money, and after securing it, they keep most of it to themselves without sharing it with others who made it possible."

Judith snorted softly. "So, you're saying billionaires are basically selfish lions with better hair?"

Isa clapped his hands, thrilled by her analogy. "Exactly! That's why I've proposed that every employee in a private company, besides their salary, will also earn a share of the annual profit. But they didn't mention it in that article."

Judith shook her head, laughing. "Isa, you're turning economics into a wildlife documentary."

Isa puffed out his chest. "Employers and employees are a pack of lions hunting for money rather than prey, which is why they deserve to share their animal prey, or human profit, just as lions do."

"That's a bit extreme!" Judith protested, sipping her coffee like it was a tranquilliser.

Isa leaned forward, eyes blazing. "If a lion were to keep his prey entirely to himself, scientists would study this abnormal behaviour. But when people do the same thing by refusing to share wealth or avoid paying taxes, they're glorified and treated like celebrities."

Judith chuckled. "Could you imagine if lions behaved like billionaires? Each lion hoarding a zebra in a private cave with a 'No Entry' sign?"

Isa slapped the table, nearly spilling his coffee. "Precisely! And eventually, they'd run out of zebras."

Judith grinned. "And start eating each other. Which, come to think of it, sounds like Wall Street."

Isa threw his hands up dramatically. "Unfortunately, this is exactly how our economy works today. Just like the limited number of zebras in the wild, there's also a limited amount of money in Vallsia. Vast amounts stored in banks don't facilitate sustainable growth because they're not spent."

Judith tilted her head, smirking. "So, your solution is to make money rot like bananas?"

Isa nodded enthusiastically. "Yes! Digital money with an expiry date will incentivise wealthy Vallsians to invest or spend before it expires."

Judith wagged her finger. "But they're already paying taxes!"

Isa rolled his eyes so hard they nearly did a full orbit. "Not all of them. Wealthy Vallsians avoid taxes by setting up corporations in tax havens."

Judith leaned back, grinning. "And your solution is?"

Isa puffed his chest like a superhero about to reveal his power. "Tax people upon every digital transaction. The government retains a flat percentage for every single transfer."

Judith laughed. "So, I'd pay income tax and VAT on top of it?"

Isa shook his head, grinning like a magician revealing a trick. "No! You'd no longer pay income tax or VAT because the tax will be deducted before your salary hits your account."

Judith raised an eyebrow. "And accountants? What happens to them?"

Isa shrugged. "They'll still track expenditures or process payroll, but no more tax returns."

Judith smirked. "So, my cousin Elijah becomes jobless?"

Isa waved his hand. "He'll survive. Maybe start a zebra farm."

Judith burst out laughing. "You're an extremist, Isa."

Isa bowed his head dramatically, as if accepting an Oscar for 'Most Radical Idea'. Judith leaned forward, grinning. "So how does your flat tax rate work with progressive taxation?"

Isa straightened up, eyes gleaming. "Progressive taxation discriminates against high earners."

Judith snorted. "High earners should pay more!"

Isa wagged his finger like a schoolteacher. "Even at the same rate, they pay more. Ten percent of €400,000 is still more than ten percent of €40,000."

Judith rolled her eyes, sipping her coffee. "Congratulations, Isa. You've officially turned breakfast into a circus."

Judith shook her head slowly, her hair swaying like a curtain in a lazy breeze, and resumed reading the Vallsian Daily on Isa's tablet. The morning light bounced off the glass table, making the tablet screen gleam like a polished mirror. Two minutes later, she jabbed at the screen with her index finger, her nail clicking against the glass like a tiny gavel. "This journalist believes your direct democracy model won't work," she announced, her tone carrying the smug satisfaction of someone about to poke holes in a balloon.

Isa leaned back in his chair, puffing out his chest like a rooster preparing for battle. "We're told that we're living in a pluralist political system, but that's not true," he asserted, waving his cigarette like a sceptre. "Every four years, we're bound to vote for a single party rather than for specific governmental policies of different parties."

Judith raised an eyebrow, sipping her coffee with exaggerated calm. "But you're already choosing a policy from various political parties."

"No! We choose a set of policies from a single political party as opposed to a policy from a wide range of political parties, which is why we don't live in true pluralism!" His voice climbed an octave, and the lion painting on the wall seemed to glare harder, as if silently judging his logic.

Judith tilted her head, smirking.

"Pluralism isn't about choosing a set of policies from a single political party. It's about choosing a single proposed development policy from various parties for a specific governmental sector, such as education, healthcare, and so on," Isa continued, gesturing so wildly that his cigarette ash nearly catapulted onto the omelette plate. "I want to live in a system whereby I could vote for a single policy to develop a specific governmental sector at a time and not for a set of policies as it currently stands."

Judith blinked, her lips twitching. "I'm not following you."

Isa groaned dramatically, throwing his head back like a man auditioning for a soap opera. "What I'm trying to say is that true pluralism should make it possible for me to vote on the proposed education policy of one political party but then vote on the proposed healthcare policy of another party, the environmental policy of another political party and so on. This is what constitutes true pluralism."

Judith scrolled the tablet with a flourish. "But this is not what you're suggesting. It says here that you want to see the end of political parties."

"Yes, because that's what animals do, and…"

Judith slammed her coffee cup down so hard the spoon inside did a somersault. "Will you give me a break from animals?" she snapped, her eyes narrowing like a cat spotting a laser pointer. "What are you trying to achieve here? Turn us into animals?"

Isa chuckled, reaching over to gently tap Judith's knee like a man trying to calm a volcano. "Relax, darling," he said mildly, flashing a grin. "Animals don't elect groups of animals as their leaders! Instead, they select a single animal as their leader."

Judith snorted. "But this is exactly what's happening in our democracy."

Isa leaned forward, his elbows sliding dangerously close to the cheese board. "We currently vote for one leader but end up with his ministers, although we never voted for them. So, people should vote for a single policy of a sectoral expert who would lead that particular governmental sector and become our next minister rather than voting for a political party and end up with ministers whom nobody voted for."

Judith threw her hands up, nearly knocking over the orange juice. "So, you're saying that we get to choose between thousands, or God knows how many, sectoral experts and their policies on the same day every four years? Surely, that would lead to widespread pandemonium."

Isa wagged his finger like a schoolteacher correcting a naughty pupil. "No, that's not what I'm suggesting," he said, trying to calm her down. "I'm saying that every four years, you get to choose the candidate who specialises in healthcare to become our health minister and lead the healthcare sector according to his or her policy for the next four years. Then six months later, you'd choose the candidate who specialises in education to lead the education sector based on his or her proposed program over the next four years, then six months later on welfare, and so on."

"Isa," she began, her voice calm but edged with curiosity, "don't you think a minister should be a good manager rather than a sectoral expert? I mean, their job is to run a ministry efficiently, not necessarily to be the Einstein of healthcare or education."

Isa straightened up setting his coffee cup down with a thud. "That's where you're wrong, darling," he declared, his tone swelling with theatrical gravitas. "The good management of a ministry is down to the Permanent Secretary, not the minister. A minister's role isn't to shuffle papers or organise filing cabinets, it's to improve a specific governmental sector through vision, based on his personal working experience."

Judith raised an eyebrow, strolling toward the table with the slow grace of someone about to deliver a knockout punch. "Vision and experience? Isa, half the ministers I've seen couldn't even manage their own calendars without three assistants and a therapy dog."

Isa chuckled, tapping the ash from his cigarette into the tray with exaggerated precision. "Exactly! That's why my model fixes this nonsense, whereby a single politician, first becomes Minister of Health, then once this political mandate ends, he becomes the Minister of Education, then ones this political mandate ends, he becomes the Minister of Environment, and so on. Ministers shouldn't be glorified managers, because they should be sectoral experts who know what they're doing and have experienced legal and budgetary obstacles. If you appoint a healthcare minister who's never set foot in a hospital except for a photo op, you end up with policies written by guesswork and Google searches."

Judith smirked, sliding into the chair opposite him and propping her chin on her hand. "So, under your system, the education minister would be... what? A retired headteacher with a vendetta against homework?"

Isa grinned, leaning forward, his elbows grazing the cheese board. "Not a vendetta... vision! Someone who's spent years in the trenches, understands the problems, and can actually propose solutions that work.

The Permanent Secretary handles the admin. The minister drives the change."

Judith laughed, shaking her head. "Isa, you're basically turning the cabinet into a superhero squad. 'Captain Healthcare', 'Professor Education', and 'The Incredible Infrastructure Man'."

Isa slapped the table, sending the grapes wobbling like tiny green marbles. "Exactly! And unlike the current system, these superheroes won't be chosen because they look good in campaign posters, they'll be chosen because they know their sector inside out."

Judith rolled her eyes, sipping her coffee. "Sounds great in theory, Isa. But in practice? You'll have experts arguing over budgets like toddlers fighting for crayons."

Isa puffed out his chest, his voice booming like a man announcing the dawn of a new era. "That's why Vallsians decide the tax rate for each policy through their vote. Let's say that if a specific expert in education wants to improve this sector by adding a tax increase of one percent, and the Vallsians vote for that, then the Minister of Finance will have to have to implement this tax increase. No more backroom deals, no more budgetary tug-of-war. Pure democracy, whereby the voters decided how much they are willing to pay, and not some teacher who gets appointed by his political party as our Minister of finance!"

Judith chuckled, standing up and stretching. "Pure chaos, more like. But hey, if you manage to pull this off, I'll personally buy you a cape."

Isa grinned, lifting his Grappa glass in salute. "Make it gold, darling. I plan to save the world."

Judith stared at him, her jaw slack, as she resumed reading the Vallian Times on Isa's tablet. "Are you suggesting that every six months, we should vote to appoint a specific candidate to lead a certain governmental sector?"

"Yes!" Isa replied emphatically, slapping the table for dramatic effect. The grapes wobbled like tiny green bowling balls. "As it currently stands, political party manifestos are nothing more than pedantic documents that explain broad goals. Very often, voters don't even bother to read them when deciding which way to vote. Instead, most voters decide on which party to vote for rather than their singular policy for the development of a specific governmental sector over the next five years. Therefore, people would vote on a policy of a specific sector, and then six months later or so, they would vote on another policy for the development of another sector, until all ministers are appointed for a five-year mandate."

Judith scrolled again, her lips curling into a mischievous smile. "But it says here that it won't work because of the budgetary chaos it will create. According to this expert, there's no way an elected budget and finance leader could deliver his policy if elected policies of other sectors will increase public spending."

Isa puffed his chest like a peacock. "One of the most fundamental rights of voters is to decide how much tax they're willing to pay to implement a specific policy they vote for and how to spend it. After all, it's their money that the government is supposed to administer. Therefore, it's the voters' exclusive right to decide how their money would be spent, not the person responsible for handling the budget."

Judith raised an eyebrow, sipping her coffee slowly. "Although this is far too complicated for me, why have you never discussed these ideas with me?"

Isa threw his hands up dramatically, nearly knocking the ashtray off the table. "You were the one that set the rule about not discussing work, not me!"

Judith smirked, leaning back in her chair. "Yes, but my work doesn't affect you, whereas this constitution will enormously impact my life."

Isa leaned forward, his voice dropping to a theatrical whisper. "So, you think I've got it all wrong?"

Judith shrugged, her lips twitching into a grin. "I'm not sure what to make of it. Your ideas are… a bit… weird."

Isa sighed, rubbing his forehead like a man burdened with the weight of genius. "I've already warned you that these ideas come from visions experienced during my setback episode, and I don't expect them to make much sense to you or anyone else."

Judith clambered onto his lap with the grace of a cat claiming its throne and rubbed Isa's cheek with her palm, hoping to soften his heart. They remained silent for a couple of minutes, the lion painting glaring down like a referee waiting to blow the whistle. Finally, Isa asked, "You disagree, don't you?"

Judith kissed his lips lightly, her breath warm against his skin, and whispered, "I'm not sure what to make of it. You could be right, but whether we like it or not, most people today define themselves through the ideologies or beliefs they've defended in the past and will continue to do so in the future." Her voice lingered in the air like a soft echo as she slid off his lap, her silk blouse brushing against his arm. She stretched like a gymnast, arms arching gracefully above her head, her spine curving until the morning light from the balcony caught her silhouette. The lion painting on the wall seemed to watch silently, its amber eyes glowing in the golden sunbeam.

Judith smoothed her hair back with both hands, her bracelets jingling faintly, and announced with a playful flick of her wrist, "I'm off to have a shower now. We don't want to be late for my niece's tenth birthday!" She turned, her bare feet padding across the polished wooden floor, leaving faint impressions in the soft rug as she disappeared into the corridor. The sound of her steps faded, replaced by the distant hum of running water.

Then, his voice rang out, echoing through the corridor like a last-minute campaign slogan, charged with urgency and conviction, "Rather than defending their ideologies or beliefs, people should defend their children by delivering a better and just world for them!"

Isa remained seated for a moment, his elbows resting on the glass table, fingers interlocked as if holding the weight of the world. The untouched grapes glistened in the bowl beside him, and the steam from his coffee curled upward like a question mark. He rose abruptly and strode toward the balcony door. The sunlight spilled across his face, highlighting the furrow in his brow. He pressed his palms against the doorframe, staring out at the garden where the wind teased the leaves into a restless dance.

For a moment, he stood frozen, a man wrestling with invisible ideologies, before tilting his head skyward.

Above him, a flock of birds sliced through the pale blue horizon in perfect formation, their wings glinting in the sunlight like silver arrowss. Isa squinted at them, his jaw tightening, and then, with the theatricality of a prophet addressing the heavens, he shouted. "What nationality are you?"

The birds, of course, ignored him, because birds have better things to do than engage in constitutional debates. They simply kept gliding, elegant and indifferent, as if mocking the absurdity of human borders. Isa threw his arms wide, nearly knocking over the ashtray perched on the balcony ledge.

"Enjoy your freedom, my feathery friends!" he bellowed, spinning halfway toward the empty dining room. "No passports! No visas! No bloody customs queues! Just pure freedom!"

# Chapter 18

Over the next six months, Isa and a large team of international experts worked seven days a week to finalise his constitution, an endeavour carried out in conference rooms so cold they could have doubled as morgues. Fluorescent lights hummed overhead like bored insects, illuminating tables buried under stacks of draft laws, sub-legal acts, and half-empty mugs of cheap UN-issue coffee that tasted vaguely of diplomatic despair. Isa paced between the tables with the self-importance of a man who genuinely believed he was saving Vallsia, often stopping mid-stride to wave a pen like a general signalling the movement of invisible troops. The experts nodded dutifully, occasionally scribbling notes while silently questioning all their life choices that had led them into this bureaucratic labyrinth.

Vallsia then held its first general elections for the leader of the educational governmental sector, an election, ironically, without political parties, which meant the candidates had to improvise their own ideological identities. Three months later, elections were held for the health governmental sector's leader, conducted in a conference hall whose peeling wallpaper and dusty ceiling chandeliers suggested it had last been maintained when the concept of hygiene was merely a rumour. Piece by piece, leader by leader, a new Vallsian governmental cabinet emerged, much like a badly assembled piece of IKEA furniture, functional, but only if nobody pushed too hard.

To everyone's surprise, Vallsia actually worked fairly well under Isa's constitution. Of course, its entirely fictitious existence helped. People worldwide, however, soon became sceptical about whether such a marvel of bureaucratic imagination would survive in the real world without the enormous UN budget, an amount of money so vast it could make even the most fiscally responsible nations salivate like stray dogs outside a butcher shop.

Following the completion of the two-year trial period of the new Vallsian government, last week the 87 UN member states that ratified the convention held national referendums. Citizens were asked whether they would prefer to live in Vallsia under Isa's constitution or continue living in their independent states, states some of them claimed to hate but, funnily enough, refused to abandon. Polling stations were crowded with people shuffling in long lines, clutching their ballots with the solemnity of individuals about to make decisions they barely understood. When votes were counted, the results were clear. Isa's constitution failed to gain enough support to give a legal birth to a new global Vallsian state. Apparently, most eligible and reasonable voters in 87 countries preferred their imperfect, corrupt, occasionally stable states over signing up for a fictional republic run by a man they had only ever seen on UN livestreams.

And so, the insane UN experiment ended, an experiment that cost billions, sparked dozens of academic conferences, and generated exactly zero practical outcomes beyond fuelling several new conspiracy theories and giving late-night comedians enough material for years.

In the meantime, Isa married Judith, by then the esteemed First Lady of a country that did not exist, and moved into a presidential palace with an enormous garden. The palace itself was a monstrous architectural tribute to overfunded committees, due to its marble floors that echoed like haunted cathedrals, golden railings polished daily by underpaid staff, and hallways so long Isa once got lost and ended up in a broom closet for forty minutes. Still, life was good for Isa. He became a father to a lovely daughter named Vajza, and a second child was already on the way. Nona and Ati moved back in together, their relationship as stable as a table with three legs but significantly more entertaining.

Although his life was no longer broadcast globally, Isa remained president of the fictitious Vallsian Republic, blissfully unaware that such a country didn't exist. Every morning, he walked through the palace garden with the dignified stride of a man leading a nation, while two gardeners exchanged looks accusing the other of being complicit in this ongoing delusion. And yes, he and his family continued to live on the UN's payroll, which raised eyebrows in certain corners of New York, but nobody dared ask how one terminates the employment of a president of an imaginary nation.

Five days after the results of the 87 national referendums were certified and confirmed by UN officials, London staged a massive Global Independence Party at Hyde Park to celebrate the spectacular failure of the Secret of the Divine Civilisation Convention to mount a global dictatorship. Fireworks lit up the sky in colours that screamed "Thank god that's over," while crowds danced, drank, and pretended they had understood the entire fiasco from the beginning. Hyde Park's grass was reduced to muddy chaos by midnight, a fitting metaphor for the global decision-making process.

Nonetheless, today, on the first spring day of 2070, humankind is on the verge of doing what it does best, which is to fuck everything up by embracing the egregious. At 03:13 am, BBC News reported that US forces launched 63 cruise missiles at military targets in Iran. Subsequently the BBC News confirmed that Iranian and Russian forces stationed along the northern edge of the Persian Gulf intercepted and destroyed 58 of the missiles, an outcome that shocked absolutely no one except the Pentagon.

It appears the world is about to get fucked on a global scale yet again by our fellow humans. But considering we owe our very existence to a fuck, you can't expect much else from our kind, then to fuck everything up.

# Author's note

Unfortunately, the truth has become a 'luxury brand' available only to a selected few and George Orwell's 1984 is no longer fiction!

Brexit and recent wars, explicitly exhibit how the invisible decision makers, The Party, turned our democracies into Oceania by exploiting the mainstream media as their Thought Police, an intrinsic part of public indoctrination. The mainstream media
perceives itself as the shepherd dog and its consumers as sheep who need safeguarding from inconvenient truths that will have an enormous impact on the livelihood of ordinary people affected by it.

This novel is a product of visions I've experienced during my enlightening bipolar setbacks, without the burden that suppresses us all, our identity. A strong identity doesn't serve any other purpose than feeding our ego, which quashes our happiness. Hitler and Brexit exemplify best what happens to nations with a strong national identity.

The negative impact that derives from a strong identity will be further explored in my second novel, Beyond The Imposed Veil, a spiritual satire that unravels what bipolars experience during setbacks, which are fundamental to human understanding of how to live a happy life

Over the remaining days of my life, I intend to write four novels that could instigate a significant societal change and, perhaps, the dawn of a new civilisation.

However, nothing meaningful will come out of a novel that nobody knows about, which is why your support is crucial, either by posting your reviews of this novel or making others aware of its existence, and I'm eternally grateful to you for doing precisely that.

# About the Author

Nolan Jazimreg is a forty-nine-year-old British architect, husband, and father to three wonderful children, Klarita, Dritushi and Diellushi.

He was born in Prishtina to an award-winning TV journalist mother, and a father who worked as a Professor of Psychology at a public university. Jazimreg spent most of his childhood in a communist system, his teenage years in a socialist one, and his adult life in capitalism.

Jazimreg experienced harsh discrimination by his state because he belonged to an ethnic minority. Throughout his teenage years, ethnic tensions amplified exponentially and ultimately led to a civil war, whereby Jazimreg fled his country to become a refugee in London.

Over 400,000 people have read Jazimreg's insights featured on his blog, nolanjazimreg.wordpress.com, which swayed the public's perception of why prominent Brexiters campaigned for the UK to leave the EU.

Considering his blog's impact on the British public, Jazimreg wrote his Amazon's #1 Mass Media book, *BREXIT: The Great British Tax Avoidance Swindle,* which framed Brexit not as a noble act of sovereignty but as a cynical scheme for the wealthy to dodge taxes, he tapped into widespread frustration.

Jazimreg plans to write three more novels, hoping they would alter readers' understanding of happiness, freedom, democracy, God, religion, heaven, or hell.

Jazimreg remains confident that his novels will inspire future generations to facilitate a new civilisation and eradicate concurrent ethnic hatred.